THE BURWASH EDITION OF THE COMPLETE
WORKS IN PROSE AND VERSE OF

RUDYARD KIPLING

VOLUME XIV

STALKY & CO.
LAND AND SEA TALES

The Collected Works Of
RUDYARD KIPLING

Stalky & Co.
Land And Sea Tales

BURWASH

AMS PRESS
NEW YORK

This is a numbered set, of which this is number . . .

Reprinted from a copy in the collection of the
Harvard University Libraries
From the edition of 1941, Garden City
First AMS EDITION published 1970
Manufactured in the United States of America

With permission of the estate of Rudyard Kipling,
Doubleday and Company, Inc., and Macmillan and Company, Ltd.

International Standard Book Number:
complete set: 0-404-03740-2
volume 14: 0-404-03754-2

Library of Congress Catalog Card Number: 75-120920

AMS PRESS, INC.
NEW YORK, N.Y. 10003

CONTENTS

STALKY & CO.

TO THE MEMORY OF

CORMELL PRICE

HEADMASTER, UNITED SERVICES COLLEGE

WESTWARD HO! BIDEFORD, NORTH DEVON

1874–1894

'LET US NOW PRAISE FAMOUS MEN'

'Let us now praise famous men'—
Men of little showing—
For their work continueth,
And their work continueth,
Broad and deep continueth,
　　Greater than their knowing!

Western wind and open surge
　　Took us from our mothers;
Flung us on a naked shore
(Twelve bleak houses by the shore!
Seven summers by the shore!)
　　'Mid two hundred brothers.

There we met with famous men
　　Set in office o'er us;
And they beat on us with rods—
Faithfully with many rods—
Daily beat us on with rods,
　　For the love they bore us.

Out of Egypt unto Troy—
　　Over Himalaya—
Far and sure our hands have gone—
Hy-Brasil or Babylon,

STALKY & CO.

Islands of the Southern Run,
  And cities of Cathaia!

And we all praise famous men—
  Ancients of the College;
For they taught us common sense—
Tried to teach us common sense—
Truth and God's Own Common Sense,
  Which is more than knowledge!

Each degree of Latitude
  Strung about Creation
Seeth one or more of us
(Of one muster all of us),
Diligent in that he does,
  Keen in his vocation.

This we learned from famous men,
  Knowing not its uses,
When they showed, in daily work,
Man must finish off his work—
Right or wrong, his daily work—
  And without excuses.

Servants of the Staff and chain,
  Mine and fuse and grapnel—
Some before the face of Kings,
Stand before the face of Kings;
Bearing gifts to divers Kings—
  Gifts of case and shrapnel.

This we learned from famous men
  Teaching in our borders,

Who declarèd it was best,
Safest, easiest, and best—
Expeditious, wise, and best—
  To obey your orders.

Some beneath the further stars
  Bear the greater burden:
Set to serve the lands they rule,
(Save he serve no man may rule),
Serve and love the lands they rule;
  Seeking praise nor guerdon.

This we learned from famous men,
  Knowing not we learned it.
Only, as the years went by—
Lonely, as the years went by—
Far from help as years went by,
  Plainer we discerned it.

Wherefore praise we famous men
  From whose bays we borrow—
They that put aside To-day—
All the joys of their To-day—
And with toil of their To-day
  Bought for us To-morrow!

Bless and praise we famous men—
  Men of little showing—
For their work continueth,
And their work continueth,
Broad and deep continueth,
  Great beyond their knowing!

CONTENTS

STALKY & CO.

Stalky & Co. was first published in 1899,
and *The Complete Stalky & Co.*, with the
additional stories, in 1929

'STALKY'

'STALKY'

'AND THEN,' it was a boy's voice, curiously level and even, 'De Vitré said we were beastly funks not to help, and *I* said there were too many chaps in it to suit us. Besides, there's bound to be a mess somewhere or other, with old De Vitré in charge. Wasn't I right, Beetle?'

'And, anyhow, it's a silly biznai, bung through. What'll they *do* with the beastly cows when they've got 'em? You can milk a cow—if she'll stand still. That's all right; but drivin' 'em about——'

'You're a pig, Beetle.'

'No, I ain't. What *is* the sense of drivin' a lot of cows up from the Burrows to—to—where is it?'

'They're tryin' to drive 'em up to Toowey's farmyard at the top of the hill—the empty one, where we smoked last Tuesday. It's a revenge. Old Vidley chivied De Vitré twice last week for ridin' his ponies on the Burrows; and De Vitré's goin' to lift as many of old Vidley's cattle as he can and plant 'em up the hill. He'll muck it, though—with Parsons, Orrin and Howlett helpin' him. They'll only yell, an' shout, an' bunk if they see Vidley.'

'*We* might have managed it,' said M'Turk slowly, turning up his coat-collar against the rain that swept over the Burrows. His hair was of the dark mahogany-red that goes with a certain temperament.

'We should,' Corkran replied with equal confidence. 'But they've gone into it as if it was a sort of spidger-hunt. I've

3

never done any cattle-liftin', but it seems to me-e-e that one might just as well be stalky about a thing as not.'

The smoking vapours of the Atlantic drove in wreaths above the boys' heads. Out of the mist to windward, beyond the grey bar of the Pebble Ridge, came the unceasing roar of mile-long Atlantic rollers. To leeward, a few stray ponies and cattle, the property of the Northam potwallopers, and the unwilling playthings of the boys in their leisure hours, showed through the haze. The three had halted by the Cattle-gate which marks the limit of cultivation, where the fields come down to the Burrows from Northam Hill. Beetle, shock-headed and spectacled, drew his nose to and fro along the wet top-bar; M'Turk shifted from one foot to the other, watching the water drain into either print; while Corkran whistled through his teeth as he leaned against a sod-bank, peering into the mist.

A grown, or sane, person might have called the weather vile; but the boys at that school had not yet learned the national interest in climate. It was a little damp, to be sure; but it was always damp in the Easter term, and sea-wet, they held, could not give one a cold under any circumstances. Mackintoshes were things to go to church in, but crippling if one had to run at short notice across heavy country. So they waited serenely in the downpour, clad as their mothers would not have cared to see.

'I say, Corky,' said Beetle, wiping his spectacles for the twentieth time, 'if we aren't goin' to help De Vitré, what are we here for?'

'We're goin' to watch,' was the answer. 'Keep your eye on your Uncle and he'll pull you through.'

'It's an awful biznai, driving cattle—in open country,' said M'Turk, who, as the son of an Irish baronet, knew something of these operations. 'They'll have to run half over the Burrows after 'em. S'pose they're ridin' Vidley's ponies?'

'De Vitré's sure to be. He's a dab on a horse. Listen! What a filthy row they're making! They'll be heard for miles.'

The air filled with whoops and shouts, cries, words of command, the rattle of broken golf-clubs, and a clatter of hooves. Three cows with their calves came up to the Cattle-gate at a milch-canter, followed by four wild-eyed bullocks and two rough-coated ponies. A fat and freckled youth of fifteen trotted behind them, riding bare-back and brandishing a hedge-stake. De Vitré, up to a certain point, was an inventive youth, with a passion for horse-exercise that the Northam farmers did not encourage. Farmer Vidley, who could not understand that a grazing pony likes being galloped about, had once called him a thief, and the insult rankled. Hence the raid.

'Come on,' he cried over his shoulder. 'Open the gate, Corkran, or they'll all cut back again. We've had no end of bother to get 'em. Oh, won't old Vidley be wild!'

Three boys on foot ran up, 'shooing' the cattle in excited and amateur fashion, till they headed them into the narrow, high-banked Devonshire lane that ran uphill.

'Come on, Corkran. It's no end of a lark,' pleaded De Vitré. But Corkran shook his head. The affair had been presented to him after dinner that day as a completed scheme, in which he might, by favour, play a minor part. And Arthur Lionel Corkran, No. 104, did not care for lieutenancies.

'You'll only be collared,' he cried, as he shut the gate. 'Parsons and Orrin are no good in a row. You'll be collared sure as a gun, De Vitré.'

'Oh, you're a beastly funk!' The speaker was already hidden by the fog.

'Hang it all,' said M'Turk. 'It's about the first time we've ever tried a cattle-lift at the Coll. Let's——'

'Not much!' said Corkran firmly. 'Keep your eye on your Uncle.' His word was law in these matters, for experience had taught them that if they manœuvred without Corkran they fell into trouble.

'You're wrathy because you didn't think of it first,' said Beetle. Corkran kicked him thrice calmly, neither he nor Beetle changing a muscle the while.

'No, I ain't; but it isn't stalky enough for me.'

'Stalky,' in the school vocabulary, meant clever, well-considered and wily, as applied to plans of action; and 'stalkiness' was the one virtue Corkran toiled after.

'Same thing,' said M'Turk. 'You think you're the only stalky chap in the Coll.'

Corkran kicked him as he had kicked Beetle; and even as Beetle, M'Turk took not the faintest notice. By the etiquette of their friendship, this was no more than formal notice of dissent from a proposition.

'They haven't thrown out any pickets,' Corkran went on (that school prepared boys for the Army). 'You ought to do that—even for apples. Toowey's farmyard may be full of farm-chaps.'

' 'Twasn't last week,' said Beetle, 'when we smoked in that cart-shed place. It's a mile from any house, too.'

Up went one of Corkran's light eyebrows. 'Oh, Beetle, I *am* so tired o' kickin' you! Does that mean it's empty *now*? They ought to have sent a fellow ahead to look. They're simply bound to be collared. An' where'll they bunk to if they have to run for it? Parsons has only been here two terms. *He* don't know the lie of the country. Orrin's a fat ass, an' Howlett bunks from a guv'nor' [vernacular for any native of

Devon engaged in agricultural pursuits] 'as far as he can see
'em. De Vitré's the only decent chap in the lot, an'—an' *I* put
him up to usin' Toowey's farmyard.'

'Well, keep your hair on,' said Beetle. 'What are we going
to do? It's hefty damp here.'

'Let's think a bit.' Corkran whistled between his teeth and
presently broke into a swift, short double-shuffle. 'We'll go
straight up the hill and see what happens to 'em. Cut across
the fields; and we'll lie up in the hedge where the lane comes
in by the barn—where we found that dead hedgehog last
term. Come on!'

He scrambled over the earth bank and dropped on to the
rain-soaked plough. It was a steep slope to the brow of the
hill where Toowey's barns stood. The boys took no account
of stiles or footpaths, crossing field after field diagonally, and
where they found a hedge, bursting through it like beagles.
The lane lay on their right flank, and they heard much lowing
and shouting in that direction.

'Well, if De Vitré isn't collared,' said M'Turk, kicking off
a few pounds of loam against a gate-post, 'he jolly well ought
to be.'

'We'll get collared, too, if you go on with your nose up like
that. Duck, you ass, and stalk along under the hedge. We can
get quite close up to the barn,' said Corkran. 'There's no
sense in not doin' a thing stalkily while you're about it.'

They wriggled into the top of an old hollow double hedge
less than thirty yards from the big black-timbered barn with
its square outbuildings. Their ten minutes' climb had lifted
them a couple of hundred feet above the Burrows. As the
mists parted here and there, they could see the great triangle
of sodden green, tipped with yellow sand-dunes and fringed
with white foam, laid out like a blurred map below. The

surge along the Pebble Ridge made a background to the wild noises in the lane.

'What did I tell you?' said Corkran, peering through the stems of the quickset which commanded a view of the farm-yard. 'Three farm-chaps—getting out dung—with pitch-forks. It's too late to head off De Vitré. We'd be collared if we showed up. Besides, they've heard 'em. They couldn't help hearing. *What* asses!'

The natives, brandishing their weapons, talked together, using many times the word 'Colleger.' As the tumult swelled, they disappeared into various pens and byres. The first of the cattle trotted up to the yard-gate, and De Vitré felicitated his band.

'That's all right,' he shouted. 'Oh, won't old Vidley be wild! Open the gate, Orrin, an' whack 'em through. They're pretty warm.'

'So'll you be in a minute,' muttered M'Turk as the raiders hurried into the yard behind the cattle. They heard a shout of triumph, shrill yells of despair; saw one Devonian guarding the gate with a pitchfork, while the others, alas! captured all four boys.

'Of all the infernal, idiotic, Lower-Second asses!' said Cork-ran. 'They haven't even taken off their House-caps.' These dainty confections of primary colours were not issued, as some believed, to encourage House-pride or *esprit de corps*, but for purposes of identification from afar, should the wearer break bounds or laws. That is why, in time of war, any one but an idiot wore his cap inside out.

'Aie! Yeou young rascals. We've got 'ee! Whutt be doin' to Muster Vidley's bullocks?'

'Oh, we found 'em,' said De Vitré, who bore himself gal-lantly in defeat. 'Would you like 'em?'

'Found 'em! They bullocks drove like that—all heavin' an'

penkin' an' hotted! Oh! Shaameful. Yeou've nigh-to killed the cows—lat alone stealin' 'em. They sends pore boys to jail for half o' this.'

'That's a lie,' said Beetle to M'Turk, turning on the wet grass.

'I know; but they always say it. 'Member when they collared us at the Monkey Farm that Sunday, with the apples in your topper?'

'My Aunt! They're goin' to lock 'em up an' send for Vidley,' Corkran whispered, as one of the captors hurried downhill in the direction of Appledore, and the prisoners were led into the barn.

'But they haven't taken their names an' numbers, anyhow,' said Corkran, who had fallen into the hands of the enemy more than once.

'But they're bottled! Rather sickly for De Vitré,' said Beetle. 'It's one lickin' anyhow, even if Vidley don't hammer him. The Head's rather hot about gate-liftin', an' poachin', an' all that sort of thing. He won't care for cattle-liftin' much.'

'It's awfully bad for cows, too, to run 'em about in milk,' said M'Turk, lifting one knee from a sodden primrose-tuft. 'What's the next move, Corky?'

'We'll get into the old cart-shed where we smoked. It's next to the barn. We can cut across over while they're inside and climb in through the window.'

'S'pose we're collared?' said Beetle, cramming his House-cap into his pocket. Caps may tumble off; so one goes into action bare-headed.

'That's just it. They'd never dream of any more chaps walkin' bung into the trap. Besides, we can get out through the roof if they spot us. Keep your eye on your Uncle. Come on,' said Corkran.

A swift dash carried them to a huge clump of nettles, beneath the unglazed back window of the cart-shed. Its open front, of course, gave on to the barnyard.

They scrambled through, dropped among the carts, and climbed up into the rudely boarded upper floor that they had discovered a week before when in search of retirement. It covered a half of the building and ended in darkness at the barn wall. The roof-tiles were broken and displaced. Through the chinks they commanded a clear view of the barnyard, half filled with disconsolate cattle, steaming sadly in the rain.

'You see,' said Corkran, always careful to secure his line of retreat, 'if they bottle us up here, we can squeeze out between these rafters, slide down the roof, an' bunk. *They* couldn't even get out through the window. They'd have to run right round the barn. Now are you satisfied, you burbler?'

'Huh! You only said that to make quite sure yourself,' Beetle retorted.

'If the boards weren't all loose, I'd kick you,' growled Corkran. 'No sense gettin' into a place you can't get out of. Shut up and listen.'

A murmur of voices reached them from the end of the attic. M'Turk tiptoed thither with caution.

'Hi! It leads through into the barn. You can get through. Come along!' He fingered the boarded wall.

'What's the other side?' said Corkran the cautious.

'Hay, you idiot.' They heard his boot-heels click on wood, and he had gone.

At some time or other sheep must have been folded in the cart-shed, and an inventive farm-hand, sooner than take the hay round, had displaced a board in the barn-side to thrust fodder through. It was in no sense a lawful path, but twelve inches in the square is all that any boy needs.

'Look here!' said Beetle, as they waited for M'Turk's return. 'The cattle are coming in out of the wet.'

'STALKY'

A brown, hairy back showed some three feet below the half-floor, as one by one the cattle shouldered in for shelter among the carts below, filling the shed with their sweet breath.

'That blocks our way out, unless we get out by the roof, an' that's rather too much of a drop, unless we have to,' said Corkran. 'They're all bung in front of the window, too. What a day we're havin'!'

'Corkran! Beetle!' M'Turk's whisper shook with delight. 'You can see 'em! I've seen 'em! They're in a blue funk in the barn, an' the two clods are makin' fun of 'em—horrid. Orrin's tryin' to bribe 'em an' Parsons is nearly blubbin'. Come an' look! I'm in the hayloft. Get through the hole. Don't make a row, Beetle.'

Lithely they wriggled between the displaced boards into the hay and crawled to the edge of the loft. Three years' skirmishing against a hard and unsympathetic peasantry had taught them the elements of strategy. For tactics they looked to Corkran; but even Beetle, notoriously absent-minded, held a lock of hay before his head as he crawled. There was no haste, no betraying giggle, no squeak of excitement. They had learned, by stripes, the unwisdom of these things. But the conference by a root-cutter on the barn floor was deep in its own affairs; De Vitré's party promising, entreating, and cajoling, while the natives laughed like Inquisitors.

'Wait till Muster Vidley an' Muster Toowey—yis, an' the policemen come,' was their only answer. ' 'Tis about time to go to milkin'. What'ull us do?'

'Yeou go milk, Tom, an' I'll stay long o' the young gentlemen,' said the bigger of the two, who answered to the name of Abraham. 'Muster Toowey, he'm laike to charge yeou for usin' his yard so free. Iss fai! Yeou'll be wopped proper. Rackon yeou'll be askin' for junkets to set in this week o' Sundays to come. But Muster Vidley, he'll give 'ee the best leatherin' of all. He'm passionful, I tal 'ee.'

Tom stumped out to milk. The barn doors closed behind him, and in the fading light a great gloom fell on all but Abraham, who discoursed eloquently on Mr. Vidley, his temper and strong arm.

Corkran turned in the hay and retreated to the attic, followed by his army.

'No good,' was his verdict. 'I'm afraid it's all up with 'em. We'd better get out.'

'Yes, but look at these beastly cows,' said M'Turk, spitting on to a heifer's back. 'It'll take us a week to shove 'em away from the window, and that brute Tom'll hear us. He's just across the yard, milkin'.'

'Tweak 'em, then,' said Corkran. 'Hang it, I'm sorry to have to go, though. If we could get that other beast out of the barn for a minute we might make a rescue. Well, it's no good. *Tweakons!*'

He drew forth a slim, well-worn home-made catapult—the 'tweaker' of those days—slipped a buckshot into its supple chamois leather pouch, and pulled to the full stretch of the elastic. The others followed his example. They only wished to get the cattle out of their way, but seeing the backs so near, they deemed it their duty each to choose his bird and to let fly with all their strength.

They were not prepared in the least for what followed. Three bullocks, trying to wheel amid six close-pressed companions, not to mention three calves, several carts, and all the lumber of a general-utility shed, do not turn end-for-end without confusion. It was lucky for the boys that they stood a little back on the floor, because one horned head, tossed in pain, flung up a loose board at the edge, and it came down

lancewise on an amazed back. Another victim floundered bodily across the shafts of a decrepit gig, smashing these and over-
setting the wheels. That was more than enough for the nerves
of the assembly. With wild bellowings and a good deal of left-
and-right butting, they dashed into the barnyard, tails on end,
and began a fine free fight on the midden. The last cow out
hooked down an old set of harness; it flapped over one eye
and trailed behind her. When a companion trod on it, which
happened every few seconds, she naturally fell on her knees;
and, being a Burrows cow, with the interests of her calf at heart,
attacked the first passer-by. Half awed, but wholly delighted,
the boys watched the outburst. It was in full flower before
they even dreamed of a second shot. Tom came out from a
byre with a pitchfork, to be chased in again by the harnessed
cow. A bullock floundered on the muck-heap, fell, rose and
bedded himself to the belly, helpless and bellowing. The
others took great interest in him.

Corkran, through the roof, scientifically 'tweaked' a frisky
heifer on the nose, and it is no exaggeration to say that she
danced on her hind legs for half a minute.

'Abram! Oh, Abram! They'm bewitched. They'm ragin'.
'Tes the milk-fever. They've been drove mad. Oh, Abram!
They'll horn the bullocks! They'll horn *me*! Abram!'

'Bide till I lock the door,' quoth Abraham, faithful to his
trust. They heard him padlock the barn door; saw him come
out with yet another pitchfork. A bullock lowered his head,
Abraham ran to the nearest pig-pen, where loud squeakings
told that he had disturbed the peace of a large family.

'Beetle,' snapped Corkran. 'Go in an' get those asses out.
Quick! We'll keep the cows happy.'

A people sitting in darkness and the shadow of monu-
mental lickings, too depressed to be angry with De Vitré,

heard a voice from on high saying, 'Come up here! Come on! Come up! There's a way out.'

They shinned up the loft-stanchions without a word; found a boot-heel which they were bidden to take for guide, and squeezed desperately through a hole in darkness, to be hauled out by Corkran.

'Have you got your caps? Did you give 'em your names an' numbers?'

'Yes. No.'

'That's all right. Drop down here. Don't stop to jaw. Over the cart—through that window. Bunk! Get *out!*'

De Vitré needed no more. They heard him squeak as he dropped among the nettles, and through the roof-chinks they watched four slight figures disappear into the rain. Tom and Abraham, from byre and pig-pen, exhorted the cattle to keep quiet.

'By Gum!' said Beetle. 'That *was* stalky! How did you think of it?'

'It was the only thing to do. Anybody could have seen that.'

'Hadn't we better bunk, too, now?' said M'Turk uneasily.

'Why? *We*'re all right. *We* haven't done anything. I want to hear what old Vidley will say. Stop tweakin', Turkey. Let 'em cool off. Golly! how that heifer danced! I swear I didn't know cows could be so lively. We're only just in time.'

'My Hat! Here's Vidley—an' Toowey,' said Beetle, as the two farmers strode into the yard.

'Gloats! oh, gloats! Fids! oh, fids! Hefty fids and gloats to us!' said Corkran.

These words, in their vocabulary, expressed the supreme of delight. 'Gloats' implied more or less of personal triumph, 'fids' was felicity in the abstract, and the boys were tasting both that day. Last joy of all, they had had the pleasure of

Mr. Vidley's acquaintance, albeit he did not love them. Toowey was more of a stranger; his orchards lying over-near to the public road.

Tom and Abraham together told a tale of stolen cattle maddened by overdriving; of cows sure to die in calving, and of milk that would never return, that made Mr. Vidley swear for three consecutive minutes in the speech of North Devon.

' 'Tes tu bad. 'Tes tu bad,' said Toowey consolingly. 'Let's 'ope they 'aven't took no great 'arm. They be wonderful wild, though.'

' 'Tes all well for yeou, Toowey, that sells them dom Collegers seventy quart a week.'

'Eighty,' Toowey replied, with the meek triumph of one who has underbidden his neighbour on public tender; 'but that's no odds to *me*. Yeou'm free to leather 'em saame as if they was yeour own sons. On my barn-floor shall 'ee leather 'em.'

'Generous old swine!' said Beetle. 'De Vitré ought to have stayed for this.'

'They'm all safe an' to rights,' said the officious Abraham, producing the key. 'Rackon us'll come in an' hold 'em for yeou. Hey! The cows are fair ragin' still. Us'll have to run for it.'

The barn being next to the shed, the boys could not see that stately entry. But they heard.

'Gone an' hided in the hay. Aie! They'm proper afraid,' cried Abraham.

'Rout un out! Rout un out!' roared Vidley, rattling a stick impatiently on the root-cutter.

'Oh, my Aunt!' said Corkran, standing on one foot.

'Shut the door. Shut the door, I tal 'ee. Rackon us can find

15

un in the dark. Us don't want un boltin' like rabbits under our elbows.' The big barn door closed with a clang.

'My Gum!' said Corkran, which was always his War Oath in time of action. He dropped down and was gone for perhaps twenty seconds.

'And *that's* all right,' he said, returning at a gentle saunter.

'Hwatt?' M'Turk almost shrieked, for Corkran, in the shed below, waved a large key.

'Stalks! Frabjous Stalks! Bottled 'em! all four!' was the reply, and Beetle fell on his bosom. 'Yiss. They'm so's to say, like, locked up. If you're goin' to laugh, Beetle, I shall have to kick you again.'

'But I must!' Beetle was blackening with suppressed mirth.

'You won't do it here, then.' He thrust the already limp Beetle through the cart-shed window. It sobered him; one cannot laugh on a bed of nettles. Then Corkran stepped on his prostrate carcass, and M'Turk followed, just as Beetle would have risen. So he was upset, and the nettles painted on his cheek a likeness of hideous eruptions.

'Thought that 'ud cure you,' said Corkran, with a sniff.

Beetle rubbed his face desperately with dock-leaves, and said nothing. All desire to laugh had gone from him. They entered the lane.

Then a clamour broke from the barn—a compound noise of horse-like kicks, shaking of door-panels, and various yells.

'They've found it out,' said Corkran. 'How strange!' He sniffed again.

'Let 'em,' said Beetle. 'No one can hear 'em. Come on up to Coll.'

'What a brute you are, Beetle! You only think of your beastly self. Those cows want milkin'. Poor dears! Hear 'em low,' said M'Turk.

'Go back an' milk 'em yourself, then.' Beetle danced with pain. 'We shall miss call-over, hangin' about like this; an' I've got two black marks this week already.'

'Then you'll have fatigue-drill on Monday,' said Corkran. 'Come to think of it, I've got two black marks *aussi*. Hm! This is serious. This is hefty serious.'

'I told you,' said Beetle, with vindictive triumph. 'An' we want to go out after that hawk's nest on Monday. We shall be swottin' dumb-bells, though. *All* your fault. If we'd bunked with De Vitré at first——'

Corkran paused between the hedgerows. 'Hold on a shake an' don't burble. Keep your eye on Uncle. Do you know, *I* believe some one's shut up in that barn. I think we ought to go and see.'

'Don't be a giddy idiot. Come on up to Coll.' But Corkran took no notice of Beetle.

He retraced his steps to the head of the lane, and, lifting up his voice, cried as in bewilderment, 'Hullo? Who's there? What's that row about? Who are you?'

'Oh, Peter!' said Beetle, skipping, and forgetting his anguish in this new development.

'Hoi! Hoi! 'Ere! Let us out!' The answers came muffled and hollow from the black bulk of the barn, with renewed thunders on the door.

'Now play up,' said Corkran. 'Turkey, you keep the cows busy. 'Member that we've just discovered 'em. *We* don't know anything. Be polite, Beetle.'

They picked their way over the muck and held speech through a crack by the door-hinge. Three more genuinely surprised boys the steady rain never fell upon. And they were so difficult to enlighten. They had to be told again and again by the captives within.

'We've been 'ere for hours an' hours.' That was Toowey. 'An' the cows to milk, an' all.' That was Vidley. 'The door she blewed against us an' jammed herself.' That was Abraham.

'Yes, we can see that. It's jammed on this side,' said Corkran. 'How careless you chaps are!'

'Oppen un. Oppen un. Bash her oppen with a rock, young gen'elmen! The cows are milk-heated an' ragin'. Haven't you boys no sense?'

Seeing that M'Turk from time to time tweaked the cattle into renewed caperings, it was quite possible that the boys had some knowledge of a sort. But Mr. Vidley was rude. They told him so through the door, professing only now to recognize his voice.

'Humour un if 'e can. I paid seven-an'-six for the padlock,' said Toowey. 'Niver mind *him*. 'Tis only old Vidley.'

'Be yeou gwaine to stay a prisoneer an' captive for the sake of a lock, Toowey? I'm shaamed of 'ee. Rowt un oppen, young gen'elmen! 'Twas a God's own mercy yeou heard us. Toowey, yeou'm a borned miser.'

'It'll be a long job,' said Corkran. 'Look here. It's near our call-over. If we stay to help you we'll miss it. We've come miles out of our way already—after you.'

'Tell yeour master, then, what kept 'ee—an arrand o' mercy, laike. I'll tal un tu when I bring the milk to-morrow,' said Toowey.

'That's no good,' said Corkran. 'We may be licked twice over by then. You'll have to give us a letter.' M'Turk, backed against the barn-wall, was firing steadily and accurately into the brown of the herd.

'Yiss, yiss. Come down to my house. My missus shall write 'ee a beauty, young gen'elmen. She makes out the bills. I'll give 'ee just such a letter o' racommendation as I'd give to my own son, if only yeou can humour the lock!'

'Niver mind the lock,' Vidley wailed. 'Let me get to me pore cows, 'fore they'm dead.'

They went to work with ostentatious rattlings and wrenchings, and a good deal of the by-play that Corkran always loved. At last—the noise of unlocking was covered by some fancy hammering with a young boulder—the door swung open and the captives marched out.

'Hurry up, Mister Toowey,' said Corkran; 'we ought to be getting back. Will you give us that note, please?'

'Some of yeou young gen'elmen was drivin' my cattle off the Burrowses,' said Vidley. 'I give 'ee fair warnin', I'll tell yeour masters. I know *yeou*!' He glared at Corkran with malignant recognition.

M'Turk looked him over from head to foot. 'Oh, it's only old Vidley. Drunk again, I suppose. Well, we can't help that. Come on, *Mister* Toowey. We'll go to your house.'

'Drunk, am I? I'll drunk 'ee! How do I know yeou bain't the saame lot? Abram, did 'ee take their names an' numbers?'

'What *is* he ravin' about?' said Beetle. 'Can't you see that if we'd taken your beastly cattle we shouldn't be hanging round your beastly barn. 'Pon my Sam, you Burrows guv'nors haven't any sense——'

'Let alone gratitude,' said Corkran. 'I suppose he *was* drunk, Mister Toowey; an' you locked him in the barn to get sober. Shockin'! Oh, shockin'!'

Vidley denied the charge in language that the boys' mothers would have wept to hear.

'Well, go and look after your cows, then,' said M'Turk. 'Don't stand there cursin' us because we've been kind enough to help you out of a scrape. Why on earth weren't your cows milked before? *You*'re no farmer. It's long past milkin'. No wonder they're half crazy. Disreputable old bog-trotter, you are! Brush your hair, sir. . . . I *beg* your pardon, Mister Toowey. Hope we're not keeping you.'

They left Vidley dancing on the muck-heap, amid the cows, and devoted themselves to propitiating Mr. Toowey on their way to his house. Exercise had made them hungry; hunger is the mother of good manners; and they won golden opinions from Mrs. Toowey.

'Three-quarters of an hour late for call-over, and fifteen minutes late for Lock-up,' said Foxy, the school Sergeant, crisply. He was waiting for them at the head of the corridor. 'Report to your House-master, please—an' a nice mess you're in, young gentlemen.'

'Quite right, Foxy. Strict attention to dooty does it,' said Corkran. 'Now where, if we asked you, would you say that his honour Mister Prout might, at this moment of time, be found prouting—eh?'

'In 'is study—as usual, Muster Corkran. He took call-over.'

'Hurrah! Luck's with us all the way. Don't blub, Foxy. I'm afraid you don't catch us this time.'

'We went up to change, sir, before comin' to you. That made us a little late, sir. We weren't really very late. We were detained—by a——'

'An errand of mercy,' said Beetle, and they laid Mrs. Toowey's laboriously written note before him. 'We thought you'd prefer a letter, sir. Toowey got himself locked into a barn, and we heard him shouting—it's Toowey who brings the Coll. milk, sir—and we went to let him out.'

'There were ever so many cows waiting to be milked,' said M'Turk; 'and of course, he couldn't get at them, sir. They said the door had jammed. There's his note, sir.'

Mr. Prout read it over thrice. It was perfectly unimpeachable; but it said nothing of a large tea supplied by Mrs. Toowey.

'Well, I don't like your getting mixed up with farmers and potwallopers. Of course you will not pay any more—er —visits to the Tooweys,' said he.

'Of course not, sir. It was really on account of the cows, sir,' replied M'Turk, glowing with philanthropy.

'And you came straight back?'

'We ran nearly all the way from the Cattle-gate,' said Corkran, carefully developing the unessential. 'That's one mile, sir. Of course, we had to get the note from Toowey first.'

'But it was because we went to change—we were rather wet, sir—that we were *really* late. After we'd reported ourselves to the Sergeant, sir, and he knew we were in Coll., we didn't like to come to your study all dirty.' Sweeter than honey was the voice of Beetle.

'Very good. Don't let it happen again.' Their House-master learned to know them better in later years.

They entered—not to say swaggered—into Number Nine form-room, where De Vitré, Orrin, Parsons, and Howlett, before the fire, were still telling their adventures to admiring associates. The four rose as one boy.

'What happened to *you?* We just saved call-over. Did you stay on? Tell us! Tell us!'

The three smiled pensively. They were not distinguished for telling more than was necessary.

'Oh, we stayed on a bit and then we came away,' said M'Turk. 'That's all.'

'You scab! You might tell a chap anyhow.'

'Think so? Well, that's awfully good of you, De Vitré. 'Pon my Sainted Sam, that's awfully good of you,' said Corkran, shouldering into the centre of the warmth and toasting one slippered foot before the blaze. 'So you really think we might tell you?'

They stared at the coals and shook with deep, delicious chuckles.

'My Hat! We *were* stalky,' said M'Turk. 'I swear we were about as stalky as they make 'em. Weren't we?'

'It was a frabjous Stalk,' said Beetle. 'Much too good to tell you brutes, though.'

The four wriggled under the insult, but made no motion to avenge it. After all, on De Vitré's showing, the three had saved the raiders from at least a public licking.

'It wasn't half bad,' said Corkran. 'Stalky *is* the word.'

'*You* were the really stalky one,' said M'Turk, one contemptuous shoulder turned to a listening world. 'By Gum! you *were* stalky.'

Corkran accepted the compliment and the name together. 'Yes,' said he; 'keep your eye on your Uncle Stalky an' he'll pull you through.'

'Well, you needn't gloat so,' said De Vitré viciously. 'You look like a stuffed cat.'

Corkran, henceforth known as Stalky, took not the slightest notice, but smiled dreamily.

'My Hat! Yes. Of course,' he murmured. 'Your Uncle Stalky —a doocid good name! Your Uncle Stalky is no end of a stalker. He's a Great Man. I swear he is. De Vitré, you're an ass—a putrid ass.'

De Vitré would have denied this but for the assenting murmurs from Parsons and Orrin.

'You needn't rub it in, then.'

'But I do. I does. You are such a whoppin' ass. D'you know it? Think over it a bit at prep. Think it up in bed. Oblige me by thinkin' of it every half-hour till further notice. Gummy! *What* an ass you are! But your Uncle Stalky'—he picked up the form-room poker and beat it against the mantelpiece—'is a Great Man!'

'Hear, hear!' said Beetle and M'Turk, who had fought under that general.

'Isn't your Uncle Stalky a great man, De Vitré? Speak the truth, you fat-headed old impostor.'

'Yes,' said De Vitré, deserted by all his band. 'I—I suppose he is.'

'Mustn't suppose. *Is* he?'

'Well, he is.'

'A Great Man?'

'A Great Man. *Now* won't you tell us?' said De Vitré pleadingly.

'Not by a heap,' said 'Stalky' Corkran.

Therefore the tale has stayed untold till to-day.

THE HOUR OF THE ANGEL[1]

Sooner or late—in earnest or in jest—
  (But the stakes are no jest) Ithuriel's Hour
Will spring on us, for the first time, the test
    Of our sole unbacked competence and power
    Up to the limit of our years and dower
Of judgment—or beyond. But here we have
Prepared long since our garland or our grave.
    For, at that hour, the sum of all our past,
    Act, habit, thought, and passion, shall be cast
    In one addition, be it more or less,
    And as that reading runs so shall we do;
    Meeting, astounded, victory at the last,
    Or, first and last, our own unworthiness.
    And none can change us though they die to save!

[1] Ithuriel was that Archangel whose spear had the magic property of showing every one exactly and truthfully what he was.

'IN AMBUSH'

'IN AMBUSH'

IN SUMMER all right-minded boys built huts in the furze-hill behind the College—little lairs whittled out of the heart of the prickly bushes, full of stumps, odd root-ends, and spikes, but, since they were strictly forbidden, palaces of delight. And for the fifth summer in succession, Stalky, M'Turk, and Beetle (this was before they reached the dignity of a study) had built, like beavers, a place of retreat and meditation, where they smoked.

Now there was nothing in their characters, as known to Mr. Prout, their House-master, at all commanding respect; nor did Foxy, the subtle red-haired school Sergeant, trust them. His business was to wear tennis-shoes, carry binoculars, and swoop hawk-like upon evil boys. Had he taken the field alone, that hut would have been raided, for Foxy knew the manners of his quarry; but Providence moved Mr. Prout, whose school-name, derived from the size of his feet, was Hoofer, to investigate on his own account; and it was the cautious Stalky who found the track of his pugs on the very floor of their lair one peaceful afternoon when Stalky would fain have forgotten Prout and his works in a volume of Surtees and a new briar-wood pipe. Crusoe, at sight of the footprint, did not act more swiftly than Stalky. He removed the pipes, swept up all loose match-ends, and departed to warn Beetle and M'Turk.

But it was characteristic of the boy that he did not approach his allies till he had met and conferred with little Hartopp, President of the Natural History Society, an institution which

Stalky held in contempt. Hartopp was more than surprised when the boy meekly, as he knew how, begged to propose himself, Beetle, and M'Turk as candidates; confessed to a long-smothered interest in first-flowerings, early butterflies, and new arrivals, and volunteered, if Mr. Hartopp saw fit, to enter on the new life at once. Being a master, Hartopp was suspicious; but he was also an enthusiast, and his gentle little soul had been galled by chance-heard remarks from the three, and specially Beetle. So he was gracious to that repentant sinner, and entered the three names in his book.

Then, and not till then, did Stalky seek Beetle and M'Turk in their House form-room. They were stowing away books for a quiet afternoon in the furze, which they called the 'wuzzy.'

'All up!' said Stalky serenely. 'I spotted Heffy's fairy feet round our hut after dinner. Blessing they're so big.'

'Con-found! Did you hide our pipes?' said Beetle.

'Oh no. Left 'em in the middle of the hut, of course. What a blind ass you are, Beetle! D'you think nobody thinks but yourself? Well, we can't use the hut any more. Hoofer will be watchin' it.'

' "Bother! Likewise blow!" ' said M'Turk thoughtfully, unpacking the volumes with which his chest was cased. The boys carried their libraries between their belt and their collar. 'Nice job! This means we're under suspicion for the rest of the term.'

'Why? All that Heffy has found is *a* hut. He and Foxy will watch it. It's nothing to do with us; only we mustn't be seen that way for a bit.'

'Yes, and where else are we to go?' said Beetle. 'You chose that place, too—an'—an' I wanted to read this afternoon.'

Stalky sat on a desk drumming his heels on the form.

'You're a despondin' brute, Beetle. Sometimes I think I

shall have to drop you altogether. Did you ever know your Uncle Stalky forget you yet? *His rebus infectis*—after I'd seen Heffy's man-tracks marchin' round our hut, I found little Hartopp—*districto ense*—wavin' a butterfly-net. I conciliated Hartopp. Told him that you'd read papers to the Bug-hunters if he'd let you join, Beetle. Told him you liked butterflies, Turkey. Anyhow, I soothed the Hartoffles, and we're Bug-hunters now.'

'What's the good of that?' said Beetle.

'Oh, Turkey, kick him!'

In the interests of science, bounds were largely relaxed for the members of the Natural History Society. They could wander, if they kept clear of all houses, practically where they chose; Mr. Hartopp holding himself responsible for their good conduct.

Beetle began to see this as M'Turk began the kicking.

'I'm an ass, Stalky!' he said, guarding the afflicted part. '*Pax*, Turkey! I'm an ass.'

'Don't stop, Turkey. Isn't your Uncle Stalky a Great Man?'

'Great Man,' said Beetle.

'All the same, bug-huntin's a filthy business,' said M'Turk. 'How the deuce does one begin?'

'This way,' said Stalky, turning to some fags' lockers behind him. 'Fags are dabs at Natural History. Here's young Braybrooke's botany-case.' He flung out a tangle of decayed roots and adjusted the slide. 'Gives one no end of a professional air, I think. Here's Clay minor's geological hammer. Beetle can carry that. Turkey, you'd better covet a butterfly-net from somewhere.'

'I'm blowed if I do!' said M'Turk simply, with immense feeling. 'Beetle, give me the hammer.'

'All right. *I'm* not proud. Chuck us down that net on top of the lockers, Stalky.'

'That's all right. It's a collapsible jamboree, too. Beastly luxurious dogs these fags are. Built like a fishin'-rod. 'Pon my Sainted Sam, but we look the complete Bug-hunters! Now, listen to your Uncle Stalky! We're goin' along the cliffs after butterflies. Very few chaps come there. We're goin' to leg it, too. You'd better leave your book behind.'

'Not much!' said Beetle firmly. 'I'm not goin' to be done out of my fun for a lot of filthy butterflies.'

'Then you'll sweat horrid. You'd better carry my Jorrocks. 'Twon't make you any hotter.'

They all sweated; for Stalky led them at a smart trot west away along the cliffs under the furze-hills, crossing combe after gorsy combe. They took no heed of flying rabbits or fluttering fritillaries, and all that Turkey said of geology was utterly unquotable.

'Are we going to Clovelly?' he puffed at last, and they flung themselves down on the short, springy turf between the drone of the sea below and the light summer wind among the inland trees. They were looking into a combe half-full of old, high furze in gay bloom that ran up to a fringe of brambles and a dense wood of mixed timber and hollies. It was as though one-half the combe were filled with golden fire to the cliff's edge. The side nearest to them was open grass, and fairly bristled with notice-boards.

'Fee-rocious old cove, this,' said Stalky, reading the nearest. ' "Prosecuted with the utmost vigour of the Law. G. M. Dabney, Col., J.P.," an' all the rest of it. Don't seem to me that any chap in his senses would trespass here, does it?'

'You've got to prove damage 'fore you can prosecute for anything! Can't prosecute for trespass,' said M'Turk, whose father held many acres in Ireland. 'That's all rot!'

'Glad of that, 'cause this looks like what we wanted. Not straight across, Beetle, you blind lunatic! Any one could spot us half a mile off. This way. Furl up your beastly butterfly-net.'

Beetle disconnected the ring, thrust the net into a pocket, shut up the handle to a two-foot stave, and slid the cane ring round his waist. Stalky led inland to the wood, which was, perhaps, a quarter of a mile from the sea, and reached the fringe of the brambles.

'*Now* we can get straight down through the furze, and never show up at all,' said the tactician. 'Beetle, go ahead and explore. Snf! Snf! Beastly stink of fox somewhere!'

On all fours, save when he clung to his spectacles, Beetle wormed into the gorse, and presently announced between grunts of pain that he had found a very fair fox-track. This was well for Beetle, since Stalky pinched him *a tergo*. Down that tunnel they crawled. It was evidently a highway for the inhabitants of the combe; and, to their inexpressible joy, ended, at the very edge of the cliff, in a few square feet of dry turf walled and roofed with impenetrable gorse.

'By Gum! There isn't a single thing to do except lie down,' said Stalky, returning a knife to his pocket. 'Look here!'

He parted the tough stems before him, and it was as a window opened on a far view of Lundy, and the deep sea sluggishly nosing the pebbles a couple of hundred feet below. They could hear young jackdaws squawking on the ledges, the hiss and jabber of a nest of hawks somewhere out of sight; and, with great deliberation, Stalky spat on to the back of a young rabbit sunning himself far down where only a cliff-rabbit could have found foot-hold. Great grey-and-black gulls screamed against the jackdaws; the heavy-scented acres of bloom round them were alive with low-nesting birds, singing or silent as the shadow of the wheeling hawks passed and returned; and on the naked turf across the combe rabbits thumped and frolicked.

'Whew! What a place! Talk of Natural History; this is it,'

said Stalky, filling himself a pipe. 'Isn't it scrumptious? Good old sea!' He spat again approvingly, and was silent.

M'Turk and Beetle had taken out their books and were lying on their stomachs, chin in hand. The sea snored and gurgled; the birds, scattered for the moment by these new animals, returned to their businesses, and the boys read on in the rich, warm, sleepy silence.

'Hullo, here's a keeper,' said Stalky, shutting *Handley Cross* cautiously, and peering through the jungle. A man with a gun appeared on the skyline to the east. 'Confound him, he's goin' to sit down!'

'He'd swear we were poachin' too,' said Beetle. 'What's the good of pheasants' eggs? They're always addled.'

'Might as well get up to the wood, *I* think,' said Stalky. 'We don't want G. M. Dabney, Col., J.P., to be bothered about us so soon. Up the wuzzy and keep quiet! He may have followed us, you know.'

Beetle was already far up the tunnel. They heard him gasp indescribably. There was the crash of a heavy body leaping through the furze.

'Aie! yeou little red rascal. I see yeou!' The keeper threw the gun to his shoulder, and fired both barrels in their direction. The pellets dusted the dry stems round them as a big fox plunged between Stalky's legs and ran over the cliff-edge.

They said nothing till they reached the wood, torn, dishevelled, hot, but unseen.

'Narrow squeak,' said Stalky. 'I'll swear some of the pellets went through my hair.'

'Did you see him?' said Beetle. 'I almost put my hand on him. Wasn't he a whopper! Didn't he stink! Hullo, Turkey, what's the matter? Are you hit?'

M'Turk's lean face had turned pearly white; his mouth,

34

generally half open, was tight shut, and his eyes blazed. They had never seen him like this save once, in a sad time of civil war.

'Do you know that that was just as bad as murder?' he said, in a grating voice, as he brushed prickles from his head.

'Well, he didn't hit us,' said Stalky. 'I think it was rather a lark. Here, where are you goin'?'

'I'm going up to the house, if there is one,' said M'Turk, pushing through the hollies. 'I am going to tell this Colonel Dabney.'

'Are you crazy? He'll swear it served us jolly well right. He'll report us. It'll be a public lickin'. Oh, Turkey, don't be an ass! Think of us!'

'You fool!' said M'Turk, turning savagely. 'D'you suppose I'm thinkin' of *us*? It's the keeper.'

'He's cracked,' said Beetle miserably, as they followed. Indeed, this was a new Turkey—a haughty, angular, nose-lifted Turkey—whom they accompanied through a shrubbery on to a lawn, where a white-whiskered old gentleman with a cleek was alternately putting and blaspheming vigorously.

'Are you Colonel Dabney?' M'Turk began in this new creaking voice of his.

'I—I am, and'—his eyes travelled up and down the boy—'who—what the devil d'you want? Ye've been disturbing my pheasants. Don't attempt to deny it. Ye needn't laugh at it.' (M'Turk's not too lovely features had twisted themselves into a horrible sneer at the word 'pheasant.') 'You've been bird's-nesting. You needn't hide your hat. I can see that you belong to the College. Don't attempt to deny it. Ye do! Your name and number at once, sir. Ye want to speak to me—Eh? You saw my notice-boards? Must have. Don't attempt to deny it. Ye did! Damnable! Oh, damnable!'

He choked with emotion. M'Turk's heel tapped the lawn and he stuttered a little—two sure signs that he was losing his temper. But why should he, the offender, be angry?

'Loo-look here, sir. Do—do you shoot foxes? Because, if you don't, your keeper does. We've seen him! I do-don't care what you call us—but it's an awful thing. It's the ruin of good feelin' among neighbours. A ma-man ought to say once and for all how he stands about preservin'. It's worse than murder, because there's no legal remedy.' M'Turk was quoting confusedly from his father, while the old gentleman made noises in his throat.

'Do you know who I am?' he gurgled at last; Stalky and Beetle quaking.

'No, sorr, nor do I care if ye belonged to the Castle itself. Answer me now, as one gentleman to another. Do ye shoot foxes or do ye not?'

And four years before Stalky and Beetle had carefully kicked M'Turk out of his Irish dialect! Assuredly he had gone mad or taken a sunstroke, and as assuredly he would be slain— once by the old gentleman and once by the Head. A public licking for the three was the least they could expect. Yet—if their eyes and ears were to be trusted—the old gentleman had collapsed. It might be a lull before the storm, but——

'I do not.' He was still gurgling.

'Then you must sack your keeper. He's not fit to live in the same county with a God-fearin' fox. An' a vixen, too—at this time o' year!'

'Did ye come up on purpose to tell me this?'

'Of course I did, ye silly man,' with a stamp of the foot. 'Would you not have done as much for me if you'd seen that thing happen on my land, now?'

Forgotten—forgotten was the College and the decency due

to elders! M'Turk was treading again the barren purple mountains of the rainy West coast, where in his holidays he was viceroy of four thousand naked acres, only son of a three-hundred-year-old house, lord of a crazy fishing-boat, and the idol of his father's shiftless tenantry. It was the landed man speaking to his equal—deep calling to deep—and the old gentleman acknowledged the cry.

'I apologise,' said he. 'I apologise unreservedly—to you, and to the Old Country. Now, will you be good enough to tell me your story?'

'We were in your combe,' M'Turk began, and he told his tale alternately as a schoolboy, and, when the iniquity of the thing overcame him, as an indignant Squire; concluding: 'So you see he must be in the habit of it. I—we—one never wants to accuse a neighbour's man; but I took the liberty in this case——'

'I see. Quite so. For a reason ye had. Infamous—oh, infamous!' The two had fallen into step beside each other on the lawn, and Colonel Dabney was talking as one man to another. 'This comes of promoting a fisherman—a fisherman—from his lobster-pots. It's enough to ruin the reputation of an archangel. Don't attempt to deny it. It is! Your father has brought you up well. He has. I'd much like the pleasure of his acquaintance. Very much indeed. And these young gentlemen? English they are. Don't attempt to deny it. They came up with you, too? Extraordinary! Extraordinary, now! In the present state of education I shouldn't have thought any three boys would be well enough grounded. . . . But out of the mouths of—— No—no! Not that by any odds. Don't attempt to deny it. Ye're not! Sherry always catches me under the liver, but—beer, now? Eh? What d'you say to beer, and something to eat? It's long since I was a boy—abominable nuisances; but exceptions prove the rule. And a vixen, too!'

They were fed on the terrace by a grey-haired housekeeper. Stalky and Beetle merely ate, but M'Turk with bright eyes continued a free and lofty discourse; and ever the old gentleman treated him as a brother.

'My dear man, of *course* ye can come again. Did I not say exceptions prove the rule? The lower combe? Man, dear, anywhere ye please, so long as you do not disturb my pheasants. The two are not incompatible. Don't attempt to deny it. They're not! I'll never allow another gun, though. Come and go as ye please. I'll not see you, and ye needn't see me. Ye've been well brought up. Another glass of beer, now? I tell you a fisherman he was and a fisherman he shall be to-night again. He shall! Wish I could drown him. I'll convoy you to the Lodge. My people are not precisely—ah—broke to boy, but they'll know *you* again.'

He dismissed them with many compliments by the high Lodge-gate in the split-oak park palings and they stood still; even Stalky, who had played second, not to say a dumb, fiddle, regarding M'Turk as one from another world. The two glasses of strong home-brewed had brought a melancholy upon the boy, for, slowly strolling with his hands in his pockets, he crooned:—

'*Oh, Paddy dear, and did ye hear the news that's goin' round?*'

Under other circumstances Stalky and Beetle would have fallen upon him, for that song was barred utterly—anathema —the sin of witchcraft. But seeing what he had wrought, they danced round him in silence, waiting till it pleased him to touch earth.

The tea-bell rang when they were still half a mile from College. M'Turk shivered and came out of dreams. The glory of his holiday estate had left him. He was a Colleger of the College, speaking English once more.

'Turkey, it was immense!' said Stalky generously. 'I didn't know you had it in you. You've got us a hut for the rest of the term, where we simply can't be collared. Fids! Fids! Oh, fids! I gloat! Hear me gloat!'

They spun wildly on their heels, jodelling after the accepted manner of a 'gloat,' which is not unremotely allied to primitive man's song of triumph, and dropped down the hill by the path from the gasometer just in time to meet their Housemaster, who had spent the afternoon watching their abandoned hut in the 'wuzzy.'

Unluckily, all Mr. Prout's imagination leaned to the darker side of life, and he looked on those young-eyed cherubim most sourly. Boys that he understood attended House-matches and could be accounted for at any moment. But he had heard M'Turk openly deride cricket—even House-matches; Beetle's views on the honour of the House he knew were incendiary; and he could never tell when the soft and smiling Stalky was laughing at him. Consequently—since human nature is what it is—those boys had been doing wrong somewhere. He hoped it was nothing very serious, but . . .

'*Ti-ra-la-la-i-tu!* I gloat! Hear me!' Stalky, still on his heels, whirled like a dancing dervish to the dining-hall.

'*Ti-ra-la-la-i-tu!* I gloat! Hear me!' Beetle spun behind him with outstretched arms.

'*Ti-ra-la-la-i-tu!* I gloat! Hear me!' M'Turk's voice cracked.

Now was there or was there not a distinct flavour of beer as they shot past Mr. Prout?

He was unlucky in that his conscience as a House-master impelled him to consult his associates. Had he taken his pipe and his troubles to little Hartopp's rooms he would, perhaps, have been saved confusion, for Hartopp believed in boys, and knew something about them. His fate led him to King, a fellow House-master, no friend of his, but a zealous hater of Stalky & Co.

'Ah-haa!' said King, rubbing his hands, when the tale was told. 'Curious! Now *my* House never dream of doing these things.'

'But you see I've no proof, exactly.'

'Proof? With the egregious Beetle! As if one wanted it! I suppose it is not impossible for the Sergeant to supply it? Foxy is considered at least a match for any evasive boy in my House. Of course they were smoking and drinking somewhere. That type of boy always does. They think it manly.'

'But they've no following in the school, and they are distinctly—er—brutal to their juniors,' said Prout, who had from a distance seen Beetle return, with interest, his butterfly-net to a tearful fag.

'Ah! They consider themselves superior to ordinary delights. Self-sufficient young animals! There's something in M'Turk's Hibernian sneer that would make me a little annoyed. And they are so careful to avoid all overt acts, too. It's sheer calculated insolence. I am strongly opposed, as you know, to interfering with another man's House; but they need a lesson, Prout. They need a sharp lesson, if only to bring down their overweening self-conceit. Were I you, I should devote myself for a week to their little performances. Boys of that order— I may flatter myself, but I think I know boys—don't join the Bug-hunters for love. Tell the Sergeant to keep his eye open; and, of course, in my peregrinations, I may casually keep mine open too.'

'*Ti-ra-la-la-i-tu!* I gloat! Hear me!' far down the corridor.

'Disgusting!' said King. 'Where do they pick up these obscene noises? One sharp lesson is what they want.'

The boys did not concern themselves with lessons for the next few days. They had all Colonel Dabney's estate to play with, and they explored it with the stealth of Red Indians and the accuracy of burglars. They could enter either by the Lodge-gates on the upper road—they were careful to ingratiate themselves with the Lodge-keeper and his wife—drop down into the combe, and return along the cliffs; or they could begin at the combe, and climb up into the road.

They were careful not to cross the Colonel's path—he had served his turn, and they would not outwear their welcome—nor did they show up on the skyline when they could move in cover. The shelter of the gorse by the cliff-edge was their chosen retreat. Beetle christened it the Pleasant Isle of Aves, for the peace and the shelter of it; and here, pipes and tobacco once cachéd in a convenient ledge an arm's length down the cliff, their position was legally unassailable.

For, observe, Colonel Dabney had not invited them to enter his house. Therefore, they did not need to ask specific leave to go visiting; and school rules were strict on that point. He had merely thrown open his grounds to them; and, since they were lawful Bug-hunters, their extended bounds ran up to his notice-boards in the combe and his Lodge-gates on the hill.

They were amazed at their own virtue.

'And even if it wasn't,' said Stalky, flat on his back, staring into the blue. 'Even suppose we were miles out of bounds, no one could get at us through this wuzzy, unless he knew the tunnel. Isn't this better than lyin' up just behind the Coll.— in a blue funk every time we had a smoke? Isn't your Uncle Stalky——?'

'No,' said Beetle—he was stretched at the edge of the cliff, thoughtfully spitting. 'We've got to thank Turkey for this. Turkey is the Great Man. Turkey, dear, you're distressin' Heffles.'

'Gloomy old ass!' said M'Turk, deep in a book.

'They've got us under suspicion,' said Stalky. 'Hoophats *is* so suspicious somehow; an' Foxy always makes every stalk he does a sort of—sort of——'

'Scalp,' said Beetle. 'Foxy's a giddy Chingangook.'

'Poor Foxy,' said Stalky. 'He's goin' to catch us one of these days. Said to me in the gym last night, "I've got my eye on you, Mister Corkran. I'm only warning you for your good." Then I said, "Well, you jolly well take it off again, or you'll get into trouble. I'm only warnin' you for your good." Foxy was wrath.'

'Yes, but it's only fair sport for Foxy,' said Beetle. 'It's Hefflelinga that has the evil mind. Shouldn't wonder if he thought we got tight.'

'I never got squiffy but once—that was in the holidays,' said Stalky reflectively; 'an' it made me horrid sick. 'Pon my Sacred Sam, though, it's enough to drive a man to drink, havin' an animal like Hoof for House-master.'

'If we attended the matches an' yelled, "Well hit, sir," an' stood on one leg an' grinned every time Heffy said, "So ho, my sons. Is it thus?" an' said, "Yes, sir," an' "No, sir," an' "Oh, sir," an' "Please, sir," like a lot o' filthy fa-ags, Heffy 'ud think no end of us,' said M'Turk, with a sneer.

'Too late to begin that.'

'It's all right. The Hefflelinga means well. *But* he is an ass. *And* we show him that we think he's an ass. An' *so* Heffy don't love us. Told me last night after prayers that he was *in loco parentis,*' Beetle grunted.

'The deuce he did!' cried Stalky. 'That means he's maturin' something unusual dam' mean. Last time he told me that, he gave me three hundred lines for dancin' the cachuca in Number Ten dormitory. *Loco parentis,* by Gum! But what's the odds, as long as you're 'appy? We're all right.'

They were, and their very rightness puzzled Prout, King, and the Sergeant. Boys with bad consciences show it. They slink out past the Fives Court in haste, and smile nervously when questioned. They return, disordered, in bare time to save a call-over. They nod and wink and giggle one to the other, scattering at the approach of a master. But Stalky and his allies had long outlived these manifestations of youth. They strolled forth unconcernedly, and returned, in excellent shape, after a light refreshment of strawberries and cream at the Lodge.

The Lodge-keeper had been promoted to keeper, *vice* the murderous fisherman, and his wife made much of the boys. The man, too, gave them a squirrel, which they presented to the Natural History Society; thereby checkmating little Hartopp, who wished to know what they were doing for Science. Foxy faithfully worked some deep Devon lanes behind a lonely cross-roads inn; and it was curious that Prout and King, members of Common-room seldom friendly, walked together in the same direction—that is to say, north-east. Now the Pleasant Isle of Aves lay due south-west.

'They're deep—day-vilish deep,' said Stalky. 'Why are they drawin' those covers?'

'Me,' said Beetle sweetly. 'I asked Foxy if he had ever tasted the beer there. That was enough for Foxy, an' it cheered him up a little. He an' Heffy were sniffin' round our old hut so long I thought they'd like a change.'

'Well, it can't last for ever,' said Stalky. 'Heffy's bankin' up like a thunder-cloud, an' King goes rubbin' his beastly hands, an' grinnin' like a hyena. It's shockin' demoralisin' for King. He'll burst some day.'

That day came a little sooner than they expected—came when the Sergeant, whose duty it was to collect defaulters, did not attend an afternoon call-over.

'Tired of pubs, eh? He's gone up to the top of the hill with his binoculars ·to spot us,' said Stalky. 'Wonder he didn't think of that before. Did you see old Heffy cock his eye at us when we answered our names? Heffy's in it, too. *Ti-ra-la-la-i-tu!* I gloat! Hear me! Come on!'

'Aves?' said Beetle.

'Of course, but I'm not smokin' *aujourd'hui*. *Parce que je* jolly well *pense* that we'll be *suivi*. We'll go along the cliffs, slow, an' give Foxy lots of time to parallel us up above.'

They strolled towards the swimming-baths, and presently overtook King.

'Oh, don't let *me* interrupt you,' he said. 'Engaged in scientific pursuits, of course? I trust you will enjoy yourselves, my young friends.'

'You see!' said Stalky, when they were out of earshot. 'He can't keep a secret. He's followin' to cut off our line of retreat. He'll wait at the Baths till Heffy comes along. They've tried every blessed place except along the cliffs, and now they think they've bottled us. No need to hurry.'

They walked leisurely over the combes till they reached the line of notice-boards.

'Listen a shake. Foxy's up wind comin' downhill like beans. When you hear him move in the bushes, go straight across to Aves. They want to catch us *flagrante delicto*.'

They dived into the gorse at right angles to the tunnel, openly crossing the grass, and lay still in Aves.

'What did I tell you?' Stalky carefully put away the pipes and tobacco. The Sergeant, out of breath, was leaning against the fence, raking the furze with his binoculars, but he might as well have tried to see through a sand-bag. Anon, Prout and King appeared behind him. They conferred.

'Aha! Foxy don't like the notice-boards, an' he don't like

the prickles either. Now we'll cut up the tunnel an' go to the Lodge. Hullo! They've sent Foxy into cover.'

The Sergeant was waist-deep in crackling, swaying furze, his ears filled with the noise of his own progress. The boys reached the shelter of the wood and looked down through a belt of hollies.

'Hellish noise!' said Stalky critically. 'Don't think Colonel Dabney will like it. I move we go up to the Lodge and get something to eat. We might as well see the fun out.'

Suddenly the keeper passed them at a trot.

'Who'm they to combe-bottom for Lard's sake? Master'll be crazy,' he said.

'Poachers simly,' Stalky replied in the broad Devon that was the boy's *langue de guerre.*

'I'll poach 'em to raights!' He dropped into the funnel-like combe, which presently began to fill with noises, notably King's voice crying, 'Go on, Sergeant! Leave him alone, you, sir. He is executing my orders.'

'Who'm yeou to give arders here, gingy whiskers? Yeou come up to the Master. Come out o' that wuzzy!' (This is to the Sergeant.) 'Yiss, I reckon us knows the boys yeou'm after. They've tu long ears an' vuzzy bellies, an' you nippies they in yeour pockets when they'm dead. Come on up to Master! He'll boy yeou all yeou'm a mind to. Yeou other folk bide yeour side fence.'

'Explain to the proprietor. You can explain, Sergeant,' shouted King. Evidently the Sergeant had surrendered to the major force.

Beetle lay at full length on the turf behind the Lodge literally biting the earth in spasms of joy.

Stalky kicked him upright. There was nothing of levity about Stalky or M'Turk save a stray muscle twitching on the cheek.

They tapped at the Lodge door, where they were always welcome.

'Come yeou right in an' set down, my little dearrs,' said the woman. 'They'll niver touch my man. He'll poach 'em to rights. Iss fai! Fresh berries an' cream. Us Dartymoor folk niver forget their friends. But them Bidevor poachers, they've no hem to their garments. Sugar? My man he've digged a badger for yeou, my dearrs. 'Tes in the linhay in a box.'

'Us'll take un with us when we'm finished here. I reckon yeou'm busy. We'll bide here an'—'tes washin'day with yeou, simly,' said Stalky. '*We*'m no company to make all vitty for. Niver yeou mind us. Yiss. There's plenty cream.'

The woman withdrew, wiping her pink hands on her apron, and left them in the parlour. There was a scuffle of feet on the gravel outside the heavily-leaded diamond panes, and then the voice of Colonel Dabney, something clearer than a bugle.

'Ye can read? You've eyes in your head? Don't attempt to deny it. Ye have!'

Beetle snatched a crochet-work antimacassar from the shiny horsehair sofa, stuffed it into his mouth, and rolled out of sight.

'You saw my notice-boards. Your duty? Curse your impudence, sir. Your duty was to keep off my grounds. Talk of duty to *me*! Why—why—why, ye misbegotten poacher, ye'll be teaching me my A B C next! Roarin' like a bull in the bushes down there! Boys? Boys? Boys? Keep your boys at home, then! I'm not responsible for your boys! But I don't believe it —I don't believe a word of it. Ye've a furtive look in your eye —a furtive, sneakin', poachin' look in your eye, that 'ud ruin the reputation of an archangel! Don't attempt to deny it! Ye have! A Sergeant? More shame to you, then, an' the worst bargain Her Majesty ever made! A Sergeant, to run about the country poachin'—on your pension! Damnable! Oh, damnable! But I'll be considerate. I'll be merciful. By gad, I'll be the very essence o' humanity! Did ye, or did ye not, see my notice-boards? Don't attempt to deny it! Ye did! Silence, Sergeant!'

Twenty-one years in the Army had left their mark on Foxy. He obeyed.

'Now. March!"

The high Lodge-gate shut with a clang. 'My duty! A Sergeant to tell me my duty!' puffed Colonel Dabney. 'Good Lard! more Sergeants!'

'It's King! It's King!' gulped Stalky, his head on the horsehair pillow. M'Turk was eating the rag-carpet before the speckless hearth, and the sofa heaved to the emotions of Beetle. Through the thick glass the figures without showed blue, distorted, and menacing.

'I—I protest against this outrage.' King had evidently been running uphill. 'The man was entirely within his duty. Let—let me give you my card.'

'He's in flannels!' Stalky buried his head again.

'Unfortunately—*most* unfortunately—I have not one with me, but my name is King, sir, a House-master of the College, and you will find me prepared—fully prepared—to answer for this man's action. We've seen three——'

'Did you see my notice-boards?'

'I admit we did; but under the circumstances——'

'I stand *in loco parentis*.' Prout's deep voice was added to the discussion. They could hear him pant.

'Fwhat?' Colonel Dabney was growing more and more Irish.

'I'm responsible for the boys under my charge.'

'Ye are, are ye? Then all I can say is that ye set them a very bad example—a dam' bad example, if I may say so. I do not own your boys. I've not seen your boys, an' I tell you that if there was a boy grinnin' in every bush on the place *still* ye've no shadow of a right here, comin' up from the combe that way, an' frightenin' everything in it. Don't attempt to deny it. Ye did! Ye should have come to the Lodge an' seen me like Christians, instead of chasin' your dam' boys through the length and breadth of my covers. *In loco parentis* ye are? Well, I've not forgotten my Latin either, an' I'll say to you: *"Quis custodiet ipsos custodes?"* If the masters trespass, how can we blame the boys?'

'But if I could speak to you privately,' said Prout.

'I'll have nothing private with you! Ye can be as private as ye please on the other side o' that gate, an'—I wish ye a very good afternoon.'

A second time the gate clanged. They waited till Colonel Dabney had returned to the house, and fell into one another's arms, crowing for breath.

'Oh, my Soul! Oh, my King! Oh, my Heffy! Oh, my Foxy! Zeal, all zeal, Mr. Easy.' Stalky wiped his eyes. 'Oh! Oh! Oh!—"I *did* boil the exciseman!" We must get out of this or we'll be late for tea.'

'Ge—ge—get the badger and make little Hartopp happy. Ma—ma—make 'em all happy,' sobbed M'Turk, groping for the door and kicking the prostrate Beetle before him.

They found the beast in an evil-smelling box, left two half-crowns for payment, and staggered home. Only the badger grunted most marvellous like Colonel Dabney, and they dropped him twice or thrice with shrieks of helpless laughter. They were but imperfectly recovered when Foxy met them by the Fives Court with word that they were to go up to their dormitory and wait till sent for.

'Well, take this box to Mr. Hartopp's rooms, then. We've

done something for the Natural History Society, at any rate,' said Beetle.

' 'Fraid that won't save you, young gen'elmen,' Foxy answered, in an awful voice. He was sorely ruffled in his mind.

"All sereno, Foxibus.' Stalky had reached the extreme stage of hiccups. 'We—we'll never desert you, Foxy. Hounds choppin' foxes in cover is more a proof of vice, ain't it? . . . No, you're right. I'm—I'm not quite well.'

'They've gone a bit too far this time,' Foxy thought to himself. 'Very far gone, I'd say, excep' there was no smell of liquor. An' yet it isn't like 'em—somehow. King and Prout they 'ad their dressin'-down same as me. That's one comfort.'

'Now, we must pull up,' said Stalky, rising from the bed on which he had thrown himself. 'We're injured innocence—as usual. *We* don't know what we've been sent up here for, do we?'

'No explanation. Deprived of tea. Public disgrace before the House,' said M'Turk, whose eyes were running over. 'It's dam' serious.'

'Well, hold on, till King loses his temper,' said Beetle. 'He's a libellous old rip, an' he'll be in a ravin' paddy-whack. Prout's too beastly cautious. Keep your eye on King, and, if he gives us a chance, appeal to the Head. That always makes 'em sick.'

They were summoned to their House-master's study, King and Foxy supporting Prout, and Foxy had three canes under his arm. King leered triumphantly, for there were tears, undried tears of mirth, on the boys' cheeks. Then the examination began.

Yes, they had walked along the cliffs. Yes, they had entered Colonel Dabney's grounds. Yes, they had seen the notice-boards (at this point Beetle sputtered hysterically). For what purpose had they entered Colonel Dabney's grounds? 'Well, sir, there was a badger.'

Here King, who loathed the Natural History Society because he did not like Hartopp, could no longer be restrained. He begged them not to add mendacity to open insolence. 'But the badger is in Mr. Hartopp's rooms, sir.' The Sergeant had kindly taken it up for them. That disposed of the badger, and the temporary check brought King's temper to boiling-point. They could hear his foot on the floor while Prout prepared his lumbering inquiries. They had settled into their stride now. Their eyes ceased to sparkle; their faces were blank; their hands hung beside them without a twitch. They were learning, at the expense of a fellow-countryman, the lesson of their race, which is to put away all emotion and entrap the alien at the proper time.

So far good. King was importing himself more freely into the trial, being vengeful where Prout was grieved. They knew the penalties of trespassing? With a fine show of irresolution, Stalky admitted that he had gathered some information vaguely bearing on this head, but he thought—— The sentence was dragged out to the uttermost: Stalky did not wish to play his trump with such an opponent. Mr. King desired no buts, nor was he interested in Stalky's evasions. They, on the other hand, might be interested in his poor views. Boys who crept—who sneaked—who lurked—out of bounds, even the generous bounds of the Natural History Society, which they had falsely joined as a cloak for their misdeeds—their vices— their villainies—their immoralities——

'He'll break cover in a minute,' said Stalky to himself. 'Then we'll run into him before he gets away.'

Such boys, scabrous boys, moral lepers—the current of his words was carrying King off his feet—evil-speakers, liars, slow-bellies—yea, incipient drunkards. . . .

He was merely working up to a peroration, and the boys knew it; but M'Turk cut through the frothing sentence, the others echoing:—

'I appeal to the Head, sir.'

'I appeal to the Head, sir.'

'I appeal to the Head, sir.'

It was their unquestioned right. Drunkenness meant expulsion after a public flogging. They had been accused of it. The case was the Head's, and the Head's alone.

'Thou hast appealed unto Caesar: unto Caesar shalt thou go.' They had heard that sentence once or twice before in their careers. 'None the less,' said King uneasily, 'you would be better advised to abide by our decision, my young friends.'

'Are we allowed to associate with the rest of the school till we see the Head, sir?' said M'Turk to his House-master, disregarding King. This at once lifted the situation to its loftiest plane. Moreover, it meant no work, for moral leprosy was strictly quarantined, and the Head never executed judgment till twenty-four cold hours later.

'Well—er—if you persist in your defiant attitude,' said King, with a loving look at the canes under Foxy's arm, 'there is no alternative.'

Ten minutes later the news was over the whole school. Stalky & Co. had fallen at last—fallen by drink. They had been drinking. They had returned blind-drunk from a hut. They were even now lying hopelessly intoxicated on the dormitory floor. A few bold spirits crept up to look, and received boots about the head.

'We've got him—got him on the Caudine Toasting-fork!' said Stalky, after those hints were taken. 'King'll have to prove his charges up to the giddy hilt.'

' "Too much ticklee, him bust," ' Beetle quoted from a book of his reading. 'Didn't I say he'd go pop if we lat un bide?'

'No prep., either. O ye incipient drunkards,' said M'Turk, 'and it's trig night, too. Hullo! Here's our dear friend Foxy. More tortures, Foxibus?'

'I've brought you something to eat, young gen'elmen,' said the Sergeant from behind a crowded tray. Their wars had ever been waged without malice, and a suspicion floated in Foxy's mind that boys who allowed themselves to be tracked so easily might, perhaps, hold something in reserve. Foxy had served through the Mutiny, when early and accurate information was worth much.

'I—I noticed you 'adn't 'ad anything to eat, an' I spoke to Gumbly, an' he said you wasn't exactly cut off from supplies. So I brought up this. It's your potted 'am tin, ain't it, Mr. Corkran?'

'Why, Foxibus, you're a brick,' said Stalky. 'I didn't think you had this much—what's the word, Beetle?'

'Bowels,' Beetle replied promptly. 'Thank you, Sergeant. That's young Carter's potted ham, though.'

'There was a C on it. I thought it was Mr. Corkran's. This is a very serious business, young gen'elmen. That's what it is. I didn't know, perhaps, but there might be something on your side which you hadn't said to Mr. King or Mr. Prout, maybe.'

'There is. Heaps, Foxibus.' This from Stalky through a full mouth.

'Then you see, if that was the case, it seemed to me I might represent it, quiet so to say, to the 'Ead when he asks me about it. I've got to take 'im the charges to-night, an'—it looks bad on the face of it.'

' 'Trocious bad, Foxy. Twenty-seven cuts in the gym before all the school, an' public expulsion. "Wine is a mocker, strong drink is ragin'," ' quoth Beetle.

'It's nothing to make fun of, young gen'elmen. I 'ave to go

to the 'Ead with the charges. An'—an' you mayn't be aware, per'aps, that I was followin' you this afternoon; havin' my suspicions.'

'Did ye see the notice-boards?' croaked M'Turk, in the very brogue of Colonel Dabney.

'Ye've eyes in your head. Don't attempt to deny it. Ye did!' said Beetle.

'A Sergeant! To run about poachin' on your pension! Damnable! Oh, damnable!' said Stalky, without pity.

'Good Lord!' said the Sergeant, sitting heavily upon a bed. 'Where—where the devil was you? I might ha' known it was a do—somewhere.'

'Oh, you clever maniac!' Stalky resumed. 'We mayn't be aware you were followin' us this afternoon, mayn't we? Thought you were stalkin' us, eh? Why, we led you bung into it, of course. Colonel Dabney—don't you think he's a nice man, Foxy?—Colonel Dabney's our pet particular friend. We've been goin' there for weeks an' weeks. He invited us. You an' your duty! Curse your duty, sir! Your duty was to keep off his covers.'

'You'll never be able to hold up your head again, Foxy. The fags 'll hoot at you,' said Beetle. 'Think of your giddy prestige!'

The Sergeant was thinking—hard.

'Look 'ere, young gen'elmen,' he said earnestly. 'You aren't surely ever goin' to tell, are you? Wasn't Mr. Prout and Mr. King in—in it too?'

'Foxibusculus, they *was*. They was—singular horrid. Caught it worse than you. We heard every word of it. You got off easy, considerin'. If I'd been Dabney I swear I'd ha' quodded you. I think I'll suggest it to him to-morrow.'

'An' it's all goin' up to the 'Ead. Oh, Good Lord!'

'Every giddy word of it, my Chingangook,' said Beetle, dancing. 'Why shouldn't it? *We*'ve done nothing wrong. *We* ain't poachers. *We* didn't cut about blastin' the characters of poor, innocent boys—sayin' they were drunk.'

'That I didn't,' said Foxy. 'I—I only said that you be'aved uncommon odd when you come back with that badger. Mr. King may have taken the wrong hint from that.'

'Course he did; an' he'll jolly well shove all the blame on you when he finds out he's wrong. *We* know King, if you don't. I'm ashamed of you. You ain't fit to be a Sergeant,' said M'Turk.

'Not with three thorough-goin' young devils like you, I ain't. I've been had. I've been ambuscaded. Horse, foot, an' guns, I've been had, an'—an' there'll be no holdin' the junior forms after this. M'r'over, the 'Ead will send me with a note to Colonel Dabney to ask if what you say about bein' invited was true.'

'Then you'd better go in by the Lodge-gates this time, instead of chasin' your dam' boys—oh, that was the Epistle to King—so it was. We-ell, Foxy?' Stalky put his chin on his hands and regarded the victim with deep delight.

'*Ti-ra-la-la-i-tu!* I gloat! Hear me!' said M'Turk. 'Foxy brought us tea when we were moral lepers. Foxy has a heart. Foxy has been in the Army, too.'

'I wish I'd ha' had you in my Company, young gen'elmen,' said the Sergeant from the depths of his heart. 'I'd ha' given you something.'

'Silence at drum-head court-martial,' M'Turk went on. 'I'm advocate for the prisoner; and, besides, this is much too good to tell all the other brutes in the Coll. They'd *never* understand. They play cricket, and say, "Yes, sir," and "Oh, sir," and "No, sir." '

'Never mind that. Go ahead,' said Stalky.

'Well, Foxy's a good little chap when he does not esteem himself so as to be clever.'

' "Take not out your 'ounds on a werry windy day," ' Stalky struck in. '*I* don't care if you let him off.'

'Nor me,' said Beetle. 'Heffy is my only joy—Heffy and King.'

'I 'ad to do it,' said the Sergeant plaintively.

'Right O! Led away by bad companions in the execution of his duty, or—or words to that effect. You're dismissed with a reprimand, Foxy. We won't tell about you. I swear we won't,' M'Turk concluded. 'Bad for the discipline of the school. Horrid bad.'

'Well,' said the Sergeant, gathering up the tea-things, 'knowin' what I know o' the young dev—gen'elmen of the College, I'm very glad to 'ear it. But what am I to tell the 'Ead?'

'Anything you jolly well please, Foxy. *We* aren't the criminals.'

To say that the Head was annoyed when the Sergeant appeared after dinner with the day's crime-sheet would be putting it mildly.

'Corkran, M'Turk, & Co., I see. Bounds as usual. Hullo! What the deuce is this? Suspicion of drinking. Whose charge?'

'Mr. King's, sir. I caught 'em out of bounds, sir: at least that was 'ow it looked. But there's a lot be'ind, sir.' The Sergeant was evidently troubled.

'Go on,' said the Head. 'Let us have your version.'

He and the Sergeant had dealt with each other for some seven years; while the Head knew that Mr. King's statements depended very largely on Mr. King's temper.

'I thought they were out of bounds along the cliffs. But it

come out they wasn't, sir. I saw them go into Colonel Dabney's woods, and—Mr. King and Mr. Prout come along—and —the fact was, sir, we was mistook for poachers by Colonel Dabney's people—Mr. King and Mr. Prout and me. There were some words, sir, on both sides. The young gen'elmen slipped 'ome somehow, and they seemed 'ighly humorous, sir. Mr. King was mistook by Colonel Dabney himself—Colonel Dabney bein' strict. Then they preferred to come straight to you, sir, on account of what—what Mr. King may 'ave said about their 'abits afterwards in Mr. Prout's study. I only said they was 'ighly humorous, laughin' an' gigglin', an' a bit above 'emselves. They've since told me, sir, in a humorous way, that they was invited by Colonel Dabney to go into 'is woods.'

'I see. They didn't tell their House-master that, of course.'

'They took up Mr. King on appeal just as soon as he spoke about their—'abits. Put in the appeal at once, sir, an' asked to be sent to the dormitory waitin' for you. I've since gathered, sir, in their humorous way, sir, that some'ow or other they've 'eard about every word Colonel Dabney said to Mr. King and Mr. Prout when he mistook 'em for poachers. I—I might ha' known when they led me on so that they 'eld the inner line of communications. It's—it's a plain do, sir, if you ask *me*; an' they're gloatin' over it in the dormitory.'

The Head saw—saw even to the uttermost farthing—and his mouth twitched a little under his moustache.

'Send them to me at once, Sergeant. This case needn't wait over.'

'Good evening,' said he, when the three appeared under escort. 'I want your undivided attention for a few minutes. You've known me for five years, and I've known you for— twenty-five. I think we understand one another perfectly. I am now going to pay you a tremendous compliment. (The brown one, please, Sergeant. Thanks. You needn't wait.) I'm going to execute you without rhyme, Beetle, or reason. I know you went to Colonel Dabney's covers because you were invited. I'm not even going to send the Sergeant with a note to ask if your statement is true; because I am convinced that, on this occasion, you have adhered strictly to the truth. I know, too, that you were not drinking. (You can take off that virtuous expression, M'Turk, or I shall begin to fear you don't understand me.) There is not a flaw in any of your characters. And that is why I am going to perpetrate a howling injustice. Your reputations have been injured, haven't they? You have been disgraced before the House, haven't you? You have a peculiarly keen regard for the honour of your House, haven't you? Well, *now* I am going to lick you.'

Six apiece was their portion upon that word.

'And this, I think'—the Head replaced the cane, and flung the written charge into the waste-paper basket—'covers the situation. When you find a variation from the normal—this will be useful to you in later life—always meet him in an abnormal way. And that reminds me. There are a pile of paperbacks on that shelf. You can borrow them if you put them back. I don't think they'll take any harm from being read in the open. They smell of tobacco rather. You will go to prep. this evening as usual. Good-night,' said that amazing man.

'Good-night, and thank you, sir.'

'I swear I'll pray for the Head to-night,' said Beetle. 'Those last two cuts were just flicks on my collar. There's a *Monte Cristo* in that lower shelf. I saw it. Bags I, next time we go to Aves!'

'Dearr man!' said M'Turk. 'No gating. No impots. No beastly questions. All settled. Hullo! what's King goin' in to him for—King and Prout?'

Whatever the nature of that interview, it did not improve

either King's or Prout's ruffled plumes, for, when they came out of the Head's house, six eyes noted that the one was red and blue with emotion as to his nose, and that the other was sweating profusely. That sight compensated them amply for the Imperial Jaw with which they were favoured by the two. It seems—and who so astonished as they?—that they had held back material facts; that they were guilty both of *suppressio veri* and *suggestio falsi* (well-known Gods against whom they often offended); further, that they were malignant in their dispositions, untrustworthy in their characters, pernicious and revolutionary in their influences, abandoned to the devils of wilfulness, pride, and a most intolerable conceit. Ninthly, and lastly, they were to have a care and to be very careful.

They were careful, as only boys can be when there is a hurt to be inflicted. They waited through one suffocating week till Prout and King were their royal selves again; waited till there was a House-match—their own House, too—in which Prout was taking part; waited, further, till he had buckled on his pads in the pavilion and stood ready to go forth. King was scoring at the window, and the three sat on a bench without.

Said Stalky to Beetle: 'I say, Beetle, *quis custodiet ipsos custodes?*'

'Don't ask me,' said Beetle. 'I'll have nothin' private with you. Ye can be as private as ye please the other end of the bench; and I wish ye a very good afternoon.'

M'Turk yawned.

'Well, ye should ha' come up to the Lodge like Christians instead o' chasin' your—a-hem—boys through the length an' breadth of my covers. *I* think these House-matches are all rot. Let's go over to Colonel Dabney's an' see if he's collared any more poachers.'

That afternoon there was joy in Aves.

SLAVES OF THE LAMP

PART I

SLAVES OF THE LAMP

PART I

THE MUSIC-ROOM on the top floor of Number Five was filled with the 'Aladdin' company at rehearsal. Dickson Quartus, commonly known as Dick Four, was Aladdin, stage-manager, ballet-master, half the orchestra, and largely librettist, for the 'book' had been rewritten and filled with local allusions. The pantomime was to be given next week, in the downstairs study occupied by Aladdin, Abanazar, and the Emperor of China. The Slave of the Lamp, with the Princess Badroul-badour and the Widow Twankey, owned Number Five study across the same landing, so that the company could be easily assembled. The floor shook to the stamp-and-go of the ballet, while Aladdin, in pink cotton tights, a blue-and-tinsel jacket, and a plumed hat, banged alternately on the piano and his banjo. He was the moving spirit of the game, as befitted a senior who had passed his Army Preliminary and hoped to enter Sandhurst next spring.

Aladdin came to his own at last, Abanazar lay poisoned on the floor, the Widow Twankey danced her dance, and the company decided it would 'come all right on the night.'

'What about the last song, though?' said the Emperor, a tallish, fair-headed boy with a ghost of a moustache, at which he pulled manfully. 'We need a rousing old tune.'

' "John Peel"? "Drink, Puppy, Drink"?' suggested Abanazar, smoothing his baggy lilac pyjamas. 'Pussy' Abanazar never looked more than one-half awake, but he owned a soft, slow smile which well suited the part of the Wicked Uncle.

'Stale,' said Aladdin. 'Might as well have "Grandfather's Clock." What's that thing you were humming at prep. last night, Stalky?'

Stalky, the Slave of the Lamp, in black tights and doublet, a black silk half-mask on his forehead, whistled lazily where he lay on the top of the piano. It was a catchy music-hall tune.

Dick Four cocked his head critically, and squinted down a large red nose.

'Once more, and I can pick it up,' he said, strumming. 'Sing the words.'

'Arrah, Patsy, mind the baby! Arrah, Patsy, mind the child!
Wrap him up in an overcoat, he's surely goin' wild!
Arrah, Patsy, mind the baby; just ye mind the child awhile!
He'll kick an' bite an' cry all night! Arrah, Patsy, mind the
*   child!'*

'Rippin'! Oh, rippin'!' said Dick Four. 'Only we shan't have any piano on the night. We must work it with the banjos— play an' dance at the same time. You try, Tertius.'

The Emperor pushed aside his pea-green sleeves of state, and followed Dick Four on a heavy nickel-plated banjo.

'Yes, but I'm dead all this time. Bung in the middle of the stage, too,' said Abanazar.

'Oh, that's Beetle's biznai,' said Dick Four. 'Vamp it up, Beetle. Don't keep us waiting all night. You've got to get Pussy out of the light somehow, and bring us all in dancin' at the end.'

'All right. You two play it again,' said Beetle, who, in a grey skirt and a wig of chestnut sausage-curls, set slantwise above a pair of spectacles mended with an old boot-lace, represented the Widow Twankey. He waved one leg in time to the hammered refrain, and the banjos grew louder.

'Um! Ah! Er—"Aladdin now has won his wife," ' he sang, and Dick Four repeated it.

' "Your Emperor is appeased." ' Tertius flung out his chest as he delivered his line.

'Now jump up, Pussy! Say, "I think I'd better come to life!" Then we all take hands and come forward: "We hope you've all been pleased." *Twiggez-vous?*'

'*Nous twiggons.* Good enough. What's the chorus for the final ballet? It's four kicks and a turn,' said Dick Four.

'Oh! Er!

> *John Short will ring the curtain down,*
> *And ring the prompter's bell;*
> *We hope you know, before you go,*
> *That we all wish you well.*'

'Rippin'! Rippin'! Now for the Widow's scene with the Princess. Hurry up, Turkey.'

M'Turk, in a violet silk skirt and a coquettish blue turban, slouched forward as one thoroughly ashamed of himself. The Slave of the Lamp climbed down from the piano, and dispassionately kicked him. 'Play up, Turkey,' he said; 'this is serious.' But there fell on the door the knock of authority. It happened to be King, in gown and mortar-board, enjoying a Saturday evening prowl before dinner.

'Locked doors! Locked doors!' he snapped, with a scowl. 'What's the meaning of this; and what, may I ask, is the intention of this—this epicene attire?'

'Pantomime, sir. The Head gave us leave,' said Abanazar, as the only member of the Sixth concerned. Dick Four stood firm in the confidence born of well-fitting tights, but Beetle strove to efface himself behind the piano. A grey princess-skirt borrowed from a day-boy's mother and a spotted cotton bodice unsystematically padded with imposition-paper make one ridiculous. And in other regards Beetle had a bad conscience.

'As usual!' sneered King. 'Futile foolery just when your careers, such as they may be, are hanging in the balance. I see! Ah, I see! The old gang of criminals—allied forces of disorder—Corkran'—the Slave of the Lamp smiled politely—'M'Turk'—the Irishman smiled—'and, of course, the unspeakable Beetle, our friend Gigadibs.' Abanazar, the Emperor, and Aladdin had more or less of characters, and King passed them over. 'Come forth, my inky buffoon, from behind yonder instrument of music! You supply, I presume, the doggerel for this entertainment. Esteem yourself to be, as it were, a poet?'

'He's found one of 'em,' thought Beetle, noting the flush on King's cheek-bone.

'I have just had the pleasure of reading an effusion of yours to my address, I believe—an effusion intended to rhyme. So—so you despise me, Master Gigadibs, do you? I am quite aware —you need not explain—that it was ostensibly *not* intended for my edification. I read it with laughter—yes, with laughter. These paper pellets of inky boys—still a boy we are, Master Gigadibs—do not disturb my equanimity.'

'Wonder which it was,' thought Beetle. He had launched many lampoons on an appreciative public ever since he discovered that it was possible to convey reproof in rhyme.

In sign of his unruffled calm, King proceeded to tear Beetle, whom he called Gigadibs, slowly asunder. From his untied

64

shoe-strings to his mended spectacles (the life of a poet at a big school is hard) he held him up to the derision of his associates—with the usual result. His wild flowers of speech—King had an unpleasant tongue—restored him to good humour at the last. He drew a lurid picture of Beetle's latter end as a scurrilous pamphleteer dying in an attic, scattered a few compliments over M'Turk and Corkran, and, reminding Beetle that he must come up for judgment when called upon, went to Common-room, where he triumphed anew over his victims.

'And the worst of it,' he explained in a loud voice over his soup, 'is that I waste such gems of sarcasm on their thick heads. It's miles above them, I'm certain.'

'We-ell,' said the school Chaplain slowly, 'I don't know what Corkran's appreciation of your style may be, but young M'Turk reads Ruskin for his amusement.'

'Nonsense! He does it to show off. I mistrust the dark Celt.'

'He does nothing of the kind. I went into their study the other night, unofficially, and M'Turk was gluing up the back of four odd numbers of *Fors Clavigera*.'

'I don't know anything about their private lives,' said a mathematical master hotly, 'but I've learned by bitter experience that Number Five study are best left alone. They are utterly soulless young devils.' He blushed as the others laughed.

But in the music-room there was wrath and bad language. Only Stalky, Slave of the Lamp, lay on the piano unmoved.

'That little swine Manders minor must have shown him your stuff. He's always suckin' up to King. Go and kill him,' he drawled. 'Which one was it, Beetle?'

'Dunno,' said Beetle, struggling out of the skirt. 'There was one about his huntin' for popularity with the small boys, and the other one was one about him in Hell, tellin' the Devil he was a Balliol man. I swear both of 'em rhymed all right. By Gum! P'raps Manders minor showed him both! *I'll* correct his caesuras for him.'

He disappeared down two flights of stairs, flushed a small pink-and-white boy in a form-room next door to King's study, which, again, was immediately below his own, and chased him up the corridor into a form-room sacred to the revels of the Lower Third. Thence he came back, greatly disordered, to find M'Turk, Stalky, and the others of the company in his study enjoying an unlimited 'brew'—coffee, cocoa, buns, new bread hot and steaming, sardine, sausage, ham-and-tongue paste, pilchards, two jams, and at least as many pounds of Devonshire cream.

'My Hat!' said he, throwing himself upon the banquet. 'Who stumped up for this, Stalky?' It was within a month of term-end, and blank starvation had reigned in the studies for weeks.

'You,' said Stalky serenely.

'Confound you! You haven't been poppin' my Sunday bags, then?'

'Keep your hair on. It's only your watch.'

'Watch! I lost it—weeks ago. Out on the Burrows, when we tried to shoot the old ram—the day our pistol burst.'

'It dropped out of your pocket (you're so beastly careless, Beetle), and M'Turk and I kept it for you. I've been wearin' it for a week, an' you never noticed. Took it into Bideford after dinner to-day. Got thirteen and sevenpence. Here's the ticket.'

'Well, that's pretty average cool,' said Abanazar behind a slab of cream and jam, as Beetle, reassured upon the safety of his Sunday trousers, showed not even surprise, much less resentment. Indeed, it was M'Turk who grew angry, saying:—

'You gave him the ticket, Stalky? You pawned it? You unmitigated beast! Why, last month you an' Beetle sold mine!
Never got a sniff of any ticket.'

'Ah, that was because you locked your trunk an' we wasted
half the afternoon hammerin' it open. We might have pawned
it if you'd behaved like a Christian, Turkey.'

'My Aunt!' said Abanazar, 'you chaps are Communists. Vote
of thanks to Beetle, though.'

'That's beastly unfair,' said Stalky, 'when I took all the
trouble to pawn it. Beetle never knew he had a watch. Oh, I
say, Rabbits-Eggs gave me a lift into Bideford this afternoon.'

Rabbits-Eggs was the local carrier—an outcrop of the early
Devonian formation. It was Stalky who had invented his un-
lovely name. 'He was pretty average drunk, or he wouldn't
have done it. Rabbits-Eggs is a little shy of me, somehow. But
I swore it was *pax* between us, an' gave him a bob. He stopped
at two pubs on the way in, so he'll be howlin' drunk to-night.
Oh, don't begin readin', Beetle; there's a council of war on.
What the deuce is the matter with your collar?'

'Chivied Manders minor into the Lower Third box-room.
Had all his beastly little friends on top of me,' said Beetle,
from behind a jar of pilchards and a book.

'You ass! Any fool could have told you where Manders
would bunk to,' said M'Turk.

'I didn't think,' said Beetle meekly, scooping out pilchards
with a spoon.

'Course you didn't. You never do.' M'Turk adjusted Beetle's collar with a savage tug. 'Don't drop oil all over my
Fors, or I'll scrag you!'

'Shut up, you—you Irish Biddy! 'Tisn't your beastly *Fors*.
It's one of mine.'

The book was a fat, brown-backed volume of the later
'Sixties, which King had once thrown at Beetle's head that

Beetle might see whence the name Gigadibs came. Beetle had quietly annexed the book, and had seen—several things. The quarter-comprehended verses lived and ate with him, as the be-dropped pages showed. He removed himself from all that world, drifting at large with wondrous Men and Women, till M'Turk hammered the pilchard spoon on his head and he snarled.

'Beetle! You're oppressed and insulted and bullied by King. Don't you feel it?'

'Let me alone! I can write some more poetry about him if I am, I suppose.'

'Mad! Quite mad!' said Stalky to the visitors, as one exhibiting strange beasts. 'Beetle reads an ass called Brownin', an' M'Turk reads an ass called Ruskin; and——'

'Ruskin isn't an ass,' said M'Turk. 'He's almost as good as the Opium-Eater. He says we're "children of noble races trained by surrounding art." That means me, and the way I decorated the study when you two badgers would have stuck up brackets and Christmas cards. Child of a noble race, trained by surrounding art, stop reading, or I'll shove a pilchard down your neck!'

'It's two to one,' said Stalky warningly, and Beetle closed the book, in obedience to the law under which he and his companions had lived for six checkered years.

The visitors looked on delighted. Number Five study had a reputation for more variegated insanity than the rest of the school put together; and, so far as its code allowed friendship with outsiders, it was polite and open-hearted to its neighbours.

'What rot do you want now?' said Beetle.

'King! War!' said M'Turk, jerking his head toward the wall, where hung a small wooden West-African war-drum, a gift to M'Turk from a naval uncle.

'Then we shall be turned out of the study again,' said Beetle, who loved his flesh-pots. 'Mason turned us out for—just warbling on it.' Mason was that mathematical master who had testified in Common-room.

'Warbling?—Oh, Lord!' said Abanazar. 'We couldn't hear ourselves speak in our study when you played the infernal thing. What's the good of getting turned out of your study, anyhow?'

'We lived in the form-rooms for a week, too,' said Beetle tragically. 'And it was beastly cold.'

'Ye-es; but Mason's rooms were filled with rats every day we were out. It took him a week to draw the inference,' said M'Turk. 'He loathes rats. Minute he let us go back the rats stopped. Mason's a little shy of us now, but there was no evidence.'

'Jolly well there wasn't,' said Stalky, 'when I got out on the roof an' dropped the beastly things down his chimney. But, look here—question is, are our characters good enough just now to stand a study row?'

'Never mind mine,' said Beetle. 'King swears I haven't any.'

'I'm not thinkin' of you,' Stalky returned scornfully. 'You aren't goin' up for the Army, you old bat. I don't want to be expelled—an' the Head's gettin' rather shy of us, too.'

'Rot!' said M'Turk. 'The Head never expels except for beastliness or stealing. But I forgot. You and Stalky *are* thieves —regular burglars.'

The visitors gasped, but Stalky interpreted the parable with large grins.

'Well, you know, that little beast Manders minor saw Beetle an' me hammerin' M'Turk's trunk open in the dormitory when we took his watch last month. Of course Manders sneaked to Mason, an' Mason solemnly took it up as a case of theft, to get even with us about the rats.'

'That just put Mason into our giddy hands,' said M'Turk blandly. 'We were nice to him, 'cause he was a new master and wanted to win the confidence of the boys. Pity he draws inferences, though. Stalky went to his study and pretended to blub, and told Mason he'd lead a new life if Mason would let him off this time, but Mason wouldn't. Said it was his duty to report him to the Head.'

'Vindictive swine!' said Beetle. 'It was all those rats! Then *I* blubbed, too, an' Stalky confessed that he'd been a thief in regular practice for six years, ever since he came to the school; an' that I'd taught him—*à la* Fagin. Mason turned white with joy. He thought he had us on toast.'

'Gorgeous! Oh, fids!' said Dick Four. 'We never heard of this.'

'Course not. Mason kept it jolly quiet. He wrote down all our statements on impot-paper. There wasn't anything he wouldn't believe,' said Stalky.

'And handed it all up to the Head, *with* an extempore prayer. It took about forty pages,' said Beetle. 'I helped him a lot.'

'And then, you crazy idiots?' said Abanazar.

'Oh, we were sent for; an' Stalky asked to have the "depositions" read out, an' the Head knocked him spinnin' into a waste-paper basket. Then he gave us eight cuts apiece—welters—for—for—takin' unheard-of liberties with a new master. I saw his shoulders shakin' when we went out. Do you know,' said Beetle pensively, 'that Mason can't look at us now in second lesson without blushin'? We three stare at him sometimes till he regularly trickles. He's an awfully sensitive beast.'

'He read *Eric; or, Little by Little*,' said M'Turk; 'so we gave him *St. Winifred's; or, The World of School*. They spent all their spare time stealing at St. Winifred's, when they weren't

70

praying or getting drunk at pubs. Well, that was only a week ago, and the Head's a little bit shy of us. He called it constructive deviltry. Stalky invented it all.'

'Not the least good havin' a row with a master unless you can make an ass of him,' said Stalky, extended at ease on the hearth-rug. 'If Mason didn't know Number Five—well, he's learnt, that's all. Now, my dearly beloved 'earers'— Stalky curled his legs under him and addressed the company —'we've got that strong, perseverin' man King on our hands. He went miles out of his way to provoke a conflict.' (Here Stalky snapped down the black silk domino and assumed the air of a judge.) 'He has oppressed Beetle, M'Turk, and me, *privatim et seriatim*, one by one, as he could catch us. But now he has insulted Number Five up in the music-room, *and* in the presence of these—these ossifers of the Ninety-third, wot look like hairdressers. Binjimin, we must make him cry *"Capivi!"* '

Stalky's reading did not include Browning or Ruskin.

'And, besides,' said M'Turk, 'he's a Philistine, a basket-hanger. He wears a tartan tie. Ruskin says that any man who wears a tartan tie will, without doubt, be damned everlastingly.'

'Bravo, M'Turk,' cried Tertius; 'I thought he was only a beast.'

'He's that, too, of course, but he's worse. He has a china basket with blue ribbons and a pink kitten on it, hung up in his window to grow musk in. You know when I got all that old oak carvin' out of Bideford Church, when they were restorin' it (Ruskin says that any man who'll restore a church is an unmitigated sweep), and stuck it up here with glue? Well, King came in and wanted to know whether we'd done it with a fret-saw! Yah! He is the King of basket-hangers!'

Down went M'Turk's inky thumb over an imaginary arena full of bleeding Kings. '*Placetne*, child of a generous race?' he cried to Beetle.

'Well,' began Beetle doubtfully, 'he comes from Balliol, but I'm goin' to give the beast a chance. You see, I can always make him hop with some more poetry. He can't report me to the Head, because it makes him ridiculous. (Stalky's quite right.) But he shall have his chance.'

Beetle opened the book on the table, ran his finger down a page, and began at random:—

> '*Or who in Moscow toward the Czar*
> *With the demurest of footfalls,*
> *Over the Kremlin's pavement white*
> *With serpentine and syenite,*
> *Steps with five other generals——*'

'That's no good. Try another,' said Stalky.

'Hold on a shake; I know what's coming.' M'Turk was reading over Beetle's shoulder:—

> '*That simultaneously take snuff,*
> *For each to have pretext enough*
> *To kerchiefwise unfold his sash,*
> *Which—softness' self—is yet the stuff*

(Gummy! What a sentence!)

> *To hold fast where a steel chain snaps*
> *And leave the grand white neck no gash.*

(Full stop.)'

'Don't understand a word of it,' said Stalky.

'More fool you! Construe,' said M'Turk. 'Those six bargees scragged the Czar and left no evidence. *Actum est* with King.'

'He gave me that book, too,' said Beetle, licking his lips:—

> *'There's a great text in Galatians,*
> *Once you trip on it entails*
> *Twenty-nine distinct damnations,*
> *One sure if another fails.'*

Then irrelevantly:—

> *'Setebos! Setebos! and Setebos!*
> *'Thinketh he liveth in the cold of the moon.'*

'He's just come in from dinner,' said Dick Four, looking through the window. 'Manders minor is with him.'

'Safest place for Manders minor just now,' said Beetle.

'Then you chaps had better clear out,' said Stalky politely to the visitors. ' 'Tisn't fair to mix you up in a study row. Besides, we can't afford to have evidence.'

'Are you going to begin at once?' said Aladdin.

'Immediately, if not sooner,' said Stalky, and turned out the gas. 'Strong, perseverin' man—King. Make him cry *"Capivi."* G'way, Binjimin.'

The company retreated to their neat and spacious study with expectant souls.

'When Stalky blows out his nostrils like a horse,' said Aladdin to the Emperor of China, 'he's on the war-path. Wonder what King will get.'

'Beans,' said the Emperor. 'Number Five generally pays in full.'

'Wonder if I ought to take any notice of it officially,' said Abanazar, who had just remembered that he was a prefect.

'It's none of your business, Pussy. Besides, if you did, we'd have them hostile to us; and we shouldn't be able to do any work,' said Aladdin. 'They've begun already.'

Now that West-African war-drum had been made to signal across estuaries and deltas. Number Five was forbidden to wake the engine within earshot of the school. But a deep devastating drone filled the passages as M'Turk and Beetle scientifically rubbed its top. Anon it changed to the blare of trumpets—of savage pursuing trumpets. Then, as M'Turk slapped one side, smooth with the blood of ancient sacrifice, the roar broke into short coughing howls such as the wounded gorilla throws in his native forest. These were followed by the wrath of King—three steps at a time, up the staircase, with a dry whirr of the gown. Aladdin and company, listening, squeaked with excitement as the door crashed open. King stumbled into the darkness, and cursed those performers by the gods of Balliol and quiet repose.

'Turned out for a week,' said Aladdin, holding the study door on the crack. 'Key to be brought down to his study in five minutes. "Brutes! Barbarians! Savages! Children!" He's rather agitated. "Arrah, Patsy, mind the baby!"' he sang in a whisper as he clung to the door-knob, dancing a noiseless war-dance.

King went downstairs again, and Beetle and M'Turk lit the gas to confer with Stalky. But Stalky had vanished.

'Looks like no end of a mess,' said Beetle, collecting his books and mathematical instrument case. 'A week in the form-rooms isn't any advantage to us.'

'Yes, but don't you see that Stalky isn't here, you owl?' said M'Turk. 'Take down the key, and look sorrowful. King'll only jaw you for half an hour. I'm going to read in the lower form-room.'

'But it's always me,' mourned Beetle.

'Wait till we see,' said M'Turk hopefully. 'I don't know any more than you do what Stalky means, but it's something. Go down and draw King's fire. You're used to it.'

No sooner had the key turned in the door than the lid of the coal-box, which was also the window-seat, lifted cautiously. It had been a tight fit, even for the lithe Stalky, his head between his knees, and his stomach under his right ear. From a drawer in the table he took a well-worn catapult, a handful of buckshot, and a duplicate key of the study. Noiselessly he raised the window and kneeled by it, his face turned to the road, the wind-sloped trees, the dark levels of the Burrows, and the white line of breakers falling nine-deep along the Pebble Ridge. Far down the steep-banked Devonshire lane he heard the husky hoot of the carrier's horn. There was a ghost of melody in it, as it might have been the wind in a gin-bottle essaying to sing 'It's a way we have in the Army.'

Stalky smiled a tight-lipped smile, and at extreme range opened fire. The old horse half wheeled in the shafts.

'Where be gwaine tu?' hiccoughed Rabbits-Eggs. Another buckshot tore through the rotten canvas tilt with a vicious zipp.

'*Habet!*' murmured Stalky, as Rabbits-Eggs swore into the patient night, protesting that he saw the 'doomed Colleger' who was assaulting him.

'And so,' King was saying in a high head voice to Beetle, whom he had kept to play with before Manders minor, well knowing that it hurts a Fifth-form boy to be held up to a fag's derision,—'and so, Master Beetle, in spite of all our verses, of which we are so proud, when we presume to come into direct conflict with even so humble a representative of authority as myself, for instance, we are turned out of our studies, are we not?'

'Yes, sir,' said Beetle, with a sheepish grin on his lips and murder in his heart. Hope had nearly left him, but he clung to a well-established faith that never was Stalky so dangerous as when he was invisible.

'You are not required to criticise, thank you. Turned out of our studies are we, just as if we were no better than little Manders minor. Only inky schoolboys we are, and must be treated as such.'

Beetle pricked up his ears, for Rabbits-Eggs was swearing savagely on the road, and some of the language entered at the upper sash. King believed in ventilation. He strode to the window, gowned and majestic, very visible in the gas-light.

'I zee un! I zee un!' roared Rabbits-Eggs, now that he had found a visible foe. (Another shot from the darkness above.) 'Yiss, yeou, yeou long-nosed, fower-eyed, gingy-whiskered beggar! Yeou'm tu old for such goin's on. Aie! Poultice yeour nose, I tal 'ee! Poultice yeour long nose!'

Beetle's heart leapt up within him. Somewhere, somehow, he knew, Stalky moved behind these manifestations. There was hope and the prospect of revenge. He would embody the suggestion about the nose in deathless verse. King threw up the window, and sternly rebuked Rabbits-Eggs. But the carrier was beyond fear or fawning. He had descended from the cart, and was stooping by the roadside.

It all fell swiftly as a dream. Manders minor raised his hand to his head with a cry, as a jagged flint cannoned on to some rich tree-calf bindings on the bookshelf. Another quoited along the writing-table. Beetle made zealous feint to stop it, and in that endeavour overturned a student's lamp, which dripped, *via* King's papers and some choice books, greasily on to a Persian rug. There was much broken glass on the window-seat; the china basket—M'Turk's aversion—cracked to flinders, had dropped her musk plant and its earth over the red rep cushions; Manders minor was bleeding profusely from a cut on the cheek-bone; and King, using strange words, every one of which Beetle treasured, ran forth to find the school Sergeant, that Rabbits-Eggs might be instantly cast into jail.

'Poor chap!' said Beetle, with a false, feigned sympathy. 'Let it bleed a little. That'll prevent apoplexy,' and he held the blind head skilfully over the table, and the papers on the table, as he guided the howling Manders to the door.

Then did Beetle, alone with the wreckage, return good for evil. How, in that office, a complete set of Gibbon was scarred all along the back as by a flint; how so much black and copying ink chanced to mingle with Manders's gore on the table-cloth; why the big gum-bottle, unstoppered, had rolled semi-circularly across the floor; and in what manner the white china door-knob grew to be painted with yet more of Manders's young blood, were matters which Beetle did not explain when the rabid King returned to find him standing politely over the reeking hearth-rug.

'You never told me to go, sir,' he said, with the air of Casabianca, and King consigned him to the outer darkness.

But it was to a boot-cupboard under the staircase on the ground floor that he hastened, to loose the mirth that was destroying him. He had not drawn breath for a first whoop of triumph when two hands choked him dumb.

'Go to the dormitory an' get me my things. Bring 'em to Number Five lavatory. I'm still in tights,' hissed Stalky, sitting on his head. 'Don't run. Walk.'

But Beetle staggered into the form-room next door, and

delegated his duty to the yet unenlightened M'Turk, with an hysterical *précis* of the campaign thus far. So it was M'Turk, of the wooden visage, who brought the clothes from the dormitory while Beetle panted on a form. Then the three buried themselves in Number Five lavatory, turned on all the taps, filled the place with steam, and dropped weeping into the baths, where they pieced out the war.

'*Moi! Je! Ich! Ego!*' gasped Stalky. 'I waited till I couldn't hear myself think, while you played the drum! Hid in the coal-locker—an' tweaked Rabbits-Eggs—an' Rabbits-Eggs rocked King. Wasn't it beautiful? Did you hear the glass?'

'Why, he—he—he—,' shrieked M'Turk, one trembling finger pointed at Beetle.

'Why, I—I—I was through it all,' Beetle howled; 'in his study, being jawed.'

'Oh, my Soul!' said Stalky with a yell, disappearing under water.

'The—the glass was nothing. Manders minor's head's cut open. La-la-lamp upset all over the rug. Blood on the books and papers. The gum! The gum! The gum! The ink! The ink! The ink! Oh, Lord!'

Then Stalky leaped out, all pink as he was, and shook Beetle into some sort of coherence; but his tale prostrated them afresh.

'I bunked for the boot-cupboard the second I heard King go downstairs. Beetle tumbled in on top of me. The spare key's hid behind the loose boards. There isn't a shadow of evidence,' said Stalky. They were all chanting together.

'And he turned us out himself—himself—him*self!*' This from M'Turk. 'He can't *begin* to suspect us. Oh, Stalky, it's the loveliest thing we've ever done.'

'Gum! Gum! Dollops of gum!' shouted Beetle, his spectacles gleaming through a sea of lather. 'Ink an' blood all mixed. I held the little beast's head all over the Latin proses for Monday. Golly, how the oil stunk! And Rabbits-Eggs told King to poultice his nose! Did you hit Rabbits-Eggs, Stalky?'

'Did I jolly well not? Tweaked him all over. Did you hear him curse? Oh, I shall be sick in a minute if I don't stop.'

But dressing was a slow process, because M'Turk was obliged to dance when he heard that the musk-basket was broken, and, moreover, Beetle retailed all King's language with emendations and purple insets.

'Shockin'!' said Stalky, collapsing in a helpless welter of half-hitched trousers. 'So dam' bad, too, for innocent boys like us! Wonder what they'd say at "St. Winifred's, *or* The World of School." By Gum! That reminds me we owe the Lower Third one for assaultin' Beetle when he chivied Manders minor. Come on! It's an alibi, Samivel; an' besides, if we let 'em off they'll be worse next time.'

The Lower Third had set a guard upon their form-room for the space of a full hour, which to a boy is a lifetime. Now they were busy with their Saturday evening businesses—cooking sparrows over the gas with rusty nibs; brewing unholy drinks in gallipots; skinning moles with pocket-knives: attending to paper trays full of silk-worms, or discussing the iniquities of their elders with a freedom, fluency, and point that would have amazed their parents. The blow fell without warning. Stalky upset a crowded form of small boys among their own cooking utensils; M'Turk raided the untidy lockers as a terrier digs at a rabbit-hole; while Beetle poured ink upon such heads as he could not appeal to with a Smith's Classical Dictionary. Three brisk minutes accounted for many silk-worms, pet larvae, French exercises, school caps, half-prepared bones and skulls, and a dozen pots of home-made sloe jam. It was a great wreckage, and the form-room looked as though three conflicting tempests had smitten it.

'Phew!' said Stalky, drawing breath outside the door (amid groans of 'Oh, you beastly ca-ads! You think yourselves awful funny,' and so forth). '*That*'s all right. Never let the sun go down upon your wrath. Rummy little devils, fags. Got no notion o' combinin'.'

'Six of 'em sat on my head when I went in after Manders minor,' said Beetle. 'I warned 'em what they'd get, though.'

'Everybody paid in full—beautiful feelin',' said M'Turk absently, as they strolled along the corridor. 'Don't think we'd better say much about King, though, do you, Stalky?'

'Not much. Our line is injured innocence, of course—same as when old Foxibus reported us on suspicion of smokin' in the Bunkers. If I hadn't thought of buyin' the pepper an' spillin' it all over our clothes, he'd have smelt us. King was gha-astly facetious about that. Called us bird-stuffers in form for a week.'

'Ah, King hates the Natural History Society because little Hartopp is president. Mustn't do anything in the Coll. without glorifyin' King,' said M'Turk. 'But he must be a putrid ass, you know, to suppose at our time o' life we'd go out and stuff birds like fags.'

'Poor old King!' said Beetle. 'He's awf'ly unpopular in Common-room, an' they'll chaff his head off about Rabbits-Eggs. Golly! How lovely! How beautiful! How holy! But you should have seen his face when the first rock came in! *And* the earth from the basket!'

So they were all stricken helpless for five minutes.

They repaired at last to Abanazar's study, and were received reverently.

'What's the matter?' said Stalky, quick to realise new atmospheres.

'You know jolly well,' said Abanazar. 'You'll be expelled if you get caught. King is a gibbering maniac.'

'Who? Which? What? Expelled for how? We only played the war-drum. We've got turned out for that already.'

'Do you chaps mean to say you didn't make Rabbits-Eggs drunk and bribe him to rock King's rooms?'

'Bribe him? No, that I'll swear we didn't,' said Stalky, with a relieved heart, for he loved not to tell lies. 'What a low mind you've got, Pussy! We've been down havin' a bath. Did Rabbits-Eggs rock King? Strong, perseverin' man King? Shockin'!'

'Awf'ly. King's frothing at the mouth. There's bell for prayers. Come on.'

'Wait a sec,' said Stalky, continuing the conversation in a loud and cheerful voice, as they descended the stairs. 'What did Rabbits-Eggs rock King for?'

'I know,' said Beetle, as they passed King's open door. 'I was in his study.'

'Hush, you ass!' hissed the Emperor of China.

'Oh, he's gone down to prayers,' said Beetle, watching the shadow of the House-master on the wall. 'Rabbits-Eggs was only a bit drunk, swearin' at his horse, an' King jawed him through the window, an' then, of course, he rocked King.'

'Do you mean to say,' said Stalky, 'that King began it?'

King was behind them, and every well-weighed word went up the staircase like an arrow. 'I can only swear,' said Beetle, 'that King cursed like a bargee. Simply disgustin'. I'm going to write to my father about it.'

'Better report it to Mason,' suggested Stalky. 'He knows our tender consciences. Hold on a shake. I've got to tie my bootlace.'

The other study hurried forward. They did not wish to be dragged into stage asides of this nature. So it was left to

M'Turk to sum up the situation beneath the guns of the enemy.

'You see,' said the Irishman, hanging on the banister, 'he begins by bullying little chaps; then he bullies the big chaps; then he bullies some one who isn't connected with the Coll., and then he catches it. Serves him jolly well right. . . . I beg your pardon, sir. I didn't see you were coming down the staircase.'

The black gown tore past like a thunderstorm, and in its wake, three abreast, arms linked, the Aladdin Company rolled up the big corridor to prayers, singing with most innocent intention:—

'Arrah, Patsy, mind the baby! Arrah, Patsy, mind the child!
Wrap him up in an overcoat, he's surely goin' wild!
Arrah, Patsy, mind the baby; just ye mind the child awhile!
He'll kick an' bite an' cry all night! Arrah, Patsy, mind the
    child!'

AN UNSAVOURY INTERLUDE

AN UNSAVOURY INTERLUDE

IT WAS A MAIDEN AUNT of Stalky who sent him both books, with the inscription, 'To dearest Artie, on his sixteenth birthday'; it was M'Turk who ordered their hypothecation; and it was Beetle, returned from Bideford, who flung them on the window-sill of Number Five study with news that Bastable would advance but ninepence on the two; *Eric; or, Little by Little*, being almost as great a drug as *St. Winifred's*. 'An' I don't think much of your aunt. We're nearly out of cartridges, too—Artie, dear.'

Whereupon Stalky rose up to grapple with him, but M'Turk sat on Stalky's head, calling him a 'pure-minded boy' till peace was declared. As they were grievously in arrears with a Latin prose; as it was a blazing July afternoon; and as they ought to have been at a House cricket-match, they began to renew their acquaintance, intimate and unholy, with the volumes.

'Here we are!' said M'Turk. ' "Corporal punishment produced on Eric the worst effects. He burned *not* with remorse or regret"—make a note o' that, Beetle—"but with shame and violent indignation. He glared"—oh, naughty Eric! Let's get to where he goes in for drink.'

'Hold on half a shake. Here's another sample. "The Sixth," he says, "is the palladium of all public schools." But this lot'—Stalky rapped the gilded book—'can't prevent fellows drinkin' an' stealin', an' lettin' fags out of window at night, an'—an' doin' what they please. Golly, what we've missed—not goin' to St. Winifred's! . . .'

'I'm sorry to see any boys of my House taking so little interest in their matches.'

Mr. Prout could move very silently if he pleased, though that is no merit in a boy's eyes. He had flung open the study-door without knocking—another sin—and looked at them suspiciously. 'Very sorry indeed, I am, to see you frowsting in your studies.'

'We've been out ever since dinner, sir,' said M'Turk wearily. One House-match is just like another, and their 'ploy' of that week happened to be rabbit-shooting with saloon-pistols.

'I can't see a ball when it's coming, sir,' said Beetle. 'I've had my gig-lamps smashed at the Nets till I got excused. I wasn't any good even as a fag, then, sir.'

'Tuck is probably your form. Tuck and brewing. Why can't you three take any interest in the honour of your House?'

They had heard that phrase till they were wearied. The 'honour of the House' was Prout's weak point, and they knew well how to flick him on the raw.

'If you order us to go down, sir, of course we'll go,' said Stalky, with maddening politeness. But Prout knew better than that. He had tried the experiment once at a big match, when the three, self-isolated, stood to attention for half an hour in full view of all the visitors, to whom fags, subsidised for that end, pointed them out as victims of Prout's tyranny. And Prout was a sensitive man.

In the infinitely petty confederacies of the Common-room, King and Macrea, fellow House-masters, had borne it in upon him that by games, and games alone, was salvation wrought. Boys neglected were boys lost. They must be disciplined. Left to himself, Prout would have made a sympathetic House-master; but he was never so left, and, with the devilish insight of youth, the boys knew to whom they were indebted for his zeal.

'Must we go down, sir?' said M'Turk.

'I don't want to order you to do what a right-thinking boy should do gladly. I'm sorry.' And he lurched out with some hazy impression that he had sown good seed on poor ground.

'Now, what does he suppose is the use of that?' said Beetle.

'Oh, he's cracked. King jaws him in Common-room about not keepin' us up to the mark, an' Macrea burbles about "dithcipline," an' old Heffy sits between 'em sweatin' big drops. I heard Oke [the Common-room butler] talkin' to Richards [Prout's House-servant] about it down in the basement the other day when I went down to bag some bread,' said Stalky.

'What did Oke say?' demanded M'Turk, throwing *Eric* into a corner.

' "Oh," he said, "they make more nise nor a nest full o' jackdaws, an' half of it like we'd no ears to our heads that waited on 'em. They talks over old Prout—what he've done an' left undone about his boys. An' how their boys be fine boys, an' his'n be dom bad." Well, Oke talked like that, you know, an' Richards got awf'ly wrathy. He has a down on King for something or other. Wonder why?'

'Why, King talks about Prout in form-room—makes allusions, an' all that—only half the chaps are such asses they can't see what he's drivin' at. And d'you remember what he said about the "Casual House" last Tuesday? He meant us. They say he says perfectly beastly things to his own House, makin' fun of Prout's,' said Beetle.

'Well, we didn't come here to mix up in their rows,' M'Turk said wrathfully. 'Who'll bathe after call-over? King's takin' it in the cricket-field. Come on.' Turkey seized his straw and led the way.

They reached the sun-blistered pavilion over against the grey Pebble Ridge just before roll-call, and, asking no questions, gathered from King's voice and manner that his House was on the road to victory.

'Ah, ha!' said he, turning to show the light of his countenance. 'Here we have the ornaments of the Casual House at last. You consider cricket beneath you, I believe'—the flannelled crowd sniggered—'and from what I have seen this afternoon, I fancy many others of your House hold the same view. And may I ask what you purpose to do with your noble selves till tea-time?'

'Going down to bathe, sir,' said Stalky.

'And whence this sudden zeal for cleanliness? There is nothing about you that particularly suggests it. Indeed, so far as I remember—I may be at fault—but a short time ago——'

'Five years, sir,' said Beetle hotly.

King scowled. 'One of you was that thing called a water-funk. Yes, a water-funk. So now you wish to wash? It is well. Cleanliness never injured a boy or—a House. We will proceed to business,' and he addressed himself to the call-over board.

'What the deuce did you say anything to him for, Beetle?' said M'Turk angrily, as they strolled towards the big, open sea-baths.

' 'Twasn't fair—remindin' one of bein' a water-funk. My first term, too. Heaps of chaps are—when they can't swim.'

'Yes, you ass; but he saw he'd fetched you. You ought never to answer King.'

'But it wasn't fair, Stalky.'

'My Hat! You've been here six years, an' you expect fairness. You *are* a ditherin' idiot.'

A knot of King's boys, also bound for the Baths, hailed them, beseeching them to wash—for the honour of their House.

'That's what comes of King's jawin' and messin'. Those young animals wouldn't have thought of it unless he'd put it into their heads. Now they'll be funny about it for weeks,' said Stalky. 'Don't take any notice.'

The boys came nearer, shouting an opprobrious word. At last they moved to windward, ostentatiously holding their noses.

'That's pretty,' said Beetle. 'They'll be sayin' our House stinks next.'

When they returned from the Baths, damp-headed, languid, at peace with the world, Beetle's forecast came only too true. They were met in the corridor by a fag—a common, Lower-Second fag—who at arm's length handed them a carefully wrapped piece of soap 'with the compliments of King's House.'

'Hold on,' said Stalky, checking immediate attack. 'Who put you up to this, Nixon? Rattray and White? [Those were two leaders in King's House.] Thank you. There's no answer.'

'Oh, it's too sickening to have this kind o' rot shoved on to a chap. What's the sense of it? What's the fun of it?' said M'Turk.

'It will go on to the end of the term, though.' Beetle wagged his head sorrowfully. He had worn many jests threadbare on his own account.

In a few days it became an established legend of the school that Prout's House did not wash and were therefore noisome. Mr. King was pleased to smile succulently in form when one of his boys drew aside from Beetle with certain gestures.

'There seems to be some disability attaching to you, my Beetle, or else why should Burton major withdraw, so to speak, the hem of his garments? I confess I am still in the dark. Will some one be good enough to enlighten me?'

Naturally, he was enlightened by half the Form.

'Extraordinary! Most extraordinary! However, each House has its traditions, with which I would not for the world interfere. *We* have a prejudice in favour of washing. Go on, Beetle—from *"Jugurtha tamen"*—and, if you can, avoid the more flagrant forms of guessing.'

Prout's House was furious because Macrea's and Hartopp's Houses joined King's to insult them. They called a House-meeting after dinner—an excited and angry meeting of all save the prefects, whose dignity, though they sympathised, did not allow them to attend. They read ungrammatical resolutions, and made speeches beginning, 'Gentlemen, we have met on this occasion,' and ending with, 'It's a beastly shame,' precisely as Houses have done since time and schools began.

Number Five study attended, with its usual air of bland patronage. At last M'Turk, of the lanthorn jaws, delivered himself:—

'You jabber and jaw and burble, and that's about all you can do. What's the good of it? King's House'll only gloat because they've drawn you, and King'll gloat, too. Besides, that resolution of Orrin's is chock-full of bad grammar, and King'll gloat over *that*.'

'I thought you an' Beetle would put it right, an'—an' we'd post it in the corridor,' said the composer meekly.

'*Pas si je le connais.* I'm not goin' to meddle with the biznai,' said Beetle. 'It's a gloat for King's House. Turkey's quite right.'

'Well, won't Stalky, then?'

But Stalky puffed out his cheeks and squinted down his nose in the style of Panurge, and all he said was, 'Oh, you abject burblers!'

'You're three beastly scabs!' was the instant retort of the democracy, and they went out amid execrations.

'This is piffling,' said M'Turk. 'Let's get our sallies, and go and shoot bunnies.'

Three saloon-pistols, with a supply of bulleted breech-caps, were stored in Stalky's trunk, and this trunk was in their dormitory, and their dormitory was a three-bed attic one, opening out of a ten-bed establishment, which, in turn, communicated with the great range of dormitories that ran practically from one end of the College to the other. Macrea's House lay next to Prout's, King's next to Macrea's, and Hartopp's beyond that again. Carefully locked doors divided House from House, but each House, in its internal arrangements,—the College had originally been a terrace of twelve large houses—was a replica of the next; one straight roof covering all.

They found Stalky's bed drawn out from the wall to the left of the dormer window, and the latter end of Richard's protruding from a two-foot-square cupboard in the wall.

'What's all this? I've never noticed it before. What are you tryin' to do, Fatty?'

'Fillin' basins, Muster Corkran.' Richards's voice was hollow and muffled. 'They've been savin' me trouble. Yiss.'

'Looks like it,' said M'Turk. 'Hi! You'll stick if you don't take care.'

Richards backed puffing.

'I can't rache un. Yiss, 'tes a stopcock, Muster M'Turk. They've took an' runned all the watter-pipes a storey higher in the Houses—runned 'em all along under the 'ang of the heaves, like. Runned 'em in last holidays. I can't rache the stopcock.'

'Let me try,' said Stalky, diving into the aperture.

'Slip 'ee to the left, then, Muster Corkran. Slip 'ee to the left, an' feel in the dark.'

To the left Stalky wriggled, and saw a long line of lead-pipe disappearing up a triangular tunnel, whose roof was the rafters and boarding of the College roof, whose floor was sharp-edged joists, and whose side was the rough studding of the lath-and-plaster wall under the dormer.

'Rummy show! How far does it go?'

'Right along, Muster Corkran—right along from end to end. Her runs under the 'ang of the heaves. Have 'ee rached the stopcock yet? Mr. King got un put in to save us carryin' watter from downstairs to fill the basins. No place for a lusty man like old Richards. I'm tu thickabout to go ferretin'. Thank 'ee, Muster Corkran.'

The water squirted through the tap just inside the cupboard, and, having filled the basins, the grateful Richards waddled away.

The boys sat round-eyed on their beds considering the possibilities of this trove. Two floors below them they could hear the hum of the angry House; for nothing is so still as a dormitory in mid-afternoon of a midsummer term.

'It has been papered over till now.' M'Turk examined the little door. 'If we'd only known before!'

'I vote we go down and explore. No one will come up this time o' day. We needn't keep *cave*.'

They crawled in, Stalky leading, drew the door behind them, and on all fours embarked on a dark and dirty road full of plaster, odd shavings, and all the raffle that builders leave in the waste room of a house. The passage was perhaps three feet wide, and, except for the straggling light round the edges of the cupboards (there was one to each dormer), almost pitchy dark.

'Here's Macrea's House,' said Stalky, his eye at the crack of the third cupboard. 'I can see Barnes's name on his trunk. Don't make such a row, Beetle! We can get right to the end of the Coll. Come on! . . . We're in King's House now—I can see a bit of Rattray's trunk. How these beastly boards hurt one's knees!' They heard his nails scraping on plaster.

'That's the ceiling below. Look out! If we smashed that, the plaster 'ud fall down in the lower dormitory,' said Beetle.

'Let's,' whispered M'Turk.

'An' be collared first thing? Not much. Why, I can shove my hand ever so far up between these boards.'

Stalky thrust an arm to the elbow between the joists.

'No good stayin' here. I vote we go back an' talk it over. It's a crummy place. Must say I'm grateful to King for his waterworks.'

They crawled out, brushed one another clean, slid the saloon-pistols down a trouser-leg, and hurried forth to a deep and solitary Devonshire lane in whose flanks a boy might sometimes slay a young rabbit. They threw themselves down under the rank elder-bushes, and began to think aloud.

'You know,' said Stalky at last, sighting at a distant sparrow, 'we could hide our sallies in there like anything.'

'Huh!' Beetle snorted, choked, and gurgled. He had been silent since they left the dormitory. 'Did you ever read a book called *The History of a House* or something? I got it out of the library the other day. A Frenchwoman wrote it—Violet somebody. But it's translated, you know; an' it's very interestin'. Tells you how a house is built.'

'Well, if you're in a sweat to find that out, you can go down to the new cottages they're building for the Coastguard.'

'My Hat! I will.' He felt in his pockets. 'Give me tuppence, some one.'

'Rot! Stay here, an' don't mess about in the sun.'

'Gi' me tuppence.'

'I say, Beetle, you aren't stuffy about anything, are you?' said M'Turk, handing over the coppers. His tone was serious, for though Stalky often, and M'Turk occasionally, manœuvred on his own account, Beetle had never been known to do so in all the history of the confederacy.

'No, I'm not. I'm thinkin'.'

'Well, we'll come too,' said Stalky, with a general's suspicion of his aides.

'Don't want you.'

'Oh, leave him alone. He's been taken worse with a poem,' said M'Turk. 'He'll go burblin' down to the Pebble Ridge and spit it all up in the study when he comes back.'

'Then why did he want the tuppence, Turkey? He's gettin' too beastly independent. Hi! There's a bunny. No, it ain't. It's a cat, by Jove! You plug first.'

Twenty minutes later, a boy with a straw hat at the back of his head, and his hands in his pockets, was staring at workmen as they moved about a half-finished cottage. He produced some ferocious tobacco, and was passed from the forecourt into the interior, where he asked many questions.

'Well, let's have your beastly epic,' said Turkey, as they burst into the study, to find Beetle deep in Viollet-le-Duc and some drawings. 'We've had no end of a lark.'

'Epic? What epic? I've been down to the Coastguard.'

'No epic? Then we will slay you, O Beadle,' said Stalky, moving to the attack. 'You've got something up your sleeve. *I* know, when you talk in that tone!'

'Your Uncle Beetle'—with an attempt to imitate Stalky's war-voice—'is a Great Man.'

'Oh no; he jolly well isn't anything of the kind. You deceive yourself, Beetle. Scrag him, Turkey!'

'A Great Man,' Beetle gurgled from the floor. '*You* are futile —look out for my tie!—futile burblers. I am the Great Man. I gloat. Ouch! Hear me!'

'Beetle, de-ah'—Stalky dropped unreservedly on Beetle's chest—'we love you, an' you're a poet. If I ever said you were a doggaroo, I apologise; but you know as well as we do that you can't do anything by yourself without mucking it.'

'I've got a notion.'

'And you'll spoil the whole show if you don't tell your Uncle Stalky. Cough it up, ducky, an' we'll see what we can do. Notion, you fat impostor—I knew you had a notion when you went away! Turkey said it was a poem.'

'I've found out how houses are built. Le' me get up. The floor-joists of one room are the ceiling-joists of the room below.'

'Don't be so filthy technical.'

'Well, the man told me. The floor is laid on top of those joists—those boards on edge that we crawled over—but the floor stops at a partition. Well, if you get behind a partition, same as you did in the attic, don't you see that you can shove anything you please under the floor between the floor-boards an' the lath-and-plaster of the ceiling below? Look here. I've drawn it.'

He produced a rude sketch, sufficient to enlighten the allies. There is no part of the modern school curriculum that deals with architecture, and none of them had yet reflected whether floors and ceilings were hollow or solid. Outside his own immediate interests the boy is as ignorant as the savage he so admires; but he has also the savage's resource.

'I see,' said Stalky. 'I shoved my hand there. An' then?'

'An' then . . . They've been callin' us stinkers, you know. We might shove somethin' under—sulphur, or something that

95

stunk pretty bad—an' stink 'em out. I know it can be done somehow.' Beetle's eyes turned to Stalky handling the diagrams.

'Stinks?' said Stalky interrogatively. Then his face grew luminous with delight. 'By Gum! I've got it. Horrid stinks! Turkey!' He leaped at the Irishman. 'This afternoon—just after Beetle went away! *She's* the very thing!'

'Come to my arms, my beamish boy,' carolled M'Turk, and they fell into each other's arms dancing. 'Oh, frabjous day! Calloo, callay! She will! She will!'

'Hold on,' said Beetle. 'I don't understand.'

'Dearr man! It shall, though. Oh, Artie, my pure-souled youth, let us tell our darlin' Reggie about Pestiferous Stinkadores.'

'Not until after call-over. Come on!'

'I say,' said Orrin stiffly, as they fell into their places along the walls of the gymnasium. 'The House are goin' to hold another meeting.'

'Hold away, then.' Stalky's mind was elsewhere.

'It's about you three this time.'

'All right, give 'em my love. . . . *Here, sir!*' and he tore down the corridor.

Gambolling like kids at play, with bounds and side-starts, with caperings and curvettings, they led the almost bursting Beetle to the rabbit-lane, and from under a pile of stones drew forth the new-slain corpse of a cat. Then did Beetle see the inner meaning of what had gone before, and lifted up his voice in thanksgiving for that the world held warriors so wise as Stalky and M'Turk.

'Well-nourished old lady, ain't she?' said Stalky. 'How long d'you suppose it'll take her to get a bit whiff in a confined space?'

'Bit whiff! What a coarse brute you are!' said M'Turk. 'Can't a poor pussy-cat get under King's dormitory floor to die without your pursuin' her with your foul innuendoes?'

'What did she die under the floor for?' said Beetle, looking to the future.

'Oh, they won't worry about *that* when they find her,' said Stalky.

'A cat may look at a King.' M'Turk rolled down the bank at his own jest. 'Pussy, you don't know how useful you're goin' to be to three pure-souled, high-minded boys.'

'They'll have to take up the floor for her, same as they did in Number Nine when the rat croaked. Big medicine—heap big medicine! Phew! Oh, Lord, I wish I could stop laughin',' said Beetle.

'Stinks! Hi, stinks! Clammy ones!' M'Turk gasped as he regained his place. 'And'—the exquisite humour of it brought them sliding down together in a tangle—'it's all for the honour of the House, too!'

'An' they're holdin' another meetin'—on us,' Stalky panted, his knees in the ditch and his face in the long grass. 'Well, let's get the bullet out of her an' hurry up. The sooner she's bedded out the better.'

Between them they did some grisly work with a penknife; between them (ask not who buttoned her to his bosom) they took up the corpse and hastened back, Stalky arranging their plan of action at the full trot.

The afternoon sun, lying in broad patches on the bed-rugs, saw three boys and an umbrella disappear into a dormitory wall. In five minutes they returned, brushed themselves all over, washed their hands, combed their hair, and descended.

'Are you sure you shoved her far enough under?' said M'Turk suddenly.

'Hang it, man, I shoved her the full length of my arm and Beetle's brolly. That must be about six feet. She's bung in the middle of King's big upper ten-bedder. Eligible central situation, *I* call it. She'll stink out his chaps, an' Hartopp's an' Macrea's, when she really begins to fume. I swear your Uncle Stalky is a Great Man. Do you realise what a Great Man he is, Beetle?'

'Well, I had the notion first, hadn't I, only——'

'You couldn't do it without your Uncle Stalky, could you?'

'They've been callin' us stinkers for a week now,' said M'Turk. 'Oh, won't they catch it!'

'Stinker! Yah! Stink-ah!' rang down the corridor.

'*And* she's there,' said Stalky, a hand on either boy's shoulder. 'She—is—there, gettin' ready to surprise 'em. Presently she'll begin to whisper to 'em in their dreams. Then she'll whiff. Golly, how she'll whiff! Oblige me by thinkin' of it for two minutes.'

They went to their study in more or less of silence. There they began to laugh—laugh as only boys can. They laughed with their foreheads on the tables, or on the floor; laughed at length, curled over the backs of chairs or clinging to a bookshelf; laughed themselves limp.

And in the middle of it Orrin entered on behalf of the House.

'Don't mind us, Orrin; sit down. You don't know how we respect an' admire you. There's something about your pure, high, young forehead, full of the dreams of innocent boyhood, that's no end fetchin'. It is, indeed.'

'The House sent me to give you this.' He laid a folded sheet of paper on the table and retired with an awful front.

'It's the resolution! Oh, read it, some one. I'm too silly-sick with laughin' to see,' said Beetle.

Stalky jerked it open with a precautionary sniff.

'Phew! Phew! Listen. *"The House notices with pain and contempt the attitude of indiference"*—how many f's in "in-difference," Beetle?'

'Two for choice.'

'Only one here—*"adopted by the occupants of Number Five Study in relation to the insults offered to Mr. Prout's House at the recent meeting in Number Twelve form-room, and the House hereby pass a vote of censure on the said Study."* That's all.'

'An' she bled all down my shirt, too!' said Beetle.

'And I'm catty all over,' said M'Turk, 'though I washed twice.'

'An' I nearly broke Beetle's brolly plantin' her where she would blossom!'

The situation was beyond speech, but not laughter. There was some attempt that night to demonstrate against the three in their dormitory; so they came forth.

'You see,' Beetle began suavely as he loosened his braces, 'the trouble with you is that you're a set of unthinkin' asses. You've no more brains than spidgers. We've told you that heaps of times, haven't we?'

'We'll give all three of you a dormitory lickin'. You always jaw at us as if you were prefects,' cried one.

'Oh no, you won't,' said Stalky, 'because you know that if you did you'd get the worst of it sooner or later. *We* aren't in any hurry. *We* can afford to wait for our little revenges. You've made howlin' asses of yourselves, an' just as soon as King gets hold of your precious resolution to-morrow you'll find that out. If you aren't sick an' sorry by to-morrow night, I'll—I'll eat my hat.'

But or ever the dinner-bell rang the next day Prout's were

sadly aware of their error. King received stray members of that House with an exaggerated attitude of fear. Did they purpose to cause him to be dismissed from the College by unanimous resolution? What were their views concerning the government of the school, that he might hasten to give effect to them? He would not offend them for worlds; but he feared—he sadly feared—that his own House, who did not pass resolutions (but washed), might somewhat deride.

King was a happy man, and his House, basking in the favour of his smile, made that afternoon a long penance to the misled Prout's. And Prout himself, with a dull and lowering visage, tried to think out the rights and wrongs of it all, only plunging deeper into bewilderment. Why should his House be called 'stinkers'? Truly, it was a small thing, but he had been trained to believe that straws show which way the wind blows, and that there is no smoke without fire. He approached King in Common-room with a sense of injustice, but King was pleased to be full of airy persiflage that tide, and brilliantly danced dialectical rings round Prout.

'Now,' said Stalky at bedtime, making pilgrimage through the dormitories before the prefects came up, '*now* what have you got to say for yourselves? Foster, Carton, Finch, Longbridge, Marlin, Brett! I heard you chaps catchin' it from King—he made hay of you—an' all you could do was to wriggle an' grin an' say, "Yes, sir," an' "No, sir," an' "Oh, sir," an' "Please, sir"! You an' your resolution! Urh!'

'Oh, shut up, Stalky.'

'Not a bit of it. You're a gaudy lot of resolutionists, you are! You've made a sweet mess of it. Perhaps you'll have the decency to leave us alone next time.'

Here the House grew angry, and in many voices pointed out how this blunder would never have come to pass if Number Five study had helped them from the first.

'But you chaps are so beastly conceited, an'—an' you swaggered into the meetin' as if we were a lot of idiots,' growled Orrin of the resolution.

'That's precisely what you *are*! That's what we've been tryin' to hammer into your thick heads all this time,' said Stalky. 'Never mind, we'll forgive you. Cheer up. You can't help bein' asses, you know,' and, the enemy's flank deftly turned, Stalky hopped into bed.

That night was the first of sorrow among the jubilant King's. By some accident of under-floor draughts the cat did not vex the dormitory beneath which she lay, but the next one to the right; stealing on the air rather as a pale-blue sensation than as any poignant offence. But the mere adumbration of an odour is enough for the sensitive nose and clean tongue of youth. Decency demands that we draw several carbolised sheets over what the dormitory said to Mr. King and what Mr. King replied. He was genuinely proud of his House and fastidious in all that concerned their well-being. He came; he sniffed; he said things. Next morning a boy in that dormitory confided to his bosom friend, a fag of Macrea's, that there was trouble in their midst which King would fain keep secret.

But Macrea's boy had also a bosom friend in Prout's, a shock-headed fag of malignant disposition, who, when he had wormed out the secret, told—told it in a high-pitched treble that rang along the corridor like a bat's squeak.

'An'—an' they've been callin' us "stinkers" all this week. Why, Harland minor says they simply can't sleep in his dormitory for the stink. Come on!'

'With one shout and with one cry' Prout's juniors hurled themselves into the war, and through the interval between first and second lesson some fifty twelve-year-olds were embroiled on the gravel outside King's windows to a tune whose *leit-motif* was the word 'stinker.'

'Hark to the minute-gun at sea!' said Stalky. They were in their study collecting books for second lesson—Latin, with King. 'I thought his azure brow was a bit cloudy at prayers.

She is comin', sister Mary,
She is——'

'If they make such a row now, what will they do when she really begins to look up an' take notice?'

'Well, no vulgar repartee, Beetle. All we want is to keep out of this row like gentlemen.'

' " 'Tis but a little faded flower." Where's my Horace? Look here, I don't understand what she means by stinkin' out Rattray's dormitory first. We holed in under White's, didn't we?' asked M'Turk, with a wrinkled brow.

'Skittish little thing! She's rompin' about all over the place, I suppose.'

'My Aunt! King'll be a cheerful customer at second lesson. I haven't prepared my Horace one little bit, either,' said Beetle. 'Come on!'

They were outside the form-room door now. It was within five minutes of the bell, and King might arrive at any moment.

Turkey elbowed into a cohort of scuffling fags, cut out Thornton tertius (he that had been Harland's bosom friend), and bade him tell his tale.

It was a simple one, interrupted by tears. Many of King's House had already battered him for libel.

'Oh, it's nothing,' M'Turk cried. 'He says that King's House stinks. That's all.'

'Stale!' Stalky shouted. 'We knew that years ago, only we didn't choose to run about shoutin' "Stinker!" We've got some manners, if they haven't. Catch a fag, Turkey, an' make sure of it.'

Turkey's long arm closed round a hurried and anxious ornament of the Lower Second.

'Oh, M'Turk, please let me go. I don't stink—I swear I don't!'

'Guilty conscience!' cried Beetle. 'Who said you did?'

'What d'you make of it?' Stalky punted the small boy into Beetle's arms.

'Snf! Snf! He does, though. I think it's leprosy—or thrush. P'raps it's both. Take it away.'

'Indeed, Master Beetle'—King generally came to the House-door for a minute or two as the bell rang—'we are vastly indebted to you for your diagnosis, which seems to reflect almost as much credit on the natural unwholesomeness of your mind as it does upon your pitiful ignorance of the diseases of which you discourse so glibly. We will, however, test your knowledge in other directions.'

That was a merry lesson, but, in his haste to scarify Beetle, King clean neglected to give him an imposition, and since at the same time he supplied him with many priceless adjectives for later use, Beetle was well content, and applied himself most seriously throughout third lesson (algebra with little Hartopp) to composing a poem entitled 'The Lazar-house.'

After dinner King took his House to bathe in the sea off the Pebble Ridge. It was an old promise; but he wished he could have evaded it, for all Prout's lined up by the Fives Court and cheered with intention. In his absence not less than half the school invaded the infected dormitory to draw their own conclusions. The cat had gained in the last twelve hours, but a battlefield of the fifth day could not have been so flamboyant as the spies reported.

'My word, she *is* doin' herself proud,' said Stalky. 'Did you ever smell anything like it? Ah, an' she isn't under White's dormitory at all yet.'

'But she will be. Give her time,' said Beetle. 'She'll twine like a giddy honeysuckle. What howlin' Lazarites they are! No House is justified in makin' itself a stench in the nostrils of decent——'

'High-minded, pure-souled boys. *Do* you burn with remorse and regret?' said M'Turk, as they hastened to meet the House coming up from the sea. King had deserted it, so speech was unfettered. Round its front played a crowd of skirmishers—all Houses mixed—flying, re-forming, shrieking insults. On its tortured flanks marched the Hoplites, seniors hurling jests one after another—simple and primitive jests of the Stone Age. To these the three added themselves, dispassionately, with an air of aloofness, almost sadly.

'An' they look all right, too,' said Stalky. 'It can't be Rattray, can it? Rattray?'

No answer.

'Rattray, dear? He seems stuffy about something or other. Look here, old man, we don't bear any malice about your sendin' that soap to us last week, do we? Be cheerful, Rat. You can live this down all right. I dare say it's only a few fags. Your House *is* so beastly slack, though.'

'You aren't going back to the House, are you?' said M'Turk. The victims desired nothing better. 'You've simply no conception of the reek up there. Of course, frowzin' as you do, you wouldn't notice it; but, after this nice wash and the clean, fresh air, even you'd be upset. Much better camp on the Burrows. We'll get you some straw. Shall we?' The House hurried in to the tune of 'John Brown's body,' sung by loving schoolmates, and barricaded themselves in their form-room. Straightway Stalky chalked a large cross, with 'Lord, have mercy upon us,' on the door, and left King to find it.

The wind shifted that night and wafted a carrion-reek into Macrea's dormitories; so that boys in night-gowns pounded on the locked door between the Houses, entreating King's to wash. Number Five study went to second lesson with not more than half a pound of camphor apiece in their clothing; and King, too wary to ask for explanations, gibbered awhile and hurled them forth. So Beetle finished yet another poem at peace in the study.

'They're usin' carbolic now. Malpas told me,' said Stalky. 'King thinks it's the drains.'

'She'll need a lot o' carbolic,' said M'Turk. 'No harm tryin', I suppose. It keeps King out of mischief.'

'I swear I thought he was goin' to kill me when I sniffed just now. He didn't mind Burton major sniffin' at me the other day, though. He never stopped Alexander howlin' "Stinker!" into our form-room before—before we doctored 'em. He just grinned,' said Stalky. 'What was he frothin' over you for, Beetle?'

'Aha! That was my subtle jape. I had him on toast. You know he always jaws about the learned Lipsius.'

' "Who at the age of four"—*that* chap?' said M'Turk.

'Yes. Whenever he hears I've written a poem. Well, just as I was sittin' down, I whispered. "How is our learned Lipsius?" to Burton major. Old Butt grinned like an owl. He didn't know what I was drivin' at; but King jolly well did. That was really why he hove us out. Ain't you grateful? Now shut up. I'm goin' to write the "Ballad of the Learned Lipsius." '

'Keep clear of anything coarse, then,' said Stalky. 'I shouldn't like to be coarse on this happy occasion.'

'Not for wo-orlds. What rhymes to "stenches," some one?'

In Common-room at lunch King discoursed acridly to Prout of boys with prurient minds, who perverted their few and baleful talents to sap discipline and corrupt their equals, to deal in foul imagery and destroy reverence.

'But you didn't seem to consider this when your House

called us—ah—"stinkers." If you hadn't assured me that you never interfere with another man's House, I should almost believe that it was a few casual remarks of yours that started all this nonsense.'

Prout had endured much, for King always took his temper to meals.

'You spoke to Beetle yourself, didn't you? Something about not bathing, and being a water-funk?' the school Chaplain put in. 'I was scoring in the pavilion that day.'

'I may have—jestingly. I really don't pretend to remember every remark I let fall among small boys; and full well I know the Beetle has no feelings to be hurt.'

'Maybe; but he, or they—it comes to the same thing—have the fiend's own knack of discovering a man's weak place. I confess I rather go out of my way to conciliate Number Five study. It may be soft, but so far, I believe, I am the only man here whom they haven't maddened by their—well—attentions.'

'That is all beside the point. I flatter myself I can deal with them alone as occasion arises. But if they feel themselves morally supported by those who should wield an absolute and open-handed justice, then I say that my lot is indeed a hard one. Of all things I detest, I admit that anything verging on disloyalty among ourselves is the first.'

The Common-room looked at one another out of the corners of their eyes, and Prout blushed.

'I deny it absolutely,' he said. 'Er—in fact, I own that I personally object to all three of them. It is not fair, there-fore, to——'

'How long do you propose to allow it?' said King.

'But surely,' said Macrea, deserting his usual ally, 'the blame, if there be any, rests with you, King. You can't hold them responsible for the—you prefer the good old Anglo-Saxon, I believe—stink in your House. My boys are complaining of it now.'

'What can you expect? You know what boys are. Naturally they take advantage of what to them is a heaven-sent opportunity,' said little Hartopp. 'What *is* the trouble in your dormitories, King?'

Mr. King explained that as he had made it the one rule of his life never to interfere with another man's House, so he expected not to be too patently interfered with. They might be interested to learn—here the Chaplain heaved a weary sigh —that he had taken all steps that, in his poor judgment, would meet the needs of the case. Nay, further, he had himself expended, with no thought of reimbursement, sums, the amount of which he would not specify, on disinfectants. This he had done because he knew by bitter—by most bitter—experience that the management of the College was slack, dilatory, and inefficient. He might even add almost as slack as the administration of certain Houses which now thought fit to sit in judgment on his actions. With a short summary of his scholastic career, and a *précis* of his qualifications, including his degrees, he withdrew, slamming the door.

'Heigho!' said the Chaplain. 'Ours is a dwarfing life—a belittling life, my brethren. God help all schoolmasters! They need it.'

'I don't like the boys, I own'—Prout dug viciously with his fork into the table-cloth—'and I don't pretend to be a strong man, as you know. But I confess I can't see any reason why I should take steps against Stalky and the others because King happens to be annoyed by—by——'

'Falling into the pit he has digged,' said little Hartopp. 'Certainly not, Prout. No one accuses *you* of setting one House against another through sheer idleness.'

'A belittling life—a belittling life.' The Chaplain rose. 'I go to correct French exercises. By dinner King will have scored off some unlucky child of thirteen. He will repeat to us every word of his brilliant repartees, and all will be well.'

'But about those three. Are they so prurient-minded?'

'Nonsense,' said little Hartopp. 'If you thought for a minute, Prout, you would see that the "precocious flow of fetid imagery" that King complains of is borrowed wholesale from King. *He* "nursed the pinion that impelled the steel." Naturally he does not approve. Come into the smoking-room for a minute. It isn't fair to listen to boys; but they should be now rubbing it into King's House outside. Little things please little minds.'

The dingy den off the Common-room was never used for anything except gowns. Its windows were ground glass; one could not see out of it, but one could hear almost every word on the gravel outside. A light and wary footstep came up from Number Five.

'Rattray!' in a subdued voice—Rattray's study fronted that way. 'D'you know if Mr. King's anywhere about? I've got a——' M'Turk discreetly left the end of his sentence open.

'No. He's gone out,' said Rattray unguardedly.

'Ah! The learned Lipsius is airing himself, is he? His Royal Highness has gone to fumigate.' M'Turk climbed on the railings, where he held forth like the never-wearied rook.

'Now in all the Coll. there was no stink like the stink of King's House, for it stank vehemently and none knew what to make of it. Save King. And he washed the fags *privatim et seriatim*. In the fishpools of Heshbon washed he them, with an apron about his loins.'

'Shut up, you mad Irishman!' There was the sound of a golf-ball spurting up the gravel.

'It's no good getting wrathy, Rattray. We've come to jape

with you. Come on, Beetle. They're all at home. You can wind 'em.'

'Where's the Pomposo Stinkadore? 'Tisn't safe for a pure-souled, high-minded boy to be seen round his House these days. Gone out, has he? Never mind. I'll do the best I can, Rattray. I'm *in loco parentis* just now.'

('One for you, Prout,' whispered Macrea, for this was Mr. Prout's pet phrase.)

'I have a few words to impart to you, my young friend. We will discourse together awhile.'

Here the listening Prout sputtered. Beetle, in a strained voice, had chosen a favourite gambit of King's.

'I repeat, Master Rattray, we will confer, and the matter of our discourse shall not be stinks, for that is a loathsome and obscene word. We will, with your good leave—granted, I trust, Master Rattray, granted, I trust—study this—this scabrous upheaval of latent demoralisation. What impresses me most is not so much the blatant indecency with which you swagger abroad under your load of putrescence' (You must imagine this discourse punctuated with golf-balls, but old Rattray was ever a bad shot) 'as the cynical immorality with which you revel in your abhorrent aromas. Far be it from me to interfere with another's House——'

('Good Lord!' said Prout, 'but this *is* King.'

'Line for line, letter for letter. Listen,' said little Hartopp.)

'But to say that you stink, as certain lewd fellows of the baser sort aver, is to say nothing—less than nothing. In the absence of your beloved House-master, for whom no one has a higher regard than myself, I will, if you will allow me, explain the grossness—the unparalleled enormity—the appalling fetor of the stenches (I believe in the good old Anglo-Saxon word), stenches, sir, with which you have seen fit to infect your House.

. . . Oh, bother! I've forgotten the rest, but it was very beautiful. Aren't you grateful to us for labourin' with you this way, Rattray? Lots of chaps 'ud never have taken the trouble, but we're grateful, Rattray.'

'Yes, we're horrid grateful,' grunted M'Turk. 'We don't forget that soap. We're polite. Why ain't you polite, Rat?'

'Hallo!' Stalky cantered up, his cap over one eye. 'Exhortin' the Whiffers, eh? I'm afraid they're too far gone to repent. Rattray! White! Perowne! Malpass! No answer. This is distressin'. This is truly distressin'. Bring out your dead, you glandered lepers!'

'You think yourself funny, don't you?' said Rattray, stung from his dignity by this last. 'It's only a rat or something under the floor. We're going to have it up to-morrow.'

'Don't try to shuffle it off on a poor dumb animal, and dead, too. I loathe prevarication. 'Pon my soul, Rattray——'

'Hold on. The Hartoffles never said " 'Pon my soul" in all his little life,' said Beetle critically.

('Ah!' said Prout to little Hartopp.)

'Upon my word, sir, upon my word, sir, I expected better things of you, Rattray. Why can you not own up to your misdeeds like a man? Have *I* ever shown any lack of confidence in *you?*'

('It's not brutality,' murmured little Hartopp, as though answering a question no one had asked. 'It's boy; only boy.')

'And this was the House——' Stalky changed from a pecking, fluttering voice to tragic earnestness—'this was the—the—open cesspit that dared to call us "stinkers." And now—and now, it tries to shelter itself behind a dead rat. You annoy me, Rattray. You disgust me! You irritate me unspeakably! Thank Heaven, I am a man of equable temper——'

('This is to your address, Macrea,' said Prout.

'I fear so, I fear so.')

'Or I should scarcely be able to contain myself before your mocking visage.'

'*Cave!*' in an undertone. Beetle had spied King sailing down the corridor.

'And what may you be doing here, my little friends?' the House-master began. 'I had a fleeting notion—correct me if I am wrong' (the listeners with one accord choked)—'that if I found you outside my House I should visit you with dire pains and penalties.'

'We were just goin' for a walk, sir,' said Beetle.

'And you stopped to speak to Rattray *en route?*'

'Yes, sir. We've been throwing golf-balls,' said Rattray, coming out of the study.

('Old Rat is more of a diplomat than I thought. So far he is strictly within the truth,' said little Hartopp. 'Observe the ethics of it, Prout.')

'Oh, you were sporting with them, were you? I must say I do not envy you your choice of associates. I fancied they might have been engaged in some of the prurient discourse with which they have been so disgustingly free of late. I should strongly advise you to direct your steps most carefully in the future. Pick up those golf-balls.' He passed on.

Next day Richards, who had been a carpenter in the Navy, and to whom odd jobs were confided, was ordered to take up a dormitory floor; for Mr. King held that something must have died there.

'We need not neglect all our work for a trumpery incident of this nature; though I am quite aware that little things please little minds. Yes, I have decreed the boards to be taken up after lunch under Richards' auspices. I have no doubt it will be vastly interesting to a certain type of so-called intellect; but any boy of my House or another's found on the dormitory stairs will *ipso facto* render himself liable to three hundred lines.'

The boys did not collect on the stairs, but most of them waited outside King's. Richards had been bound to cry the news from the attic window, and, if possible, to exhibit the corpse.

' 'Tes a cat, a dead cat!' Richards' face showed purple at the window. He had been in the chamber of death and on his knees for some time.

'Cat be blowed!' cried M'Turk. 'It's a dead fag left over from last term. Three cheers for King's dead fag!'

They cheered lustily.

'Show it, show it! Let's have a squint at it!' yelled the juniors. 'Give her to the Bug-hunters.' (This was the Natural History Society.) 'The cat looked at the King—and died of it! Hoosh! Yai! Yaow! Maiow! Ftzz!' were some of the cries that followed.

Again Richards appeared.

'She've been'—he checked himself suddenly—'dead a long taime.'

The school roared.

'Well, come on out for a walk,' said Stalky in a well-chosen pause. 'It's all very disgustin', an' I do hope that the Lazar-house won't do it again.'

'Do what?' a King's boy cried furiously.

'Kill a poor innocent cat every time you want to get off washin'. It's awf'ly hard to distinguish between you as it is. I prefer the cat, I must say. She isn't quite so whiff. What are you goin' to do, Beetle?'

'*Je vais gloater. Je vais gloater tout le* blessed afternoon.

AN UNSAVOURY INTERLUDE

Jamais j'ai gloaté comme je gloaterai aujourd'hui. Nous bunkerons aux Bunkers.'

And it seemed good to them so to do.

Down in the basement, where the gas flickers and the boots stand in racks, Richards, amid his blacking-brushes, held forth to Oke of the Common-room, Gumbly of the dining-halls, and fair Lena of the laundry.

'Yiss. Her were in a shockin' staate an' condition. Her nigh made me sick, I tal 'ee. But I rowted un out, an' I rowted un out, an' I made all shipshape, though her smelt like to bilges.'

'Her died mousin', I rackon, poor thing,' said Lena.

'Then her moused different to any made cat o' God's world, Lena. I up with the top-board, an' she were lyin' on her back, an' I turned un ovver with the brume-handle, an' 'twas her back was all covered with the plaster from 'twixt the lathin'. Yiss, I tal 'ee. An' under her head there lay, like, so's to say, a little pillow o' plaster druv up in front of her by raison of her slidin' along on her back. No cat niver went mousin' on her back, Lena. Some one had shoved her along right underneath, so far as they could shove un. Cats don't make theyselves pillows for to die on. Shoved along, she were, when she was settin' for to be cold, laike.'

'Oh, yeou'm too clever to live, Fatty. Yeou go get wed an' taught some sense,' said Lena, the affianced of Gumbly.

'Larned a little 'fore iver some maidens was born. Sarved in the Queen's Navy, I have, where yeou'm taught to use yeour eyes. Yeou go 'tend yeour own business, Lena.'

'Do 'ee mean what yeou've been tellin' us?' said Oke.

'Ask me no questions, I'll give 'ee no lies. Bullet-hole clane thru from side to side, an' tu heart-ribs broke like withies. I seed un when I turned un ovver. They'm clever, oh, they'm clever, but they'm not tu clever for old Richards! 'Twas on the born tip o' my tongue to tell, but . . . he said us niver washed, he did. Let his dom boys call us "stinkers," he did. Sarved un dom well raight, I say!'

Richards spat on a fresh boot and fell to his work, chuckling.

THE IMPRESSIONISTS

THE IMPRESSIONISTS

THEY HAD DROPPED into the Chaplain's study for a Saturday night smoke—all four House-masters—and the three briars and the one cigar reeking in amity proved the Rev. John Gillett's good generalship. Since the discovery of the cat, King had been too ready to see affront where none was meant, and the Reverend John, buffer-state and general confidant, had worked for a week to bring about a good understanding. He was fat, clean-shaven, except for a big moustache, of an imperturbable good temper, and, those who loved him least said, a guileful Jesuit. He smiled benignantly upon his handiwork —four sorely-tried men talking without very much malice.

'Now remember,' he said, when the conversation turned that way, 'I impute nothing. But every time that any one has taken direct steps against Number Five study, the issue has been more or less humiliating to the taker.'

'I can't admit that. I pulverise the egregious Beetle daily for his soul's good; and the others with him,' said King.

'Well, take your own case, King, and go back a couple of years. Do you remember when Prout and you were on their track—for hutting and trespass, wasn't it? Have you forgotten Colonel Dabney?'

The others laughed. King did not care to be reminded of his career as a poacher.

'That was one instance. Again, when you had rooms below them—I always said that that was entering the lion's den— you turned them out.'

'For making disgusting noises. Surely, Gillett, you don't excuse——'

'All I say is that you turned them out. That same evening your study was wrecked.'

'By Rabbits-Eggs—most beastly drunk—from the road,' said King. 'What has that——?'

The Reverend John went on.

'Lastly, they conceive that aspersions are cast upon their personal cleanliness—a most delicate matter with all boys. Ve-ry good. Observe how, in each case, the punishment fits the crime. A week after your House calls them "stinkers," King, your House is, not to put too fine a point on it, stunk out by a dead cat who chooses to die in the one spot where she can annoy you most. Again the long arm of coincidence! *Summa*. You accuse them of trespass. Through some absurd chain of circumstances—they may or may not be at the other end of it—you and Prout are made to appear as trespassers. You evict them. For a time your study is made untenable. I have drawn the parallel in the last case. Well?'

'She was under the centre of White's dormitory,' said King. 'There are double floor-boards there to deaden noise. No boy, even in my own House, could possibly have pried up the boards without leaving some trace—and Rabbits-Eggs was phenomenally drunk that other night.'

'They are singularly favoured by fortune. That is all I ever said. Personally, I like them immensely, and I believe I have a little of their confidence. I confess I like being called "Padre." They are at peace with me; consequently I am not treated to bogus confessions of theft.'

'You mean Mason's case?' said Prout heavily. 'That always struck me as peculiarly scandalous. I thought the Head should have taken up the matter more thoroughly. Mason may be misguided, but at least he is thoroughly sincere and means well.'

THE IMPRESSIONISTS

'I confess I cannot agree with you, Prout,' said the Reverend John. 'He jumped at some silly tale of theft on their part; accepted another boy's evidence without, so far as I can see, any inquiry; and—frankly, I think he deserved all he got.'

'They deliberately outraged Mason's best feelings,' said Prout. 'A word to me on their part would have saved the whole thing. But they preferred to lure him on; to play on his ignorance of their characters——'

'That may be,' said King, 'but I don't like Mason. I dislike him for the very reason that Prout advances to his credit. He means well.'

'Our criminal tradition is not theft—among ourselves, at least,' said little Hartopp.

'For the head of a House that raided seven head of cattle from the innocent potwallopers of Northam, isn't that rather a sweeping statement?' said Macrea.

'Precisely so,' said Hartopp, unabashed. 'That, with gate-lifting, and a little poaching and hawk-hunting on the cliffs, is our salvation.'

'It does us far more harm as a school—' Prout began.

'Than any hushed-up scandal could? Quite so. Our reputation among the farmers is most unsavoury. But I would much sooner deal with any amount of ingenious crime of that nature than—some other offences.'

'They may be all right, but they are unboylike, abnormal, and, in my opinion, unsound,' Prout insisted. 'The moral effect of their performances must pave the way for greater harm. It makes me doubtful how to deal with them. I might separate them.'

'You might, of course; but they have gone up the school together for six years. *I* shouldn't care to do it,' said Macrea.

'They use the editorial "we," ' said King irrelevantly. 'It annoys me. "Where's your prose, Corkran?" "Well, sir, we haven't quite done it yet. We'll bring it in a minute," and so on. And the same with the others.'

'There's great virtue in that "we," ' said little Hartopp. 'You know I take them for trig. M'Turk may have some conception of the meaning of it; but Beetle is as the brutes that perish about sines and cosines. He copies serenely from Stalky, who positively rejoices in mathematics.'

'Why don't you stop it?' said Prout.

'It rights itself at the exams. Then Beetle shows up blank sheets, and trusts to his "English" to save him from a fall. I fancy he spends most of his time with me in writing verse.'

'I wish to Heaven he would transfer a little of his energy in that direction to Elegiacs.' King jerked himself upright. 'He is, with the single exception of Stalky, the very vilest manufacturer of "barbarous hexameters" that I have ever dealt with.'

'The work is combined in that study,' said the Chaplain. 'Stalky does the mathematics, M'Turk the Latin, and Beetle attends to their English and French. At least, when he was in the sick-house last month——'

'Malingering,' Prout interjected.

'Quite possibly. I found a very distinct falling off in their *Roman d'un Jeune Homme Pauvre* translations.'

'I think it is profoundly immoral,' said Prout. 'I've always been opposed to the study system.'

'It would be hard to find any study where the boys don't help each other; but in Number Five the thing has probably been reduced to a system,' said little Hartopp. 'They have a system in most things.'

'They confess as much,' said the Reverend John. 'I've seen

M'Turk being hounded up the stairs to elegise the "Elegy in a Churchyard," while Beetle and Stalky went to puntabout.'

'It amounts to systematic cribbing,' said Prout, his voice growing deeper and deeper.

'No such thing,' little Hartopp returned. 'You can't teach a cow the violin.'

'In intention it is cribbing.'

'But we spoke under the seal of the confessional, didn't we?' said the Reverend John.

'You say you've heard them arranging their work in this way, Gillett,' Prout persisted.

'Good Heavens! Don't make me Queen's evidence, my dear fellow. Hartopp is equally incriminated. If they ever found out that I had sneaked, our relations would suffer—and I value them.'

'I think your attitude in this matter is weak,' said Prout, looking round for support. 'It would be really better to break up the study—for a while—wouldn't it?'

'Oh, break it up by all means,' said Macrea. 'We shall see then if Gillett's theory holds water.'

'Be wise, Prout. Leave them alone or calamity will overtake you; and what is much more important, they will be annoyed with me. I am too fat, alas! to be worried by bad boys. Where are you going?'

'Nonsense! They would not dare—but I am going to think this out,' said Prout. 'It needs thought. In intention they cribbed, and I must think out my duty.'

'He's perfectly capable of putting the boys on their honour. It's *I* that am a fool!' The Reverend John looked round remorsefully. 'Never again will I forget that a master is not a man. Mark my words,' said the Reverend John. 'There will be trouble.'

STALKY & CO.

But by the yellow Tiber
Was tumult and affright.

Out of the blue sky (they were still rejoicing over the cat war) Mr. Prout had dropped into Number Five, read them a lecture on the enormity of cribbing, and bidden them return to the form-rooms on Monday. They had raged, solo and chorus, all through the peaceful Sabbath, for their sin was more or less the daily practice of all the studies.

'What's the good of cursin'?' said Stalky at last. 'We're all in the same boat. We've got to go back an' consort with the House. A locker in the form-room, an' a seat at prep. in Number Twelve.' He looked regretfully round the cosy study which M'Turk, their leader in matters of Art, had decorated with a dado, a stencil, and cretonne hangings.

'Yes! Heffy lurchin' into the form-rooms like a frowzy old retriever, to see if we aren't up to something. You know he never leaves his House alone, these days,' said M'Turk. 'Oh, it will be giddy!'

' "Why aren't you down watchin' cricket? I like a robust, healthy boy. You mustn't frowst in a form-room. Why don't you take an interest in your House?" Yah!' Beetle quoted.

'Yes, why don't we! Let's! We'll take an interest in the House. We'll take no end of interest in the House. He hasn't had us in the form-rooms for a year. We've learned a lot since then. Oh, we'll make it a be-autiful House before we've done! 'Member that chap in *Eric* or *St. Winifred's*—Belial somebody? I'm goin' to be Belial,' said Stalky, with an ensnaring grin.

'Right O!' said Beetle, 'and I'll be Mammon. I'll lend money at usury—that's what they do at all schools accordin' to the *B.O.P.* Penny a week on a shillin'. That'll startle Heffy's weak intellect. You can be Lucifer, Turkey.'

'What have I got to do?' M'Turk also smiled.

'Head conspiracies—an' cabals—an' boycotts. Go in for that "stealthy intrigue" that Heffy is always talkin' about. Come on!'

The House received them on their fall with the mixture of jest and sympathy always extended to boys turned out of their study. The known aloofness of the three made them more interesting.

'Quite like old times, ain't it?' Stalky selected a locker and flung in his books. 'We've come to sport with you, my young friends, for a while, because our beloved House-master has hove us out of our diggin's.'

'Serve you jolly well right,' said Orrin, 'you cribbers!'

'This will never do,' said Stalky. 'We can't maintain our giddy prestige, Orrin, de-ah, if you make these remarks.'

They wrapped themselves lovingly about the boy, thrust him to the opened window, and drew down the sash to the nape of his neck. With an equal swiftness they tied his thumbs together behind his back with a piece of twine, and then, because he kicked furiously, removed his shoes.

There Mr. Prout happened to find him a few minutes later, guillotined and helpless, surrounded by a convulsed crowd who would not assist.

Stalky, in an upper form-room, had gathered himself allies against vengeance. Orrin presently tore up at the head of a boarding-party, and the form-room grew one fog of dust through which boys wrestled, stamped, shouted, and yelled. A desk was carried away in the tumult, a knot of warriors reeled into and split a door-panel, a window was broken, and a gas-jet fell. Under cover of the confusion the three escaped to the corridor, whence they called in and sent up passers-by to the fray.

'Rescue, King's! King's! King's! Number Twelve form-room! Rescue, Prout's—Prout's! Rescue, Macrea's! Rescue, Hartopp's!'

The juniors hurried out like bees a-swarm, asking no questions, clattered up the staircase, and added themselves to the embroilment.

'Not bad for the first evening's work,' said Stalky, rearranging his collar. 'I fancy Prout'll be somewhat annoyed. We'd better establish an alibi.' So they sat on Mr. King's railings till prep.

'You see,' quoth Stalky, as they strolled up to prep. with the ignoble herd, 'if you get the Houses well mixed up an' scufflin', it's even bettin' that some ass will start a real row. Hullo, Orrin, you look rather metagrobolised.'

'It was all your fault, you beast! You started it. We've got two hundred lines apiece, and Heffy's lookin' for you. Just see what that swine Malpass did to my eye!'

'I like your saying *we* started it. Who called us cribbers? Can't your infant mind connect cause an' effect yet? Some day you'll find out that it don't pay to jest with Number Five.'

'Where's that shillin' you owe me?' said Beetle suddenly.

Stalky could not see Prout behind him, but returned the lead without a quaver.

'I only owed you ninepence, you old usurer.'

'You've forgotten the interest,' said M'Turk. 'A halfpenny a week per bob is Beetle's charge. You must be filthy rich, Beetle.'

'Well, Beetle lent me sixpence.' Stalky came to a full stop and made as to work it out on his fingers. 'Sixpence on the nineteenth, didn't he?'

'Yes; but you've forgotten you paid no interest on the other bob—the one I lent you before.'

'But you took my watch as security.' The game was developing itself almost automatically.

'Never mind. Pay me my interest, or I'll charge you interest on interest. Remember I've got your note-of-hand!' shouted Beetle.

'You're a cold-blooded Jew,' Stalky groaned.

'Hush!' said M'Turk very loudly indeed; then started as Prout came upon them.

'I didn't see you in that disgraceful affair in the form-room just now,' said he.

'What, sir? We've just come up from Mr. King's,' said Stalky. 'Please, sir, what am I to do about prep.? They've broken the desk you told me to sit at, an' the form's just swimmin' with ink.'

'Find another seat—find another seat. D'you expect me to dry-nurse you? I wish to know whether you are in the habit of advancing money to your associates, Beetle?'

'No, sir; not as a general rule, sir.'

'It is a most reprehensible habit. I thought that my House, at least, would be free from it. Even with my opinion of you, I hardly thought it was one of your vices.'

'There's no harm in lending money, sir, is there?'

'I am not going to bandy words with you on your notions of morality. How much have you lent Corkran?'

'I—I don't quite know,' said Beetle. It is difficult to improvise a going concern on the spur of the minute.

'You seemed certain enough just now.'

'I think it's two and fourpence,' said M'Turk, with a glance of cold scorn at Beetle.

In the hopelessly involved finances of the study there was just that sum to which both M'Turk and Beetle laid claim, as their share in the pledging of Stalky's second-best Sunday trousers. But Stalky had maintained for two terms that the money was his commission for effecting the pawn; and had, of course, spent it on a study 'brew.'

'Understand this, then. You are not to continue your operations as a money-lender. Two and fourpence, you said, Corkran?'

Stalky had said nothing, and continued so to do.

'Your influence for evil is quite strong enough without buying a hold over your companions.' He felt in his pockets, and (oh, joy!) produced a florin and fourpence. 'Bring me what you call Corkran's note-of-hand, and be thankful that I do not carry the matter any further. The money is stopped from your pocket-money, Corkran. The receipt to my study, at once.'

Little they cared! Two and fourpence in a lump is worth six weekly sixpences any hungry day of the week.

'But what the dooce *is* a note-of-hand?' said Beetle. 'I only read about it in a book.'

'Now you've jolly well got to make one,' said Stalky.

'Yes—but our ink don't turn black till next day. S'pose he'll spot that?'

'Not him. He's too worried,' said M'Turk. 'Sign your name on a bit of impot-paper, Stalky, and write, "I O U two and fourpence." Aren't you grateful to me for getting that out of Prout? Stalky'd never have paid. . . . Why, you ass!'

Mechanically Beetle had handed over the money to Stalky as treasurer of the study. The custom of years is not lightly broken.

In return for the document, Prout explained to Beetle the enormity of money-lending, which, like everything except compulsory cricket, corrupted Houses and destroyed good feeling among boys, made youth cold and calculating, and opened the door to all evil. Finally, did Beetle know of any other cases? If so, it was his duty as proof of repentance to let his House-master know. No names need be mentioned.

Beetle did not know—at least, he was not quite sure, sir. How could he give evidence against his friends? The House might, of course—here he feigned an anguished delicacy—be full of it. He was not in a position to say. He had not met with any open competition in his trade; but if Mr. Prout considered it was a matter that affected the honour of the House (Mr. Prout did consider it precisely that), perhaps the House-prefects would be better . . .

He spun it out till half-way through prep.

'And,' said the amateur Shylock, returning to the form-room and dropping at Stalky's side, 'if he don't think the House is putrid with it, I'm several Dutchmen—that's all. . . . I've been to Mr. Prout's study, sir.' This to the prep.-master. 'He said I could sit where I liked, sir. . . . Oh, he is just tricklin' with emotion. . . . Yes, sir, I'm only askin' Corkran to let me have a dip in his ink.'

After prayers, on the road to the dormitories, Harrison and Craye, senior House-prefects, zealous in their office, waylaid them with great anger.

'What have you been doing to Heffy this time, Beetle? He's been jawin' us all the evening.'

'What has His Serene Transparency been vexin' you for?' said M'Turk.

'About Beetle lendin' money to Stalky,' began Harrison; 'and then Beetle went and told him that there was any amount of money-lendin' in the House.'

'No, you don't,' said Beetle, sitting on a boot-basket. 'That's just what I didn't tell him. I spoke the giddy truth. He asked me if there was much of it in the House; an' I said I didn't know.'

'He thinks you're a set of filthy Shylocks,' said M'Turk. 'It's

just as well for you he don't think you're burglars. You know
he never gets a notion out of his conscientious old head.'

'Well-meanin' man. Did it all for the best.' Stalky curled
gracefully round the stair-rail. 'Head in a drainpipe. Full
confession in the left boot. Bad for the honour of the House
—very.'

'Shut up,' said Harrison. 'You chaps always behave as if
you were jawin' us when we come to jaw you.'

'You're a lot too cheeky,' said Craye.

'I don't quite see where the cheek comes in, except on your
part, in interferin' with a private matter between me an'
Beetle after it has been settled by Prout.' Stalky winked cheerfully at the others.

'That's the worst of clever little swots,' said M'Turk, ad-
dressing the gas. 'They get made prefects before they have any
tact; and then they annoy chaps who could really help 'em to
look after the honour of the House.'

'We won't trouble you to do that!' said Craye hotly.

'Then what are you badgerin' us for?' said Beetle. 'On your
own showin', you've been so beastly slack, lookin' after the
House, that Prout believes it's a nest of money-lenders. I've
told him that I've lent money to Stalky, an' no one else. I
don't know whether he believes me, but that finishes my case.
The rest is *your* business.'

'Now we find out'—Stalky's voice rose—'that there is apparently an organised conspiracy throughout the House. For
aught we know, the fags may be lendin' and borrowin' *far*
beyond their means. *We* aren't responsible for it. We're only
the rank and file.'

'Are you surprised we don't wish to associate with the
House?' said M'Turk with dignity. 'We've kept ourselves to
ourselves in our study till we were turned out, and now we

find ourselves let in for—for this sort of thing. It's simply disgraceful.'

'Then you hector and bullyrag us on the stairs,' said Stalky, 'about matters that are your business entirely. You know we aren't prefects.'

'You threatened us with a prefects' lickin' just now,' said Beetle, boldly inventing as he saw the bewilderment in the faces of the enemy.

'And if you expect you'll gain anything from us by your way of approachin' us, you're jolly well mistaken. That's all. Good-night.'

They clattered upstairs, injured virtue on every inch of their backs.

'But—but what the dickens have *we* done?' said Harrison, amazedly, to Craye.

'I don't know. Only—it always happens that way when one has anything to do with them. They're so beastly plausible.'

And Mr. Prout called the good boys into his study anew, and succeeded in sinking both his and their innocent minds ten fathoms deeper in blindfolded bedazement. He spoke of steps and measures, of tone and loyalty in the House and to the House, and urged them to take up the matter tactfully.

So they demanded of Beetle whether he had any connection with any other establishment. Beetle promptly went to his House-master, and wished to know by what right Harrison and Craye had reopened a matter already settled between him and his House-master. In injured innocence no boy excelled Beetle.

Then it occurred to Prout that he might have been unfair to the culprit, who had not striven to deny or palliate his offence. He sent for Harrison and Craye, reprehending them very gently for the tone they had adopted to a repentant sinner, and when they returned to their study, they used the language of despair. They then made headlong inquisition through the House, driving the fags to the edge of hysterics, and unearthing, with tremendous pomp and parade, the natural and inevitable system of small loans that prevails among small boys.

'You see, Harrison, Thornton minor lent me a penny last Saturday, because I was fined for breaking the window; and I spent it at Keyte's. I didn't know there was any harm in it. And Wray major borrowed twopence from me when my uncle sent me a post-office order—I cashed it at Keyte's—for five bob; but he'll pay me back before the holidays. We didn't know there was anything wrong in it.'

They waded through hours of this kind of thing, but found no usury, or anything approaching to Beetle's gorgeous scale of interest. The seniors—for the school had no tradition of deference to prefects outside compulsory games—told them succinctly to go about their business. They would not give evidence on any terms. Harrison was one idiot, and Craye was another; but the greatest of all, they said, was their House-master.

When a House is thoroughly upset, however good its conscience, it breaks into knots and coteries—small gatherings in the twilight, box-room committees, and groups in the corridor. And when from group to group, with an immense affectation of secrecy, three wicked boys steal, crying 'Cave' when there is no need of caution, and whispering 'Don't tell!' on the heels of trumpery confidences that instant invented, a very fine air of plot and intrigue can be woven round such a House.

At the end of a few days, it dawned on Prout that he moved in an atmosphere of perpetual ambush. Mysteries hedged him on all sides, warnings ran before his heavy feet, and counter-signs were muttered behind his attentive back. M'Turk and Stalky invented many absurd and idle phrases—catchwords that swept through the House as fire through stubble. It was a rare jest, and the only practical outcome of the Usury Commission, that one boy should say to a friend, with awful gravity, 'Do you think there's much of it going on in the House?' The other would reply, 'Well, one can't be too careful, you know.' The effect on a House-master of humane conscience and good intent may be imagined. Again, a man who has sincerely devoted himself to gaining the esteem of his charges does not like to hear himself described, even at a distance, as 'Popularity Prout' by a dark and scowling Celt with a fluent tongue. A rumour that stories—unusual stories—are told in the form-rooms, between the lights, by a boy who does not command his confidence, agitates such a man; and even elaborate and tender politeness—for the courtesy that wise grown men offer to a bewildered child was the courtesy which Stalky wrapped round Prout—restores not his peace of mind.

'The tone of the House seems changed—changed for the worse,' said Prout to Harrison and Craye. 'Have you noticed it? I don't for an instant impute——'

He never imputed anything; but, on the other hand, he never did anything else, and, with the best intentions in the world, he had reduced the House-prefects to a state as nearly bordering on nervous irritation as healthy boys can know. Worst of all, they began at times to wonder whether Stalky & Co. had not some truth in their often repeated assertions that Prout was 'a gloomy ass.'

'As you know, I am not the kind of man who puts himself out for every little thing he hears. *I* believe in letting the

House work out their own salvation—with a light guiding
hand on the reins, of course. But there is a perceptible lack
of reverence—a lower tone in matters that touch the honour
of the House, a sort of hardness.'

> *'Oh, Prout he is a nobleman, a nobleman, a nobleman!*
> *Our Heffy is a nobleman—*
> *He does an awful lot,*
> *Because his popularity—*
> *Oh, pop-u-pop-u-larity—*
> *His giddy popularity*
> *Would suffer did he not!'*

The study door stood ajar; and the song, borne by twenty
clear voices, came faint from a form-room. The fags rather
liked the tune; the words were Beetle's.

'That's a thing no sensible man objects to,' said Prout, with
a lop-sided smile; 'but, you know, straws show which way the
wind blows. Can you trace it to any direct influence? I am
speaking to you now as heads of the House.'

'There isn't the least doubt of it,' said Harrison angrily. 'I
know what you mean, sir. It all began when Number Five
study came to the form-rooms. There's no use blinkin' it,
Craye. You know that, too.'

'They make things rather difficult for us, sometimes,' said
Craye. 'It's more their manner than anything else, that Harrison means.'

'Do they hamper you in the discharge of your duties, then?'

'Well, no, sir. They only look on and grin—and turn up
their noses generally.'

'Ah,' said Prout sympathetically.

'I think, sir,' said Craye, plunging into the business boldly, 'it would be a great deal better if they were sent back to their study—better for the House. They are rather old to be knocking about the form-rooms.'

'They are younger than Orrin, or Flint, and a dozen others that I can think of.'

'Yes, sir; but that's different, somehow. They're rather influential. They have a knack of upsettin' things in a quiet way that one can't take hold of. At least, if one does——'

'And you think they would be better in their own study again?'

Emphatically Harrison and Craye were of that opinion. As Harrison said to Craye, afterwards, 'They've weakened our authority. They're too big to lick; they've made an exhibition of us over this usury business, and we're a laughing-stock to the rest of the school. I'm going up ['for Sandhurst' understood] next term. They've managed to knock me out of half my work already, with their—their lunacy. If they go back to their study we may have a little peace.'

'Hullo, Harrison.' M'Turk ambled round the corner, with a roving eye on all possible horizons. 'Bearin' up, old man? That's right. Live it down! Live it down!'

'What d'you mean?'

'You look a little pensive,' said M'Turk. 'Exhaustin' job superintendin' the honour of the House, ain't it? By the way, how are you off for mares'-nests?'

'Look here,' said Harrison, hoping for instant reward. 'We've recommended Prout to let you go back to your study.'

'The dooce you have! And who under the sun are *you*, to interfere between us and our House-master? Upon my Sam, you two try us very hard—you do, indeed. Of course, we don't know how far you abuse your position to prejudice us with Mr. Prout; but when you deliberately stop me to tell me

you've been makin' arrangements behind our back—in secret
—with Prout—I—I don't know really what we ought to do.'

'That's beastly unfair!' cried Craye.

'It is.' M'Turk had adopted a ghastly solemnity that sat
well on his long, lean face. 'Hang it all! A prefect's one
thing and an usher's another; but you seem to combine 'em.
You recommend this—you recommend that! *You* say how and
when we go back to our study!'

'But—but—we thought you'd like it, Turkey. We did,
indeed. You know you'll be ever so much more comfortable
there.' Harrison's voice was almost tearful.

M'Turk turned away as if to hide his emotions.

'They're broke!' He hunted up Stalky and Beetle in a box-
room. 'They're sick! They've been beggin' Heffy to let us go
back to Number Five. Poor devils! Poor little devils!'

'It's the olive branch,' was Stalky's comment. 'It's the giddy
white flag, by Gum! Come to think of it, we *have* metagrobolised 'em.'

Just after tea that day, Mr. Prout sent for them to say that
if they chose to ruin their future by neglecting their work, it
was entirely their own affair. He wished them, however, to
understand that their presence in the form-rooms could not be
tolerated one hour longer. He personally did not care to think
of the time he must spend in eliminating the traces of their
evil influences. How far Beetle had pandered to the baser side
of youthful imagination he would ascertain later; and Beetle
might be sure that if Mr. Prout came across any soul-corrupt-
ing consequences——

'Consequences of what, sir?' said Beetle, genuinely bewildered this time; and M'Turk quietly kicked him on the ankle
for being 'fetched' by Prout.

Beetle, the House-master continued, knew very well what

was intended. Evil and brief had been their careers under his eye; and as one standing *in loco parentis* to their yet uncontaminated associates, he was bound to take his precautions. The return of the study key closed the sermon.

'But what was the baser-side-of-imagination business?' said Beetle on the stairs.

'I never knew such an ass as you are for justifyin' yourself,' said M'Turk. 'I hope I jolly well skinned your ankle. Why do you let yourself be drawn by everybody?'

'Draws be blowed! I must have tickled him up in some way I didn't know about. If I'd had a notion of that before, of course I could have rubbed it in better. It's too late now. What a pity! "Baser side." What was he drivin' at?'

'Never mind,' said Stalky. 'I knew we could make it a happy little House. I said so, remember—but I swear I didn't think we'd do it so soon.'

'No,' said Prout most firmly in Common-room. 'I maintain that Gillett is wrong. True, I let them return to their study.'

'With your known views on cribbing, too?' purred little Hartopp. 'What an immoral compromise!'

'One moment,' said the Reverend John. 'I—we—all of us have exercised an absolutely heartbreaking discretion for the last ten days. Now we want to know. Confess—have you known a happy minute since——'

'As regards my House, I have not,' said Prout. 'But you are entirely wrong in your estimate of those boys. In justice to the others—in self-defence——'

'Ha! I said it would come to that,' murmured the Reverend John.

'——I was forced to send them back. Their moral influence was unspeakable—simply unspeakable.'

And bit by bit he told his tale, beginning with Beetle's usury, and ending with the House-prefects' appeal.

'Beetle in the *rôle* of Shylock is new to me,' said King, with twitching lips. 'I heard rumours of it——'

'Before!' said Prout.

'No, after you had dealt with them; but I was careful not to inquire. I never interfere with——'

'I myself,' said Hartopp, 'would cheerfully give him five shillings if he could work out one simple sum in compound interest without three gross errors.'

'Why—why—why!' Mason, the mathematical master, stuttered, a fierce joy on his face. 'You've been had—precisely the same as me!'

'And so you held an inquiry?' Little Hartopp's voice drowned Mason's ere Prout caught the import of the sentence.

'The boy himself hinted at the existence of a good deal of it in the House,' said Prout.

'He is past master in that line,' said the Chaplain. 'But, as regards the honour of the House——'

'They lowered it in a week. I have striven to build it up for years. My own House-prefects—and boys do not willingly complain of each other—besought me to get rid of them. You say you have their confidence, Gillett: they may tell you another tale. As far as I am concerned, they may go to the devil in their own way. I'm sick and tired of them,' said Prout bitterly.

But it was the Reverend John, with a smiling countenance, who went to the devil just after Number Five had cleared away a very pleasant little brew (it cost them two and fourpence) and was settling down to prep.

'Come in, Padre, come in,' said Stalky, thrusting forward the best chair. 'We've only met you official-like these last ten days.'

'You were under sentence,' said the Reverend John. 'I do not consort with malefactors.'

'Ah, but we're restored again,' said M'Turk. 'Mr. Prout has relented.'

'Without a stain on our characters,' said Beetle. 'It was a painful episode, Padre, most painful.'

'Now, consider for a while, and perpend, *mes enfants*. It is about your characters that I've called to-night. In the language of the schools, what the dooce *have* you been up to in Mr. Prout's House? It isn't anything to laugh over. He says that you so lowered the tone of the House he had to pack you back to your study. Is that true?'

'Every word of it, Padre.'

'Don't be flippant, Turkey. Listen to me. I've told you very often that no boys in the school have a greater influence for good or evil than you have. You know I don't talk about ethics and moral codes, because I don't believe that the young of the human animal realises what they mean for some years to come. All the same, I don't want to think you've been perverting the juniors. Don't interrupt, Beetle. Listen to me! Mr. Prout has a notion that you have been corrupting your associates somehow or other.'

'Mr. Prout has so many notions, Padre,' said Beetle wearily. 'Which one is this?'

'Well, he tells me that he heard you telling a story in the twilight in the form-room, in a whisper. And Orrin said, just as he opened the door, "Shut up, Beetle; it's too beastly." Now then?'

'You remember Mrs. Oliphant's *Beleaguered City* that you lent me last term?' said Beetle.

The Padre nodded.

'I got the notion out of that. Only, instead of a city, I made it the Coll. in a fog—besieged by ghosts of dead boys, who hauled chaps out of their beds in the dormitory. All the names are *quite* real. You tell it in a whisper, you know—with the names. Orrin didn't like it one little bit. None of 'em have ever let me finish it. It gets just awful at the end.'

'But why in the world didn't you explain to Mr. Prout, instead of leaving him under the impression——'

'Padre Sahib,' said M'Turk, 'it isn't the least good explainin' to Mr. Prout. If he hasn't one impression, he's bound to have another.'

'He'd do it with the best o' motives. He's *in loco parentis*,' purred Stalky.

'You young demons!' the Reverend John replied. 'And am I to understand that the—the usury business was another of your House-master's impressions?'

'Well—we helped a little in that,' said Stalky. 'I did owe Beetle two and fourpence—at least, Beetle says I did, but I never intended to pay him. Then we started a bit of an argument on the stairs, an'—an' Mr. Prout dropped into it accidental. That was how it was, Padre. He paid me cash down like a giddy Dook (stopped it out of my pocket-money just the same), an' Beetle gave him my note-of-hand all correct. I don't know what happened after that.'

'I was too truthful,' said Beetle. 'I always am. You see, he was under an impression, Padre, and I suppose I ought to have corrected that impression; but, of course, I couldn't be quite certain that his House wasn't given over to money-lendin', could I? I thought the House-prefects might know more about it than I did. They ought to. They're giddy palladiums of public schools.'

'They did, too—by the time they'd finished,' said M'Turk. 'As nice a pair of conscientious, well-meanin', upright, pure-souled boys as you'd ever want to meet, Padre. They turned the House upside down—Harrison and Craye—with the best motives in the world.'

'They said so.

> *They said it very loud and clear,*
> *They went and shouted in our ear,'*

said Stalky.

'My own private impression is that all three of you will infallibly be hanged,' said the Reverend John.

'Why, *we* didn't do anything,' replied M'Turk. 'It was all Mr. Prout. Did you ever read a book about Japanese wrestlers? My uncle—he's in the Navy—gave me a beauty once.'

'Don't try to change the subject, Turkey.'

'I'm not, sir. I'm givin' an illustration—same as a sermon. These wrestler-chaps have got some sort of trick that lets the other chap do all the work. Then they give a little wriggle, and he upsets himself. It's called *shibbuwichee* or *tokonoma*, or somethin'. Mr. Prout's a *shibbuwicher*. It isn't our fault.'

'Did you suppose we went round corruptin' the minds of the fags?' said Beetle. 'They haven't any, to begin with; and if they had, they're corrupted long ago. I've been a fag, Padre.'

'Well, I fancied I knew the normal range of your iniquities; but if you take so much trouble to pile up circumstantial evidence against yourselves, you can't blame any one if——'

'We don't blame any one, Padre. We haven't said a word against Mr. Prout, have we?' Stalky looked at the others. 'We love him. He hasn't a notion how we love him.'

'H'm! You dissemble your love very well. Have you ever thought who got you turned out of your study, in the first place?'

'It was Mr. Prout who turned us out,' said Stalky, with significance.

'Well, I was that man. I didn't mean it; but some words of mine, I'm afraid, gave Mr. Prout the impression——'

Number Five laughed aloud.

'You see, it's just the same thing with you, Padre,' said M'Turk. 'He *is* quick to get an impression, ain't he? But you mustn't think we don't love him, 'cause we do. There isn't an ounce of vice about him.'

A double knock fell on the door.

'The Head to see Number Five study in his study at once,' said the voice of Foxy, the school Sergeant.

'Whew!' said the Reverend John. 'It seems to me that there is a great deal of trouble coming for some people.'

'My word! Mr. Prout's gone and told the Head,' said Stalky. 'He's a moral double-ender. Not fair, luggin' the Head into a House-row.'

'I should recommend a copy-book on a—h'm—safe and certain part,' said the Reverend John disinterestedly.

'Huh! He licks across the shoulders, an' it would slam like a beastly barn-door,' said Beetle. 'Good-night, Padre. We're in for it.'

Once more they stood in the presence of the Head—Belial, Mammon, and Lucifer. But they had to deal with a man more subtle than them all. Mr. Prout had talked to him, heavily and sadly, for half an hour; and the Head had seen all that was hidden from the House-master.

'You've been bothering Mr. Prout,' he said pensively. 'House-masters aren't here to be bothered by boys more than is necessary. I don't like being bothered by these things. You are bothering *me*. That is a very serious offence. You see it?'

'Yes, sir.'

'Well, now, I purpose to bother you, on personal and private grounds, because you have broken into my time. You are much too big to lick, so I suppose I shall have to mark my displeasure in some other way. Say, a thousand lines apiece, a week's gating, and a few things of that kind. Much too big to lick, aren't you?'

'Oh no, sir,' said Stalky cheerfully; for a week's gating in the summer term is serious.

'Ve-ry good. Then we will do what we can. I *wish* you wouldn't bother me.'

It was a fair, sustained, equable stroke, with a little draw to it, but what they felt most was his unfairness in stopping to talk between executions. Thus:—

'Among the—lower classes this would lay me open to a charge of—assault. You should be more grateful for your—privileges than you are. There is a limit—one finds it by experience, Beetle—beyond which it is never safe to pursue private vendettas, because—don't move—sooner or later one comes—into collision with the—higher authority, who has studied the animal. *Et ego*—M'Turk, please—in *Arcadia vixi*. There's a certain flagrant injustice about this that ought to appeal to—your temperament. And that's all! You will tell your Housemaster that you have been formally caned by me.'

'My word!' said M'Turk, wriggling his shoulder-blades all down the corridor. 'That was business! The Prooshian Bates has an infernal straight eye.'

'Wasn't it wily of me to ask for the lickin',' said Stalky, 'instead of those impots?'

'Rot! We were in for it from the first. *I* knew the cock of his old eye,' said Beetle. 'I was within an inch of blubbin'.'

'Well, I didn't exactly smile,' Stalky confessed.

'Let's go down to the lavatory an' have a look at the damage. One of us can hold the glass an t'others can squint.'

They proceeded on these lines for some ten minutes. The

wales were very red and very level. There was not a penny to choose between any of them for thoroughness, efficiency, and a certain clarity of outline that stamps the work of the artist.

'What are you doing down there?' Mr. Prout was at the head of the lavatory stairs, attracted by the noise of splashing.

'We've only been caned by the Head, sir, an' we're washin' off the blood. The Head said we were to tell you. We were comin' to report ourselves in a minute, sir. (*Sotto voce.*) That's a score for Heffy!'

'Well, he deserves to score something, poor devil,' said M'Turk, putting on his shirt. 'We've sweated a stone and a half off him since we began.'

'But look here, why aren't we wrathy with the Head? He said it was a flagrant injustice. So it is!' said Beetle.

'Dearr man,' said M'Turk, and vouchsafed no further answer.

It was Stalky who laughed till he had to hold on by the edge of a basin.

'You *are* a funny ass! What's that for?' said Beetle.

'I'm—I'm thinking of the flagrant injustice of it!'

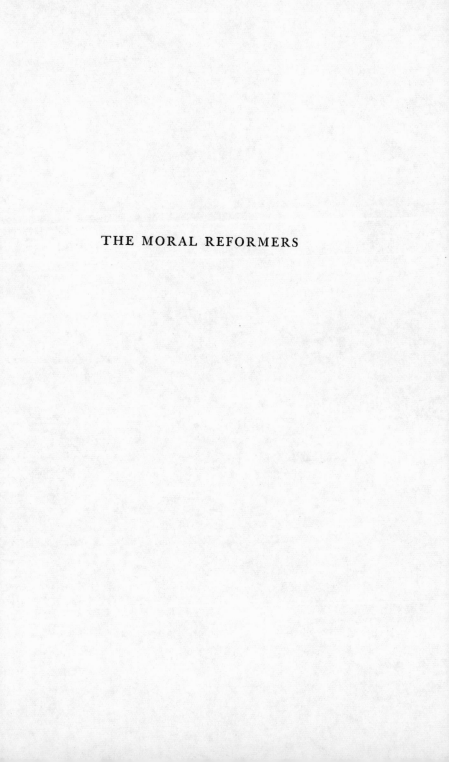

THE MORAL REFORMERS

THE MORAL REFORMERS

THERE WAS NO DISGUISING the defeat. The victory was to Prout, but they grudged it not. If he had broken the rules of the game by calling in the Head, they had had a good run for their money.

The Reverend John sought the earliest opportunity of talking things over. Members of a bachelor Common-room, in a school where masters' studies are designedly dotted among studies and form-rooms, can, if they choose, see a great deal of their charges. Number Five had spent some cautious years in testing the Reverend John. He was emphatically a gentleman. He knocked at a study door before entering; he comported himself as a visitor and not a strayed lictor; he never prosed, and he never carried over into official life the confidences of idle hours. Prout was ever an unmitigated nuisance; King came solely as the avenger of blood; even little Hartopp, talking Natural History, seldom forgot his office; but the Reverend John was a guest desired and beloved by Number Five.

Behold him, then, in their only arm-chair, a bent briar between his teeth, chin down in three folds on his clerical collar, and blowing like an amiable whale, while Number Five discoursed of life as it appeared to them, and specially of that last interview with the Head—in the matter of usury.

'One licking once a week would do you an immense amount of good,' he said, twinkling and shaking all over; 'and, as you say, you were entirely in the right.'

'Ra-ather, Padre! We could have proved it if he'd let us talk,' said Stalky; 'but he didn't. The Head's a downy bird.'

'He understands you perfectly. Ho! ho! Well, you worked hard enough for it.'

'But he's awfully fair. He doesn't lick a chap in the morning an' preach at him in the afternoon,' said Beetle.

'He can't; he ain't in Orders, thank goodness,' said M'Turk. Number Five held the very strongest views on clerical head-masters, and were ever ready to meet their pastor in argument.

'Almost all other schools have clerical Heads,' said the Reverend John gently.

'It isn't fair on the chaps,' Stalky replied. 'Makes 'em sulky. Of course, it's different with you, sir. You belong to the school —same as we do. I mean ordinary clergymen.'

'Well, I am a most ordinary clergyman; and Mr. Hartopp's in Orders too.'

'Ye—es, but he took 'em after he came to the Coll. We saw him go up for his exam. *That's* all right,' said Beetle. 'But just think if the Head went and got ordained!'

'What would happen, Beetle?'

'Oh, the Coll. 'ud go to pieces in a year, sir. There's no doubt o' that.'

'How d'you know?' The Reverend John was smiling.

'We've been here nearly six years now. There are precious few things about the Coll. we don't know,' Stalky replied. 'Why, even you came the term after I did, sir. I remember your asking our names in form your first lesson. Mr. King, Mr. Prout, and the Head, of course, are the only masters senior to us—in that way.'

'Yes, we've changed a good deal—in Common-room.'

'Huh!' said Beetle, with a grunt. 'They came here, an' they went away to get married. Jolly good riddance, too!'

'Doesn't our Beetle hold with matrimony?'

'No, Padre; don't make fun of me. I've met chaps in the

holidays who've got married House-masters. It's perfectly awful! They have babies and teething and measles and all that sort of thing right bung *in* the school; and the masters' wives give tea-parties—tea-parties, Padre!—and ask the chaps to breakfast.'

'That don't matter so much,' said Stalky. 'But the House-masters let their Houses alone, and they leave everything to the prefects. Why, in one school, a chap told me, there were big baize doors and a passage about a mile long between the House and the master's house. They could do just what they pleased.'

'Satan rebuking sin with a vengeance.'

'Oh, larks are right enough; but you know what we mean, Padre. After a bit it gets worse an' worse. Then there's a big bust-up and a row that gets into the papers, and a lot of chaps are expelled, you know.'

'Always the wrong uns; don't forget that. Have a cup of cocoa, Padre?' said M'Turk, with the kettle.

'No, thanks. I'm smoking. Always the wrong uns? Pro-ceed, my Stalky.'

'And then'—Stalky warmed to the work—'everybody says, "Who'd ha' thought it? Shockin' boys! Wicked little kids!" It all comes of havin' married House-masters, I think.'

'A Daniel come to judgment!'

'But it does,' M'Turk interrupted. 'I've met chaps in the holidays, an' they've told me the same thing. It looks awfully pretty for one's people to see—a nice separate house with a nice lady in charge an' all that. But it isn't. It takes the House-masters off their work, and it gives the prefects a heap too much power, an'—an'—it rots up everything. You see, it isn't as if we were just an ordinary school. We take crammers' rejections as well as good little boys like Stalky. We've got to do that to make our name, of course, and we get 'em into Sandhurst somehow or other, don't we?'

'True, O Turk! Like a book thou talkest, Turkey.'

'And so we want rather different masters, don't you think so, to other places? We aren't like the rest of the schools.'

'It leads to all sorts of bullyin', too, a chap told me,' said Beetle.

'Well, you *do* need most of a single man's time, I must say.' The Reverend John considered his hosts critically. 'But do you never feel that the world—the Common-room—is too much with you sometimes?'

'Not exactly—in summer, anyhow.' Stalky's eye roved contentedly to the window. 'Our bounds are pretty big, too, an' they leave us to ourselves a good deal.'

'For example, here am I sitting in your study, very much in your way, eh?'

'Indeed you aren't, Padre. Sit down. Don't go, sir. You know we're glad whenever you come.'

There was no doubting the sincerity of the voices. The Reverend John flushed a little with pleasure and refilled his briar.

'And we generally know where the Common-room are,' said Beetle triumphantly. 'Didn't you come through our lower dormitories last night after ten, sir?'

'I went to smoke a pipe with your House-master. No, I didn't give him any impressions. I took a short cut through your dormitories.'

'I sniffed a whiff of 'baccy this mornin'. Yours is stronger than Mr. Prout's. *I* knew,' said Beetle, wagging his head.

'Good Heavens!' said the Reverend John absently. It was some years before Beetle perceived that this was rather a tribute to innocence than observation. The long, light, blindless dormitories, devoid of inner doors, were crossed at all hours of the night by masters visiting one another; for bachelors sit up later than married folk. Beetle had never dreamed that there might be a purpose in this steady policing.

'Talking about bullying,' the Reverend John resumed, 'you all caught it pretty hot when you were fags, didn't you?'

'Well, we must have been rather awful little beasts,' said Beetle, looking serenely over the gulf between eleven and sixteen. 'My Hat, what bullies they were then—Fairburn, "Gobby" Maunsell, an' all that gang!'

' 'Member when "Gobby" called us the Three Blind Mice, an' we had to get up on the lockers an' sing while he buzzed inkpots at us?' said Stalky. 'They *were* bullies if you like!'

'But there isn't any of it now,' said M'Turk soothingly.

'That's where you make a mistake. We're all inclined to say that everything is all right as long as we ourselves aren't hurt. I sometimes wonder if it is extinct—bullying.'

'Fags bully each other horrid; but the upper forms are supposed to be swottin' for exams, sir. They've got something else to think about,' said Beetle.

'Why? What do you think?' Stalky was watching the Chaplain's face.

'I have my doubts.' Then, explosively, 'On my word, for three moderately intelligent boys you aren't very observant. I suppose you were too busy making things warm for your House-master to see what lay under your noses when you were in the form-rooms last week?'

'What, sir? I—I swear we didn't see anything,' said Beetle.

'Then I'd advise you to look. When a little chap is whimpering in a corner and wears his clothes like rags, and never does any work, and is notoriously the dirtiest little "corridor-caution" in the Coll., something's wrong somewhere.'

'That's Clewer,' said M'Turk under his breath.

'Yes, Clewer. He comes to me for his French. It's his first term, and he's almost as complete a wreck as you were, Beetle. He's not naturally clever, but he has been hammered till he's nearly an idiot.'

'Oh no. They sham silly to get off more lickin's,' said Beetle. '*I* know that.'

'I've never actually seen him knocked about,' said the Reverend John.

'The genuine article don't do that in public,' said Beetle. 'Fairburn never touched me when any one was looking on.'

'You needn't swagger about it, Beetle,' said M'Turk. 'We all caught it in our time.'

'But I got it worse than any one,' said Beetle. 'If you want an authority on bullyin', Padre, come to me. Corkscrews—brush-drill—keys—head-knucklin'—arm-twistin'—rockin'—Ag Ags—an' all the rest of it.'

'Yes. I do want you as an authority, or rather I want your authority to stop it—all of you.'

'What about Abana and Pharpar, Padre—Harrison and Craye? They are Mr. Prout's pets,' said M'Turk a little bitterly. 'We aren't even sub-prefects.'

'I've considered that, but, on the other hand, since most bullying is mere thoughtlessness——'

'Not one little bit of it, Padre,' said M'Turk. 'Bullies like bullyin'. They mean it. They think it up in lesson and practise it in the quarters.'

'Never mind. If the thing goes up to the prefects it may make another House-row. You've had one already. Don't laugh. Listen to me. I ask you—my own Tenth Legion—to take the thing up quietly. I want little Clewer made fairly clean and decent——'

'Blowed if *I* wash him!' whispered Stalky.

'Decent and self-respecting. As for the other boy, whoever he is, you can use your influence'—a purely secular light flickered in the Chaplain's eye—'in any way you please to—to dissuade him. That's all. I'll leave it to you. Good-night, *mes enfants*.'

'Well, what are we goin' to do?' Number Five stared at each other.

'Young Clewer would give his eyes for a place to be quiet in. *I* know that,' said Beetle. 'If we made him a study-fag, eh?'

'No!' said M'Turk firmly. 'He's a dirty little brute, and he'd mess up everything. Besides, we ain't goin' to have any beastly Erickin'. D'you want to walk about with your arm round his neck?'

'He'd clean out the jam-pots, anyhow; an' the burnt-porridge saucepan. It's filthy now.'

'Not good enough,' said Stalky, bringing up both heels with a crash on the table. 'If we find the merry jester who's been bullyin' him an' make him happy, that'll be all right. Why didn't we spot him when we were in the form-rooms, though?'

'Maybe a lot of fags have made a dead set at Clewer. They do that sometimes.'

'Then we'll have to kick the whole of the Lower School in our House—on spec. Come on,' said M'Turk.

'Keep your hair on! We mustn't make a fuss about the biznai. Whoever it is, he's kept quiet or we'd have seen him,' said Stalky. 'We'll walk round an' sniff about till we're sure.'

They drew the House form-rooms, accounting for every junior and senior against whom they had suspicions—investigated, at Beetle's suggestion, the lavatories and box-rooms, but without result. Everybody seemed to be present save Clewer.

'Rum!' said Stalky, pausing outside a study door. 'Golly!'

A thin piping mixed with tears came muffled through the panels.

'As beautiful Kitty one morning was tripping——'

'Louder, you young devil, or I'll buzz a book at you!'

'With a pitcher of milk——

Oh, Campbell, please don't!

To the fair of——'

A book crashed on something soft, and squeals arose.

'Well, I never thought it was a study-chap, anyhow. That accounts for our not spotting him,' said Beetle. 'Sefton and Campbell are rather hefty chaps to tackle. Besides, one can't go into their study like a form-room.'

'What swine!' M'Turk listened. 'Where's the fun of it? I suppose Clewer's faggin' for them.'

'They aren't prefects. That's one good job,' said Stalky, with his war-grin. 'Sefton and Campbell! Um! Campbell *and* Sefton! Ah! One of 'em's a crammer's pup.'

The two were precocious hairy youths between seventeen and eighteen, sent to the school in despair by parents who hoped that six months' steady cram might, perhaps, jockey them into Sandhurst. Nominally they were in Mr. Prout's House; actually they were under the Head's eye; and since he was very careful never to promote strange new boys to prefect-ships, they considered they had a grievance against the school. Sefton had spent three months with a London crammer, and the tale of his adventures there lost nothing in the telling. Campbell, who had a fine taste in clothes and a fluent vocabulary, followed his lead in looking down loftily on the rest of the world. This was only their second term, and the school, used to what it profanely called 'crammers' pups,' had treated them with rather galling reserve. But their whiskers—Sefton owned a real razor—and their moustaches were beyond question impressive.

'Shall we go in an' dissuade 'em?' M'Turk asked. 'I've never had much to do with 'em, but I'll bet my hat Campbell's a funk.'

'No—o! That's *oratio directa*,' said Stalky, shaking his head. 'I like *oratio obliqua*. 'Sides, where'd our moral influence be then? Think o' that!'

'Rot! What are you goin' to do?' Beetle turned into Lower Number Nine form-room, next door to the study.

'Me?' The lights of war flickered over Stalky's face. 'Oh, I want to jape with 'em. Shut up a bit!'

He drove his hands into his pockets and stared out of window at the sea, whistling between his teeth. Then a foot tapped the floor; one shoulder lifted; he wheeled, and began the short quick double-shuffle—the war-dance of Stalky in meditation. Thrice he crossed the empty form-room, with compressed lips and expanded nostrils, swaying to the quick-step. Then he halted before the dumb Beetle and softly knuckled his head, Beetle bowing to the strokes. M'Turk nursed one knee and rocked to and fro. They could hear Clewer howling as though his heart would break.

'Beetle is the sacrifice,' Stalky said at last. 'I'm sorry for you, Beetle. 'Member Galton's *Art of Travel* [one of the forms had been studying that pleasant work] an' the kid whose bleatin' excited the tiger?'

'Oh, curse!' said Beetle uneasily. It was not his first season as a sacrifice. 'Can't you get on without me?'

' 'Fraid not, Beetle, dear. You've got to be bullied by Turkey an' me. The more you howl, o' course, the better it'll be.

Turkey, go an' covet a stump and a box-rope from somewhere. We'll tie him up for a kill—*à la* Galton. 'Member when "Molly" Fairburn made us cock-fight with our shoes off, an' tied up our knees?'

'But that hurt like sin.'

'Course it did. What a clever chap you are, Beetle! Turkey'll knock you all over the place. 'Member we've had a big row all round, an' I've trapped you into doin' this. Lend us your wipe.'

Beetle was trussed for cock-fighting; but, in addition to the stump between elbow and knee, his knees were bound with a box-rope. In this posture, at a push from Stalky he rolled over sideways, covering himself with dust.

'Ruffle his hair, Turkey. Now you get down, too. "The bleatin' of the kid excites the tiger." You two are in such a sweatin' wax with me that you only curse. 'Member that. I'll tickle you up with a stump. You'll have to blub, Beetle.'

'Right O! I'll work up to it in half a shake,' said Beetle.

'Now begin—and remember the bleatin' o' the kid.'

'Shut up, you brutes! Let me up! You've nearly cut my knees off. Oh, you *are* beastly cads! Do shut up. 'Tisn't a joke!' Beetle's protest was, in tone, a work of art.

'Give it to him, Turkey! Kick him! Roll him over! Kill him! Don't funk, Beetle, you brute. Kick him again, Turkey.'

'He's not blubbin' really. Roll up, Beetle, or I'll kick you into the fender,' roared M'Turk.

They made a hideous noise among them, and the bait allured their quarry.

'Hullo! What's the giddy jest?' Sefton and Campbell entered to find Beetle on his side, his head against the fender, weeping copiously, while M'Turk prodded him in the back with his toes.

'It's only Beetle,' Stalky explained. 'He's shammin' hurt. I can't get Turkey to go for him properly.'

Sefton promptly kicked both boys, and his face lighted. 'All right, I'll attend to 'em. Get up an' cock-fight, you two. Give me the stump. I'll tickle 'em. Here's a giddy jest! Come on, Campbell. Let's cook 'em.'

Then M'Turk turned on Stalky and called him very evil names.

'You said you were goin' to cock-fight too, Stalky. Come on!'

'More ass you for believin' me, then!' shrieked Stalky.

'Have you chaps had a row?' said Campbell.

'Row?' said Stalky, 'Huh! I'm only educatin' them. D'you know anythin' about cock-fighting, Seffy?'

'Do I know? Why, at Maclagan's, where I was crammin' in Town, we used to cock-fight in his drawing-room, and little Maclagan daren't say anything. But we were just the same as men there, of course. Do I know? I'll show you.'

'Can't I get up?' moaned Beetle, as Stalky sat on his shoulder.

'Don't jaw, you fat piffler. You're goin' to fight Seffy.'

'He'll slay me!'

'Oh, lug 'em into our study,' said Campbell. 'It's nice an' quiet in there. I'll cock-fight Turkey. This is an improvement on young Clewer.'

'Right O! I move it's shoes-off for them an' shoes-on for us,' said Sefton joyously, and the two were flung down on the study floor. Stalky rolled them behind an arm-chair.

'Now I'll tie you two up an' direct the bull-fight. Golly, what wrists you have, Seffy. They're too thick for a wipe; got a box-rope?' said he.

'Lots in the corner,' Sefton replied. 'Hurry up! Stop blubbin', you brute, Beetle. We're goin' to have a giddy campaign. Losers have to sing for the winners—sing odes in honour of the conqueror. You call yourself a beastly poet, don't you,

Beetle? I'll poet you.' He wriggled into position by Campbell's side.

Swiftly and scientifically the stumps were thrust through the natural crooks, and the wrists tied with well stretched box-ropes to an accompaniment of insults from M'Turk, bound, betrayed, and voluble behind the chair.

Stalky set away Campbell and Sefton, and strode over to his allies, locking the door on the way.

'And that's all right,' said he in a changed voice.

'What the devil——?' Sefton began. Beetle's false tears had ceased; M'Turk, smiling, was on his feet. Together they bound the knees and ankles of the enemy even more straitly.

Stalky took the arm-chair and contemplated the scene with his blandest smile. A man trussed for cock-fighting is, perhaps, the most helpless thing in the world.

' "The bleatin' of the kid excites the tiger." Oh, you frabjous asses!' He lay back and laughed till he could no more. The victims took in the situation but slowly.

'We'll give you the finest lickin' you ever had in your young lives when we get up!' thundered Sefton from the floor. 'You'll laugh the other side of your mouth before you've done. What the deuce d'you mean by this?'

'You'll see in two shakes,' said M'Turk. 'Don't swear like that. What we want to know is, why you two hulkin' swine have been bullyin' Clewer?'

'It's none of your business.'

'What did you bully Clewer for?' The question was repeated with maddening iteration by each in turn. They knew their work.

'Because we jolly well chose,' was the answer at last. 'Let's get up.' Even then they could not realise the game.

'Well, now we're goin' to bully you because we jolly well

choose. We're goin' to be just as fair to you as you were to Clewer. He couldn't do anything against you. You can't do anything to us. Odd, ain't it?'

'Can't we? You wait an' see.'

'Ah,' said Beetle reflectively, 'that shows you've never been properly jested with. A public lickin' ain't in it with a gentle jape. Bet a bob you'll weep an' promise anything.'

'Look here, young Beetle, we'll half kill you when we get up. I'll promise you that, at any rate.'

'You're goin' to be half killed first, though. Did you give Clewer Head-knuckles?'

'Did you give Clewer Head-knuckles?' M'Turk echoed. At the twentieth repetition—no boy can stand the torture of one unvarying query, which is the essence of bullying—came confession.

'We did, confound you!'

'Then you'll be knuckled'; and knuckled they were, according to ancient experience. Head-knuckling is no trifle. 'Molly' Fairburn of the old days could not have done better.

'Did you give Clewer Brush-drill?'

This time the question was answered sooner, and Brush-drill was dealt out for the space of five minutes by Stalky's watch. They could not even writhe in their bonds. No brush is employed in Brush-drill.

'Did you give Clewer the Key?'

'No; we didn't. I swear we didn't!' from Campbell, rolling in agony.

'Then we'll give it to you, so you can see what it would be like if you had.'

The torture of the Key—which has no key at all—hurts excessively. They endured several minutes of it, and their language necessitated the gag.

'Did you give Clewer Corkscrews?'

'Yes. Oh, curse your silly souls! Let us alone, you cads.'

They were corkscrewed, and the torture of the Corkscrew—this has nothing to do with corkscrews—is keener than the torture of the Key.

The method and silence of the attacks was breaking their nerves. Between each new torture came the pitiless, dazing rain of questions, and when they did not answer to the point, Isabella-coloured handkerchiefs were thrust into their mouths.

'Now are those all the things you did to Clewer? Take out the gag, Turkey, and let 'em answer.'

'Yes, I swear that was all. Oh, you're killing us, Stalky!' cried Campbell.

'Pre-cisely what Clewer said to you. I heard him. Now we're goin' to show you what real bullyin' is. What I don't like about you, Sefton, is, you come to the Coll. with your stick-up collars an' patent-leather boots, an' you think you can teach us something about bullyin'. *Do* you think you can teach us anything about bullyin'? Take out the gag and let him answer.'

'No!'—ferociously.

'He says no. Rock him to sleep. Campbell can watch.'

It needs three boys and two boxing-gloves to rock a boy to sleep. Again the operation has nothing to do with its name. Sefton was 'rocked' till his eyes set in his head and he gasped and crowed for breath, sick and dizzy.

'My Aunt!' said Campbell, appalled, from his corner, and turned white.

'Put him away,' said Stalky. 'Bring on Campbell. Now this *is* bullyin'. Oh, I forgot! I say, Campbell, what did you bully Clewer for? Take out his gag an' let him answer.'

'I—I don't know. Oh, let me off! I swear I'll make it *pax*. Don't "rock" me!'

'"The bleatin' of the kid excites the tiger." He says he don't know. Set him up, Beetle. Give me the glove an' put in the gag.'

In silence Campbell was 'rocked' sixty-four times.

'I believe I'm goin' to die!' he gasped.

'He says he is goin' to die. Put him away. Now, Sefton! Oh, I forgot! Sefton, what did you bully Clewer for?'

The answer is unprintable; but it brought not the faintest blush to Stalky's downy cheek.

'Make him an Ag Ag, Turkey!'

And an Ag Ag was he made, forthwith. The hard-bought experience of nearly eighteen years was at his disposal, but he did not seem to appreciate it.

'He says we are sweeps. Put him away! Now, Campbell! Oh, I forgot! I say, Campbell, what did you bully Clewer for?'

Then came the tears—scalding tears; appeals for mercy and abject promises of peace. Let them cease the tortures and Campbell would never lift hand against them. The questions began again—to an accompaniment of keen persuasions.

'You seem hurt, Campbell. Are you hurt?'

'Yes. Awfully!'

'He says he is hurt. Are you broke?'

'Yes, yes! I swear I am. Oh, stop!'

'He says he is broke. Are you humble?'

'Yes!'

'He says he is humble. Are you devilish humble?'

'Yes!'

'He says he is devilish humble. Will you bully Clewer any more?'

'No. No—ooh!'

'He says he won't bully Clewer. Or any one else?'

'No. I swear I won't!'

'Or any one else. What about that lickin' you an' Sefton were goin' to give us?'

'I won't! I won't! I swear I won't!'

'He says he won't lick us. Do you esteem yourself to know anything about bullyin'?'

'No, I don't!'

'He says he doesn't know anything about bullyin'. Haven't we taught you a lot?'

'Yes—yes!'

'He says we've taught him a lot. Aren't you grateful?'

'Yes!'

'He says he is grateful. Put him away. Oh, I forgot! I say, Campbell, what did you bully Clewer for?'

He wept anew; his nerves being raw. 'Because I was a bully. I suppose that's what you want me to say?'

'He says he is a bully. Right he is. Put him in the corner. No more japes for Campbell. Now, Sefton!'

'You devils! You young devils!' This and much more as Sefton was punted across the carpet by skilful knees.

' "The bleatin' of the kid excites the tiger." We're goin' to make you beautiful. Where does he keep his shaving-things?' (Campbell told.) 'Beetle, get some water. Turkey, make the lather. We're goin' to shave you, Seffy, so you'd better lie jolly still, or you'll get cut. I've never shaved any one before.'

'Don't! Oh, don't! Please don't!'

'Gettin' polite, eh? I'm only goin' to take off one ducky little whisker——'

'I'll—I'll make it *pax*, if you don't. I swear I'll let you off your lickin' when I get up!'

'And half that moustache we're so proud of. He says he'll let us off our lickin'. Isn't he kind?'

M'Turk laughed into the nickel-plated shaving-cup, and settled Sefton's head between Stalky's vice-like knees.

'Hold on a shake,' said Beetle, 'you can't shave long hairs. You've got to cut all that moustache short first, an' then scrope him.'

'Well, I'm not goin' to hunt about for scissors. Won't a match do? Chuck us the match-box. He *is* a hog, you know; we might as well singe him. Lie still!'

He lit a vesta, but checked his hand. 'I only want to take off half, though.'

'That's all right.' Beetle waved the brush. 'I'll lather up to the middle—see? and you can burn off the rest.'

The thin-haired first moustache of youth fluffed off in flame to the lather-line in the centre of the lip, and Stalky rubbed away the burnt stumpage with his thumb. It was not a very gentle shave, but it abundantly accomplished its purpose.

'Now the whisker on the other side. Turn him over!' Between match and razor this, too, was removed. 'Give him his shaving-glass. Take the gag out. I want to hear what he'll say.'

But there were no words. Sefton gazed at the lop-sided wreck in horror and despair. Two fat tears rolled down his cheek.

'Oh, I forgot! I say, Sefton, what did you bully Clewer for?'

'Leave me alone! Oh, you infernal bullies, leave me alone! Haven't I had enough!'

'He says we must leave him alone,' said M'Turk.

'He says we are bullies, an' we haven't even begun yet,' said Beetle. 'You're ungrateful, Seffy. Golly! You do look an atrocity and a half!'

'He says he has had enough,' said Stalky. 'He errs!'

'Well, to work, to work!' chanted M'Turk, waving a stump. 'Come on, my giddy Narcissus. Don't fall in love with your own reflection!'

'Oh, let him off,' said Campbell from his corner; 'he's blub-bin', too.'

Sefton cried like a twelve-year-old with pain, shame, wounded vanity, and utter helplessness.

'You'll make it *pax*, Sefton, won't you? You can't stand up to those young devils——'

'Don't be rude, Campbell, de-ah,' said M'Turk, 'or you'll catch it again!'

'You *are* devils, you know,' said Campbell.

'What? For a little bullyin'—same as you've been givin' Clewer! How long have you been jestin' with him?' said Stalky. 'All this term?'

'We didn't always knock him about, though!'

'You did when you could catch him,' said Beetle, cross-legged on the floor, dropping a stump from time to time across Sefton's instep. 'Don't I know it!'

'I—perhaps we did.'

'And you went out of your way to catch him? Don't I know it! Because he was an awful little beast, eh? Don't I know it! Now, you see, *you*'re awful beasts, and you're gettin' what he got—for bein' a beast. Just because we choose.'

'We never really bullied him—like you've done us.'

'Yah!' said Beetle. 'They never really bully—"Molly" Fairburn didn't. Only knock 'em about a little bit. That's what they say. Only kick their souls out of 'em, and they go and blub in the box-rooms. Shove their heads into the ulsters an' blub. Write home three times a day—yes, you brute, I've done that—askin' to be taken away. You've never been bullied properly, Campbell. I'm sorry you made *pax*.'

'I'm not!' said Campbell, who was a humorist in a way. 'Look out, you're slaying Sefton!'

In his excitement Beetle had used the stump unreflectingly, and Sefton was now shouting for mercy.

'An' you!' he cried, wheeling where he sat. 'You've never been bullied, either. Where were you before you came here?'

'I—I had a tutor.'

'Yah! You would. You never blubbed in your life. But you're blubbin' now, by Gum. Aren't you blubbin'?'

'Can't you see, you blind beast?' Sefton fell over sideways, tear-tracks furrowing the dried lather. Crack came the cricket-stump on the curved later-end of him.

'Blind, am I,' said Beetle, 'and a beast? Shut up, Stalky. I'm goin' to jape a bit with our friend, à la "Molly" Fairburn. *I* think I can see. Can't I see, Sefton?'

'The point is well taken,' said M'Turk, watching the stump at work. 'You'd better say that he sees, Seffy.'

'You do—you can! I swear you do!' yelled Sefton, for strong arguments were coercing him.

'Aren't my eyes lovely?' The stump rose and fell steadily throughout this catechism.

'Yes.'

'A gentle hazel, aren't they?'

'Yes—oh yes!'

'What a liar you are! They're sky-blue. Ain't they sky-blue?'

'Yes—oh yes!'

'You don't know your mind from one minute to another. You must learn—you must learn.'

'What a bait you're in!' said Stalky. 'Keep your hair on, Beetle.'

'I've had it done to me,' said Beetle. 'Now—about my being a beast.'

'*Pax*—oh, *pax*!' cried Sefton; 'make it *pax*. I'll give up! Let me off! I'm broke! I can't stand it!'

'Ugh! Just when we were gettin' our hand in!' grunted M'Turk. 'They didn't let Clewer off, I'll swear.'

'Confess—apologise—quick!' said Stalky.

From the floor Sefton made unconditional surrender, more abjectly even than Campbell. He would never touch any one again. He would go softly all the days of his life.

'We've got to take it, I suppose?' said Stalky. 'All right, Sefton. You're broke? Very good. Shut up, Beetle! But before we let you up, you an' Campbell will kindly oblige us with "Kitty of Coleraine"—*à la* Clewer.'

'That's not fair,' said Campbell, 'we've surrendered.'

'Course you have. Now you're goin' to do what we tell you—same as Clewer would. If you hadn't surrendered you'd ha' been really bullied. Havin' surrendered—do you follow, Seffy?—you sing odes in honour of the conquerors. Hurry up!'

They dropped into chairs luxuriously. Campbell and Sefton looked at each other, and, neither taking comfort from that view, struck up 'Kitty of Coleraine.'

'Vile bad!' said Stalky, as the miserable wailing ended. 'If you hadn't surrendered it would have been our painful duty to buzz books at you for singin' out o' tune. Now then.'

He freed them from their bonds, but for several minutes they could not rise. Campbell was first on his feet, smiling uneasily. Sefton staggered to the table, buried his head in his arms, and shook with sobs. There was no shadow of fight in either—only amazement, distress, and shame.

'Ca—can't he shave clean before tea, please?' said Campbell. 'It's ten minutes to bell.'

Stalky shook his head. He meant to escort the half-shaved one to that meal.

M'Turk yawned in his chair and Beetle mopped his face. They were all dripping with excitement and exertion.

'If I knew anything about it, I swear I'd give you a moral lecture,' said Stalky severely.

'Don't jaw; they've surrendered,' said M'Turk. 'This moral suasion biznai takes it out of a chap.'

'Don't you see how gentle we've been? We might have called Clewer in to look at you,' said Stalky. 'The bleatin' of the tiger excites the kid. But we didn't. We've only got to tell a few chaps in Coll. about this and you'd be hooted all over the shop. Your life wouldn't be worth havin'. But we aren't goin' to do that, either. We're strictly moral suasers, Campbell; so, unless you or Seffy split about this, no one will.'

'I swear you're a brick,' said Campbell. 'I suppose I was rather a brute to Clewer.'

'It looked like it,' said Stalky. 'But I don't think Seffy need come into hall with cock-eye whiskers. Horrid bad for the fags if they saw him. He can shave. Ain't you grateful, Sefton?'

The head did not lift. Sefton was deeply asleep.

'That's rummy,' said M'Turk, as a snore mixed with a sob. 'Cheek, I think; or else he's shammin'.'

'No, 'tisn't,' said Beetle, 'When "Molly" Fairburn had attended to me for an hour or so I used to go bung off to sleep on a form sometimes. Poor devil! But he called me a beastly poet, though.'

'Well, come on.' Stalky lowered his voice. 'Good-bye, Campbell. 'Member, if you don't talk, nobody will.'

There should have been a war-dance, but that all three were so utterly tired that they almost went to sleep above the tea-cups in their study, and slept till prep.

'A most extraordinary letter. Are *all* parents incurably mad? What do you make of it?' said the Head, handing a closely-written eight pages to the Reverend John.

' "The only son of his mother, and she a widow." That is the least reasonable sort.' The Chaplain read with pursed lips.

'If half those charges are true he should be in the sick-house; whereas he is disgustingly well. Certainly he has shaved. I noticed that.'

'Under compulsion, as his mother points out. How delicious! How salutary!'

'*You* haven't to answer her. It isn't often I don't know what has happened in Coll.; but this is beyond me.'

'If you asked me I should say "Seek not to propitiate." When one is forced to take crammers' pups——'

'He was perfectly well at extra-tuition—with me—this morning,' said the Head absently. 'Unusually well-behaved, too.'

'——they either educate the school, or the school, as in this case, educates them. I prefer our own methods,' the Chaplain concluded.

'You think it was that?' A lift of the Head's eyebrow.

'I'm sure of it! And nothing excuses his trying to give the Coll. a bad name.'

'That's the line I mean to take with him,' the Head answered.

The Augurs winked.

A few days later the Reverend John called on Number Five. 'Why haven't we seen you before, Padre?' said they.

'I've been watching times and seasons and events and men—and boys,' he replied. 'I am pleased with my Tenth Legion. I make them my compliments. Clewer was throwing ink-balls in form this morning, instead of doing his work. He is now doing fifty lines for—unheard-of audacity.'

'You can't blame us, sir,' said Beetle. 'You told us to remove the—er—pressure. That's the worst of a fag.'

'I've known boys five years his senior throw ink-balls, Beetle. To such an one have I given two hundred lines—not so long ago. And now I come to think of it, were those lines ever shown up?'

'Were they, Turkey?' said Beetle unblushingly.

'Don't you think Clewer looks a little cleaner, Padre?' Stalky interrupted.

'We're no end of moral reformers,' said M'Turk.

'It was all Stalky, but it was a lark,' said Beetle.

'I have noticed the moral reform in several quarters. Didn't I tell you you had more influence than any boys in the Coll. if you cared to use it?'

'It's a trifle exhaustin' to use frequent—our kind of moral suasion. Besides, you see, it only makes Clewer cheeky.'

'I wasn't thinking of Clewer; I was thinking of—the other people, Stalky.'

'Oh, we didn't bother much about the other people,' said M'Turk. 'Did we?'

'But *I* did—from the beginning.'

'Then you knew, sir?'

A downward puff of smoke.

'Boys educate each other, they say, more than we can or dare. If I had used one half of the moral suasion you may or may not have employed——'

'With the best motives in the world. Don't forget our pious motives, Padre,' said M'Turk.

'I suppose I should be now languishing in Bideford jail, shouldn't I? Well, to quote the Head, in a little business which we have agreed to forget, that strikes me as flagrant injustice. . . . What are you laughing at, you young sinners? Isn't it true? I will not stay to be shouted at. What I looked into this den of iniquity for was to find out if any one cared to come down for a bathe off the Ridge. But I see you won't.'

'Won't we, though! Half a shake, Padre Sahib, till we get our towels, and *nous sommes avec vous!*'

THE UNITED IDOLATERS

TO THE COMPANIONS

HORACE, Bk. V, Ode 17

How comes it that, at even-tide,
  When level beams should show most truth,
Man, failing, takes unfailing pride
  In memories of his frolic youth?

Venus and Liber fill their hour;
  The games engage, the law-courts prove;
Till hardened life breeds love of power
  Or Avarice, Age's final love.

Yet at the end, these comfort not—
  Nor any triumph Fate decrees—
Compared with glorious, unforgot-
  ten innocent enormities

Of frontless days before the beard,
  When, instant on the casual jest,
The God Himself of Mirth appeared
  And snatched us to His heaving breast.

And we—not caring who He was
  But certain He would come again—
Accepted all He brought to pass
  As Gods accept the lives of men . . .

Then He withdrew from sight and speech,
  Nor left a shrine. How comes it now,
While Charon's keel grates on the beach,
  He calls so clear: 'Rememberest thou?'?

THE UNITED IDOLATERS

HIS NAME WAS BROWNELL and his reign was brief. He came from the Central Anglican Scholastic Agency, a soured, clever, reddish man picked up by the Head at the very last moment of the summer holidays in default of Macrea (of Macrea's House) who wired from Switzerland that he had smashed a knee mountaineering, and would not be available that term.

Looking back at the affair, one sees that the Head should have warned Mr. Brownell of the College's outstanding peculiarity, instead of leaving him to discover it for himself the first day of the term, when he went for a walk to the beach, and saw 'Potiphar' Mullins, Head of Games, smoking without conceal on the sands. 'Pot,' having the whole of the Autumn Football challenges, acceptances, and Fifteen reconstructions to work out, did not at first comprehend Mr. Brownell's shrill cry of: 'You're smoking! You're smoking, sir!' but he removed his pipe, and answered, placably enough: 'The Army Class is allowed to smoke, sir.'

Mr. Brownell replied: 'Preposterous!'

Pot, seeing that this new person was uninformed, suggested that he should refer to the Head.

'You may be sure I shall—sure I shall, sir! Then we shall see!'

Mr. Brownell and his umbrella scudded off, and Pot returned to his match-plannings. Anon, he observed, much as the Almighty might observe black-beetles, two small figures coming over the Pebble Ridge a few hundred yards to his right. They were a Major and his Minor, the latter a new boy and, as such, entitled to his brother's countenance for exactly three days—after which he would fend for himself. Pot waited till they were well out on the great stretch of mother-o'-pearl sands; then caused his ground-ash to describe a magnificent whirl of command in the air.

'Come on,' said the Major. 'Run!'

'What for?' said the Minor, who had noticed nothing.

''Cause we're wanted. Leg it!'

'Oh, I can do *that*,' the Minor replied and, at the end of the sprint, fetched up a couple of yards ahead of his brother, and much less winded.

'Your Minor?' said Pot, looking over them, seawards.

'Yes, Mullins,' the Major replied.

'All right. Cut along!' They cut on the word.

'Hi! Fludd Major! Come back!'

Back fled the elder.

'Your wind's bad. Too fat. You grunt like a pig. Mustn't do it! Understand? Go away!'

'What was all that for?' the Minor asked on the Major's return.

'To see if we could run, you fool!'

'Well, I ran faster than you, anyhow,' was the scandalous retort.

'Look here, Har—Minor, if you go on talkin' like this, you'll get yourself kicked all round Coll. An' you mustn't stand like you did when a prefect's talkin' to you.'

The Minor's eyes opened with awe. 'I thought it was only one of the masters,' said he.

'Masters! It was Mullins—Head o' Games. You *are* a putrid young ass!'

By what seemed pure chance, Mr. Brownell ran into the

school Chaplain, the Reverend John Gillett, beating up against the soft September rain that no native ever troubled to wear a coat for.

'I was trying to catch you after lunch,' the latter began. 'I wanted to show you our objects of local interest.'

'Thank you! I've seen all *I* want,' Mr. Brownell answered. 'Gillett, *is* there anything about me which suggests the Congenital Dupe?'

'It's early to say, yet,' the Chaplain answered. 'Who've you been meeting?'

'A youth called Mullins, I believe.' And, indeed, there was Potiphar, ground-ash, pipe, and all, quarter-decking serenely below the Pebble Ridge.

'Oh! I see. Old Pot—our Head of Games.'

'He was smoking. He's smoking *now*! Before those two little boys, too!' Mr. Brownell panted. 'He had the audacity to tell me that——'

'Yes,' the Reverend John cut in. 'The Army Class is allowed to smoke—not in their studies, of course, but within limits, out of doors. You see, we have to compete against the crammers' establishments, where smoking's usual.'

This was true! Of the only school in England was this the cold truth, and for the reason given, in that unprogressive age!

'Good Heavens!' said Mr. Brownell to the gulls and the grey sea. 'And I was never warned!'

'The Head *is* a little forgetful. *I* ought to have—— But it's all right,' the Chaplain added soothingly. 'Pot won't—er—give you away.'

Mr. Brownell, who knew what smoking led to, testified out of his twelve years' experience of what he called the Animal Boy. He left little unexplored or unexplained.

'There may be something in what you say,' the Reverend John assented. 'But as a matter of fact, their actual smoking doesn't amount to much. They talk a great deal about their brands of tobacco. Practically, it makes them rather keen on putting down smoking among the juniors—as an encroachment on their privilege, you see. They lick 'em twice as hard for it as *we*'d dare to.'

'Lick!' Mr. Brownell cried. 'One expels! One expels! *I* know the end of these practices.' He told his companion, in detail, with anecdotes and inferences, a great deal more about the Animal Boy.

'Ah!' said the Reverend John to himself. 'You'll leave at the end of the term; but you'll have a deuce of a time first.' Aloud: 'We-ell, I suppose no one can be sure of any school's tendency at any given moment, but, personally, I should incline to believe that we're reasonably free from the—er—monastic microbes of—er—older institutions.'

'But a school's a school. You can't get out of *that*! It's preposterous! You must admit *that*,' Mr. Brownell insisted.

They were within hail of Pot by now, and the Reverend John asked him how Affairs of State stood.

'All right, thank you, sir. How are you, sir?'

'Loungin' round and sufferin', my son. What about the dates for the Exeter and Tiverton matches?'

'As late in the term as we can get 'em, don't you think, sir?'

'Quite! Specially Blundell's. They're our dearest foe,' he explained to the frozen Mr. Brownell. 'Aren't we rather light in the scrum just now, Mullins?'

' 'Fraid so, sir: but Packman's playin' forward this term.'

'*At* last!' cried the Reverend John. (Packman was Pot's second-in-command, who considered himself a heaven-born half-back, but Pot had been working on him diplomatically.) 'He'll be a pillar, at any rate. Lend me one of your fusees, please. I've only got matches.'

Mr. Brownell was unused to this sort of talk. 'A bad beginning to a bad business,' he muttered, as they returned to College.

Pot finished out his meditations; from time to time rubbing up the gloss on his new seven-and-sixpenny silver-mounted, rather hot, myall-wood pipe, with its very thin crust in the bowl.

As the Studies brought back brackets and pictures for their walls, so did they bring odds and ends of speech—theatre, opera, and music-hall gags—from the great holiday world; some of which stuck for a term, and others were discarded. Number Five was unpacking, when Dick Four (King's House) of the red nose and dramatic instincts, who with Pussy and Tertius inhabited the study below, loafed up and asked them 'how their symptoms seemed to segashuate.' They said nothing at the time, for they knew Dick had a giddy naval uncle who took him to the Pavilion and the Cri, and all would be explained later. But, before they met again, Beetle came across two fags at war in a box-room, one of whom cried to the other: 'Turn me loose, or I'll knock the natal stuffin' out of you.' Beetle demanded why he, being offal, presumed to use this strange speech. The fag said it came out of a new book about rabbits and foxes and turtles and niggers, which was in his locker. (*Uncle Remus* was a popular holiday gift-book in Shotover's year: when Cetewayo lived in Melbury Road, Arabi Pasha in Egypt, and Spofforth on the Oval.) Beetle had it out and read for some time, standing by the window, ere he carried it off to Number Five and began at once to give a wonderful story of a Tar Baby. Stalky tore it from him because he sputtered incoherently; M'Turk, for the same cause, wrenching it from Stalky. There was no prep. that night. The book was amazing, and full of quotations that one could hurl like javelins. When they came down to prayers, Stalky, to show he was abreast of the latest movement, pounded on the door of Dick Four's study, shouting a couplet that pleased him:—

> *'Ti-yi! Tungalee!*
> *I eat um pea! I pick um pea!'*

Upon which Dick Four, hornpiping and squinting, and not at all unlike a bull-frog, came out and answered from the bottom of his belly, whence he could produce incredible noises:—

> *'Ingle-go-jang, my joy, my joy!*
> *Ingle-go-jang, my joy!*
> *I'm right at home, my joy, my joy!——'*

The chants seemed to answer the ends of their being created for the moment. They all sang them the whole way up the corridor, and, after prayers, bore the burdens dispersedly to their several dormitories, where they found many who knew the book of the words, but who, boylike, had waited for a lead ere giving tongue. In a short time the College was as severely infected with *Uncle Remus* as it had been with *Pinafore* and *Patience*. King realised it specially because he was running Macrea's House in addition to his own and, Dick Four said, was telling his new charges what he thought of his 'esteemed colleague's' methods of House-control.

The Reverend John was talking to the Head in the latter's study, perhaps a fortnight later.

'If you'd only wired *me*,' he said. 'I could have dug up something that might have tided us over. This man's dangerous.'

'*Mea culpa!*' the Head replied. 'I had so much on hand. Our Governing Council alone—— But what do *We* make of him?'

'Trust Youth! *We* call him "Mister." '

' "Mister Brownell"?'

'Just "Mister." It took *Us* three days to plumb his soul.'

'And he doesn't approve of Our institutions? You say he is On the Track—eh? He suspects the worst?'

The school Chaplain nodded.

'We-ell. *I* should say that that was the one tendency we had *not* developed. Setting aside we haven't even a curtain in a dormitory, let alone a lock to any form-room door—there has to be tradition in these things.'

'So I believe. So, indeed, one knows. And—'tisn't as if I ever preached on personal purity either.'

The Head laughed. 'No, or you'd join Brownell at term-end. By the way, what's this new line of Patristic discourse you're giving us in church? I found myself listening to some of it last Sunday.'

'Oh! My Early Christianity sermons? I bought a dozen ready made in Town just before I came down. Some one who knows his Gibbon must have done 'em. Aren't they good?' The Reverend John, who was no hand at written works, beamed self-approvingly. There was a knock and Pot entered.

The weather had defeated him, at last. All footer-grounds, he reported, were unplayable, and must be rested. His idea, to keep things going, was Big and Little Side Paper-chases thrice a week. For the juniors, a shortish course on the Burrows, which he intended to oversee personally the first few times, while Packman lunged Big Side across the inland and upland ploughs, for proper sweats. There was some question of bounds that he asked authority to vary; and, would the Head please say which afternoons would interfere least with the Army Class, Extra Tuition?

As to bounds, the Head left those, as usual, entirely to Pot. The Reverend John volunteered to shift one of his extra-tu. classes from four to five P.M. till after prayers—nine to ten. The whole question was settled in five minutes.

'*We* hate paper-chases, don't we, Pot?' the Headmaster asked as the Head of Games rose.

'Yes, sir, but it keeps 'em in training. Good night, sir.'

'To go back——' drawled the Head when the door was well shut. 'No-o. I do *not* think so! . . . Ye-es! He'll leave at the end of the term . . . A-aah! How does it go? "Don't 'spute wid de squinch-owl. Jam de shovel in de fier." Have you come across that extraordinary book, by the way?'

'Oh yes. *We*'ve got it badly too. It has some sort of elemental appeal, I suppose.'

Here Mr. King came in with a neat little scheme for the re-organisation of certain details in Macrea's House, where he had detected reprehensible laxities. The Head sighed. The Reverend John only heard the beginnings of it. Then he slid out softly. He remembered he had not written to Macrea for quite a long time.

The first Big Side Paper-chase, in blinding wet, was as vile as even the groaning and bemired Beetle had prophesied. But Dick Four had managed to run his own line when it skirted Bideford, and turned up at the lavatories half an hour late cherishing a movable tumour beneath his sweater.

'Ingle-go-jang!' he chanted, and slipped out a warm but coy land-tortoise.

'My Sacred Hat!' cried Stalky. 'Brer Terrapin! Where you catchee? What you makee-do *aveck*?'

This was Stalky's notion of how they talked in *Uncle Remus*; and he spake no other tongue for weeks.

'I don't know yet; but I had to get him. Man with a barrow full of 'em in Bridge Street. Gave me my choice for a bob. Leave him alone, you owl! He won't swim where you've been washing your filthy self! "*I*'m right at home, my joy, my joy."' Dick's nose shone like Bardolph's as he bubbled in the bath.

Just before tea-time, he, Pussy, and Tertius broke in upon Number Five, processionally, singing:—

> '*Ingle-go-jang, my joy, my joy!*
> *Ingle-go-jang, my joy!*
> *I'm right at home, my joy, my joy!*
> *Ingle-go-jang, my joy!*'

Brer Terrapin, painted *or* and *sable*—King's House-colours —swung by a neatly contrived belly-band from the end of a broken jumping-pole. They thought rather well of taking him in to tea. They called at one or two studies on the way, and were warmly welcomed; but when they reached the still shut doors of the dining-hall (Richards, ex-Petty Officer, R.N., was always unpunctual—but they needn't have called him 'Stinking Jim') the whole school shouted approval. After the meal, Brer Terrapin was borne the round of the form-rooms from Number One to Number Twelve, in an unbroken roar of homage.

'To-morrow,' Dick Four announced, 'we'll sacrifice to him. Fags in blazin' paper-baskets!' and with thundering 'Ingle-go-jangs' the Idol retired to its shrine.

It had been a satisfactory performance. Little Hartopp,

surprised labelling 'rocks' in Number Twelve, which held the
Natural History.Museum, had laughed consumedly; and the
Reverend John, just before prep., complimented Dick that he
had not a single dissenter to his following. In this respect the
affair was an advance on Byzantium and Alexandria, which,
of course, were torn by rival sects led by militant Bishops or
zealous heathen. *Vide,* (Beetle,) *Hypatia,* and (if Dick Four
ever listened, instead of privily swotting up his Euclid, in
chapel) the Reverend John's own sermons. Mr. King, who
had heard the noise but had not appeared, made no comment
till dinner, when he told the Common-room ceiling that he
entertained the lowest opinion of Uncle Remus's buffoonery,
but opined that it might interest certain types of intellect.
Little Hartopp, school Librarian, who had, by special request,
laid in an extra copy of the book, differed acridly. He had, he
said, heard or overheard every salient line of *Uncle Remus*
quoted, appositely too, by boys whom he would not have
credited with intellectual interests. Mr. King repeated that
he was wearied by the senseless and childish repetitions of
immature minds. He recalled the *Patience* epidemic. Mr.
Prout did not care for *Uncle Remus*—the dialect put him
off—but he thought the Houses were getting a bit out of
hand. There was nothing one could lay hold of, of course—
'As yet,' Mr. Brownell interjected darkly. 'But this larking
about in form-rooms,' he added, 'had potentialities which, if
he knew anything of the Animal Boy, would develop—or had
developed.'

'I shouldn't wonder,' said the Reverend John. 'This is the
first time to my knowledge that Stalky has ever played second
fiddle to any one. Brer Terrapin was entirely Dick Four's notion. By the way, he was painted *your* House-colours, King.'

'Was he?' said King artlessly. 'I have always held that our

THE UNITED IDOLATERS

Dickson Quartus had the rudiments of imagination. We will look into it—look into it.'

'In our loathsome calling, more things are done by judicious letting alone than by any other,' the Reverend John grunted.

'I can't subscribe to that,' said Mr. Prout. '*You* haven't a House,' and for once Mr. King backed Prout.

'Thank Heaven I haven't! Or I should be like you two. Leave 'em alone! Leave 'em alone! Haven't you ever seen puppies fighting over a slipper for hours?'

'Yes, but Gillett admits that Dickson Quartus was the only begetter of this manifestation. I wasn't aware that the—er—Testacean had been tricked out in *my* colours,' said King.

And at that very hour, Number Five study—prep. thrown to the winds—were toiling inspiredly at a Tar Baby made up of Beetle's sweater and half-a-dozen lavatory-towels; a condemned cretonne curtain, and, ditto, baize table-cloth for 'natal stuffin'; an ancient, but air-tight puntabout-ball for the head; all three play-box ropes for bindings; and most of Richards' weekly blacking-allowance for Prout's House's boots, to give tone to the whole.

'Gummy!' said Beetle, when their curtain-pole had been taken down and Tar Baby hitched to the end of it by a loop in its voluptuous back. 'It looks pretty average indecent, somehow.'

'You can use it this way, too,' Turkey demonstrated, handling the curtain-pole like a flail. 'Now, shove it in the fireplace to dry an' we'll wash up.'

'But—but,' said Stalky, fascinated by the unspeakable front and behind of the black and bulging horror. 'How *come* he lookee so hellish?'

'Dead easy! If you do anything with your whole heart, Ruskin says, you always pull off something dam'-fine. Brer Terrapin's only a natural animal; but Tar Baby's Art,' M'Turk explained.

'I see! "If you're anxious for to shine in the high aesthetic line." Well, Tar Baby's the filthiest thing *I*'ve even seen in my life,' Stalky concluded. 'King'll be rabid.'

The United Idolaters set forth, side by side, at five o'clock next afternoon; Brer Terrapin, wide awake, and swimming hard into nothing; Tar Baby lurching from side to side with a lascivious abandon that made Foxy, the school Sergeant, taking defaulters' drill in the corridor, squawk like an outraged hen. And when they ceremoniously saluted each other, like aristocratic heads on revolutionary pikes, it beat the previous day's performance out of sight and mind. The very fags, offered up, till the bottoms of the paper-baskets carried away, as heave-offerings before them, fell over each other for the honour; and House by House, when the news spread, dropped its doings, and followed the Mysteries—not without song . . .

Some say it was a fag of Prout's who appealed for rescue from Brer Terrapin to Tar Baby; others, that the introits to the respective creeds ('Ingle-go-jang'—'Ti-yi-Tungalee!') carried in themselves the seeds of dissent. At any rate, the cleavage developed as swiftly as in a new religion, and by tea-time, when they were fairly hoarse, the rolling world was rent to the death between Ingles *versus* Tungles, and Brer Terrapin had swept out Number Eleven form-room to the war-cry: 'Here I come a-bulgin' and a-bilin'.' Prep. stopped further developments, but they agreed that, as a recreation for wet autumn evenings, the jape was unequalled, and called for its repetition on Saturday.

That was a brilliant evening, too. Both sides went into prayers practically re-dressing themselves. There was a smell of singed fag down the lines and a watery eye or so; but nothing to which the most fastidious could have objected. The Reverend John hinted something about roof-lifting noises.

'Oh *no*, Padre Sahib. We were only billin' an' cooin' a bit,' Stalky explained. 'We haven't really begun. There's goin' to be a tug-o'-war next Saturday with Miss Meadows' bedcord——'

' "Which in dem days would ha' hilt a mule," ' the Reverend John quoted. 'Well, I've got to be impartial. I wish you both good luck.'

The week, with its three paper-chases, passed uneventfully, but for a certain amount of raiding and reprisals on new lines that might have warned them they were playing with fire. The juniors had learned to use the sacred war-chants as signals of distress; oppressed Ingles squealing for aid against oppressing Tungles, and *vice versa*; so that one never knew when a peaceful form-room would flare up in song and slaughter. But not a soul dreamed, for a moment, that that Saturday's jape would develop into—what it did! They were rigidly punctilious about the ritual; exquisitely careful as to the weights on Miss Meadows' bed-cord, kindly lent by Richards, who said he knew nothing about mules, but guaranteed it would hold a barge's crew; and if Dick Four chose to caparison himself as Archimandrite of Joppa, black as burned cork could make him, why, Stalky, in a nightgown kilted up beneath his sweater, was equally the Pope Symmachus, just converted from heathendom but given to alarming relapses.

It began after tea—say 6.50 P.M. It got into its stride by 7.30 when Turkey, with pillows bound round the ends of forms, invented the Royal Battering-Ram Corps. It grew and —it grew till a quarter to nine when the prefects, most of whom had fought on one side or the other, thought it time to stop and went in with ground-ashes and the bare hand for ten minutes. . . .

Honours for the action were not awarded by the Head till Monday morning when he dealt out one dozen lickings to selected seniors, eight 'millies' (one thousand lines), fourteen 'usuals' (five hundred lines), minor impositions past count, and a stoppage of pocket-money on a scale and for a length of time unprecedented in modern history.

He said the College was within an ace of being burned to the ground when the gas-jet in Number Eleven form-room— where they tried to burn Tar Baby, fallen for the moment into the hands of the enemy—was wrenched off, and the lit gas spouted all over the ceiling till some one plugged the pipe with dormitory soap. He said that nothing save his consideration for their future careers kept him from expelling the wanton ruffians who had noosed all the desks in Number Twelve and swept them up in one cracking mound, barring a couple that had pitch-poled through the window. This, again, had been no man's design but the inspiration of necessity when Tar Baby's bodyguard, surrounded but defiant, was only rescued at the last minute by Turkey's immortal flank-attack with the battering-rams that carried away the door of Number Nine. He said that the same remarks applied to the fireplace and mantelpiece in Number Seven which everybody had seen fall out of the wall of their own motion after Brer Terrapin had hitched Miss Meadows' bed-cord to the bars of the grate.

He said much more, too; but as King pointed out in Common-room that evening, his canings were inept, he had *not* confiscated the Idols and, above all, had not castigated, as King would have castigated, the disgusting childishness of all concerned.

'Well,' said little Hartopp, 'I saw the prefects choking them off as we came into prayers. You've reason to reckon that in the scale of suffering.'

'And more than half the damage was done under *your* banner, King,' the Reverend John added.

'That doesn't affect my judgment; though, as a matter of fact, I believe Brer Terrapin triumphed over Tar Baby all along the line. Didn't he, Prout?'

'It didn't seem to me a fitting time to ask. The Tar Babies were handicapped, of course, by not being able to—ah—tackle a live animal.'

'I confess,' Mr. Brownell volunteered, 'it was the studious perversity of certain aspects of the orgy which impressed *me*. And yet, what can one exp——'

'How do you mean?' King demanded. 'Dickson Quartus may be eccentric, but——'

'I was alluding to the vile and calculated indecency of that black doll.'

Mr. Brownell had passed Tar Baby going down to battle, all round and ripe, before Turkey had begun to use it as Bishop Odo's holy-water sprinkler.

'It is possible you didn't——'

'*I* never noticed anything,' said Prout. 'If there had been, I should have been the first——'

Here little Hartopp sniggered, which did not cool the air.

'Peradventure,' King began with due intake of the breath—. 'Peradventure even *I* might have taken cognizance of the matter both for my own House's sake and for my colleague's . . . No! Folly I concede. Utter childishness and complete

absence of discipline in *all* quarters, as the natural corollary
to dabbling in so-called transatlantic humour, I frankly admit. But that there was anything esoterically obscene in the
outbreak I absolutely deny.'

'They've been fighting for weeks over those things,' said
Mr. Prout. 'Silly, of course, but I don't see how it can be
dangerous.'

'Quite true. Any House-master of experience knows *that*,
Brownell,' the Reverend John put in reprovingly.

'Given a normal basis of tradition and conduct—certainly,'
Mr. Brownell answered. 'But with such amazing traditions as
exist here, no man with any experience of the Animal Boy
can draw your deceptive inferences. That's all *I* mean.'

Once again, and not for the first time, but with greater
heat he testified what smoking led to—what, indeed, he was
morally certain existed in full blast under their noses . . .

Gloves were off in three minutes. Pessimists, no more than
poets, love each other and, even when they work together, it
is one thing to pessimise congenially with an ancient and
tried associate who is also a butt, and another to be pessimised
over by an inexperienced junior, even though the latter's college career may have included more exhibitions—nay, even
pot-huntings—than one's own. The Reverend John did his
best to pour water on the flames. Little Hartopp, perceiving
that it was pure oil, threw in canfuls of his own, from the
wings. In the end, words passed which would have made the
Common-room uninhabitable for the future, but that Macrea
had written (the Reverend John had seen the letter) saying
that his knee was fairly re-knit and he was prepared to take
on again at half-term. This happened to be the only date
since the Creation beyond which Mr. Brownell's self-respect
would not permit him to stay one hour. It solved the situation, amid puffings and blowings and bitter epigrams, and

a most distinguished stateliness of bearing all round, till Mr. Brownell's departure.

'My dear fellow!' said the Reverend John to Macrea, on the first night of the latter's return. 'I *do* hope there was nothing in my letters to you—you asked me to keep you posted—that gave you any idea King wasn't doing his best with your House according to his lights?'

'Not in the least,' said Macrea. 'I've the greatest respect for King, but after all, one's House is one's House. One can't stand it being tinkered with by well-meaning outsiders.'

To Mr. Brownell on Bideford station-platform, the Reverend John's last words were:—

'Well, well. You mustn't judge us too harshly. I dare say there's a great deal in what you say. Oh, yes! King's conduct was inexcusable, absolutely inexcusable! About the smoking? Lamentable, but we must all bow down, more or less, in the House of Rimmon. *We* have to compete with the crammers' shops.'

To the Head, in the silence of his study, next day: 'He didn't seem to me the kind of animal who'd keep to advantage in our atmosphere. Luckily he lost his temper (King and he are own brothers) and he couldn't withdraw his resignation.'

'Excellent. After all, it's only a few pounds to make up. I'll slip it in under our recent—er—barrack damages. And what do *We* think of it all, Gillett?'

'*We* do not think at all—any of us,' said the Reverend John. 'Youth is its own prophylactic, thank Heaven.'

And the Head, not usually devout, echoed, 'Thank Heaven!'

'It was worth it,' Dick Four pronounced on review of the profit-and-loss account with Number Five in his study.

'Heap-plenty-*bong-assez*,' Stalky assented.

'But why. didn't King ra'ar up an' cuss Tar Baby?' Beetle asked.

'You preter-pluperfect, fat-ended fool!' Stalky began—

'Keep your hair on! We *all* know the Idolaters wasn't our Uncle Stalky's idea. But why didn't King——'

'Because Dick took care to paint Brer Terrapin King's House-colours. You can always conciliate King by soothin' his putrid *esprit-de-maisong*. Ain't that true, Dick?'

Dick Four, with the smile of modest worth unmasked, said it was so.

'An' now,' Turkey yawned, 'King an' Macrea'll jaw for the rest of the term how he ran his House when Macrea was tryin' to marry fat widows in Switzerland. Mountaineerin'! Bet Macrea never went near a mountain.'

'One good job, though. I go back to Macrea for Maths. He *does* know something,' said Stalky.

'Why? Didn't "Mister" know anythin'?' Beetle asked.

''Bout as much as *you*,' was Stalky's reply.

'*I* don't go about pretendin' to. What was he like?'

' "Mister"? Oh, rather like King—King and water.'

Only water was not precisely the fluid that Stalky thought fit to mention.

THE CENTAURS

Up came the young Centaur-colts from the plains they were
    fathered in—
    Curious, awkward, afraid.
Burrs in their hocks and their tails, they were gathered in
    Mobs and run up to the yard to be made.

Starting and shying at straws, with sidlings and plungings,
    Buckings and whirlings and bolts;
Greener than grass, but full-ripe for their bridlings and
    lungings,
    Up to the yards and to Chiron they bustled the colts . . .

First the light web and the cavesson; then the linked keys
    To jingle and turn on the tongue. Then, with cocked ears,
The hour of watching and envy, while comrades at ease
    Passaged and backed, making naught of these terrible gears.

Next, over-pride and its price at the low-seeming fence,
    Too oft and too easily taken—the world-beheld fall!
And none in the yard except Chiron to doubt the immense,
    Irretrievable shame of it all! . . .

Last, the trained squadron, full-charge—the sound of a going
    Through dust and spun clods, and strong kicks, pelted
    home as they went,
And repaid at top speed; till the order to halt without slowing
    Brought every colt on his haunches—and Chiron content!

REGULUS

REGULUS

Regulus, a Roman general, defeated the Carthaginians 256 B.C., but was next year defeated and taken prisoner by the Carthaginians, who sent him to Rome with an embassy to ask for peace or an exchange of prisoners. Regulus strongly advised the Roman Senate to make no terms with the enemy. He then returned to Carthage and was put to death.

THE FIFTH FORM had been dragged several times in its collective life, from one end of the school Horace to the other. Those were the years when Army examiners gave thousands of marks for Latin, and it was Mr. King's hated business to defeat them.

Hear him, then, on a raw November morning at second lesson.

'Aha!' he began, rubbing his hands. '*Cras ingens iterabimus aequor.* Our portion to-day is the Fifth Ode of the Third Book, I believe—concerning one Regulus, a gentleman. And how often have we been through it?'

'Twice, sir,' said Malpass, head of the Form.

Mr. King shuddered. 'Yes, twice, quite literally,' he said. 'To-day, with an eye to your Army *viva-voce* examinations— ugh!—I shall exact somewhat freer and more florid renditions. With feeling and comprehension if that be possible. I except'—here his eye swept the back benches—'our friend and companion Beetle, from whom, now as always, I demand an absolutely literal translation.' The Form laughed subserviently.

'Spare his blushes! Beetle charms us first.'

Beetle stood up, confident in the possession of a guaranteed construe, left behind by M'Turk, who had that day gone into the sick-house with a cold. Yet he was too wary a hand to show confidence.

'*Credidimus,* we—believe—we have believed,' he opened in hesitating slow time, '*tonantem Jovem,* thundering Jove—*regnare,* to reign—*caelo,* in heaven. *Augustus,* Augustus—*habebitur,* will be held or considered—*praesens divus,* a present God—*adjectis Britannis,* the Britons being added—*imperio,* to the Empire—*gravibusque Persis,* with the heavy—er—stern Persians.'

'What?'

'The grave or stern Persians.' Beetle pulled up with the 'Thank-God-I-have-done-my-duty' air of Nelson in the cockpit.

'I am quite aware,' said King, 'that the first stanza is about the extent of your knowledge, but continue, sweet one, continue. *Gravibus,* by the way, is usually translated as "troublesome."'

Beetle drew a long and tortured breath. The second stanza (which carries over to the third) of that Ode is what is technically called a 'stinker.' But M'Turk had done him handsomely.

'*Milesne Crassi,* had—has the soldier of Crassus—*vixit,* lived—*turpis maritus,* a disgraceful husband——'

'You slurred the quantity of the word after *turpis,*' said King. 'Let's hear it.'

Beetle guessed again, and for a wonder hit the correct quantity. 'Er—a disgraceful husband—*conjuge barbara,* with a barbarous spouse.'

'Why do you select *that* disgustful equivalent out of all the dictionary?' King snapped. 'Isn't "wife" good enough for you?'

'Yes, sir. But what do I do about this bracket, sir? Shall I take it now?'

'Confine yourself at present to the soldier of Crassus.'

'Yes, sir. *Et,* and—*consenuit,* has he grown old—*in armis,* in the—er—arms—*hostium socerorum,* of his father-in-law's enemies.'

'Who? How? Which?'

'Arms of his enemies' fathers-in-law, sir?'

'Tha-anks. By the way, what meaning might you attach to *in armis?*'

'Oh, weapons—weapons of war, sir.' There was a virginal note in Beetle's voice as though he had been falsely accused of uttering indecencies. 'Shall I take the bracket now, sir?'

'Since it seems to be troubling you.'

'*Pro Curia,* O for the Senate House—*inversique mores,* and manners upset—upside down.'

'Ve-ry like your translation. Meantime, the soldier of Crassus?'

'*Sub rege Medo,* under a Median King—*Marsus et Apulus,* he being a Marsian and an Apulian.'

'Who? The Median King?'

'No, sir. The soldier of Crassus. *Oblittus* agrees with *Milesne Crassi,* sir,' volunteered too hasty Beetle.

'Does it? It doesn't with *me.*'

'*Oh-blight-us,*' Beetle corrected hastily, 'forgetful—*ancili-orum,* of the shields, or trophies—*et nominis,* and the—his name—*et togae,* and the toga—*eternaeque Vestae,* and eternal Vesta—*incolumi Jove,* Jove being safe—*et urbe Roma,* and the Roman city.' With an air of hardly restrained zeal— 'Shall I go on, sir?'

Mr. King winced. 'No, thank you. You have indeed given us a translation! May I ask if it conveys any meaning whatever to your so-called mind?'

'Oh, I think so, sir.' This with gentle toleration for Horace and all his works.

'We envy you. Sit down.'

Beetle sat down relieved, well knowing that a reef of uncharted genitives stretched ahead of him, on which in spite of M'Turk's sailing-directions he would infallibly have been wrecked.

Rattray, who took up the task, steered neatly through them and came unscathed to port.

'Here we require drama,' said King. 'Regulus himself is speaking now. Who shall represent the provident-minded Regulus? Winton, will you kindly oblige?'

Winton of King's House, a long, heavy, tow-headed Second Fifteen forward, overdue for his First Fifteen colours, and in aspect like an earnest, elderly horse, rose up, and announced, among other things, that he had seen 'signs affixed to Punic deluges.' Half the Form shouted for joy, and the other half for joy that there was something to shout about.

Mr. King opened and shut his eyes with great swiftness. '*Signa adfixa delubris*,' he gasped. 'So *delubris* is "deluges," is it? Winton, in all our dealings, have I ever suspected you of a jest?'

'No, sir,' said the rigid and angular Winton, while the Form rocked about him.

'And yet you assert *delubris* means "deluges." Whether I am a fit subject for such a jape is, of course, a matter of opinion, but. . . . Winton, you are normally conscientious. May we assume you looked out *delubris*?'

'No, sir.' Winton was privileged to speak that truth dangerous to all who stand before Kings.

'Made a shot at it then?'

Every line of Winton's body showed he had done nothing of the sort. Indeed, the very idea that 'Pater' Winton (and a boy is not called 'Pater' by companions for his frivolity) would make a shot at anything was beyond belief. But he replied, 'Yes,' and all the while worked with his right heel as though he were heeling a ball at puntabout.

Though none dared to boast of being a favourite with King, the taciturn, three-cornered Winton stood high in his House-master's opinion. It seemed to save him neither rebuke nor punishment, but the two were in some fashion sympathetic.

'Hm!' said King drily. 'I was going to say—*Flagitio additis damnum*, but I think—I think I see the process. Beetle, the translation of *delubris*, please.'

Beetle raised his head from his shaking arm long enough to answer: 'Ruins, sir.'

There was an impressive pause while King checked off crimes on his fingers. Then to Beetle the much-enduring man addressed winged words:—

'Guessing,' said he—'Guessing, Beetle, as usual, from the look of *delubris* that it bore some relation to *diluvium* or deluge, you imparted the result of your half-baked lucubrations to Winton, who seems to have been lost enough to have accepted it. Observing, next, your companion's fall, from the presumed security of your undistinguished position in the rear-guard, you took another pot-shot. The turbid chaos of your mind threw up some memory of the word "dilapidations" which you have pitifully attempted to disguise under the synonym of "ruins." '

As this was precisely what Beetle had done he looked hurt but forgiving. 'We will attend to this later,' said King. 'Go on, Winton, and retrieve yourself.'

Delubris happened to be the one word which Winton had not looked out and had asked Beetle for, when they were settling into their places. He forged ahead with no further trouble. Only when he rendered *scilicet* as 'forsooth,' King erupted.

'Regulus,' he said, 'was *not* a leader-writer for the penny press, nor, for that matter, was Horace. Regulus says: "The soldier ransomed by gold will come keener for the fight—will he, by—by Gum!" *That*'s the meaning of *scilicet*. It indicates contempt—bitter contempt. "Forsooth," forsooth! You'll be talking about "speckled beauties" and "eventually transpire" next. Howell, what do you make of that doubled *Vidi ego—ego vidi*? It wasn't put in to fill up the metre, you know.'

'Isn't it intensive, sir?' said Howell, afflicted by a genuine interest in what he read. 'Regulus was a bit in earnest about Rome making no terms with Carthage—and he wanted to let the Romans understand it, didn't he, sir?'

'Less than your usual grace, but the fact. Regulus *was* in earnest. He was also engaged at the same time in cutting his own throat with every word he uttered. He knew Carthage, which (your examiners won't ask you this, so you needn't take notes) was a sort of God-forsaken nigger Manchester. Regulus was not thinking about his own life. He was telling Rome the truth. He was playing for his side. Those lines from the eighteenth to the fortieth ought to be written in blood. Yet there are things in human garments which will tell you that Horace was a *flâneur*—a man about town. Avoid such beings. Horace knew a very great deal. *He* knew! *Erit ille fortis*—"will he be brave who once to faithless foes has knelt?" And again (stop pawing with your hooves, Thornton!) *hic unde vitam sumeret inscius*. That means roughly—but I perceive I am ahead of my translators. Begin at *hic unde,* Vernon, and let us see if you have the spirit of Regulus.'

Now no one expected fireworks from gentle Paddy Vernon, sub-prefect of Hartopp's House, but, as must often be the case with growing boys, his mind was in abeyance for the time being, and he said, all in a rush, on behalf of Regulus: '*O magna Carthago probrosis altior Italiae ruinis,* O Carthage, thou wilt stand forth higher than the ruins of Italy.'

Even Beetle, most lenient of critics, was interested at this point, though he did not join the half-groan of reprobation from the wiser heads of the Form.

'*Please* don't mind me,' said King, and Vernon very kindly did not. He ploughed on thus: 'He (Regulus) is related to have removed from himself the kiss of the shameful wife and of his small children as less by the head, and, being stern, to have placed his virile visage on the ground.'

Since King loved 'virile' about as much as he did 'spouse' or 'forsooth' the Form looked up hopefully. But Jove thundered not.

'Until,' Vernon continued, 'he should have confirmed the sliding fathers as being the author of counsel never given under an alias.'

He stopped, conscious of stillness round him like the dread calm of the typhoon's centre. King's opening voice was sweeter than honey.

'I am painfully aware by bitter experience that I cannot give you any idea of the passion, the power, the—the essential guts of the lines which you have so foully outraged in our presence. But——' the note changed, 'so far as in me lies, I will strive to bring home to you, Vernon, the fact that there exist in Latin a few pitiful rules of grammar, of syntax, nay, even of declension, which were not created for your incult sport—your Bœotian diversion. You will, therefore, Vernon, write out and bring to me to-morrow a word-for-word English-Latin translation of the Ode, together with a full list of all adjectives—an adjective is not a verb, Vernon, as the Lower Third will tell you—all adjectives, their number, case, and gender. Even now I haven't begun to deal with you faith-fully.'

'I—I'm very sorry, sir,' Vernon stammered.

'You mistake the symptoms, Vernon. You are possibly dis-comfited by the imposition, but sorrow postulates some sort of mind, intellect, *nous*. Your rendering of *probrosis* alone stamps you as lower than the beasts of the field. Will some one take the taste out of our mouths? And—talking of tastes——' He coughed. There was a distinct flavour of chlo-rine gas in the air. Up went an eyebrow, though King knew perfectly well what it meant.

'Mr. Hartopp's Sti—Science class next door,' said Malpass.

'Oh yes. I had forgotten. Our newly established Modern Side, of course. Perowne, open the windows; and Winton, go on once more from *interque maerentes*.'

'And hastened away,' said Winton, 'surrounded by his mourning friends, into—into illustrious banishment. But I got that out of Conington, sir,' he added in one conscientious breath.

'I am aware. The master generally knows his ass's crib, though I acquit *you* of any intention that way. Can you suggest anything for *egregius exul*? Only "egregious exile"? I fear "egregious" is a good word ruined. No! You can't in this case improve on Conington. Now then for *atqui sciebat quae sibi barbarus tortor pararet*. The whole force of it lies in the *atqui*.'

'Although he knew,' Winton suggested.

'Stronger than that, I think.'

'He who knew well,' Malpass interpolated.

'Ye-es. "Well though he knew." I don't like Conington's "Well-witting." It's Wardour Street.'

'Well though he knew what the savage torturer was—was getting ready for him,' said Winton.

'Ye-es. Had in store for him.'

'Yet he brushed aside his kinsmen and the people delaying his return.'

'Ye-es; but then how do you render *obstantes*?'

'If it's a free translation mightn't *obstantes* and *morantem* come to about the same thing, sir?'

'Nothing comes to "about the same thing" with Horace, Winton. As I have said, Horace was not a journalist. No, I take it that his kinsmen bodily withstood his departure, whereas the crowd—*populumque*—the democracy stood about futilely pitying him and getting in the way. Now for that noblest of endings—*quam si clientum*,' and King ran off into the quotation:—

> 'As though, some tedious business o'er
> Of clients' court, his journey lay
> Towards Venafrum's grassy floor
> Or Sparta-built Tarentum's bay.

All right, Winton. Beetle, when you've quite finished dodging the fresh air yonder, give me the meaning of *tendens*—and turn down your collar.'

'Me, sir? *Tendens*, sir? Oh! Stretching away in the direction of, sir.'

'Idiot! Regulus was not a feature of the landscape. He was a man, self-doomed to death by torture. *Atqui sciebat*—knowing it—having achieved it for his country's sake—can't you hear that *atqui* cut like a knife?—he moved off with some dignity. That is why Horace out of the whole golden Latin tongue chose the one word *tendens*—which is utterly untranslatable.'

The gross injustice of being asked to translate it converted Beetle into a young Christian martyr, till King buried his nose in his handkerchief again.

'I think they've broken another gas-bottle next door, sir,' said Howell. 'They're always doing it.' The Form coughed as more chlorine came in.

'Well, I suppose we must be patient with the Modern Side,' said King. 'But it is almost insupportable for this Side. Vernon, what are you grinning at?'

Vernon's mind had returned to him glowing and inspired. He chuckled as he underlined his Horace.

'It appears to amuse you,' said King. 'Let us participate. What is it?'

'The last two lines of the Tenth Ode, in this Book, sir,' was Vernon's amazing reply.

'What? Oh, I see. *Non hoc semper erit liminis aut aquae caelestis patiens latus.*'[1] King's mouth twitched to hide a grin. 'Was that done with intention?'

'I—I thought it fitted, sir.'

'It does. It's distinctly happy. What put it into your thick head, Paddy?'

'I don't know, sir, except we did the Ode last term.'

'And you remembered? The same head that minted *pro-*

---

[1] 'This side will not always be patient of rain and waiting on the threshold.'

brosis as a verb! Vernon, you are an enigma. No! This Side will *not* always be patient of unheavenly gases and waters. I will make representations to our so-called Moderns. Meantime (who shall say I am not just?) I remit you your accrued pains and penalties in regard to *probrosim, probrosis, probosit* and other enormities. I oughtn't to do it, but this Side is occasionally human. By no means bad, Paddy.'

'Thank you, sir,' said Vernon, wondering how inspiration had visited him.

Then King, with a few brisk remarks about Science, headed them back to Regulus, of whom and of Horace and Rome and evil-minded commercial Carthage and of the democracy eternally futile, he explained, in all ages and climes, he spoke for ten minutes; passing thence to the next Ode—*Delicta majorum*—where he fetched up, full-voiced, upon—'*Dis te minorem quod geris imperas*' (Thou rulest because thou bearest thyself as lower than the Gods)—making it a text for a discourse on manners, morals, and respect for authority as distinct from bottled gases, which lasted till the bell rang. Then Beetle, concertinaing his books, observed to Winton, 'When King's really on tap he's an interestin' dog. Hartopp's chlorine uncorked him.'

'Yes; but why did you tell me *delubris* was "deluges," you silly ass?' said Winton.

'Well, that uncorked him too. Look out, you hoof-handed old owl!' Winton had cleared for action as the Form poured out like puppies at play and was scragging Beetle. Stalky from behind collared Winton low. The three fell in confusion.

'*Dis te minorem quod geris imperas,*' quoth Stalky, ruffling Winton's lint-white locks. 'Mustn't jape with Number Five study. Don't be too virtuous. Don't brood over it. 'Twon't count against you in your future caree-ah. Cheer up, Pater.'

'Pull him off my—er—essential guts, will you?' said Beetle from beneath. 'He's squashin' 'em.'

They dispersed to their studies.

No one, the owner least of all, can explain what is in a growing boy's mind. It might have been the blind ferment of adolescence; Stalky's random remarks about virtue might have stirred him; like his betters he might have sought popularity by way of clowning; or, as the Head asserted years later, the only known jest of his serious life might have worked on him, as a sober-sided man's one love colours and dislocates all his after days. But, at the next lesson, mechanical drawing with Mr. Lidgett, who as drawing-master had very limited powers of punishment, Winton fell suddenly from grace and let loose a live mouse in the form-room. The whole Form, shrieking and leaping high, threw at it all the plaster cones, pyramids, and fruit in high relief—not to mention ink-pots—that they could lay hands on. Mr. Lidgett reported at once to the Head; Winton owned up to his crime, which, venial in the Upper Third, pardonable at a price in the Lower Fourth, was, of course, rank ruffianism on the part of a Fifth Form boy; and so, by graduated stages, he arrived at the Head's study just before lunch, penitent, perturbed, annoyed with himself, and —as the Head said to King in the corridor after the meal— more human than he had known him in seven years.

'You see,' the Head drawled on, 'Winton's only fault is a certain costive and unaccommodating virtue. So this comes very happily.'

'I've never noticed any sign of it,' said King. Winton was in King's House, and though King as pro-consul might, and did, infernally oppress his own Province, once a black-and-yellow cap was in trouble at the hands of the Imperial authority King fought for him to the very last steps of Caesar's throne.

'Well, you yourself admitted just now that a mouse was beneath the occasion,' the Head answered.

'It was.' Mr. King did not love Mr. Lidgett. 'It should have been a rat. But—but—I hate to plead it—it's the lad's first offence.'

'Could you have damned him more completely, King?'

'Hm. What is the penalty?' said King, in retreat, but keeping up a rear-guard action.

'Only my usual few lines of Virgil to be shown up by tea-time.'

The Head's eyes turned slightly to that end of the corridor where Mullins, Head of Games ('Pot,' 'old Pot,' or 'Potiphar' Mullins), was pinning up the usual Wednesday notice —'Big, Middle, and Little Side Football—A to K, L to Z, 3 to 4.45 P.M.'

You cannot write out the Head's usual few (which means five hundred) Latin lines and play football for one hour and three-quarters between the hours of 1.30 and 5 P.M. Winton had evidently no intention of trying to do so, for he hung about the corridor with a set face and an uneasy foot. Yet it was law in the school, compared with which that of the Medes and Persians was no more than a non-committal resolution, that any boy, outside the First Fifteen, who missed his football for any reason whatever, and had not a written excuse, duly signed by competent authority, to explain his absence, would receive not less than three strokes with a ground-ash from the Head of Games, generally a youth between seventeen and eighteen years, rarely under eleven stone (Pot was nearer thirteen), and always in hard condition.

King knew without inquiry that the Head had given Winton no such excuse.

'But he is practically a member of the First Fifteen. He has played for it all this term,' said King. 'I believe his Cap should have arrived last week.'

'His Cap has not been given him. Officially, therefore, he is naught. I rely on old Pot.'

'But Mullins is Winton's study-mate,' King persisted.

Pot Mullins and Pater Winton were cousins and rather close friends.

'That will make no difference to Mullins—or Winton, if I know 'em,' said the Head.

'But—but,' King played his last card desperately, 'I was going to recommend Winton for extra sub-prefect in my House, now Carton has gone.'

'Certainly,' said the Head. 'Why not? He will be excellent by tea-time, I hope.'

At that moment they saw Mr. Lidgett, tripping down the corridor, waylaid by Winton.

'It's about that mouse business at mechanical drawing,' Winton opened, swinging across his path.

'Yes, yes, highly disgraceful,' Mr. Lidgett panted.

'I know it was,' said Winton. 'It—it was a cad's trick be-cause——'

'Because you knew I couldn't give you more than fifty lines,' said Mr. Lidgett.

'Well, anyhow, I've come to apologise for it.'

'Certainly,' said Mr. Lidgett, and added, for he was a kindly man, 'I think that shows quite right feeling. I'll tell the Head at once I'm satisfied.'

'No—no!' The boy's still unmended voice jumped from the growl to the squeak. 'I didn't mean *that*! I—I did it on principle. Please don't—er—do anything of the kind.'

Mr. Lidgett looked him up and down and, being an artist, understood.

'Thank you, Winton,' he said. 'This shall be between ourselves.'

'You heard?' said King, indecent pride in his voice.

'Of course. You thought he was going to get Lidgett to beg him off the impot.'

King denied this with so much warmth that the Head laughed and King moved away in a huff.

'By the way,' said the Head, 'I've told Winton to do his lines in your form-room—not in his study.'

'Thanks,' said King over his shoulder, for the Head's orders had saved Winton and Mullins, who was doing extra Army work in the study, from an embarrassing afternoon together.

An hour later, King wandered into his still form-room as though by accident. Winton was hard at work.

'Aha!' said King, rubbing his hands. 'This does not look like games, Winton. Don't let me arrest your facile pen. Whence this sudden love for Virgil?'

'Impot from the Head, sir, for that mouse business this morning.'

'Rumours thereof have reached us. That was a lapse on your part into Lower Thirdery which I don't quite understand.'

The 'tump-tump' of the puntabouts before the sides settled to games came through the open window. Winton, like his House-master, loved fresh air. Then they heard Paddy Vernon, sub-prefect on duty, calling the roll in the field and marking defaulters. Winton wrote steadily. King curled himself up on a desk, hands round knees. One would have said that the man was gloating over the boy's misfortune, but the boy understood.

'*Dis te minorem quod geris imperas*,' King quoted presently.
'It is necessary to bear oneself as lower than the local gods—
even than drawing-masters who are precluded from effective
retaliation. I *do* wish you'd tried that mouse game with me,
Pater.'

Winton grinned; then sobered. 'It was a cad's trick, sir, to
play on Mr. Lidgett.' He peered forward at the page he was
copying.

'Well, "the sin *I* impute to each frustrate ghost"——' King
stopped himself. 'Why do you goggle like an owl? Hand me
the Mantuan and I'll dictate. No matter. Any rich Virgilian
measures will serve. I may peradventure recall a few.' He
began:—

'*Tu regere imperio populos Romane memento;*
Hae tibi erunt artes pacisque imponere morem,
Parcere subjectis et debellare superbos.

There you have it all, Winton. Write that out twice and yet
once again.'

For the next forty minutes, with never a glance at the
book, King paid out the glorious hexameters (and King could
read Latin as though it were alive), Winton hauling them in
and coiling them away behind him as trimmers in a tele-
graph-ship's hold coil away deep-sea cable. King broke from
the Aeneid to the Georgics and back again, pausing now and
then to translate some specially loved line or to dwell on the
treble-shot texture of the ancient fabric. He did not allude to
the coming interview with Mullins except at the last, when
he said, 'I think at this juncture, Pater, I need not ask you
for the precise significance of *atqui sciebat quae sibi barbarus*
tortor pararet.'

REGULUS

The ungrateful Winton flushed angrily, and King loafed out to take five o'clock call-over, after which he invited little Hartopp to tea and a talk on chlorine gas. Hartopp accepted the challenge like a bantam, and the two went up to King's study about the same time as Winton returned to the form-room beneath it to finish his lines.

Then half-a-dozen of the Second Fifteen who should have been washing strolled in to condole with Pater Winton, whose misfortune and its consequences were common talk. No one was more sincere than the long, red-headed, knotty-knuckled Paddy Vernon, but, being a careless animal, he joggled Winton's desk.

'Curse you for a silly ass!' said Winton. 'Don't do that.'

No one is expected to be polite while under punishment, so Vernon, sinking his sub-prefectship, replied peacefully enough:

'Well, don't be wrathy, Pater.'

'I'm not,' said Winton. 'Get out! This ain't your House form-room.'

'Form-room don't belong to you. Why don't you go to your own study?' Vernon replied.

'Because Mullins is there waitin' for the victim,' said Stalky delicately, and they all laughed. 'You ought to have shaken that mouse out of your trouser-leg, Pater. That's the way *I* did in my youth. Pater's revertin' to his second childhood. Never mind, Pater, we all respect you and your future caree-ah.'

Winton, still writhing, growled. Vernon, leaning on the desk, somehow shook it again. Then he laughed.

'What are you grinning at?' Winton asked.

'I was only thinkin' of *you* being sent up to take a lickin' from Pot. I swear I don't think it's fair. You've never shirked a game in your life, and you're as good as in the First Fifteen already. Your Cap ought to have been delivered last week, oughtn't it?'

It was law in the school that no man could by any means enjoy the privileges and immunities of the First Fifteen till the black velvet cap with the gold tassel, made by dilatory Exeter outfitters, had been actually set on his head. Ages ago, a large-built and unruly Second Fifteen had attempted to change this law, but the prefects of that age were still larger, and the lively experiment had never been repeated.

'Will you,' said Winton very slowly, 'kindly mind your own damned business, you cursed, clumsy, fat-headed fool?'

The form-room was as silent as the empty field in the darkness outside. Vernon shifted his feet uneasily.

'Well, *I* shouldn't like to take a lickin' from Pot,' he said.

'Wouldn't you?' Winton asked, as he paged the sheets of lines with hands that shook.

'No, I shouldn't,' said Vernon, his freckles growing more distinct on the bridge of his white nose.

'Well, I'm going to take it'—Winton moved clear of the desk as he spoke. 'But *you*'re going to take a lickin' from me first.' Before any one realised it, he had flung himself neighing against Vernon. No decencies were observed on either side, and the rest looked on amazed. The two met confusedly, Vernon trying to do what he could with his longer reach; Winton, insensible to blows, only concerned to drive his enemy into a corner and batter him to pulp. This he managed over against the fireplace, where Vernon dropped half-stunned. 'Now I'm going to give you your lickin',' said Winton. 'Lie there till I get a ground-ash and I'll cut you to pieces. If you move, I'll chuck you out of the window.' He wound his hands into the boy's collar and waistband, and had actually heaved him half off the ground before the others with one accord dropped on his head, shoulders, and legs. He fought them crazily in an awful hissing silence. Stalky's sensitive nose was rubbed along the floor; Beetle received a jolt in the wind that sent him whistling and crowing against the wall; Perowne's forehead was cut, and Malpass came out with an eye that explained itself like a dying rainbow through a whole week.

'Mad! Quite mad!' said Stalky, and for the third time wriggled back to Winton's throat. The door opened and King came in, Hartopp's little figure just behind him. The mound on the floor panted and heaved but did not rise, for Winton still squirmed vengefully. 'Only a little play, sir,' said Perowne. 'Only hit my head against a form.' This was quite true.

'Oh,' said King. '*Dimovit obstantes propinquos.* You, I presume, are the *populus* delaying Winton's return to—Mullins, eh?'

'No, sir,' said Stalky behind his claret-coloured handkerchief. 'We're the *maerentes amicos*.'

'Not bad! You see, some of it sticks after all,' King chuckled to Hartopp, and the two masters left without further inquiries.

The boys sat still on the now passive Winton.

'Well,' said Stalky at last, 'of all the putrid he-asses, Pater, you are the——'

'I'm sorry. I'm awfully sorry,' Winton began, and they let him rise. He held out his hand to the bruised and bewildered Vernon. 'Sorry, Paddy. I—I must have lost my temper. I—I don't know what's the matter with me.'

'Fat lot of good that'll do my face at tea,' Vernon grunted. 'Why couldn't you say there was something wrong with you instead of lamming out like a lunatic? Is my lip puffy?'

'Just a trifle. Look at my beak! Well, we got all these pretty marks at footer—owin' to the zeal with which we played the game,' said Stalky, dusting himself. 'But d'you think you're fit to be let loose again, Pater? Sure you don't want to kill another sub-prefect? I wish *I* was Pot. I'd cut your sprightly young soul out.'

'I s'pose I ought to go to Pot now,' said Winton.

'And let all the other asses see you lookin' like this! Not much. We'll all come up to Number Five study and wash off in hot water. Beetle, you aren't damaged. Go along and light the gas-stove.'

'There's a tin of cocoa in my study somewhere,' Perowne shouted after him. 'Rootle round till you find it, and take it up.'

Separately, by different roads, Vernon's jersey pulled half over his head, the boys repaired to Number Five study. Little Hartopp and King, I am sorry to say, leaned over the banisters of King's landing and watched.

'Ve-ry human,' said little Hartopp. 'Your virtuous Winton, having got himself into trouble, takes it out of my poor old Paddy. I wonder what precise lie Paddy will tell about his face.'

'But surely you aren't going to embarrass him by asking?' said King.

'*Your* boy won,' said Hartopp.

'To go back to what we were discussing,' said King quickly, 'do you pretend that your modern system of inculcating unrelated facts about chlorine, for instance, all of which may be proved fallacies by the time the boys grow up, can have any real bearing on education—even the low type of it that examiners expect?'

'I maintain nothing. But is it any worse than your Chinese reiteration of uncomprehended syllables in a dead tongue?'

REGULUS

'Dead, forsooth!' King fairly danced. 'The only living tongue on earth! Chinese! On my word, Hartopp!'

'And at the end of seven years—how often have I said it?' Hartopp went on,—'seven years of two hundred and twenty days of six hours each, your victims go away with nothing, absolutely nothing, except, perhaps, if they've been very attentive, a dozen—no, I'll grant you twenty—one score of totally unrelated Latin tags which any child of twelve could have absorbed in two terms.'

'But—but can't you realise that if our system brings later—at any rate—at a pinch—a simple understanding—grammar and Latinity apart—a mere glimpse of the significance (foul word!) of, we'll say, one Ode of Horace, one twenty lines of Virgil, we've got what we poor devils of ushers are striving after?'

'And what might that be?' said Hartopp.

'Balance, proportion, perspective—life. Your scientific man is the unrelated animal—the beast without background. Haven't you ever realised *that* in your atmosphere of stinks?'

'Meantime you make them lose life for the sake of living, eh?'

'Blind again, Hartopp! I told you about Paddy's quotation this morning. (But he made *probrosis* a verb, he did!) You yourself heard young Corkran's reference to *maerentes amicos*. It sticks—a little of it sticks among the barbarians.'

'Absolutely and essentially Chinese,' said little Hartopp, who, alone of the Common-room, refused to be outfaced by King. 'But I don't yet understand how Paddy came to be licked by Winton. Paddy's supposed to be something of a boxer.'

'Beware of vinegar made from honey,' King replied. 'Pater, like some other people, is patient and long-suffering, but he

215

has his limits. The Head is oppressing him damnably, too. As I pointed out, the boy has practically been in the First Fifteen since term began.'

'But, my dear fellow, I've known you give a boy an impot and refuse him leave off games, again and again.'

'Ah, but that was when there was real need to get at some oaf who couldn't be sensitised in any other way. Now, in our esteemed Head's action I see nothing but——'

The conversation from this point does not concern us.

Meantime Winton, very penitent and especially polite towards Vernon, was being cheered with cocoa in Number Five study. They had some difficulty in stemming the flood of his apologies. He himself pointed out to Vernon that he had attacked a sub-prefect for no reason whatever, and, therefore, deserved official punishment.

'I can't think what was the matter with me to-day,' he mourned. 'Ever since that blasted mouse business——'

'Well, then, don't think,' said Stalky. 'Or do you want Paddy to make a row about it before all the Coll.?'

Here Vernon was understood to say that he would see Winton and all the Coll. somewhere else.

'And if you imagine Perowne and Malpass and me are goin' to give evidence at a prefects' meetin' just to soothe your beastly conscience, you jolly well err,' said Beetle. 'I know what you did.'

'What?' croaked Pater, out of the valley of his humiliation.

'You went Berserk. I've read all about it in *Hypatia*.'

'What's "going Berserk"?' Winton asked.

'Never you mind,' was the reply. 'Now, don't you feel awfully weak and seedy?'

'I *am* rather tired,' said Winton, sighing.

'That's what you ought to be. You've gone Berserk and pretty soon you'll go to sleep. But you'll probably be liable to fits of it all your life,' Beetle concluded. 'Shouldn't wonder if you murdered some one some day.'

'Shut up—you and your Berserks!' said Stalky. 'Go to Mullins now and get it over, Pater.'

'I call it filthy unjust of the Head,' said Vernon. 'Anyhow, you've given me my lickin', old man. I hope Pot'll give you yours.'

'I'm awfully sorry—awfully sorry,' was Winton's last word.

It was the custom in that consulship to deal with games' defaulters between five o'clock call-over and tea. Mullins, who was old enough to pity, did not believe in letting boys wait through the night till the chill of the next morning for their punishments. He was finishing off the last of the small fry and their excuses when Winton arrived.

'But, please, Mullins'—this was Babcock tertius, a dear little twelve-year-old mother's darling—'I had an awful hack on the knee. I've been to the Matron about it and she gave me some iodine. I've been rubbing it in all day. I thought that would be an excuse off.'

'Let's have a look at it,' said the impassive Mullins. 'That's a shin-bruise—about a week old. Touch your toes. I'll give you the iodine.'

Babcock yelled loudly as he had many times before. The face of Jevons, aged eleven, a new boy that dark wet term, low in the House, low in the Lower School, and lowest of all in his homesick little mind, turned white at the horror of the sight. They could hear his working lips part stickily as Babcock wailed his way out of hearing.

'Hullo, Jevons! What brings you here?' said Mullins.

'Pl-ease, sir, I went for a walk with Babcock tertius.'

'Did you? Then I bet you went to the tuck-shop—and you paid, didn't you?'

A nod. Jevons was too terrified to speak.

'Of course, and I bet Babcock told you that old Pot 'ud let you off because it was the first time.'

Another nod with a ghost of a smile in it.

'All right.' Mullins picked Jevons up before he could guess what was coming, laid him on the table with one hand, with the other gave him three emphatic spanks, then held him high in air.

'Now you tell Babcock tertius that he's got you a licking from me, and see you jolly well pay it back to him. And when you're Head of Games don't you let any one shirk his footer without a written excuse. Where d'you play in your game?'

'Forward, sir.'

'You can do better than that. I've seen you run like a young buck-rabbit. Ask Dickson from me to try you as three-quarter next game, will you? Cut along.'

Jevons left, warm for the first time that day, enormously set up in his own esteem, and very hot against the deceitful Babcock.

Mullins turned to Winton. 'Your name's on the list, Pater.' Winton nodded.

'I know it. The Head landed me with an impot for that mouse business at mechanical drawing. No excuse.'

'He meant it then?' Mullins jerked his head delicately towards the ground-ash on the table. 'I heard something about it.'

Winton nodded. 'A rotten thing to do,' he said. 'Can't think what I was doing ever to do it. It counts against a fellow so; and there's some more too——'

'All right, Pater. Just stand clear of our photo-bracket, will you?'

The little formality over, there was a pause. Winton swung round, yawned in Pot's astonished face and staggered towards the window-seat.

'What's the matter with you, Dick? Ill?'

'No. Perfectly all right, thanks. Only—only a little sleepy.' Winton stretched himself out, and then and there fell deeply and placidly asleep.

'It isn't a faint,' said the experienced Mullins, 'or his pulse wouldn't act. 'Tisn't a fit or he'd snort and twitch. It can't be sunstroke, this term, and he hasn't been over-training for anything.' He opened Winton's collar, packed a cushion under his head, threw a rug over him and sat down to listen to the regular breathing. Before long Stalky arrived, on pretence of borrowing a book. He looked at the window-seat.

'Noticed anything wrong with Winton lately?' said Mullins.

'Notice anything wrong with my beak?' Stalky replied. 'Pater went Berserk after call-over, and fell on a lot of us for jestin' with him about his impot. You ought to see Malpass's eye.'

'You mean that Pater fought?' said Mullins.

'Like a devil. Then he nearly went to sleep in our study just now. I expect he'll be all right when he wakes up. Rummy business! Conscientious old bargee. You ought to have heard his apologies.'

'But Pater can't fight one little bit,' Mullins repeated.

''Twasn't fightin'. He just tried to murder every one.' Stalky described the affair, and when he left Mullins went off to take counsel with the Head, who, out of a cloud of blue smoke, told him that all would yet be well.

'Winton,' said he, 'is a little stiff in his moral joints. He'll get over that. If he asks you whether to-day's doings will count against him in his——'

'But you know it's important to him, sir. His people aren't —very well off,' said Mullins.

'That's why I'm taking all this trouble. You must reassure him, Pot. I have overcrowded him with new experiences. Oh, by the way, has his Cap come?'

'It came at dinner, sir.' Mullins laughed.

Sure enough, when he waked at tea-time, Winton proposed to take Mullins all through every one of his day's lapses from grace, and 'Do you think it will count against me?' said he.

'Don't you fuss so much about yourself and your silly career,' said Mullins. 'You're all right. And oh—here's your First Cap at last. Shove it up on the bracket and come on to tea.'

They met King on their way, stepping statelily and rubbing his hands. 'I have applied,' said he, 'for the services of an additional sub-prefect in Carton's unlamented absence. Your name, Winton, seems to have found favour with the powers that be, and—and all things considered—I am disposed to give my support to the nomination. You are therefore a quasi-lictor.'

'Then it didn't count against me,' Winton gasped as soon as they were out of hearing.

A Head of Games can jest with a sub-prefect publicly.

'You utter ass!' said Mullins, and caught him by the back of his stiff neck and ran him down to the hall, where the sub-prefects, who sit below the salt, made him welcome with the economical bloater-paste of mid-term.

King and little Hartopp were sparring in the Reverend John Gillett's study at 10 P.M.—classical *versus* modern as usual.

'Character—proportion—background,' snarled King. 'That is the essence of the Humanities.'

'Analects of Confucius,' little Hartopp answered.

'Time,' said the Reverend John behind the soda-water. 'You men oppress me. Hartopp, what did you say to Paddy in your dormitories to-night? Even *you* couldn't have overlooked his face.'

'But I did,' said Hartopp calmly. 'I wasn't even humorous about it, as some clerics might have been. I went straight through and said naught.'

'Poor Paddy! Now, for my part,' said King, 'and you know I am not lavish in my praises, I consider Winton a first-class type; absolutely first-class.'

'Ha-ardly,' said the Reverend John. 'First-class of the second class, I admit. The very best type of second class, but'—he shook his head—'it should have been a rat. Pater'll never be anything more than a Colonel of Engineers.'

'What do you base that verdict on?' said King stiffly.

'He came to me after prayers—with all his conscience.'

'Poor old Pater. Was it the mouse?' said little Hartopp.

'That, and what he called his uncontrollable temper, and his responsibilities as sub-prefect.'

'And you?'

'If we had had what is vulgarly called a pi-jaw he'd have had hysterics. So I recommended a dose of Epsom salts. He'll take it, too—conscientiously. Don't eat me, King. Perhaps he'll be a K.C.B.'

Ten o'clock struck and the Army Class boys in the further studies coming to their Houses after an hour's extra work passed along the gravel path below. Some one was chanting, to the tune of 'White sand and grey sand,' *Dis te minorem quod geris imperas.* He stopped outside Mullins' study. They heard Mullins' window slide up and then Stalky's voice:

'Ah! Good-evenin', Mullins, my *barbarus tortor*. We're the waits. We have come to inquire after the local Berserk. Is he doin' as well as can be expected in his new caree-ah?'

'Better than you will, in a sec, Stalky,' Mullins grunted.

'Glad of that. We thought he'd like to know that Paddy has been carried to the sick-house in ravin' delirium. They think it's concussion of the brain.'

'Why, he was all right at prayers,' Winton began earnestly, and they heard a laugh in the background as Mullins slammed down the window.

' 'Night, Regulus,' Stalky sang out, and the light footsteps went on.

'You see. It sticks. A little of it sticks among the barbarians,' said King.

'Amen,' said the Reverend John. 'Go to bed.'

A TRANSLATION

HORACE, Bk. V, Ode 3

There are whose study is of smells,
  And to attentive schools rehearse
How something mixed with something else
  Makes something worse.

Some cultivate in broths impure
  The clients of our body—these,
Increasing without Venus, cure,
  Or cause, disease.

Others the heated wheel extol,
  And all its offspring, whose concern
Is how to make it farthest roll
  And fastest turn.

Me, much incurious if the hour
  Present, or to be paid for, brings
Me to Brundusium by the power
  Of wheels or wings;

Me, in whose breast no flame hath burned
  Life-long, save that by Pindar lit,
Such lore leaves cold: I am not turned
  Aside to it

More than when, sunk in thought profound
My steward (friend but slave) brings round
  Of what the unaltering Gods require,
    Logs for my fire.

A LITTLE PREP.

A LITTLE PREP.

Qui procul hinc—the legend's writ,
   The frontier grave is far away;
Qui ante diem periit,
   Sed miles, sed pro patriâ.
                              NEWBOLT.

THE EASTER TERM was but a month old when Stettson major,
a day-boy, contracted diphtheria, and the Head was very angry.
He decreed a new and narrower set of bounds—the infection
had been traced to an outlying farmhouse—urged the prefects
to lick all trespassers severely, and promised extra attentions
from his own hand. There were no words bad enough for
Stettson major, quarantined at his mother's house, who had
lowered the school average of health. This he said in the gymnasium after prayers. Then he wrote some two hundred letters
to as many anxious parents and guardians, and bade the school
carry on. The trouble did not spread, but, one night, a dog-cart
drove to the Head's door, and in the morning the Head had
gone, leaving all things in charge of Mr. King, senior House-
master. The Head often ran up to Town, where the school
devoutly believed he bribed officials for early proofs of the
Army Examination papers; but this absence was unusually
prolonged.

   'Downy old bird!' said Stalky to the allies, one wet afternoon,
in the study. 'He must have gone on a bend an' been locked
up, under a false name.'

227

'What for?' Beetle entered joyously into the libel.

'Forty shillin's or a month for hackin' the chucker-out of the Pavvy on the shins. Bates always has a spree when he goes to Town. Wish he was back, though. I'm about sick o' King's "whips an' scorpions" an' lectures on public-school spirit—yah!—and scholarship!'

' "Crass an' materialised brutality of the middle-classes—readin' solely for marks. Not a scholar in the whole school," ' M'Turk quoted, pensively boring holes in the mantelpiece with a hot poker.

'That's rather a sickly way of spending an afternoon. Stinks, too. Let's come out an' smoke. Here's a treat.' Stalky held up a long Indian cheroot. 'Bagged it from my pater last holidays. I'm a bit shy of it, though; it's heftier than a pipe. We'll smoke it palaver-fashion. Hand it round, eh? Let's lie up behind the old harrow on the Monkey-farm Road.'

'Out of bounds. Bounds beastly strict these days, too. Besides, we shall cat.' Beetle sniffed the cheroot critically. 'It's a regular Pomposo Stinkadore.'

'You can. I shan't. What d'you say, Turkey?'

'Oh, may's well, I s'pose.'

'Chuck on your cap, then. It's two to one, Beetle. Hout you come!'

They saw a group of boys by the notice-board in the corridor; little Foxy, the school Sergeant, among them.

'More bounds, I expect,' said Stalky. 'Hullo, Foxibus, who are you in mournin' for?' There was a broad band of crape round Foxy's arm.

'He was in my old Regiment,' said Foxy, jerking his head towards the notices, where a newspaper cutting was thumb-tacked between call-over lists.

'By Gum!' quoth Stalky, uncovering as he read. 'It's old

Duncan—Fat-Sow Duncan—killed on duty at something or other Kotal. *"Rallyin' his men with conspicuous gallantry."* He would, of course. *"The body was recovered."* That's all right. They cut 'em up sometimes, don't they, Foxy?'

'Horrid,' said the Sergeant briefly.

'Poor old Fat-Sow! I was a fag when he left. How many does that make to us, Foxy?'

'Mr. Duncan, he is the ninth. He came here when he was no bigger than little Grey tertius. My old Regiment, too. Yiss, nine to us, Mr. Corkran, up to date.'

The boys went out into the wet, walking swiftly.

'Wonder how it feels—to be shot an' all that,' said Stalky, as they splashed down a lane. 'Where did it happen, Beetle?'

'Oh, out in India somewhere. We're always rowin' there. But look here, Stalky, what is the good o' sittin' under a hedge an' cattin'? It's be-eastly cold. It's be-eastly wet, an' we'll be collared as sure as a gun.'

'Shut up! Did you ever know your Uncle Stalky get you into a mess yet?' Like many other leaders, Stalky did not dwell on past defeats.

They pushed through a dripping hedge, landed among water-logged clods, and sat down on a rust-coated harrow. The cheroot burned with sputterings of saltpetre. They smoked it gingerly, each passing to the other between closed forefinger and thumb.

'Good job we hadn't one apiece, ain't it?' said Stalky, shivering, through set teeth. To prove his words he immediately laid all before them, and they followed his example. . . .

'I told you,' moaned Beetle, sweating clammy drops. 'Oh, Stalky, you *are* a fool!'

'Je cat, tu cat, il cat. Nous cattons!' M'Turk handed up his contribution and lay hopelessly on the cold iron.

'Something's wrong with the beastly thing. I say, Beetle, have you been droppin' ink on it?'

But Beetle was in no case to answer. Limp and empty, they sprawled across the harrow, the rust marking their ulsters in red squares and the abandoned cheroot-end reeking under their very cold noses. Then—they had heard nothing—the Head himself stood before them—the Head who should have been in Town bribing examiners—the Head fantastically attired in old tweeds and a deer-stalker!

'Ah,' he said, fingering his moustache. 'Very good. I might have guessed who it was. You will go back to the College and give my compliments to Mr. King and ask him to give you an extra-special licking. You will then do me five hundred lines. I shall be back to-morrow. Five hundred lines by five o'clock to-morrow. You are also gated for a week. This is not exactly the time for breaking bounds. *Extra*-special, please.'

He disappeared over the hedge as lightly as he had come. There was a murmur of women's voices in the deep lane.

'Oh, you Prooshian brute!' said M'Turk as the voices died away. 'Stalky, it's all your silly fault.'

'Kill him! Kill him!' gasped Beetle.

'I ca-an't. I'm going to cat again . . . I don't mind that, but King'll gloat over us horrid. Extra-special, ooh!'

Stalky made no answer—not even a soft one. They went to College and received that for which they had been sent. King enjoyed himself most thoroughly, for by virtue of their seniority the boys were exempt from his hand, save under special order. Luckily, he was no expert in the gentle art.

' "Strange, how desire doth outrun performance," ' said Beetle irreverently, quoting from some Shakespeare play that they were cramming that term. They regained their study and settled down to the imposition.

'You're quite right, Beetle.' Stalky spoke in silky and propitiating tones. 'Now, if the Head had sent us up to a prefect, we'd have got something to remember!'

'Look here,' M'Turk began with cold venom, 'we aren't going to row you about this business, because it's too bad for a row; but we want you to understand you're jolly well excommunicated, Stalky. You're a plain ass.'

'How was I to know that the Head 'ud collar us? What was he doin' in those ghastly clothes, too?'

'Don't try to raise a side-issue,' Beetle grunted severely.

'Well, it was all Stettson major's fault. If he hadn't gone an' got diphtheria 'twouldn't have happened. But don't you think it rather rummy—the Head droppin' on us that way?'

'Shut up! You're dead!' said Beetle. 'We've chopped your spurs off your beastly heels. We've cocked your shield upside down, and—and I don't think you ought to be allowed to brew for a month.'

'Oh, stop jawin' at me. I want——'

'Stop? Why—why, we're gated for a week.' M'Turk almost howled as the agony of the situation overcame him. 'A lickin' from King, five hundred lines, *and* a gating. D'you expect us to kiss you, Stalky, you beast?'

'Drop rottin' for a minute. I want to find out about the Head bein' where he was.'

'Well, you have. You found him quite well and fit. Found him making love to Stettson major's mother. That was her in the lane—I heard her. And *so* we were ordered a licking before a day-boy's mother. Bony old widow, too,' said M'Turk. 'Anything else you'd like to find out?'

'I don't care. I swear I'll get even with him some day,' Stalky growled.

'Looks like it,' said M'Turk. 'Extra-special, week's gating and

five hundred . . . and now you're goin' to row about it! Help
scrag him, Beetle!' Stalky had thrown his Virgil at them.

The Head returned next day without explanation, to find
the lines waiting for him and the school a little relaxed under
Mr. King's viceroyalty. Mr. King had been talking at and
round and over the boys' heads, in a lofty and promiscuous
style, of public-school spirit and the traditions of ancient seats;
for he always improved an occasion. Beyond waking in two
hundred and fifty young hearts a lively hatred of all other
foundations, he accomplished little—so little, indeed, that
when, two days after the Head's return, he chanced to come
across Stalky & Co., gated but ever resourceful, playing marbles
in the corridor, he said that he was not surprised—not in the
least surprised. This was what he had expected from persons
of their morale.

'But there isn't any rule against marbles, sir. Very interestin'
game,' said Beetle, his knees white with chalk and dust. Then
he received two hundred lines for insolence, besides an order
to go to the nearest prefect for judgment and slaughter.

This is what happened behind the closed doors of Flint's
study, and Flint was then Head of Games:—

'Oh, I say, Flint. King has sent me to you for playin' marbles
in the corridor an' shoutin' "alley tor" an' "knuckle down." '

'What does he suppose I have to do with that?' was the
answer.

'Dunno. Well?' Beetle grinned wickedly. 'What am I to tell
him? He's rather wrathy about it.'

'If the Head chooses to put a notice in the corridor forbiddin'
marbles, I can do something; but I can't move on a House-
master's report. He knows that as well as I do.'

The sense of this oracle Beetle conveyed, all unsweetened, to
King, who hastened to interview Flint.

A LITTLE PREP.

Now Flint had been seven and a half years at the College, counting six months with a London crammer, from whose roof he had returned, homesick, to the Head for the final Army polish. There were four or five other seniors who had gone through much the same mill, not to mention boys, rejected by other establishments on account of a certain overwhelmingness, whom the Head had wrought into very fair shape. It was not a Sixth to be handled without gloves, as King found.

'Am I to understand it is your intention to allow Board-school games under your study windows, Flint? If so, I can only say——' He said much, and Flint listened politely.

'Well, sir, if the Head sees fit to call a prefects' meeting we are bound to take the matter up. But the tradition of the school is that the prefects can't move in any matter affecting the whole school without the Head's direct order.'

Much more was then delivered; both sides a little losing their temper.

After tea, at an informal gathering of prefects in his study, Flint related the adventure.

'He's been playin' for this for a week, and now he's got it. You know as well as I do that if he hadn't been gassin' at us the way he has, that young devil Beetle wouldn't have dreamed of marbles.'

'We know that,' said Perowne, 'but that isn't the question. On Flint's showin' King has called the prefects names enough to justify a first-class row. Crammers' rejections, ill-regulated hobbledehoys, wasn't it? Now it's impossible for prefects——'

'Rot,' said Flint, 'King's the best classical cram we've got; and 'tisn't fair to bother the Head with a row. He's up to his eyes with extra-tu. and Army work as it is. Besides, as I told King, we aren't a public school. We're a limited liability company payin' four per cent. My father's a shareholder, too.'

'What's that got to do with it?' said Venner, a red-headed boy of eighteen.

'Well, seems to me that we should be interferin' with ourselves. We've got to get into the Army or—get out, haven't we? King's hired by the Council to teach us. All the rest's flumdiddle. Can't you see?'

It might have been because he felt the air was a little thunderous that the Head took his after-dinner cheroot to Flint's study; but he so often began an evening in a prefect's room that nobody suspected when he drifted in politely, after the knocks that etiquette demanded.

'Prefects' meeting?' A cock of one wise eyebrow.

'Not exactly, sir; we're just talking things over. Won't you take the easy chair?'

'Thanks. Luxurious infants, you are.' He dropped into Flint's big half-couch and puffed for a while in silence. 'Well, since you're all here, I may confess that I'm the mute with the bow-string.'

The young faces grew serious. The phrase meant that certain of their number would be withdrawn from all further games for extra-tuition. It might also mean future success at Sandhurst; but it was present ruin for the First Fifteen.

'Yes, I've come for my pound of flesh. I ought to have had you out before the Exeter match; but it's our sacred duty to beat Exeter.'

'Isn't the Old Boys' match sacred, too, sir?' said Perowne. The Old Boys' match was the event of the Easter term.

'We'll hope they aren't in training. Now for the list. First I want Flint. It's the Euclid that does it. You must work deductions with me. Perowne, extra mechanical drawing. Dawson goes to Mr. King for extra Latin, and Venner to me for German. Have I damaged the First Fifteen much?' He smiled sweetly.

'Ruined it, I'm afraid, sir,' said Flint. 'Can't you let us off till the end of the term?'

'Impossible. It will be a tight squeeze for Sandhurst this year.'

'And all to be cut up by those vile Afghans, too,' said Dawson. 'Wouldn't think there'd be so much competition, would you?'

'Oh, that reminds me. Crandall is coming down with the Old Boys—I've asked twenty of them, but we shan't get more than a weak team. I don't know whether he'll be much use, though. He was rather knocked about, recovering poor old Duncan's body.'

'Crandal major—the Gunner?' Perowne asked.

'No, the minor—"Toffee" Crandall—in a Native Infantry regiment. He was almost before your time, Perowne.'

'The papers didn't say anything about him. We read about Fat-Sow, of course. What's Crandall done, sir?'

'I've brought over an Indian paper that his mother sent me. It was rather a—hefty, I think you say—piece of work. Shall I read it?'

The Head knew how to read. When he had finished the quarter-column of small type everybody thanked him politely.

'Good for the old Coll.!' said Perowne. 'Pity he wasn't in time to save Fat-Sow, though. That's nine to us, isn't it, in the last three years?'

'Yes . . . And I took old Duncan off all games for extra-tu. five years ago this term,' said the Head. 'By the way, who do you hand over the Games to, Flint?'

'Haven't thought yet. Who'd you recommend, sir?'

'No, thank you. I've heard it casually hinted behind my back that the Prooshian Bates is a downy bird, but he isn't going to make himself responsible for a new Head of Games. Settle it among yourselves. Good night.'

'And that's the man,' said Flint, when the door shut, 'that you want to bother with a dame-school row.'

'I was only pullin' your fat leg,' Perowne returned hastily. 'You're so easy to draw, Flint.'

'Well, never mind that. The Head's knocked the First Fifteen to bits, and we've got to pick up the pieces, or the Old Boys will have a walk-over. Let's promote all the Second Fifteen and make Big Side play up. There's heaps of talent somewhere that we can polish up between now and the match.'

The case was represented so urgently to the school that even Stalky and M'Turk, who affected to despise football, played one Big-Side game seriously. They were forthwith promoted ere their ardour had time to cool, and the dignity of their Caps demanded that they should keep some show of virtue. The match-team was worked at least four days out of seven, and the school saw hope ahead.

With the last week of the term the Old Boys began to arrive, and their welcome was nicely proportioned to their worth. Gentlemen cadets from Sandhurst and Woolwich, who had only left a year ago, but who carried enormous side, were greeted with a cheerful 'Hullo! What's the Shop like?' from those who had shared their studies. Militia subalterns had more consideration, but it was understood they were not precisely of the true metal. Recreants who, failing for the Army, had gone into business or banks were received for old sake's sake, but in no way made too much of. But when the real subalterns, officers and gentlemen full-blown—who had been to the ends of the earth and back again and so carried no side—came on the scene strolling about with the Head, the school divided right and left in admiring silence. And when one laid hands on Flint, even upon the Head of Games, crying, 'Good Heavens! What do you mean by growing in this way? You were a beastly little fag when I left,' visible halos encircled Flint. They would walk to and fro in the corridor with the little red school Sergeant, telling news of old regiments; they would burst into form-rooms sniffing the well-remembered smells of ink and whitewash; they would find nephews and cousins in the lower forms and present them with enormous wealth; or they would invade the gymnasium and make Foxy show off the new stock on the bars.

Chiefly, though, they talked with the Head, who was father-confessor and agent-general to them all; for what they shouted in their unthinking youth, they proved in their thoughtless manhood—to wit, that the Prooshian Bates was 'a downy bird.' Young blood who had stumbled into an entanglement with a pastry-cook's daughter at Plymouth; experience who had come into a small legacy but mistrusted lawyers; ambition halting at cross-roads, anxious to take the one that would lead him farthest; extravagance pursued by the money-lender; arrogance in the thick of a regimental row—each carried his trouble to the Head; and Chiron showed him, in language quite unfit for little boys, a quiet and safe way round, out, or under. So they overflowed his house, smoked his cigars, and drank his health as they had drunk it all the earth over when two or three of the old school had forgathered.

'Don't stop smoking for a minute,' said the Head. 'The more you're out of training the better for us. I've demoralised the First Fifteen with extra-tu.'

'Ah, but we're a scratch lot. Have you told 'em we shall need a substitute even if Crandall can play?' said a Lieutenant of Engineers with the D.S.O. to his credit.

'He wrote me he'd play, so he can't have been much hurt. He's coming down to-morrow morning.'

'Crandall minor that was, and brought off poor Duncan's

body?' The Head nodded. 'Where are you going to put him? We've turned you out of house and home already, Head Sahib.' This was a Squadron-Commander of Bengal Lancers, home on leave.

'I'm afraid he'll have to go up to his old dormitory. You know Old Boys can claim that privilege. Yes, I think leetle Crandall minor must bed down there once more.'

'Bates Sahib'—a Gunner flung a heavy arm round the Head's neck—'you've got something up your sleeve. Confess! I know that twinkle.'

'Can't you see, you cuckoo?' a Submarine Miner interrupted. 'Crandall goes up to the dormitory as an object-lesson, for moral effect and so forth. Isn't that true, Head Sahib?'

'It is. You know too much, Purvis. I licked you for that in '79.'

'You did, sir, and it's my private belief you chalked the cane.'

'N-no. But I've a very straight eye. Perhaps that misled you.'

That opened the flood-gates of fresh memories, and they all told tales out of school.

When Crandall minor that was—Lieutenant R. Crandall of an ordinary Indian regiment—arrived from Exeter on the morning of the match, he was cheered along the whole front of the College, for the prefects had repeated the sense of that which the Head had read them in Flint's study. When Prout's House understood that he would claim his Old Boy's right to a bed for one night, Beetle ran into King's House next door and executed a public 'gloat' up and down the enemy's big form-room; departing in a haze of ink-pots.

'What d'you take any notice of those rotters for?' said Stalky, playing substitute for the Old Boys, magnificent in black jersey, white knickers, and black stockings. 'I talked to *him* up in the dormitory when he was changin'. Pulled his sweater down for him. He's cut about all over the arms—horrid purply ones. He's goin' to tell us about it to-night. I asked him to when I was lacin' his boots.'

'Well, you *have* got cheek,' said Beetle enviously.

'Slipped out before I thought. But he wasn't a bit angry. He's no end of a chap. I swear I'm goin' to play up like beans. Tell Turkey!'

The technique of that match belongs to a bygone age. Scrimmages were tight and enduring; hacking was direct and to the purpose; and round the scrimmage stood the school, crying, 'Put down your heads and shove!' Toward the end everybody lost all sense of decency, and mothers of day-boys too close to the touch-line heard language not included in the bills. No one was actually carried off the field, but both sides felt happier when time was called, and Beetle helped Stalky and M'Turk into their overcoats. The two had met in the many-legged heart of things, and, as Stalky said, had 'done each other proud.' As they swaggered woodenly behind the teams—substitutes do not rank as equals of hairy men—they passed a pony-carriage near the wall, and a husky voice cried, 'Well played. Oh, played indeed!' It was Stettson major, white-cheeked and hollow-eyed, who had fought his way to the ground under escort of an impatient coachman.

'Hullo, Stettson,' said Stalky, checking. 'Is it safe to come near you yet?'

'Oh yes. I'm all right. They wouldn't let me out before, but I had to come to the match. Your mouth looks pretty plummy.'

'Turkey trod on it accidental-done-a-purpose. Well, I'm glad you're better, because we owe you somethin'. You and your membranes got us into a sweet mess, young man.'

'I heard of that,' said the boy, giggling. 'The Head told me.'

'Dooce he did! When?'

'Oh, come on up to Coll. My shin'll stiffen if we stay jawin' here.'

'Shut up, Turkey. I want to find out about this. Well?'

'He was stayin' at our house all the time I was ill.'

'What for? Neglectin' the Coll. that way? Thought he was in Town.'

'I was off my head, you know, and they said I kept on callin' for him.'

'Cheek! You're only a day-boy.'

'He came just the same, and he about saved my life. I was all bunged up one night—just goin' to croak, the doctor said—and they stuck a tube or somethin' in my throat, and the Head sucked out the stuff.'

'Ugh! Shot if *I* would!'

'He ought to have got diphtheria himself, the doctor said. So he stayed on at our house instead of going back. I'd ha' croaked in another twenty minutes, the doctor says.'

Here the coachman, being under orders, whipped up and nearly ran over the three.

'My Hat!' said Beetle. 'That's pretty average heroic.'

'Pretty average!' M'Turk's knee in the small of his back cannoned him into Stalky, who punted him back. 'You ought to be hung!'

'And the Head ought to get the V.C.,' said Stalky. 'Why, he might have been dead *and* buried by now. But he wasn't. But he didn't. Ho! ho! He just nipped through the hedge like a lusty old blackbird. Extra-special, five hundred lines, an' gated for a week—all sereno!'

'I've read o' somethin' like that in a book,' said Beetle. 'Gummy, what a chap! Just think of it!'

'I'm thinking,' said M'Turk; and he delivered a wild Irish yell that made the team turn round.

A LITTLE PREP.

'Shut your fat mouth,' said Stalky, dancing with impatience. 'Leave it to your Uncle Stalky, and he'll have the Head on toast. If you say a word, Beetle, till I give you leave, I swear I'll slay you. *Habeo Capitem crinibus minimis.* I've got him by the short hairs! Now look as if nothing had happened.'

There was no need of guile. The school was too busy cheering the drawn match. It hung round the lavatories regardless of muddy boots while the team washed. It cheered Crandall minor whenever it caught sight of him, and it cheered more wildly than ever after prayers, because the Old Boys in evening dress, openly twirling their moustaches, attended, and instead of standing with the masters, ranged themselves along the wall immediately before the prefects; and the Head called them over, too—majors, minors, and tertiuses, after their old names.

'Yes, it's all very fine,' he said to his guests after dinner, 'but the boys are getting a little out of hand. There will be trouble and sorrow later, I'm afraid. You'd better turn in early, Crandall. The dormitory will be sitting up for you. I don't know to what dizzy heights you may climb in your profession, but I do know you'll never get such absolute adoration as you're getting now.'

'Confound the adoration. I want to finish my cigar, sir.'

'It's all pure gold. Go where glory waits, Crandall—minor.'

The setting of that apotheosis was a ten-bed attic dormitory, communicating through doorless openings with three others. The gas flickered over the raw pine washstands. There was an incessant whistling of draughts, and outside the naked windows the sea beat on the Pebble Ridge.

'Same old bed—same old mattress, I believe,' said Crandall, yawning. 'Same old everything. Oh, but I'm lame! I'd no notion you chaps could play like this.' He caressed a battered shin. 'You've given us all something to remember you by.'

It needed a few minutes to put them at their ease; and, in

some way they could not understand, they were more easy when Crandall turned round and said his prayers—a ceremony he had neglected for some years.

'Oh, I *am* sorry. I've forgotten to put out the gas.'

'Please don't bother,' said the prefect of the dormitory. 'Worthington does that.'

A nightgowned twelve-year-old, who had been waiting to show off, leaped from his bed to the bracket and back again, by way of a washstand.

'How d'you manage when he's asleep?' said Crandall, chuckling.

'Shove a cold cleek down his neck.'

'It was a wet sponge when I was junior in the dormitory. . . . Hullo! What's happening?'

The darkness had filled with whispers, the sound of trailing rugs, bare feet on bare boards, protests, giggles, and threats such as:

'Be quiet, you ass! . . . *Squattez-vous* on the floor, then! . . . I swear you aren't going to sit on *my* bed! . . . Mind the tooth-glass,' and so forth.

'Sta—Corkran said,' the prefect began, his tone showing his sense of Stalky's insolence, 'that perhaps you'd tell us about that business with Duncan's body.'

'Yes—yes—yes,' ran the keen whispers. 'Tell us.'

'There's nothing to tell. What on earth are you chaps hoppin' about in the cold for?'

'Never mind us,' said the voices. 'Tell about Fat-Sow.'

So Crandall turned on his pillow and spoke to the generation he could not see.

'Well, about three months ago he was commandin' a treasure-guard—a cart full of rupees to pay troops with—five thousand rupees in silver. He was comin' to a place called Fort Pearson, near Kalabagh.'

A LITTLE PREP.

'I was born there,' squeaked a small fag. 'It was called after my uncle.'

'Shut up—you and your uncle! Never mind *him*, Crandall.'

'Well, ne'er mind. The Afridis found out that this treasure was on the move, and they ambushed the whole show a couple of miles before he got to the fort, and cut up the escort. Duncan was wounded, and the escort hooked it. There weren't more than twenty Sepoys all told, and there were any amount of Afridis. As things turned out, I was in charge at Fort Pearson. Fact was, I'd heard the firing and was just going to see about it, when Duncan's men came up. So we all turned back together. They told me something about an officer, but I couldn't get the hang of things till I saw a chap under the wheels of the cart out in the open, propped up on one arm, blazing away with a revolver. You see, the escort had abandoned the cart, and the Afridis—they're an awfully suspicious gang—thought the retreat was a trap—sort of draw, you know—and the cart was the bait. So they had left poor old Duncan alone. Minute they spotted how few *we* were, it was a race across the flat who should reach old Duncan first. We ran, and they ran, and we won, and after a little hackin' about they pulled off. I never knew it was one of us till I was right on top of him. There are heaps of Duncans in the Service, and of course the name didn't remind me. He wasn't changed at all hardly. He'd been shot through the lungs, poor old man, and he was pretty thirsty. I gave him a drink and sat down beside him, and—funny thing, too—he said, "Hullo, Toffee!" and I said, "Hullo, Fat-Sow! Hope you aren't hurt," or something of the kind. But he died in a minute or two—never lifted his head off my knees. . . . I say, you chaps out there will get your death of cold. Better go to bed.'

'All right. In a minute. But your cuts—your cuts. How did you get wounded?'

'That was when we were taking the body back to the Fort. They came on again, and there was a bit of a scrimmage.'

'Did you kill any one?'

'Yes. Shouldn't wonder. Good night.'

'Good night. Thank you, Crandall. Thanks awf'ly, Crandall. Good night.'

The unseen crowds withdrew. His own dormitory rustled into bed and lay silent for a while.

'I say, Crandall'—Stalky's voice was tuned to a wholly foreign reverence.

'Well, what?'

'Suppose a chap found another chap croakin' with diphtheria—all bunged up with it—and they stuck a tube in his throat and the chap sucked the stuff out, what would you say?'

'Um,' said Crandall reflectively. 'I've only heard of one case, and that was a doctor. He did it for a woman.'

'Oh, this wasn't a woman. It was only a boy.'

'Makes it all the finer, then. It's about the bravest thing a man can do. Why?'

'Oh, I heard of a chap doin' it. That's all.'

'Then he's a brave man.'

'Would *you* funk it?'

'Ra-ather. Anybody would. Fancy dying of diphtheria in cold blood.'

'Well—ah! Er! Look here!' That sentence ended in a grunt, for Stalky had leaped out of bed and with M'Turk was sitting on the head of Beetle, who would have sprung the mine there and then.

Next day, which was the last of the term and given up to a few wholly unimportant examinations, began with wrath and war. Mr. King had discovered that nearly all his House—it lay, as you know, next door but one to Prout's in the long range of buildings—had unlocked the doors between the dormitories and had gone in to listen to a story told by Crandall. He went to the Head, clamorous, injured, appealing; for he never approved of allowing so-called young men of the world to contaminate the morals of boyhood. 'Very good,' said the Head. He would attend to it.

'Well, I'm awf'ly sorry,' said Crandall guiltily. 'I don't think I told 'em anything they oughtn't to hear. Don't let them get into trouble on my account.'

'Tck!' the Head answered, with the ghost of a wink. 'It isn't the boys that make trouble; it's the masters. However, Prout and King don't approve of dormitory gatherings on this scale, and one must back up the House-masters. Moreover, it's hopeless to punish two Houses only, so late in the term. We must be fair and include everybody. Let's see. They have a holiday task for the Easters, which, of course, none of them will ever look at. We will give the whole school, except prefects and study-boys, regular prep. to-night; and the Common-room will have to supply a master to take it. We must be fair to all.'

'Prep. on the last night of the term. Whew!' said Crandall, thinking of his own wild youth. 'I fancy there will be larks.'

The school, frolicking among packed trunks, whooping down the corridor, and 'gloating' in form-rooms, received the news with amazement and rage. No school in the world did prep. on the last night of the term. This thing was monstrous, tyrannical, subversive of law, religion, and morality. They would go into the form-rooms, and they would take their degraded holiday task with them, but—here they smiled and speculated what manner of man the Common-room would send up against them. The lot fell on Mason, credulous and enthusiastic, who loved youth. No other master was anxious to take that prep., for the school lacked the steadying influence of tradition; and men accustomed to the ordered routine of ancient foundations found it occasionally insubordinate. The four long form-rooms, in which all below the rank of study-boys worked, received him with thunders of applause. Ere he had coughed twice they favoured him with a metrical summary of the marriage-laws of Great Britain, as recorded by the High Priest of the Israelites and commented on by the leader of the host. The lower forms reminded him that it was the last day, and that therefore he must 'take it all in play.' When he dashed off to rebuke them, the Lower Fourth and Upper Third began with one accord to be sick, loudly and realistically. Mr. Mason tried, of all vain things under heaven, to argue with them, and a bold soul at a back desk bade him 'take fifty lines for not 'olding up 'is 'and before speaking.' As one who prided himself upon the precision of his English this cut Mason to the quick, and while he was trying to discover the offender, the Upper and Lower Second, three form-rooms away, turned out the gas and threw ink-pots. It was a pleasant and stimulating prep. The study-boys and prefects heard the echoes of it far off, and the Common-room at dessert smiled.

Stalky waited, watch in hand, till half-past eight.

'If it goes on much longer the Head will come up,' said he. 'We'll tell the studies first, and then the form-rooms. Look sharp!'

He allowed no time for Beetle to be dramatic or M'Turk to drawl. They poured into study after study, told their tale, and went again so soon as they saw they were understood, waiting for no comment; while the noise of that unholy prep. grew and deepened. By the door of Flint's study they met Mason flying towards the corridor.

'He's gone to fetch the Head. Hurry up! Come on!'

A LITTLE PREP.

They broke into Number Twelve form-room abreast and panting.

'The Head! The Head! The Head!' That call stilled the tumult for a minute, and Stalky leaping to a desk shouted, 'He went and sucked the diphtheria stuff out of Stettson major's throat when we thought he was in Town. Stop rottin', you asses! Stettson major would have croaked if the Head hadn't done it. The Head might have died himself. Crandall says it's the bravest thing any livin' man can do, and'—his voice cracked—'the Head don't know we know!'

M'Turk and Beetle, jumping from desk to desk, drove the news home among the junior forms. There was a pause, and then, Mason behind him, the Head entered. It was in the established order of things that no boy should speak or move under his eye. He expected the hush of awe. He was received with cheers—steady, ceaseless cheering. Being a wise man he went away, and the forms were silent and a little frightened.

'It's all right,' said Stalky. 'He can't do much. 'Tisn't as if you'd pulled the desks up like we did when old Carlton took prep. once. Keep it up! Hear 'em cheering in the studies!' He rocketed out with a yell, to find Flint and the prefects lifting the roof off the corridor.

When the Head of a limited liability company, paying four per cent, is cheered on his saintly way to prayers, not only by four form-rooms of boys waiting punishment, but by his trusted prefects, he can either ask for an explanation or go his road with dignity, while the senior House-master glares like an excited cat and points out to a white and trembling mathematical master that certain methods—not his, thank God— usually produce certain results. Out of delicacy the Old Boys did not attend that call-over; and it was to the school drawn up in the gymnasium that the Head spoke icily.

'It is not often that I do not understand you; but I confess I do not to-night. Some of you, after your idiotic performances at prep., seem to think me a fit person to cheer. I am going to show you that I am not.'

Crash—crash—crash—came the triple cheer that disproved it, and the Head glowered under the gas.

'That is enough. You will gain nothing. The little boys' (the Lower School did not like that form of address) 'will do me three hundred lines apiece in the holidays. I shall take no further notice of them. The Upper School will do me one thousand lines apiece in the holidays, to be shown up the evening of the day they come back. And further——'

'Gummy, what a glutton!' Stalky whispered.

'For your behaviour towards Mr. Mason I intend to lick the whole of the Upper School to-morrow when I give you your journey-money. This will include the three study-boys I found dancing on the form-room desks when I came up. Prefects will stay after call-over.'

The school filed out in silence, but gathered in groups by the gymnasium door waiting what might befall.

'And now, Flint,' said the Head, 'will you be good enough to give me some explanation of your conduct?'

'Well, sir,' said Flint desperately, 'if you save a chap's life at the risk of your own when he's dyin' of diphtheria, and the Coll. finds it out, wha-what can you expect, sir?'

'Um, I see. Then that noise was not meant for—ah, cheek. I can connive at immorality, but I cannot stand impudence. However, it does not excuse their insolence to Mr. Mason. I'll forgo the lines this once, remember; but the lickings hold good.'

When this news was made public, the school, lost in wonder and admiration, gasped at the Head as he went to his house. Here was a man to be reverenced. On the rare occasions when he caned he did it very scientifically, and the execution of a hundred boys would be epic—immense.

'It's all right, Head Sahib. *We* know,' said Crandall, as the Head slipped off his gown with a grunt in his smoking-room. 'I found out just now from our substitute. He was gettin' my opinion of your performance last night in the dormitory. I didn't know then that it was you he was talkin' about. Crafty young animal. Freckled chap with eyes—Corkran, I think his name is.'

'Oh, I know him, thank you,' said the Head; and reflectively, 'Ye-es, I should have included them even if I hadn't seen 'em.'

'If the old Coll. weren't a little above themselves already, we'd chair you down the corridor,' said the Engineer. 'Oh, Bates, how could you? You might have caught it yourself, and where would we have been then?'

'I always knew you were worth twenty of us any day. Now I'm sure of it,' said the Squadron-Commander, looking round for contradictions.

'He isn't fit to manage a school, though. Promise you'll never do it again, Bates Sahib. We—we can't go away comfy in our minds if you take these risks,' said the Gunner.

'Bates Sahib, you aren't ever goin' to cane the whole Upper School, are you?' said Crandall.

'I can connive at immorality, as I said, but I can't stand impudence. Mason's lot is quite hard enough even when I back him. Besides, the men at the golf-club heard them singing "Aaron and Moses." I shall have complaints about that from the parents of day-boys. Decency must be preserved.'

'We're coming to help,' said all the guests.

The Upper School were caned one after the other, their overcoats over their arms, the brakes waiting in the road below to take them to the station, their journey-money on the table. The Head began with Stalky, M'Turk, and Beetle. He dealt faithfully by them.

'And here's your journey-money. Good-bye, and pleasant holidays.'

'Good-bye. Thank you, sir. Good-bye.'

They shook hands.

'Desire don't outrun performance—*much*—this mornin'. We got the cream of it,' said Stalky. 'Now wait till a few chaps come out, and we'll really cheer him.'

'Don't wait on our account, please,' said Crandall, speaking for the Old Boys. 'We're going to begin now.'

It was very well so long as the cheering was confined to the corridor, but when it spread to the gymnasium, when the boys awaiting their turn cheered, the Head gave it up in despair, and the remnant flung themselves upon him to shake hands.

Then they seriously devoted themselves to cheering till the brakes were hustled off the premises in dumb show.

'Didn't I say I'd get even with him?' said Stalky on the box-seat, as they swung into the narrow Northam street. 'Now all together—takin' time from your Uncle Stalky:—

> *It's a way we have in the Army,*
> *It's a way we have in the Navy,*
> *It's a way we have in the Public Schools,*
> *Which nobody can deny!'*

THE FLAG OF THEIR COUNTRY

THE FLAG OF THEIR COUNTRY

IT WAS WINTER and bitter cold of mornings. Consequently Stalky and Beetle—M'Turk being of the offensive type that makes ornate toilet under all circumstances—drowsed till the last moment before turning out to call-over in the gas-lit gymnasium. It followed that they were often late; and since every unpunctuality earned them a black mark, and since three black marks a week meant defaulters' drill, equally it followed that they spent hours under the Sergeant's hand. Foxy drilled the defaulters with all the pomp of his old parade-ground.

'Don't think it's any pleasure to me' (his introduction never varied). 'I'd much sooner be smoking a quiet pipe in my own quarters—but I see we 'ave the Old Brigade on our 'ands this afternoon. If I only 'ad you regular, Muster Corkran,' said he, dressing the line.

'You've had me for nearly six weeks, you old glutton. Number off from the right!'

'Not *quite* so previous, please. I'm taking this drill. Left, half—turn! Slow—march.' Twenty-five sluggards, all old offenders, filed into the gymnasium. 'Quietly provide yourselves with the requisite dumb-bells; returnin' quietly to your place. Number off from the right, in *a* low voice. Odd numbers one pace to the front. Even numbers stand fast. Now, leanin' forward from the 'ips, takin' your time from me.'

The dumb-bells rose and fell, clashed and were returned as one. The boys were experts at the weary game.

'Ve-ry good. I shall be sorry when any of you resume your 'abits of punctuality. Quietly return dumb-bells. We will now try some simple drill.'

'Ugh! I know that simple drill.'

'It would be 'ighly to your discredit if you did not, Muster Corkran. *At* the same time, it is not so easy as it looks.'

'Bet you a bob, I can drill as well as you, Foxy.'

'We'll see later. Now try to imagine you ain't defaulters at all, but an 'arf company on parade, me bein' your commandin' officer. There's no call to laugh. If you're lucky, most of you will 'ave to take drills 'arf your life. Do me a little credit. You've been at it long enough, goodness knows.'

They were formed into fours, marched, wheeled, and countermarched, the spell of ordered motion strong on them. As Foxy said, they had been at it a long time.

The gymnasium door opened, revealing M'Turk in charge of an old gentleman.

The Sergeant, leading a wheel, did not see. 'Not so bad,' he murmured. 'Not 'arf so bad. The pivot-man of the wheel *honly* marks time, Muster Swayne. Now, Muster Corkran, you say you know the drill? Oblige me by takin' over the command and, reversin' my words step by step, relegate them to their previous formation.'

'What's this? What's this?' cried the visitor authoritatively.

'A—a little drill, sir,' stammered Foxy, saying nothing of first causes.

'Excellent—excellent. I only wish there were more of it,' he chirruped. 'Don't let me interrupt. You were just going to hand over to some one, weren't you?' He sat down, breathing frostily in the chill air.

'I shall muck it. I know I shall,' whispered Stalky uneasily; and his discomfort was not lightened by a murmur from the rear rank that the old gentleman was General Collinson, a member of the College Board of Council.

'Eh—what?' said Foxy.

'Collinson, K.C.B.—He commanded the Pompadours—my father's old Regiment,' hissed Swayne major.

'Take your time,' said the visitor. '*I* know how it feels. Your first drill—eh?'

'Yes, sir.' He drew an unhappy breath. ' 'Tention. Dress!' The echo of his own voice restored his confidence.

The wheel was faced about, flung back, broken into fours, and restored to line without a falter. The official hour of punishment was long past, but no one thought of that. They were backing up Stalky—Stalky in deadly fear lest his voice should crack.

'He does you credit, Sergeant,' was the visitor's comment. 'A good drill—and good material to drill. Now, it's an extraordinary thing: I've been lunching with your Head-master and he never told me you had a cadet-corps in the College.'

'We 'aven't, sir. This is only a little drill,' said the Sergeant.

'But aren't they keen on it?' said M'Turk, speaking for the first time, with a twinkle in his deep-set eyes.

'Why aren't *you* in it, though, Willy?'

'Oh, I'm not punctual enough,' said M'Turk. 'The Sergeant only takes the pick of us.'

'Dismiss! Break off!' cried Foxy, fearing an explosion in the ranks. 'I—I ought to have told you, sir, that——'

'But you should have a cadet-corps.' The General pursued his own line of thought. 'You *shall* have a cadet-corps, too, if my recommendation in Council is any use. I don't know when I've been so pleased. Boys animated by a spirit like yours should set an example to the whole school.'

'They do,' said M'Turk.

'Bless my soul! Can it be so late? I've kept my fly waiting half an hour. Well, I must run away. Nothing like seeing things for oneself. Which end of the building does one get out at? Will you show me, Willy? Who was that boy who took the drill?'

'Corkran, I think his name is.'

'You ought to know him. That's the kind of boy you should cultivate. Evidently an unusual sort. A wonderful sight. Five-and-twenty boys, who, I dare say, would much sooner be playing cricket—' (it was the depth of winter; but grown people, especially those who have lived long in foreign parts, make these little errors, and M'Turk did not correct him)— 'drilling for the sheer love of it. A shame to waste so much good stuff; but I think I can carry my point.'

'An' who's your friend with the white whiskers?' demanded Stalky, on M'Turk's return to the study.

'General Collinson. He comes over to shoot with my father sometimes. Rather a decent old bargee, too. He said I ought to cultivate your acquaintance, Stalky.'

'Did he tip you?'

M'Turk exhibited a blessed whole sovereign.

'Ah,' said Stalky, annexing it, for he was treasurer. 'We'll have a hefty brew. You'd pretty average cool cheek, Turkey, to jaw about our keenness an' punctuality.'

'Didn't the old boy know we were defaulters?' said Beetle.

'Not him. He came down to lunch with the Head. I found him pokin' about the place on his own hook afterwards, an' I thought I'd show him the giddy drill. When I found he was so pleased, I wasn't goin' to damp his giddy ardour. He mightn't ha' given me the quid if I had.'

'Wasn't old Foxy pleased? Did you see him get pink behind the ears?' said Beetle. 'It was an awful score for him. Didn't we back him up beautifully? Let's go down to Keyte's an' get some cocoa and sassingers.'

They overtook Foxy, speeding down to retail the adventure to Keyte, who in his time had been Troop-Sergeant-Major in a cavalry regiment, and now, a war-worn veteran, was local postmaster and confectioner.

'You owe us something,' said Stalky, with meaning.

'I'm 'ighly grateful, Muster Corkran. I've 'ad to run against you pretty hard in the way o' business, now and then, but I will say that outside o' business—bounds an' smokin', an' such like—I don't wish to have a more trustworthy young gen'el-man to 'elp me out of a hole. The way you 'andled the drill was beautiful, though I say it. Now, if you come regular henceforward——'

'But he'll have to be late three times a week,' said Beetle. 'You can't expect a chap to do that—just to please you, Foxy.'

'Ah, that's true. Still, if you could manage it—and you, Muster Beetle—it would give you a big start when the cadet-corps is formed. I expect the General will recommend it.'

They raided Keyte's very much at their own sweet will, for the old man, who knew them well, was deep in talk with Foxy.

'I make what we've taken seven and six,' Stalky called at last over the counter; 'but you'd better count for yourself.'

'No—no. I'd take your word any day, Muster Corkran.— In the Pompadours, was he, Sergeant? We lay with them once —at Umballa, I think it was.'

'I don't know whether this ham-and-tongue tin is eighteen pence or one an' four.'

'Say one an' fourpence, Muster Corkran. . . . Of course, Sergeant, if it was any use to give my time, I'd be pleased to do it, but I'm too old. I'd like to see a drill again.'

'Oh, come on, Stalky,' cried M'Turk. 'He isn't listenin' to you. Chuck over the money.'

'I want the quid changed, you ass. Keyte! Private Keyte! Corporal Keyte! Terroop-Sergeant-Major Keyte, will you give me change for a quid?'

'Yes—yes, of course. Seven an' six.' He stared abstractedly, pushed the silver over, and melted away into the darkness of the back room.

'Now those two'll jaw about the Mutiny till teatime,' said Beetle.

'Old Keyte was at Sobraon,' said Stalky. 'Hear him talk about that sometimes! Beats Foxy hollow.'

The Head's face, inscrutable as ever, was bent over a pile of letters.

'What do you think?' he said at last to the Reverend John Gillett.

'It's a good idea. There's no denying that—an estimable idea.'

'We concede that much. Well?'

'I have my doubts about it—that's all. The more I know of boys the less do I profess myself capable of following their moods; but I own I shall be very much surprised if the scheme takes. It—it isn't the temper of the school. We prepare for the Army.'

'My business—in this matter—is to carry out the wishes of the Council. They demand a volunteer cadet-corps. A volunteer cadet-corps will be furnished. I have suggested, however, that we need not embark upon the expense of uniforms till we are drilled. General Collinson is sending us fifty lethal weapons —cut-down Sniders, he calls them—all carefully plugged.'

'Yes, that is necessary in a school that uses loaded saloon-pistols to the extent we do.' The Reverend John smiled.

'Therefore there will be no outlay except the Sergeant's time.'

'But if he fails you will be blamed.'

'Oh, assuredly. I shall post a notice in the corridor this afternoon, and——'

'I shall watch the result.'

'Kindly keep your 'ands off the new arm-rack.'

Foxy wrestled with a turbulent crowd in the gymnasium. 'Nor it won't do even a condemned Snider any good to be continual snappin' the lock, Muster Swayne.—Yiss, the uniforms will come later, when we're more proficient; at present we will confine ourselves to drill. I am 'ere for the purpose of takin' the names o' those willin' to join.—Put down that Snider, Muster Hogan!'

'What are you goin' to do, Beetle?' said a voice.

'I've had all the drill *I* want, thank you.'

'What! After all you've learned? Come on. Don't be a scab! They'll make you corporal in a week,' cried Stalky.

'I'm not goin' up for the Army.' Beetle touched his spectacles.

'Hold on a shake, Foxy,' said Hogan. 'Where are you goin' to drill us?'

'Here—in the gym—till you are fit an' capable to be taken out on the road.' The Sergeant threw a chest.

'For all the Northam cads to look at? Not good enough, Foxibus.'

'Well, we won't make a point of it. You learn your drill first, an' later we'll see.'

'Hullo,' said Ansell of Macrea's, shouldering through the mob. 'What's all this about a giddy cadet-corps?'

'It will save you a lot o' time at Sandhurst,' the Sergeant replied promptly. 'You'll be dismissed your drills early if you go up with a good groundin' before-'and.'

'Hm! Don't mind learnin' my drill, but I'm not goin' to ass

about the country with a toy Snider. Perowne, what are you goin' to do? Hogan's joinin'.'

'Don't know whether I've the time,' said Perowne. 'I've got no end of extra-tu. as it is.'

'Well, call this extra-tu.,' said Ansell. ' 'Twon't take us long to mug up the drill.'

'Oh, that's right enough, but what about marchin' in public?' said Hogan, not foreseeing that three years later he should die in the Burmese sunlight outside Minhla Fort.

'Afraid the uniform won't suit your creamy complexion?' M'Turk asked with a villainous sneer.

'Shut up, Turkey. You aren't goin' up for the Army.'

'No, but I'm goin' to send a substitute. Hi! Morrell an' Wake! You two fags by the arm-rack, you've got to volunteer.'

Blushing deeply—they had been too shy to apply before—the youngsters sidled towards the Sergeant.

'But I don't want the little chaps—not at first,' said the Sergeant disgustedly. 'I want—I'd like some of the Old Brigade —the defaulters—to stiffen 'em a bit.'

'Don't be ungrateful, Sergeant. They're nearly as big as you get 'em in the Army now.' M'Turk read the papers of those years and could be trusted for general information, which he used as he used his 'tweaker.' Yet he did not know that Wake minor would be a Bimbashi of the Egyptian Army ere his thirtieth year.

Hogan, Swayne, Stalky, Perowne, and Ansell were deep in consultation by the vaulting-horse, Stalky as usual laying down the law. The Sergeant watched them uneasily, knowing that many waited on their lead.

'Foxy don't like my recruits,' said M'Turk, in a pained tone, to Beetle. 'You get him some.'

Nothing loath, Beetle pinioned two more fags—each no taller than a carbine.

'Here you are, Foxy. Here's food for powder. Strike for your hearts an' homes, you young brutes—an' be jolly quick about it.'

'Still he isn't happy,' said M'Turk.

> *'For the way we have with our Army*
> *Is the way we have with our Navy.'*

Here Beetle joined in. They had found the poem in an old volume of *Punch,* and it seemed to cover the situation:—

> *'An' both of 'em lead to adversity,*
> *Which nobody can deny!'*

'You be quiet, young gentlemen. If you can't 'elp—don't 'inder.' Foxy's eye was still on the council by the horse. Carter, White, and Tyrrell, all boys of influence, had joined it. The rest fingered the rifles irresolutely.

'Half a shake,' cried Stalky. 'Can't we turn out those rotters before we get to work?'

'Certainly,' said Foxy. 'Any one wishful to join will stay 'ere. Those who do not so intend will go out, quietly closin' the door be'ind 'em.'

Half-a-dozen of the earnest-minded rushed at M'Turk and Beetle, and they had just time to escape into the corridor.

'Well, why don't you join?' Beetle asked, resettling his collar.

'Why didn't you?'

'What's the good? We aren't goin' up for the Army. Besides, I know the drill—all except the manual, of course. Wonder what they're doin' inside?'

'Makin' a treaty with Foxy. Didn't you hear Stalky say: "That's what we'll do—an' if he don't like it he can lump it"?

They'll use Foxy for a cram. Can't you see, you idiot? They're goin' up for Sandhurst or the Shop in less than a year. They'll learn their drill an' then they'll drop it like a shot. D'you suppose chaps with their amount of extra-tu. are takin' up volunteerin' for fun?'

'Well, I don't know. I thought of doin' a poem about it—rottin' 'em, you know—"The Ballad of the Dogshooters"—eh?'

'I don't think you can, because King'll be down on the corps like a cartload o' bricks. He hasn't been consulted. He's sniffin' round the notice-board now. Let's lure him.' They strolled up carelessly towards the House-master—a most meek couple.

'How's this?' said King, with a start of feigned surprise. 'Methought you would be learning to fight for your country.'

'I think the company's full, sir,' said M'Turk.

'It's a great pity,' sighed Beetle.

'Forty valiant defenders, have we, then? How noble! What devotion! I presume that it is possible that a desire to evade their normal responsibilities may be at the bottom of this zeal. Doubtless they will be accorded special privileges, like the Choir and the Natural History Society—one must not say Bug-hunters.'

'Oh, I suppose so, sir,' said M'Turk cheerily. 'The Head hasn't said anything about it yet, but he will, of course.'

'Oh, sure to.'

'It is just possible, my Beetle,' King wheeled on the last speaker, 'that the House-masters—a necessary but somewhat neglected factor in our humble scheme of existence—may have a word to say on the matter. Life, for the young at least, is not all weapons and munitions of war. Education is incidentally one of our aims.'

'What a consistent pig he is!' cooed M'Turk, when they were out of earshot. 'One always knows where to have him.

Did you see how he rose to that draw about the Head and special privileges?'

'Confound him, he might have had the decency to have backed the scheme. I could do such a lovely ballad, rottin' it; an' now I'll have to be a giddy enthusiast. It don't bar our pullin' Stalky's leg in the study, does it?'

'Oh no; but in the Coll. we must be pro-cadet-corps like anything. Can't you make up a giddy epigram, *à la* Catullus, about King objectin' to it?' Beetle was at this noble task when Stalky returned all hot from his first drill.

'Hullo, my ramrod-bunger!' began M'Turk. 'Where's your dead dog? Is it Defence or Defiance?'

'Defiance,' said Stalky, and leaped on him at that word. 'Look here, Turkey, you mustn't rot the corps. We've arranged it beautifully. Foxy swears he won't take us out into the open till we want to go.'

'*Dis*-gustin' exhibition of immature infants apin' the idiosyncrasies of their elders. Snff!'

'Have you drawn King, Beetle?' Stalky asked in a pause of the scuffle.

'Not exactly; but that's his genial style.'

'Well, listen to your Uncle Stalky—who is a Great Man. Moreover an' subsequently, Foxy's goin' to let us drill the corps in turn—*privatim et seriatim*—so that we'll all know how to handle a half company anyhow. *Ergo,* an' *propter hoc,* when we go to the Shop we shall be dismissed drill early; thus, my beloved 'earers, combinin' education with wholesome amusement.'

'I knew you'd make a sort of extra-tu. of it, you cold-blooded brute,' said M'Turk. 'Don't you want to die for your giddy country?'

'Not if I can jolly well avoid it. So you mustn't rot the corps.'

'We'd decided on that, years ago,' said Beetle scornfully. 'King'll do the rottin'.'

'Then you've got to rot King, my giddy poet. Make up a good catchy Limerick, and let the fags sing it.'

'Look here, you stick to volunteerin', an' don't jog the table.'

'He won't have anything to take hold of,' said Stalky, with dark significance.

They did not know what that meant till, a few days later, they proposed to watch the corps at drill. They found the gymnasium door locked and a fag on guard.

'This is sweet cheek,' said M'Turk, stooping.

'Mustn't look through the key-hole,' said the sentry.

'I like that. Why, Wake, you little beast, I made you volunteer.'

'Can't help it. My orders are not to allow any one to look.'

'S'pose we do?' said M'Turk. 'S'pose we jolly well slay you?'

'My orders are, I am to give the name of anybody who interferes with me on my post, to the corps, an' they'd deal with him after drill, accordin' to martial law.'

'What a brute Stalky is!' said Beetle. They never doubted for a moment who had devised that scheme.

'You esteem yourself a giddy centurion, don't you?' said Beetle, listening to the crash and rattle of grounded arms within.

'My orders are, not to talk except to explain my orders—they'll lick me if I do.'

M'Turk looked at Beetle. The two shook their heads and turned away.

'I swear Stalky *is* a Great Man,' said Beetle after a long pause. 'One consolation is that this sort of secret-society biznai will drive King wild.'

It troubled many more than King, but the members of the corps were muter than oysters. Foxy, being bound by no vow, carried his woes to Keyte.

'I never come across such nonsense in my life. They've tiled the lodge, inner and outer guard all complete, and then they get to work, keen as mustard.'

'But what's it all for?' asked the ex-Troop-Sergeant-Major.

'To learn their drill. You never saw anything like it. They begin after I've dismissed 'em—practisin' tricks; but out into the open they will not come—not for ever so. The 'ole thing is pre-posterous. If you're a cadet-corps, I say, be a cadet-corps, instead o' hidin' be'ind locked doors.'

'And what do the authorities say about it?'

'That beats me again.' The Sergeant spoke fretfully. 'I go to the 'Ead an' 'e gives me no help. There's times when I think he's makin' fun o' me. I've never been a Volunteer-sergeant, thank God—but I've always had the consideration to pity 'em. I'm glad o' that.'

'I'd like to see 'em,' said Keyte. 'From your statements, Sergeant, I can't get at what they're after.'

'Don't ask me, Major! Ask that freckle-faced young Corkran. He's their generalissimo.'

One does not refuse a warrior of Sobraon, or deny the only pastry-cook within bounds. So Keyte came, by invitation, leaning upon a stick, tremulous with old age, to sit in a corner and watch.

'They shape well. They shape uncommon well,' he whispered between evolutions.

'Oh, *this* isn't what they're after. Wait till I dismiss 'em.'

At the 'break-off' the ranks stood fast. Perowne fell out, faced them, and, refreshing his memory by glimpses at a red-bound, metal-clasped book, drilled them for ten minutes. (This is that Perowne who was shot in Equatorial Africa by his own men.)

Ansell followed him, and Hogan followed Ansell. All three were implicitly obeyed.

Then Stalky laid aside his Snider, and, drawing a long breath, favoured the company with a blast of withering invective.

''Old 'ard, Muster Corkran. That ain't in any drill,' cried Foxy.

'All right, Sergeant. You never know what you may have to say to your men.—For pity's sake, try to stand up without leanin' against each other, you blear-eyed, herrin'-gutted gutter-snipes. It's no pleasure to *me* to comb you out. That ought to have been done before you came here, you—you Militia broom-stealers!'

'The old touch—the old touch. We know it,' said Keyte, wiping his rheumy eyes. 'But where did he pick it up?'

'From his father—or his uncle. Don't ask me! Half of 'em must have been born within earshot o' the barracks.' (Foxy was not far wrong in his guess.) 'I've heard more back-talk since this volunteerin' nonsense began than I've heard in a year in the Service.'

'There's a rear-rank man lookin' as though his belly were in the pawn-shop. Yes, you, Private Ansell,' and Stalky tongue-lashed the victim for three minutes, in gross and in detail.

'Hullo!' He returned to his normal tone. 'First blood to me. You flushed, Ansell. You wriggled.'

'Couldn't help flushing,' was the answer. 'Don't think I wriggled, though.'

'Well, it's your turn now.' Stalky resumed his place in the ranks.

'Lord, Lord! It's as good as a play,' chuckled the attentive Keyte.

THE FLAG OF THEIR COUNTRY

Ansell, too, had been blessed with relatives in the Service, and slowly, in a lazy drawl—his style was more reflective than Stalky's—descended the abysmal depths of personality.

'Blood to me!' he shouted triumphantly. 'You couldn't stand it, either.' Stalky was a rich red, and his Snider shook visibly.

'I didn't think I would,' he said, struggling for composure, 'but after a bit I got in no end of a bait. Curious, ain't it?'

'Good for the temper,' said the slow-moving Hogan, as they returned arms to the rack.

'Did you ever?' said Foxy, hopelessly, to Keyte.

'I don't know much about volunteers, but it's the rummiest show I ever saw. I can see what they're gettin' at, though. Lord! how often I've been told off an' dressed down in my day! They shape well—extremely well they shape.'

'If I could get 'em out into the open, there's nothing I couldn't do with 'em, Major. Perhaps when the uniforms come down, they'll change their tune.'

Indeed it was time that the corps made some concession to the curiosity of the school. Thrice had the guard been maltreated and thrice had the corps dealt out martial law to the offender. The school raged. What was the use, they asked, of a cadet-corps which none might see? Mr. King congratulated them on their invisible defenders, and they could not parry his thrusts. Foxy was growing sullen and restive. A few of the corps openly expressed doubts as to the wisdom of their course; and the question of uniforms loomed on the near horizon. If those were issued, they would be forced to wear them.

But as so often happens in this life, the matter was suddenly settled from without.

The Head had duly informed the Council that their recommendation had been acted upon, and that, so far as he could learn, the boys were drilling.

He said nothing of the terms on which they drilled. Nat-

urally, General Collinson was delighted and told his friends.
One of his friends rejoiced in a friend, a member of Parlia-
ment—a zealous, an intelligent, and, above all, a patriotic
person, anxious to do the most good in the shortest possible
time. But we cannot answer, alas! for the friends of our friends.
If Collinson's friend had introduced him to the General, the
latter would have taken his measure and saved much. But the
friend merely spoke of his friend; and since no two people in
this world see eye to eye, the picture conveyed to Collinson
was inaccurate. Moreover, the man was an M.P., an impeccable
Conservative, and the General had the English soldier's lurk-
ing respect for any member of the Court of Last Appeal. The
man was going down into the West country, to spread light
in some benighted constituency. Wouldn't it be a good idea if,
armed with the General's recommendation, he, taking the admirable and newly-established cadet-corps for his text, spoke
a few words—'Just talked to the boys a little—eh? You know
the kind of thing that would be acceptable; and he'd be the
very man to do it. The sort of talk that boys understand, you
know.'

'They didn't talk to 'em much in my time,' said the General
suspiciously.

'Ah! but times change—with the spread of education and so
on. The boys of to-day are the men of to-morrow. An impression in youth is likely to be permanent. And in these times, you
know, with the country going to the dogs!'

'You're quite right.' The Island was then entering on five
years of Mr. Gladstone's rule; and the General did not like
what he had seen of it. He would certainly write to the Head,
for it was beyond question that the boys of to-day made the
men of to-morrow. That, if he might say so, was uncommonly
well put.

In reply, the Head stated that he should be delighted to welcome Mr. Raymond Martin, M.P., of whom he had heard so much; to put him up for the night, and to allow him to address the school on any subject that he conceived would interest them. If Mr. Martin had not yet faced an audience of this particular class of British youth, the Head had no doubt that he would find it an interesting experience.

'And I don't think I am very far wrong in that last,' he confided to the Reverend John. 'Do you happen to know anything of one Raymond Martin?'

'I was at College with a man of that name,' the Chaplain replied. 'He was without form and void, so far as I remember, but desperately earnest.'

'He will address the Coll. on "Patriotism" next Saturday.'

'If there is one thing our boys detest more than another it is having their Saturday evenings broken into. Patriotism has no chance beside "brewing." '

'Nor art either. D'you remember our "Evening with Shakespeare"?' The Head's eyes twinkled. 'Or the humorous gentleman with the magic-lantern?'

'An' who the dooce is this Raymond Martin, M.P.?' demanded Beetle, when he read the notice of the lecture in the corridor. 'Why do the brutes always turn up on a Saturday?'

'Ouh! Reomeo, Reomeo! Wherefore art thou Reomeo?' said M'Turk over his shoulder, quoting the Shakespeare artiste of last term. 'Well, he won't be as bad as *her*, I hope. Stalky, are you properly patriotic? Because if you ain't, this chap's goin' to make you.'

'Hope he won't take up the whole of the evenin'. I suppose we've got to listen to him.'

'Wouldn't miss him for the world,' said M'Turk. 'A lot of

chaps thought that Romeo-Romeo woman was a bore. *I* didn't.
I liked her! 'Member when she began to hiccup in the middle
of it? P'raps he'll hiccup. Whoever gets into the gym first,
bags seats for the other two.'

There was no nervousness, but a brisk and cheery affability
about Mr. Raymond Martin, M.P., as he drove up, watched by
many eyes, to the Head's house.

'Looks a bit of a bargee,' was M'Turk's comment. 'Shouldn't
be surprised if he was a Radical. He rowed the driver about
the fare. I heard him.'

'That was his giddy patriotism,' Beetle explained.

After tea they joined the rush for seats, secured a private
and invisible corner, and began to criticise. Every gas-jet was
lit. On the little dais at the far end stood the Head's official
desk, whence Mr. Martin would discourse, and a ring of
chairs for the masters.

Entered then Foxy, with official port, and leaned something
like a cloth rolled round a stick against the desk. No one in
authority was yet present, so the school applauded, crying:
'What's that, Foxy? What are you stealin' the gentleman's
brolly for?—We don't birch here. We cane! Take away that
bauble!—Number off from the right'—and so forth, till the
entry of the Head and the masters ended all demonstrations.

'One good job—the Common-room hate this as much as we
do. Watch King wrigglin' to get out of the draught.'

'Where's the Raymondiferous Martin? Punctuality, my beloved 'earers, is the image o' war——'

'Shut up. Here's the giddy Dook. Golly, what a dewlap!'
Mr. Martin, in evening-dress, was undeniably throaty—a tall,
generously designed, pink-and-white man. Still, Beetle need
not have been coarse.

'Look at his back while he's talkin' to the Head. Vile bad form to turn your back on the audience! He's a Philistine—a Bopper—a Jebusite an' a Hivite.' M'Turk leaned back and sniffed contemptuously.

In a few colourless words the Head introduced the speaker and sat down amid applause. When Mr. Martin took the applause to himself, they naturally applauded more than ever. It was some time before he could begin. He had no knowledge of the school—its tradition or heritage. He did not know that the last census showed that eighty per cent of the boys had been born abroad—in camp, cantonment, or upon the high seas; or that seventy-five per cent were sons of officers in one or other of the Services—Willoughbys, Paulets, De Castros, Maynes, Randalls, after their kind—looking to follow their fathers' profession. The Head might have told him this, and much more; but, after an hour-long dinner in his company, the Head decided to say nothing whatever. Mr. Raymond Martin seemed to know so much already.

He plunged into his speech with a long-drawn, rasping 'Well, boys,' that, though they were not conscious of it, set every young nerve a-jar. He supposed they knew—hey?—what he had come down for? It was not often that he had an opportunity to talk to boys. He supposed that boys were very much the same kind of persons—some people thought them rather funny persons—as they had been in his youth.

'This man,' said M'Turk, with conviction, 'is *the* Gadarene Swine.'

But they must remember that they would not always be boys. They would grow up into men, because the boys of to-day made the men of to-morrow, and upon the men of to-morrow the fair fame of their glorious native land depended.

'If this goes on, my beloved 'earers, it will be my painful

duty to rot this bargee.' Stalky drew a long breath through his nose.

'Can't do that,' said M'Turk: 'He ain't chargin' anything for his Romeo.'

And so they ought to think of the duties and responsibilities of the life that was opening before them. Life was not all—he enumerated a few games, and, that nothing might be lacking to the sweep and impact of his fall, added 'marbles.' 'Yes, life was not,' he said, 'all marbles.'

There was one tense gasp—among the juniors almost a shriek—of quivering horror. He was a heathen—an outcast—beyond the extremest pale of toleration—self-damned before all men! Stalky bowed his head in his hands. M'Turk, with a bright and cheerful eye, drank in every word, and Beetle nodded solemn approval.

Some of them, doubtless, expected in a few years to have the honour of a commission from the Queen, and to wear a sword. Now, he himself had had some experience of these duties, as a Major in a Volunteer regiment, and he was glad to learn that they had established a volunteer corps in their midst. The establishment of such an establishment conduced to a proper and healthy spirit, which, if fostered, would be of great benefit to the land they loved and were so proud to belong to. Some of those now present expected, he had no doubt—some of them anxiously looked forward to leading their men against the bullets of England's foes; to confronting the stricken field in all the pride of their youthful manhood.

Now the reserve of a boy is tenfold deeper than the reserve of a maid, she being made for one end only by blind Nature, but man for several. With a large and healthy hand, he tore down these veils, and trampled them under the well-intentioned feet of eloquence. In a raucous voice he cried aloud little matters, like the hope of Honour and the dream of Glory, that boys do not discuss even with their most intimate equals; cheerfully assuming that, till he spoke, they had never considered these possibilities. He pointed them to shining goals, with fingers which smudged out all radiance on all horizons. He profaned the most secret places of their souls with outcries and gesticulations. He bade them consider the deeds of their ancestors in such fashion that they were flushed to their tingling ears. Some of them—the rending voice cut a frozen stillness—might have had relatives who perished in defence of their country. (They thought, not a few of them, of an old sword in a passage, or above a breakfast-room table, seen and fingered by stealth since they could walk.) He adjured them to emulate those illustrious examples; and they looked all ways in their extreme discomfort.

Their years forbade them even to shape their thoughts clearly to themselves. They felt savagely that they were being outraged by a fat man who considered marbles a game.

And so he worked towards his peroration—which, by the way, he used later with overwhelming success at a meeting of electors—while they sat, flushed and uneasy, in sour disgust. After many many words, he reached for the cloth-wrapped stick and thrust one hand in his bosom. This—this was the concrete symbol of their land—worthy of all honour and reverence! Let no boy look on this flag who did not purpose to worthily add to its imperishable lustre. He shook it before them—a large calico Union Jack, staring in all three colours—and waited for the thunder of applause that should crown his effort.

They looked in silence. They had certainly seen the thing before—down at the coastguard station, or through a telescope, half-mast high when a brig went ashore on Braunton sands;

above the roof of the Golf Club, and in Keyte's window, where a certain kind of striped sweetmeat bore it in paper on each box. But the College never displayed it; it was no part of the scheme of their lives; the Head had never alluded to it; their fathers had not declared it unto them. It was a matter shut up, sacred and apart. What, in the name of everything caddish, was he driving at, who waved that horror before their eyes? Happy thought! Perhaps he was drunk.

The Head saved the situation by rising swiftly to propose a vote of thanks, and at his first motion the school clapped furiously, from a sense of relief.

'And I am sure,' he concluded, the gaslight full on his face, 'that you will all join me in a very hearty vote of thanks to Mr. Raymond Martin for the most enjoyable address he has given us.'

To this day we shall never know the rights of the case. The Head vows that he did no such thing; or that, if he did, it must have been something in his eye; but those who were present are persuaded that he winked, once, openly and solemnly, after the word 'enjoyable.' Mr. Raymond Martin got his applause full tale. As he said, 'Without vanity, I think my few words went to their hearts. I never knew boys could cheer like that.'

He left as the prayer-bell rang, and the boys lined up against the wall. The flag lay still unrolled on the desk, Foxy regarding it with pride, for he had been touched to the quick by Mr. Martin's eloquence. The Head and the Common-room, standing back on the dais, could not see the glaring offence, but a prefect left the line, rolled it up swiftly, and as swiftly tossed it into a glove-and-foil locker.

Then, as though he had touched a spring, broke out the low murmur of content, changing to quick-volleyed handclapping.

THE FLAG OF THEIR COUNTRY

They discussed the speech in the dormitories. There was not one dissentient voice. Mr. Raymond Martin, beyond question, was born in a gutter, and bred in a Board-school, where they played marbles. He was further (I give the barest handful from great store) a Flopshus Cad, an Outrageous Stinker, a Jelly-bellied Flag-flapper (this was Stalky's contribution), and several other things which it is not seemly to put down.

The volunteer cadet-corps fell in next Monday, depressedly, with a face of shame. Even then, judicious silence might have turned the corner.

Said Foxy: 'After a fine speech like what you 'eard night before last, you ought to take 'old of your drill with *re*-newed activity. I don't see how you can avoid comin' out an' marchin' in the open now.'

'Can't we get out of it, then, Foxy?' Stalky's fine old silky tone should have warned him.

'No, not with his giving the flag so generously. He told me before he left this morning that there was no objection to the corps usin' it as their own. It's a handsome flag.'

Stalky returned his rifle to the rack in dead silence, and fell out. His example was followed by Hogan and Ansell.

Perowne hesitated. 'Look here, oughtn't we——?' he began.

'I'll get it out of the locker in a minute,' said the Sergeant, his back turned. 'Then we can——'

'Come on!' shouted Stalky. 'What the devil are you waiting for? Dismiss! Break off.'

'Why—what the—where the——?'

The rattle of Sniders, slammed into the rack, drowned his voice, as boy after boy fell out.

'I—I don't know that I shan't have to report this to the Head,' he stammered.

'Report, then, and be damned to you,' cried Stalky, white to the lips, and ran out.

'Rummy thing!' said Beetle to M'Turk. 'I was in the study, doin' a simply lovely poem about the Jelly-bellied Flag-flapper, an' Stalky came in, an' I said "Hullo!" an' he cursed me like a bargee, an' then he began to blub like anything. Shoved his head on the table and howled. Hadn't we better do something?'

M'Turk was troubled. 'P'raps he's smashed himself up somehow.'

They found him, with very bright eyes, whistling between his teeth.

'Did I take you in, Beetle? I though I would. Wasn't it a good draw? Didn't you think I was blubbin'? Didn't I do it well? Oh, you fat old ass!' And he began to pull Beetle's ears and cheeks, in the fashion that was called 'milking.'

'I knew you were blubbin',' Beetle replied composedly. 'Why aren't you at drill?'

'Drill! What drill?'

'Don't try to be a clever fool. Drill in the gym.'

' 'Cause there isn't any. The volunteer cadet-corps is broke up—disbanded—dead—putrid—corrupt—stinkin'. An' if you look at me like that, Beetle, I'll slay you too. . . . Oh yes, an' I'm goin' to be reported to the Head for swearin'.'

THE PROPAGATION OF KNOWLEDGE

THE BIRTHRIGHT

The miracle of our land's speech—so known
And long received, none marvel when 'tis shown!

We have such wealth as Rome at her most pride
Had not or (having) scattered not so wide;
Nor with such arrant prodigality
Beneath her any pagan's foot let lie . . .
Lo! Diamond that cost some half their days
To find and t'other half to bring to blaze:
Rubies of every heat, wherethrough we scan
The fiercer and more fiery heart of man:
Emerald that with the uplifted billow vies,
And Sapphires evening remembered skies:
Pearl perfect, as immortal tears must show,
Bred, in deep waters, of a piercing woe;
And tender Turkis, so with charms y-writ,
Of woven gold, Time dares not bite on it.
Thereafter, in all manners worked and set,
Jade, coral, amber, crystal, ivories, jet,—
Showing no more than various fancies, yet
Each a Life's token or Love's amulet. . . .
Which things, through timeless arrogance of use,
We neither guard nor garner, but abuse;
So that our scholars—nay, our children—fling
In sport or jest treasure to arm a King;
And the gross crowd, at feast or market, hold
Traffic perforce with dust of gems and gold!

THE PROPAGATION OF KNOWLEDGE

THE ARMY CLASS 'ENGLISH,' which included the Upper Fifth, was trying to keep awake; for 'English' (Literature—Augustan epoch—eighteenth century) came at last lesson, and that, on a blazing July afternoon, meant after every one had been bathing. Even Mr. King found it hard to fight against the snore of the tide along the Pebble Ridge, and spurred himself with strong words.

Since, said he, the pearls of English Literature existed only to be wrenched from their settings and cast before young swine rooting for marks, it was his loathed business—in anticipation of the Army Preliminary Examination which, as usual, would be held at the term's end, under the auspices of an official Examiner sent down *ad hoc*—to prepare for the Form a General Knowledge test-paper, which he would give them next week. It would cover their studies, up to date, of the Augustans and *King Lear*, which was the selected—and strictly expurgated—Army Exam. play for that year. Now, English Literature, as he might have told them, was *not* divided into water-tight compartments, but flowed like a river. For example, Samuel Johnson, glory of the Augustans and no mean commentator of Shakespeare, was but one in a mighty procession which——

At this point Beetle's nodding brows came down with a grunt on the desk. He had been soaking and sunning himself in the open sea-baths built out on the rocks under the cliffs, from two-fifteen to four-forty.

The Army Class took Johnson off their minds. With any luck, Beetle would last King till the tea-bell. King rubbed his hands and began to carve him. He had gone to sleep to show his contempt (*a*) for Mr. King, who might or might not matter, and (*b*) for the Augustans, who none the less were not to be sneered at by one whose vast and omnivorous reading, for which such extraordinary facilities had been granted [this was because the Head had allowed Beetle the run of his library], naturally overlooked such *epigonoi* as Johnson, Swift, Pope, Addison, and the like. Harrison Ainsworth and Marryat doubtless appealed——

Even so, Beetle, salt-encrusted all over except his spectacles, and steeped in delicious languors, was sliding back to sleep again, when 'Taffy' Howell, the leading light of the Form, who knew his Marryat as well as Stalky did his Surtees, began in his patent, noiseless whisper: ' "Allow me to observe—in the most delicate manner in the world—just to hint——" '

'Under pretext of studying literature, a desultory and unformed mind would naturally return, like the dog of Scripture——'

' "You're a damned, trencher-scrapin', napkin-carryin', shillin'-seekin', up-an'-down-stairs &c." ', Howell breathed.

Beetle choked aloud on the sudden knowledge that King was the ancient and eternal Chucks—later Count Shucksen—or *Peter Simple*. He had not realised it before.

'Sorry, sir. I'm afraid I've been asleep, sir,' he sputtered.

The shout of the Army Class diverted the storm. King was grimly glad that Beetle had condescended to honour truth so far. Perhaps he would now lend his awakened ear to a summary of the externals of Dr. Johnson, as limned by Macaulay. And he read, with intention, the just historian's outline of a grotesque figure with untied shoe-strings, that twitched and grunted, gorged its food, bit its finger-nails, and neglected its ablutions. The Form hailed it as a speaking likeness of Beetle; nor were they corrected.

Then King implored him to vouchsafe his comrades one single fact connected with Dr. Johnson which might at any time have adhered to what, for decency's sake, must, Mr. King supposed, be called his mind.

Beetle was understood to say that the only thing he could remember was in French.

'You add, then, the Gallic tongue to your accomplishments? The information plus the accent? 'Tis well! Admirable Crichton, proceed!'

And Beetle proceeded with the text of an old Du Maurier drawing in a back-number of *Punch*:—

> '*De tous ces défunts cockolores*
> *Le moral Fénelon,*
> *Michel Ange et Johnson*
> (*Le Docteur*) *sont les plus awful bores.*'

To which Howell, wooingly, just above his breath:
' "Oh, *won't* you come up, come up?" '
Result, as the tea-bell rang, one hundred lines, to be shown up at seven forty-five that evening. This was meant to blast the pleasant summer interval between tea and prep. Howell, a favourite in 'English' as well as Latin, got off; but the Army Class crashed in to tea with a new Limerick.

The imposition was a matter of book-keeping, so far as Beetle was concerned; for it was his custom of rainy afternoons to fabricate store of lines in anticipation of just these accidents. They covered such English verse as interested him at the moment, and helped to fix the stuff in his memory. After tea, he drew the required amount from his drawer in Number Five study, thrust it into his pocket, went up to the Head's house, and settled himself in the big Outer Library where, ever since the Head had taken him off all mathematics, he did précis-work and French translation. Here he buried himself in a close-printed, thickish volume which had been his chosen browse for some time. A hideous account of a hanging, drawing, and quartering had first attracted him to it; but later he discovered the book (*Curiosities of Literature* was its name) full of the finest confused feeding—such as forgeries and hoaxes, Italian literary societies, religious and scholastic controversies of old when men (even that most dreary John Milton, of *Lycidas*) slanged each other, not without dust and heat, in scandalous pamphlets; personal peculiarities of the great; and a hundred other fascinating inutilities. This evening he fell on a description of wandering, mad Elizabethan beggars, known as Tom-a-Bedlams, with incidental references to Edgar who plays at being a Tom-a-Bedlam in *Lear*, but whom Beetle did not consider at all funny. Then, at the foot of a left-hand page, leaped out on him a verse—of incommunicable splendour, opening doors into inexplicable worlds—from a song which Tom-a-Bedlams were supposed to sing. It ran:—

> *With a heart of furious fancies*
> *Whereof I am commander,*
> *With a burning spear and a horse of air,*
> *To the wilderness I wander.*
> *With a knight of ghosts and shadows*
> *I summoned am to tourney,*
> *Ten leagues beyond the wide world's end—*
> *Methinks it is no journey.*

He sat, mouthing and staring before him, till the prep.-bell rang and it was time to take his lines up to King's study and lay them, as hot from the press, in the impot-basket appointed. He carried his dreams on to Number Five. They knew the symptoms of old.

'Readin' again,' said Stalky, like a wife welcoming her spouse from the pot-house.

'Look here, I've found out something——' Beetle began. 'Listen——'

'No, you don't—till afterwards. It's Turkey's prep.' This meant it was a Horace Ode through which Turkey would take them for a literal translation, and all possible pitfalls. Stalky gave his businesslike attention, but Beetle's eye was glazed and his mind adrift throughout, and he asked for things to be repeated. So, when Turkey closed the Horace, justice began to be executed.

'I'm all right,' he protested. 'I swear I heard a lot of what Turkey said. Shut up! Oh, shut *up*! *Do* shut up, you putrid asses.' Beetle was speaking from the fender, his head between Turkey's knees, and Stalky largely over the rest of him.

'What's the metre of the beastly thing?' M'Turk waved his Horace. 'Look it up, Stalky. Twelfth of the Third.'

'*Ionicum a minore*,' Stalky reported, closing his book in turn. 'Don't let him forget it'; and Turkey's Horace marked the metre on Beetle's skull, with special attention to elisions. It hurt.

> '*Miserar' est neq' amori dare ludum neque dulci*
> *Mala vino laver' aut ex——*

'Got it? You liar! You've no ear at all! Chorus, Stalky!' Both Horaces strove to impart the measure, which was altogether different from its accompaniment. Presently Howell dashed in from his study below.

'Look *out*! If you make this infernal din we'll have some one up the staircase in a sec.'

'We're teachin' Beetle Horace. He was goin' to burble us some muck he'd read,' the tutors explained.

''Twasn't muck! It was about those Tom-a-Bedlams in *Lear*.'

'Oh!' said Stalky. 'Why didn't you say so?'

''Cause you didn't listen. They had drinkin'-horns an' badges, an' there's a Johnson note on Shakespeare about the meanin' of Edgar sayin' "My horn's dry." But Johnson's dead-wrong about it. Aubrey says——'

'Who's Aubrey?' Howell demanded. 'Does King know about him?'

'Dunno. Oh yes, an' Johnson started to learn Dutch when he was seventy.'

'What the deuce for?' Stalky asked.

'For a change after his Dikker, I suppose,' Howell suggested.

'And I looked up a lot of other English stuff, too. I'm goin' to try it all on King.'

'Showin'-off as usual,' said the acid M'Turk, who, like his race, lived and loved to destroy illusions.

'No. For a draw. He's an unjust dog! If you read, he says you're showin'-off. If you don't, you're a mark-huntin' Philistine. What does he want you to do, curse him?'

'Shut up, Beetle!' Stalky pronounced. 'There's more than draws in this. You've cribbed your maths off me ever since you came to Coll. You don't know what a cosine is, even *now*. Turkey does all your Latin.'

'I like that! Who does both your *Picciolas*?'

'French don't count. It's time you began to work for your

giddy livin' an' help us. *You* aren't goin' up for anythin' that matters. Play for your side, as Heffles says, or die the death! You don't want to die the death, again, do you? Now let's hear about that stinkard Johnson swottin' Dutch. You're sure it was Samivel, not Binjimin? You *are* so dam' inaccurate!'

Beetle conducted an attentive class on the curiosities of literature for nearly a quarter of an hour. As Stalky pointed out, he promised to be useful.

The Horace Ode next morning ran well; and King was content. Then, in full feather, he sailed round the firmament at large, and, somehow, apropos to something or other, used the word 'della Cruscan'—'if any of you have the faintest idea of its origin.' Some one hadn't caught it correctly; which gave Beetle just time to whisper 'Bran—an' mills' to Howell, who said promptly: 'Hasn't it somethin' to do with mills—an' bran, sir?' King cast himself into poses of stricken wonder. 'Oddly enough,' said he, 'it has.'

They were then told a great deal about some silly Italian Academy of Letters which borrowed its office furniture from the equipment of mediaeval flour-mills. And: 'How has our Ap-Howell come by his knowledge?' Howell, being, indeed, Welsh, thought that it might have been something he had read in the holidays. King openly purred over him.

'If that had been *me*,' Beetle observed while they were toying with sardines between lessons, 'he'd ha' dropped on me for showin'-off.'

'See what we're savin' you from,' Stalky answered. 'I'm playin' Johnson, 'member, this afternoon.'

That, too, came cleanly off the bat; and King was gratified by this interest in the Doctor's studies. But Stalky hadn't a ghost of a notion how he had come by the fact.

'Why didn't you say your father told you?' Beetle asked at tea.

'My-y Lord! Have you ever seen the guv'nor?' Stalky collapsed shrieking among the piles of bread and butter. 'Well, look here. Taffy goes in to-morrow about those drinkin'-horns an' Tom-a-Bedlams. You cut up to the library after tea, Beetle. You know what King's English papers are like. Look out useful stuff for answers an' we'll divvy at prep.'

At prep., then, Beetle, loaded with assorted curiosities, made his forecast. He argued that there were bound to be a good many 'what-do-you-know-abouts' those infernal Augustans. Pope was generally a separate item; but the odds were that Swift, Addison, Steele, Johnson, and Goldsmith would be lumped under one head. Dryden was possible, too, though rather outside the Epoch.

'Dryden. Oh! "Glorious John!" Know *that* much, anyhow,' Stalky vaunted.

'Then lug in Claude Halcro in *The Pirate*,' Beetle advised. 'He's always sayin' "Glorious John." King's a hog on Scott, too.'

'No-o. I don't read Scott. You take this Hell Crow chap, Taffy.'

'Right. What about Addison, Beetle?' Howell asked.

'Drank like a giddy fish.'

'We all know that,' chorused the gentle children.

'He said, "See how a Christian can die"; an' he hadn't any conversation, 'cause some one or other——'

'Guessin' again, *as* usual,' M'Turk sneered. 'Who?'

'Cynical man called Mandeville—said he was a silent parson in a tie-wig.'

'Right O! I'll take the silent parson with wig and 'purtenances. Taffy can have the dyin' Christian,' Stalky decided.

Howell nodded, and resumed: 'What about Swift, Beetle?'

'Died mad. Two girls. Saw a tree, an' said: "I shall die at the top." Oh yes, an' his private amusements were "ridiculous an' trivial." '

Howell shook a wary head. 'Dunno what that might let me in for with King. You can have it, Stalky.'

'I'll take that,' M'Turk yawned. 'King doesn't matter a curse to me, and he knows it. "Private amusements contemptible." ' He breathed all Ireland into the last perverted word.

'Right,' Howell assented. 'Bags I the dyin' tree, then.'

'Cheery lot, these Augustans,' Stalky sighed. 'Any more of 'em been croakin' lately, Beetle?'

'My Hat!' the far-seeing Howell struck in. 'King always gives us a stinker half-way down. What about Richardson—that *Clarissa* chap, y'know?'

'I've found out lots about him,' said Beetle promptly. 'He was the "Shakespeare of novelists." '

'King won't stand that. He says there's only one Shakespeare. Mustn't rot about Shakespeare to King,' Howell objected.

'An' he was "always delighted with his own works," ' Beetle continued.

'Like you,' Stalky pointed out.

'Shut up. Oh yes, an'——' he consulted some hieroglyphics on a scrap of paper—'the—the impassioned Diderot (dunno who *he* was) broke forth: "O Richardson, thou singular genius!" '

Howell and Stalky rose together, each clamouring that he had bagged that first.

'I *must* have it!' Howell shouted. 'King's never seen me breakin' forth with the impassioned Diderot. He's *got* to! Give me Diderot, you impassioned hound!'

'Don't upset the table. There's tons more. An' his genius was "fertile and prodigal." '

'All right! *I* don't mind bein' "fertile and prodigal" for a change,' Stalky volunteered. 'King's going to enjoy this exam. If he was the Army Prelim. chap we'd score.'

'The Prelim. questions will be pretty much like King's stuff,' Beetle assured them.

'But it's always a score to know what your examiner's keen on,' Howell said, and illustrated it with an anecdote. 'Uncle of mine stayin' with my people last holidays——'

'Your Uncle Diderot?' Stalky asked.

'No, you ass! Captain of Engineers. He told me he was up for a Staff exam. to an old Colonel-bird who believed that the English were the Lost Tribes of Israel, or something like that. He'd written tons o' books about it.'

'All Sappers are mad,' said Stalky. 'That's one of the things the guv'nor *did* tell me.'

'Well, ne'er mind. My uncle played up, o' course. Said he'd always believed it, too. And *so* he got nearly top-marks for field-fortification. Didn't know a thing about it, either, he said.'

'Good biznai!' said Stalky. 'Well, go on, Beetle. What about Steele?'

'Can't I keep anything for myself?'

'Not *much*! King'll ask you where you got it from, an' you'd show off, an' he'd find out. This ain't your silly English Literature, you ass. It's our marks. Can't you see that?'

Beetle very soon saw it was exactly as Stalky had said.

Some days later a happy, and therefore not too likeable, King was explaining to the Reverend John in his own study how effort, zeal, scholarship, the Humanities, and perhaps a little natural genius for teaching, could inspire even the mark-hunting minds of the young. His text was the result of his General Knowledge paper on the Augustans and *King Lear*.

'Howell,' he said, 'I was not surprised at. He *has* intelligence. But, frankly, I did not expect young Corkran to burgeon. Almost one might believe he occasionally read a book.'

'And M'Turk too?'

'Yes. He had somehow arrived at a rather just estimate of Swift's lighter literary diversions. They *are* contemptible. And in the Lear questions—they were all attracted by Edgar's character—Stalky had dug up something about Aubrey on Tom-a-Bedlams from some unknown source. Aubrey, of all people! I'm sure I only alluded to him once or twice.'

'Stalky among the prophets of "English"! And he didn't remember where he'd got it either?'

'No. Boys are amazingly purblind and limited. But if they keep this up at the Army Prelim., it is conceivable the Class may not do itself discredit. I told them so.'

'I congratulate you. Ours is the hardest calling in the world, with the least reward. By the way, who are they likely to send down to examine us?'

'It rests between two, I fancy. Martlett—with me at Balliol —and Hume. *They* wisely chose the Civil Service. Martlett has published a brochure on Minor Elizabethan Verse—journeyman work, of course—enthusiasms, but no grounding. Hume I heard of lately as having infected himself in Germany with some transatlantic abomination about Shakespeare and Bacon. He was Sutton.' (The Head, by the way, was a Sutton man.)

King returned to his examination-papers and read extracts from them, as mothers repeat the clever sayings of their babes.

'Here's old Taffy Howell, for instance—apropos to Diderot's eulogy of Richardson. "The impassioned Diderot broke forth: 'Richardson, thou singular genius!' " '

It was the Reverend John who stopped himself, just in time, from breaking forth. He recalled that, some days ago, he had heard Stalky on the stairs of Number Five, hurling the boots of many fags at Howell's door and bidding the 'impassioned Diderot' within 'break forth' at his peril.

'Odd,' said he, gravely, when his pipe drew again. 'Where did Diderot say that?'

'I've forgotten for the moment. Taffy told me he'd picked it up in the course of holiday reading.'

'Possibly. One never knows what heifers the young are ploughing with. Oh! How did Beetle do?'

'The necessary dates and his handwriting defeated him, I'm glad to say. I cannot accuse myself of having missed any opportunity to castigate that boy's inordinate and intolerable conceit. But I'm afraid it's hopeless. I think I touched him somewhat, though, when I read Macaulay's stock piece on Johnson. The others saw it at once.'

'Yes, you told me about that at the time,' said the Reverend John, hurriedly.

'And our esteemed Head having taken him off maths for this précis-writing—whatever that means!—has turned him into a most objectionable free-lance. He was without any sense of reverence before, and promiscuous cheap fiction—which is all that his type of reading means—aggravates his worst points. When it came to a trial he was simply nowhere.'

'Ah, well! Ours is a hard calling—specially if one's sensitive. Luckily, I'm too fat.' The Reverend John went out to bathe off the Pebble Ridge, girt with a fair linen towel whose red fringe signalled from half a mile away.

There lurked on summer afternoons, round the Fives Court or the gym, certain watchful outcasts who had exhausted their weekly ration of three baths, and who were too well known to Cory the bathman to outface him by swearing that they hadn't. These came in like sycophantic pups at walk, and when the Reverend John climbed the Pebble Ridge, more than a dozen of them were at his heels, with never a towel among them. One could only bathe off the Ridge with a House-master, but by custom, a dozen details above a certain age, no matter whence recruited, made a 'House' for bathing, if any kindly master chose so to regard them. Beetle led the low, growing reminder: 'House! House, sir? We've got a House now, Padre.'

'Let it be law as it is desired,' boomed the Reverend John. On which word they broke forward, hirpling over the unstable pebbles and stripping as they ran, till, when they touched the sands, they were as naked as God had made them, and as happy as He intended them to be.

It was half-flood—dead-smooth, except for the triple line of combers, a mile from wing to wing, that broke evenly with a sound of ripping canvas, while their sleek rear-guards formed up behind. One swam forth, trying to copy the roll, rise, and dig-out of the Reverend John's side-stroke, and manœuvred to meet them so that they should crash on one's head, when for an instant one glanced down arched perspectives of beryl, before all broke in fizzy, electric diamonds, and the pulse of the main surge slung one towards the beach. From a good comber's crest one was hove up almost to see Lundy on the horizon. In its long cream-streaked trough, when the top had turned over and gone on, one might be alone in mid-Atlantic. Either way it was divine. Then one capered on the sands till one dried off; retrieved scattered flannels, gave thanks in chorus to the Reverend John, and lazily trailed up to five o'clock call-over, taken on the lower cricket field.

'Eight this week,' said Beetle, and thanked Heaven aloud.

'Bathing seems to have sapped your mind,' the Reverend John remarked. 'Why did you do so vilely with the Augustans?'

'They *are* vile, Padre. So's *Lear*.'

'The other two did all right, though.'

'I expect they've been swottin',' Beetle grinned.

'I've expected that, too, in my time. But I want to hear about the "impassioned Diderot," please.'

'Oh, that was Howell, Padre. You mean when Diderot broke forth: "Richardson, thou singular genius"? He'd read it in the holidays somewhere.'

'I *beg* your pardon. Naturally, Taffy would read Diderot in the holidays. Well, I'm sorry I can't lick you for this; but if any one ever finds out anything about it, you've only yourself to thank.'

Beetle went up to Coll. and to the Outer Library, where he had 'on tap the last of a book called *Elsie Venner*, by a man called Oliver Wendell Holmes—all about a girl who was interestingly allied to rattlesnakes. He finished what was left of her, and cast about for more from the same hand, which he found on the same shelf, with the trifling difference that the writer's Christian name was now Nathaniel, and he did not deal in snakes. The authorship of Shakespeare was his theme —not that Shakespeare with whom King oppressed the Army Class, but a low-born, poaching, ignorant, immoral village lout who could not have written one line of any play ascribed to him. (Beetle wondered what King would say to Nathaniel if ever they met.) The real author was Francis Bacon, of Bacon's Essays, which did not strike Beetle as any improvement. He had 'done' the Essays last term. But evidently Nathaniel's views annoyed people, for the margins of his book— it was second-hand, and the old label of a public library still adhered—flamed with ribald, abusive, and contemptuous comments by various hands. They ranged from 'Rot!' 'Rubbish!' and such-like to crisp counter-arguments. And several times some one had written: 'This beats Delia.' One copious annotator dissented, saying: 'Delia is supreme in this line,' 'Delia

beats this hollow.' 'See Delia's *Philosophy*, page so and so.'
Beetle grieved he could not find anything about Delia (he had
often heard King's views on lady-writers as a class) beyond a
statement by Nathaniel, with pencilled exclamation-points
rocketing all round it, that 'Delia Bacon discovered in Francis
Bacon a good deal more than Macaulay.' Taking it by and
large, with the kind help of the marginal notes, it appeared
that Delia and Nathaniel between them had perpetrated every
conceivable outrage against the Head-God of King's idolatry:
and King was particular about his idols. Without pronouncing
on the merits of the controversy, it occurred to Beetle that a
well-mixed dose of Nathaniel ought to work on King like a
seidlitz powder. At this point a pencil and a half sheet of
impot-paper came into action, and he went down to tea so
swelled with Baconian heresies and blasphemies that he could
only stutter between mouthfuls. He returned to his labours
after the meal, and was visibly worse at prep.

'I say,' he began, 'have you ever heard that Shakespeare
never wrote his own beastly plays?'

'Fat lot of good to us!' said Stalky. 'We've got to swot 'em
up just the same. Look here! This is for English parsin' to-
morrow. It's *your* biznai.' He read swiftly from the school
Lear (Act II. Sc. 2) thus:—

    Steward: '*Never any:*
   It pleased the King his master, very late,
   To strike at me, upon his misconstruction;
   When he, conjunct, an' flatterin' his displeasure,
   Tripped me behind: bein' down, insulted, railed,
   And put upon him such a deal of man,
   That worthy'd him, got praises of the King
   For him attemptin' who was self-subdued;

STALKY & CO.

And, in the fleshment of this dread exploit,
Drew on me here again.

'Now then, my impassioned bard, *construez!* That's Shake-speare.'

'Give it up! He's drunk,' Beetle declared at the end of a blank half-minute.

'No, he isn't,' said Turkey. 'He's a steward—on the estate—chattin' to his employers.'

'Well—look here, Turkey. You ask King if Shakespeare ever wrote his own plays, an' he won't give a dam' what the steward said.'

'I've not come here to play with ushers,' was M'Turk's view of the case.

'I'd do it,' Beetle protested, 'only he'd slay *me!* He don't love me when I ask about things. I can give you the stuff to draw him—tons of it!' He broke forth into a précis, interspersed with praises, of Nathaniel Holmes and his commentators—especially the latter. He also mentioned Delia, with sorrow that he had not read her. He spoke through nearly the whole of prep.; and the upshot of it was that M'Turk relented and promised to approach King next 'English' on the authenticity of Shakespeare's plays.

The time and tone chosen were admirable. While King was warming himself by a preliminary canter round the Form's literary deficiencies, Turkey coughed in a style which suggested a reminder to a slack employee that it was time to stop chattering and get to work. As King began to bristle, Turkey inquired: 'I'd be glad to know, sir, if it's true that Shakespeare did not write his own plays at all?'

'Good God!' said King most distinctly. Turkey coughed again piously. 'They all say so in Ireland, sir.'

'Ireland—Ireland—Ireland!' King overran Ireland with one blast of flame that should have been written in letters of brass for instruction to-day. At the end, Turkey coughed once more, and the cough said: 'It is Shakespeare, and not my country, that you are hired to interpret to me.' He put it directly, too: 'An' is it true at all about the alleged plays, sir?'

'It is not,' Mr. King whispered, and began to explain, on lines that might, perhaps, have been too freely expressed for the parents of those young (though it gave their offspring delight), but with a passion, force, and wealth of imagery which would have crowned his discourse at any university. By the time he drew towards his peroration the Form was almost openly applauding. Howell noiselessly drummed the cadence of 'Bonnie Dundee' on his desk; Paddy Vernon framed a dumb 'Played! Oh, *well* played, sir!' at intervals; Stalky kept tally of the brighter gems of invective; and Beetle sat aghast but exulting among the spirits he had called up. For though their works had never been mentioned, and though Mr. King said he had merely glanced at the obscene publications, he seemed to know a tremendous amount about Nathaniel and Delia— especially Delia.

'I told you so!' said Beetle, proudly, at the end.

'What? *Him!* I wasn't botherin' myself to listen to him an' his Delia,' M'Turk replied.

Afterwards King fought his battle over again with the Reverend John in the Common-room.

'Had I been that triple ass Hume, I might have risen to the bait. As it is, I flatter myself I left them under no delusions as to Shakespeare's authenticity. Yes, a small drink, please. Virtue has gone out of me indeed. But *where* did they get it from?'

'The devil! The young devil!' the Reverend John muttered, half aloud.

'I could have excused devilry. It was ignorance. Sheer, crass, insolent provincial ignorance! I tell you, Gillett, if the Romans had dealt faithfully with the Celt, *ab initio,* this—this would never have happened.'

'Quite so. I should like to have heard your remarks.'

'I've told 'em to tell me what they remember of them, with their own conclusions, in essay form next week.'

Since he had loosed the whirlwind, the fair-minded Beetle offered to do Turkey's essay for him. On Turkey's behalf, then, he dealt with Shakespeare's lack of education, his butchering, poaching, drinking, horse-holding, and errand-running as Nathaniel had described them; lifted from the same source pleasant names, such as 'rustic' and 'sorry poetaster,' on which last special hopes were built; and expressed surprise that one so ignorant 'could have done what he was attributed to.' His own essay contained no novelties. Indeed, he withheld one or two promising 'subsequently transpireds' for fear of distracting King.

But, when the essays were read, Mr. King confined himself wholly to Turkey's pitiful, puerile, jejune, exploded, unbaked, half-bottomed thesis. He touched, too, on the 'lie in the soul,' which was, fundamentally, vulgarity—the negation of Reverence and the Decencies. He broke forth into an impassioned defence of 'mere atheism,' which he said was often no more than mental flatulence—transitory and curable by knowledge of life—in no way comparable, for essential enormity, with the debasing pagan abominations to which Turkey had delivered himself. He ended with a shocking story about one Jowett, who seemed to have held some post of authority where King came from, and who had told an atheistical undergraduate that if he could not believe in a Personal God by five that afternoon he would be expelled—as, with tears of rage in his eyes, King regretted that he could not expel M'Turk. And Turkey blew his nose in the middle of it.

But the aim of education being to develop individual judgment, King could not well kill him for his honest doubts about Shakespeare. And he himself had several times quoted, in respect to other poets: 'There lives more faith in honest doubt, Believe me, than in half the creeds.' So he treated Turkey in form like a coiled puff-adder; and there was a tense peace among the Augustans. The only ripple was the day before the Army Examiner came, when Beetle inquired if he 'need take this exam., sir, as I'm not goin' up for anything.' Mr. King said there was great need—for many reasons, none of them flattering to vanity.

As far as the Army Class could judge, the Examiner was not worse than his kind, and the written 'English' paper ran closely on the lines of King's mid-term General Knowledge test. Howell played his 'impassioned Diderot' to the Richardson lead; Stalky his parson in the wig; M'Turk his contemptible Swift; Beetle, Steele's affectionate notes out of the spunging-house to 'Dearest Prue,' all in due order. There were, however, one or two leading questions about Shakespeare. A boy's hand shot up from a back bench.

'In answering Number Seven—reasons for Shakespeare's dramatic supremacy,' he said, 'are we to take it Shakespeare *did* write the plays he is supposed to have written, sir?'

The Examiner hesitated an instant. 'It is generally assumed that he did.' But there was no reproof in his words. Beetle began to sit down slowly.

Another hand and another voice: 'Have we got to say we believe he did, sir? Even if we do *nott*?'

'You are not called upon to state your beliefs. But we can go into that at *viva voce* this afternoon—if it interests you.'

'Thank you, sir.'

'What did you do that for?' Paddy Vernon demanded at dinner.

'It's the Lost Tribes of Israel game, you ass,' said Howell.

'To make sure,' Stalky amplified. 'If he was like King, he'd have shut up Beetle an' Turkey at the start, but he'd have thought King gave us the Bacon notion. Well, he didn't shut 'em up; so they're playin' it again this afternoon. If he stands it then, he'll be sure King gave us the notion. Either way, it's dead-safe for us—*an*' King.'

At the afternoon's *viva voce*, before they sat down to the Augustans, the Examiner wished to hear, 'with no bearing on the examination, of course,' from those two candidates who had asked him about Question Seven. Which were they?

'Take off your gigs, you owl,' said Stalky between his teeth. Beetle pocketed them and looked into blurred vacancy with a voice coming out of it that asked: 'Who—what gave you that idea about Shakespeare?' From Stalky's kick he knew the question was for him.

'Some people say, sir, there's a good deal of doubt about it nowadays, sir.'

'Ye-es, that's true, but——'

'It's his knowin' so much about legal phrases.' Turkey was in support—a lone gun barking somewhere to his right.

'That is a crux, I admit. Of course, whatever one may think privately, officially Shakespeare *is* Shakespeare. But how have *you* been taught to look at the question?'

'Well, Holmes says it's impossible he could——'

'On the legal phraseology alone, sir,' M'Turk chimed in.

'Ah, but the theory is that Shakespeare's experiences in the society of that day brought him in contact with all the leading intellects.' The Examiner's voice was quite colloquial now.

300

'But they didn't think much of actors then, sir, did they?'
This was Howell cooing like a cushat dove. 'I mean——'

The Examiner explained the status of the Elizabethan actor
in some detail, ending: 'And that makes it the more curious,
doesn't it?'

'And this Shakespeare was supposed to be writin' plays and
actin' in 'em *all* the time?' M'Turk asked, with sinister meaning.

'Exactly what I—what lots of people have pointed out.
Where did he get the time to acquire all his special knowledge?'

'Then it looks as if there was something in it, doesn't it, sir?'

'That,' said the Examiner, squaring his elbows at ease on
the desk, 'is a very large question which——'

'Yes, sir!'—in half-a-dozen eagerly attentive keys. . . .

For decency's sake a few Augustan questions were crammed
in conscience-strickenly, about the last ten minutes. Howell
took them since they involved dates, but the answers, though
highly marked, were scarcely heeded. When the clock showed
six-thirty the Examiner addressed them as 'Gentlemen'; and
said he would have particular pleasure in speaking well of this
Army Class, which had evinced such a genuine and unusual
interest in English Literature, and which reflected the greatest
credit on their instructors. He passed out: the Form upstanding, as custom was.

'He's goin' to congratulate King,' said Howell. 'Don't make
a row! "Don't—make—a—noise—Or else you'll wake the
Baby!" '. . .

Mr. King of Balliol, after Mr. Hume of Sutton had complimented him, as was only just, before all his colleagues in
Common-room, was kindly taken by the Reverend John to his
study, where he exploded on the hearth-rug.

'He—he thought *I* had loosed this—this rancid Baconian rot among them. He complimented me on my breadth of mind—my being abreast of the times! You heard him? That's how they think of Sutton. It's an open stye! A lair of bestial! They have a chapel there, Gillett, and they pray for their souls—their *souls!*'

'His particular weakness apart, Hume was perfectly sincere about what you'd done for the Army Class. He'll report in that sense, too. That's a feather in your cap, and a deserved one. He said their interest in Literature was unusual. That is *all* your work, King.'

'But I bowed down in the House of Rimmon while he Baconised all over me!—poor devil of an usher that I am! You heard it! I ought to have spat in his eye! Heaven knows I'm as conscious of my own infirmities as my worst enemy can be; but what have I done to deserve this? What *have* I done?'

'That's just what I was wondering,' the Reverend John replied. 'Have you, perchance, done anything?'

'Where? How?'

'In the Army Class, for example.'

'Assuredly not! My Army Class? I couldn't wish for a better—keen, interested enough to read outside their allotted task—intelligent, receptive! They're head and shoulders above last year's. The idea that I, forsooth, should, even by inference, have perverted their minds with this imbecile and unspeakable girls'-school tripe that Hume professes! *You* at least know that I have my standards; and in Literature and in the Classics, I hold *maxima debetur pueris reverentia.*'[1]

'It's singular, not plural, isn't it?' said the Reverend John. 'But you're absolutely right as to the principle! . . . Ours is a deadly calling, King—especially if one happens to be sensitive.'

[1] The greatest respect is due to young persons.

THE SATISFACTION OF A GENTLEMAN

THE SATISFACTION OF A GENTLEMAN

LONG BEFORE THE DAYS of *Cyrano de Bergerac*, the Coll. knew
that you might discuss his red nose with Dickson Quartus
in all amity and safety, so long as it did not turn blue, and
he did not gnash his teeth and speak with tongues. If that
happened—why, anything might happen; and the worst generally happened after long stretches of lean living. For example, 'Pussy' Abanazar and Tertius, his study-mates, being the
junior sub-prefects of that winter term, were in the field, taking Lower School footer—which, of course, took both of their
fags—and Dick coming up from place-kicking found the study
fire out, too.

Naturally, he went up to Number Five, immediately overhead, and borrowed from Beetle, *in riposo* on the domestic
hearth, a shovelful of burning coals. Coming down with it,
he almost ran into Mr. King, his own House-master, at the
bottom of the stairs, and from sheer nervous shock tilted out
the whole affair at, if not over, his feet. There was some
energetic dancing and denouncing, as Beetle noted through
the banisters, and when it had ceased Dick had five hundred
lines, which did not prevent him from being very happy with
Beetle over the spirited action of King's hind-legs among the
cinders.

Last lesson that day was English Literature—*Paradise Lost*
—and when Harrison major, whose voice is as a lost sheep's,
bleated about Satan treading on 'burning marl,' Beetle sputtered aloud.

King might or might not have guessed the connection. But
he said nothing beyond, 'Two hundred Latin lines.' Dick

condoled with Beetle after tea; but also developed his own grievance, which was that Beetle had heaped too many coals of fire on him.

'I like that!' was the retort. 'I kept *on* tellin' you your shovel wouldn't hold 'em, you blue-snouted Mandrill.' Beetle knew much about the coloration of Mandrills, and would often describe it to Dick.

But this time Dick's nose blue-fired where it stood; he gnashed his teeth, and emitted the war-cry of the Royal Line of Ashantee. (His naval uncle had fought in those parts and, Dick swore, had taught him all the languages.) What followed, though painful for Beetle, who was alone (and Pussy was with Dick), was merely an affair of outposts. The Temple of Janus was opened ceremonially later. After prayers, Number Five, who were sitting up from nine to ten for 'extra work,' caught a fag of their House about to undress, hustled it into a nightgown over all for tabard, and sent it to Dick's study with a stolen gym boxing-glove, which Turkey called 'the Cartel.' Dick spared the quavering herald, and pranced up to Number Five, robed in a tablecloth, at the very top of his rarely shown form. As Head of the Gaboon and the Dahomey Customs, he talked Fantee, which includes —with whistlings and quackings—Rabelaisian accounts of the manners of the West Coast, and the etiquette of native courts thereabouts; for his uncle had been an observant officer. It altogether destroyed Number Five. They clung to the table, beseeching Dick to stop and let them get breath; and they topped off the ribald hour with pickled onions and raspberry vinegar for a pledge of naked war.

When they went up to their study next morning, after second lesson, they found, when they could see, everything in it furred with a ghastly, greasy deposit; and a smell fouler than the sight. Dick had shut down their chimney damper, set an old 'gutty' golf-ball in a sardine-tin on the new-made fire, jammed their window, plugged up with paper beneath their door, and let nature do the rest. Their pictures left white squares on the walls when they took them down. Turkey felt it most, for Art was his province. Beetle wanted to bore holes in the floor, and pour melted lead through; but, as Stalky pointed out, Pussy and Tertius were sub-prefects, and one could not include their study in the field of unrestricted warfare.

'Dick's flank is covered all right,' he said. 'Beetle ought to have thought of that. Yes, you ass, I *have* thought of snuff; but don't *you* try to think, or you'll hash it. Leave him alone!'

So when the King of Ashantee quacked his triumph at next call-over, they all looked straitly to their own front, and lifted neither hand nor hoof. Only Pussy, on an exquisite note between apology and authority, reminded Stalky that the day following would be a House-match (Macrea's *v.* King's), which would claim him, Tertius and Dick from three to five. As sub-prefect he could have commanded a truce, but as ally of Dick he had sanctioned the war and had taken part in the execution of Beetle—Death by the Hundred Slices between two forms.

'That's all right,' Stalky answered him. '*We* wouldn't dree-eam of goin' into studies when they're empty.'

'Dick didn't think,' Pussy went on. It was the extreme limit of concession.

'Don't you worry, Kitten. He's goin' to.' After which, Stalky removed from Beetle six penny stamps reserved for correspondence.

'Want 'em all?' said Beetle.

'I didn't. But I will now, you selfish hound. I do all the work an'——'

'*All* right. 'Tisn't *my* fault if I can't write home,' said the robbed one in a relieved voice, and went on plaintively: 'Who's bagged my new socks, curse you?'

'Those Mandrill ones? Wouldn't be found dead in 'em. Turkey most likely. He's eesthetic.'

Beetle sighed. They were a church-going pair of a provocative peacock-blue, which, when coquettishly exhibited across an aisle, would make Dick's nose glow through half the sermon.

On Saturday afternoon, with everybody down at the House-match, Stalky brought out the communal frying-pan, and laid in it large slabs of the fattest bacon.

'Old Mother Hunt gave me all that for fourpence. She thinks it's a bit off. Fry it, Beetle.'

The slices rendered as generously as blubber. When the pan was about half full of fat, Stalky fished out three slices and tied each slice to a string from a new penny string-ball. Then he and the others leaned out of their window, and bobbed them against the window of the study below. In that crisp October air, each bob left a white blob of coagulated fat on the pane. When a slice ceased to register, it was hauled up and reconditioned. At intervals, some one would go down to report on the effect from the ground-level, or to direct the more delicate stipplings. They put on a second coat to make sure, and judged that it would do.

The returning enemy were too full of their game to notice anything till they had washed, and were well at home again. Then, peering from above, Number Five saw Pussy's huge paw put forth, and an experimenting finger drawn through the creamy deposit on the panes.

'Go an' jape with them, Turkey. Get Dick's head well out. Keep that fat just off the bubble, Beetle,' said Stalky.

Turkey presented himself on the area-railings outside the lower study and, as usual, let others make conversation. He had gifts that way. Things had not gone much beyond 'Filthy swine!' when the King of Ashantee, ousting his slower-minded mates, leaned forth, and addressed himself directly to Turkey, with two golf-balls, one after the other. Here Stalky took the pan from Beetle, and decanted, say, one pint of pure bacon fat on to Dick's scalp, where it set at once into a frosty wig. The bag of flour, dashed down after it, was sheer waste of the sixth of Beetle's penny stamps. Without a glance at the result, Turkey sauntered back, and pushed the study table against the door.

'All right. To-morrow's Sunday,' said Stalky. 'Good for Dick's topper. But don't you notice him. He's the Lord's Anointed.'

Saturday prayers were worth attending; but next day's divine service was—just that! Dick's locks had clotted into irregular overlapping scales which, when flattened by a desperate hand, sprang up again unrelatedly. Even his study-mates mocked him, but, for Number Five, it was as though he had never been upon earth or in memory. They merely put it about that his was a disease which comes from not brushing the hair, and that presently it would bleed.

That same Sabbath eve—disregarding advice and scorning reinforcements—the Head of the Gaboon tore upstairs alone to call upon them, when, seeing that he appeared to be armed, they fell on him—ankle, waist and neck—without a word. At last he was understood to say something about 'slugs in a saw-pit.' They let him up.

'It's your gloat,' he gasped. 'Let's top off with a duel in the

Bunkers. I challenge the lot of you. Death before dishonour!
An' give me some of that raspberry vinegar.'

'Your sally any good?' M'Turk asked. He had Number
Five's armoury in his own care.

'Hellish stiff. I was bringing it for you to clean a bit. I've
got cartridges but no oil.' He picked up from the floor a
lock-jawed twenty-two rim-fire Belgian saloon-pistol, which
Turkey took over at once.

'Get expelled for duellin',' Beetle observed sourly.

'You abject cur! You're the only one with gig-lamps, too,'
Stalky rebuked.

'*You* called me The Mandrill,' said the Head of the Gaboon. 'An' what was that beastliness of yours about my hair
bleedin',—thou—thou varlet?' (That was Dick's word of the
week, so to say.)

'Oh, *Plica Polonica*,' said Beetle, and brightly summarised
as much as he could recall of Polish Plat out of a Heaven-sent
old encyclopedia.

'*Two* shots at Beetle for that,' said Dick icily.

'You shall have 'em!' cried generous Stalky. 'But look here,
you can't take us *all* on. What about a quadrilateral duel?'
Stalky saw himself excelling Marryat.

'What for? You each get plugged at three times, same as
me. *I* don't mind.'

'What distance?' said Turkey, with his head in his playbox
among the oiled rags.

'Dunno, quite. Ten paces too much?' Stalky suggested.

'Rot!' Beetle protested. 'You can make a Burrows donkey
bray his head off at a hundred yards with dust-shot. I've done
it.'

'You unfeelin' brute! Now you can do a little brayin' on
your own, an' see how you like it. I vote we make it twelve

paces for the duels, an' after that we'll pick sides and have a general stalk in the Bunkers.'

'Who's to give the range *then*?' Beetle asked.

'Guess it, you old burbler. Besides, dust-shot don't hardly sting even at point-blank.'

Beetle explained what his spiritual adventures must be ere he lent himself to such speculations. His piety wearied them.

'If you say much more we'll decree you a rabbit—same as Maunsell did young Vivian. *He* made him cock-up at point-blank.' Stalky was referring to an episode of their early and oppressed past.

'Yes, an' Gartside major got hold of it an' half cut Maunsell's fat soul out of him in the dormitory. That shows what prefects think of duellin'! An' s'pose King spots us in the Bunkers with his filthy telescope? I've looked through it. I swear you can see the crabs runnin' about on Braunton Sands.' Beetle delivered this all in one passionate breath.

'You're sickenin',' said Turkey. 'Maunsell was bullyin' young Vivian. D'you mean to say *you're* bein' bullied? An', tell me now, has King or Prout or Foxy—has anyone—ever told ye that duellin' is forbidden at Coll.? Don't prevaricate. Have you ever seen it posted in the corridor?'

'Then get Pussy and Tertius for seconds,' Beetle howled.

'I'd not dream of runnin' in on them for a little thing like this,' Turkey concluded, and Dick added:

'Besides, this is a private affair. It's the satisfaction of a gentleman, thou scurvy varlet.'

'Oh, shut up an' listen to your Uncle. The Bunkers to-morrow after call-over. Shots all round—*an'* one extra for Beetle. First blood satisfies Honour. Then we'll pick sides an' have a general stalk till we're out of ammunition.'

'Good business,' said the foe. '*And* a brew for the survivors after tea! My uncle hath remembered me. Selah! We'd better have it up here and ask Pussy and Tertius. It's safer.'

At that epoch, the young of the English, alone of their kind, understood the exact difference between official and unofficial. Pussy and Tertius said they would be happy to attend the brew and, being men of substance, sent, as it were, milk and honey in advance. They had not been officially informed what the banquet would celebrate, but prying suspicion is beneath true authority.

'Anyhow,' said Pussy to his colleague, 'I've been through Dick's cartridges to make sure. *All* dust-shot.'

At three, then, next day, after Beetle, the housekeeper, had set out the table for a brew of six, four boys in prudent overcoats ('sallies' pack clumsily beneath short jackets) pushed into the wind for the rushy sand-dunes at the far end of the Pebble Ridge. It is true that certain old men who, though not in the Army, impiously wore red coats, used a fringe of the landscape for a senile diversion known as Golf—Turkey had played it for some weeks and pronounced it 'sickenin' '— but once off the line of their activities—the 'fairway,' they called it—a boy might have been in the Sahara.

The Equinox drove the sand into their faces or round their legs, as they dived among the sheep-haunted hollows. The upstanding winter tide roared and trampled along the Pebble Ridge outside till they had to shout to each other, and racing slashes of low sunlight from seaward lit the sands and the bents with fierce coppery glares. In a secluded dell, out of the worst of the wind, Turkey posted Stalky and Dick Four— each edge-on, House-cap pulled down to the eyebrows, left elbow crooked, covering mouth and nose, and pistol ready to level over the crook at the Caution and to fire at the Word.

For such had been the tradition of the Giants of the Prime —great names—now even greater Captains who, of course, stood fire daily.

'Squad!' croaked Turkey in Foxy's best manner. 'Fire!' Both pistols popped together. It was a clean miss.

'Didn't you even hear mine?' Stalky called.

The King of Coomassie shook his head gingerly. It was difficult for him to keep his cap on his matted hair.

'Never mind. I'll get you at the stalk.' Then Stalky in turn placed Turkey and Dick. They fired.

'Heard something that time,' said Dick appreciatively. Turkey had raised his left elbow, knowing that his pistol threw low.

Beetle took the field of honour without parade. His first shot was well to the left.

'Your man is in front of ye,' said M'Turk grimly. 'Reload as ye stand.'

'*Now* you pay for Mandrill!' Dick shouted. But on the 'Fire' Beetle blazed skyward, which, with that uncertain sort of ammunition and by the help of a passing gust, was just enough to sling the charge well forward. The King of Ashantee rubbed his cheek and swore in purest English.

'Blood!' Turkey paced in. 'Tip of Dick's ear bleedin'.'

'Pimple! Pimple!' roared the King. 'I've been scratchin' it for weeks.'

Turkey dabbed with a handkerchief and held up the evidence.

'Blood! Honour satisfied. Let-off for you, Beetle!'

But Beetle was already treading his own conception of a reel to the chant of: '*I*'ve drilled the *Man*drill—the *Man*drill —the *Man*drill!'

'Bunk!' Stalky warned him. 'Run, you ass!' The Head of the

Gaboon was gnashing his teeth and reloading with intent. 'We'll start the stalk now. I'm on our side, Beetle.'

'Are ye? Then I'm on Dick's,' said M'Turk, wheeling, and fired into the skirts of the flying overcoat.

Beetle was out of that hollow and across several others before he found a ragged bunker—the old 'Cockscomb'—whose crest had been undercut by rabbits. Here he lay down and reloaded, resolved to sell his life dear, but not to go looking for many buyers. He knew what Stalky could be as an ally, and it worried him; but, from broken words that rode the gale, it sounded as though Stalky must have stalked Dick Four, and so committed himself to a definite policy. Beetle's was to reach, as soon as might be, those very old red-coated men whom he had so often scorned. Deeply as they loathed his likes, they would not allow him to be peppered in their fairway. He crawled unfastidiously to the next bunker furthest from the sea, descended its face, and disturbed an old ewe. She bolted up wind, and brought down on him out of a side-ravine Dick Four, wrestling with a jammed pistol and roaring like a gorilla. Just when Beetle—as he ever afterwards explained—was about to blow his silly brains out, Dick scooped up tons of sand and tossed them into the blast. Beetle ate of it what he could not avoid, rubbed enough of the rest out of his spectacles and eyes to see a little, and ploughed on, the skirts of his unbuttoned overcoat ever being blown forward between his legs. Renewed poppings and yells from the rear indicated either that he had been 'decreed a rabbit' *in absentia*, or that civil war had broken out. But, like unthinking youth, he did not look back.

He arrived, well on all fours, at the lip of a big crater known in those pure days as The Pit. Directly beneath him stood an ancient in a red coat, scrabbling, like King David, with a niblick. While Beetle, on both elbows, removed his spectacles to get a little more damp sand off them, the unkind wind hove his coattails clean over his head, and plunged him into darkness. Almost at the same instant he felt a pain behind, which urged him to plunge out of it. . . . And thus it was that this innocent boy, with life's golden promise before him, and that withered zealot, trifling blasphemously through his few remaining days, met all of a heap, on much the same selection of *mots justes*—cries of lost souls and defeated generals.

'Blast you! Who *are* you?' the elder began; but Beetle, his spectacles in his hand, disengaged and fled on—he felt at the moment that he could run for ever—to the protection of the fairway. Here, as he cleaned and reshipped his glasses, he realised that his personal grief was now more like the dying memory of an efficient ground-ash than any portent of fatal haemorrhage. Presently, life, as it tingled through his young system, seemed rather prosperous. At any rate, he had drilled the Mandrill; escaped further active service; the old goat in The Pit had not seen him with his spectacles on, which ought to be a perfect alibi; and a brew of brews awaited him. He returned towards Coll.

A sobbing voice hailed, and Stalky ranged or, rather, tottered alongside. Without turning his head, Beetle asked him what he had done *that* for.

'Because you deserted! You left me to fight a rear-guard action alone, you cad!' Then, clinging to Beetle's cold shoulder: 'I didn't mean to. I *swear* I didn't till your coat blew up! Then I couldn't help it. Wasn't it a beauty? Did it sting much? Never mind! Turkey's got it in the ankle—point-

blank. He left his silly foot stickin' out of some rushes an'
Dick thought it was you! Turkey's a bit wrathy.'

Turkey limped up with Dick. They were obviously es-
tranged. Dick was talking about 'lousy Fenians,' and Turkey's
nose was high in air.

'Well?' said Beetle, a thought comforted. Stalky continued:

'Turkey got my cap. I stuck it up to draw his fire. Then he
got me on the hand!' A dirty rag round a palm was proof.
'Oh, but before that, I got Dick where I got you, but *much*
tighter. Turkey changed sides after Dick plugged him. That
was really why I had to plug *you*—to make things fair. See,
you old burbler?'

'But,' Dick was pleading with Turkey, 'how the devil was
I to know you were wearing Beetle's ungodly socks? I couldn't
smell 'em in this wind, could I? It was your fault for baggin'
'em!'

Beetle chortled. There seemed to be some justice in things
after all.

'I hope Turkey plugged you, you murderer,' he rounded on
Dick.

'Only once.' Dick rubbed his neck again. He might have
lightly brushed a bough of gorse.

'That's nothing.' Beetle looked pointedly at his own salient
work on the rim of the ear.

'Yours was an infernal fluke,' said Dick hotly. 'You were in a
blue funk all the time,—thou—thou noisome varlet.'

'Thou notch-eared knave,' was the reply.

But the crisis had passed, and Dick beamed; he, too, had
a sound taste in epithets.

They were going through pockets for overlooked cartridges (one has to explain so much if any are found), and
throwing them into Goosey Pool, when, out of the autumn

dusk, a robin-like old man hopped, and almost pecked, at
Turkey. The others delicately walked on; Beetle for once
leading.

'You were the boy who swore at me just now,' the stranger
began.

Turkey took no notice, except that his nose went up a little
more.

'I was in a bunker, and you knocked into me. Using filthy
language, sir!'

'An' what were ye doin' in the bunker? An' which bunker
was it?' Turkey spoke like all the wearied and disbelieving
magistracy of the Ireland of those days.

'The Pit,' said the Ancient, being a golfer—which is to say
a monomaniac.

Turkey came to life with a jerk.

'Bunkered? In The Pit? With this wind blowin'? Goin' or
comin' ye could *nott*!'

'But I tell you I *did*.' The other seemed to have forgotten
his original grievance.

'Ah, then, ye're not worth a curse—an' never will be.'

Turkey rejoined his companions, to whom Beetle was giving a theory of cause and effect. The four linked arms and
swept up the old sunken lane to Coll. Honour was satisfied;
there remained but their own young appetites. When, just
before last lesson, Beetle connected the rubber tube from the
gas-bracket to their dear little stove—turning the jet down
to that exact degree which will bring milk-cocoa to perfec-
tion in one hour and a half—and counted the potted ham-
and-tongue jars, the chicken-and-ham sausage, the sardine-
tins, the three jams, the condensed milk, the two pounds of
Devonshire cream, and the whole pound of real butter, he
would not have changed his lot with kings. Nor, as he went

to the form-room, did it strike him that a spare, accurately dressed person standing in the Head's porch had anything to do with the old goat he had heard, rather than seen, cursing in The Pit.

Ten minutes before the close of last lesson (their mouths were watering already), Foxy knocked and laid a well-known slip on King's desk.

'The Head to see,' King read, and paused to let suspense soak in. 'Ah! Only our usual three—*plus* Dickson Quartus. This, I fear, portends tragedy. All four of you—*at* once—*if* you please!'

They agreed that, for the first time in their knowledge of him, the Head must have been drunk. Nothing else explained his performance.

'The way he *talked* was enough,' said Dick Four. 'All the studies brew, and he knows it. But he went on as if he'd heard of it for the first time.'

'At the top of his voice, too. When Bates is wrathy, he whispers. But he shouted like Rabbits-Eggs. That proves it,' said Stalky.

'Then, all that putrid rot about "the criminality" of havin' a tube. *All* the studies have 'em. He said it was theft—of gas! *There* you are!' Dick continued.

'An' his rot about "gorgin'." He *knows* we can't live on the muck they give us. He—he said brewin' was "an insult to the bountiful provision made for us by the authorities." Mad! Ravin' mad!' This was Beetle's kinder judgment.

Turkey scratched an ankle and spoke:—

'Authority! He's never said a word about any authority except himself since I've been here.'

'Then you think he's tight, too?'

'I do not. If he'd drunk enough to make him talk like that, he'd have been lyin' on the floor to say it.'

'Anyhow, he licked like hell,' Beetle went on.

'He did *nott*, either. His arm was never shoulder-high once.'

'But if he wasn't tight, what made him count the cuts aloud? No one does that, except Justus Prout,' said Stalky.

Dick Four pointed at the untouched table.

'He hasn't confiscated the grub. Better eat it and have Pussy and Tertius in for cover.'

'Better make sure first,' said Beetle. '*I* don't want the Head japin' with me again just now. I'll ask Foxy.'

He found him in the gym as usual.

'No orders about it at all,' said the Sergeant, and there was an unfathomable twinkle in his little red eye.

But Turkey sat on the window-seat asking of nobody:—

'For what would he be roarin' like that? The man was out of his nature, I tell ye.'

Years—some years—later, Captain 'Pussy' Abanazar, R.E., seconded for duty in the Indian Political, at home on leave, was invited by the Head to spend a few days of the Easters at Coll., in a mild, early, Devon spring. Half-a-dozen of the Army Class stayed up to read for near exams., and perhaps as many juniors whose people were abroad. When the last shouting brake-load had left, and emptiness filled the universe, the Head turned into a most delightful and comprehending uncle, so that that forlorn band remembered those Easters through the rest of their lives. And when Captain Abanazar rolled in, and was to each of them equally a demi-god and an elder brother of the right sort (he tipped like Croesus), their cups overflowed.

One soft evening in the Head's private study, with the sea churning up old memories all along the Ridge, Pussy asked:

'Bates Sahib, do you remember lickin' Number Five and Dick Four for brewin' in——' He gave the year and added: 'My first term as a sub, you know.'

The Head smiled and nodded.

'And giving 'em a pi-jaw?'

'Pi-jaws aren't my line. There *was* a jaw, though. Why? What did they think about it?'

'They didn't understand it at all. I believe they thought you were tight.'

'Would I had been! But it was worse. It was cowardice, Pussy—it was bowing down in the House of Rimmon. And they noticed what I said?'

'I should say they did!'

'No wonder! We had a Board of Directors in those days— retired Colonels—martial men with the habit of command. I'm glad I never had that.'

'Yes, we all deplored your lack of it, sir.'

'Don't misunderstand me. They were excellent men. I'm sure we were all deeply indebted to them. One of the very best was a Colonel—Coll—Con—wait a minute—Curthwen. But he's in Abraham's bosom now. (Awkward bedfellow!) He knew about education and the prices of things. *So* useful at Board meetings. I always moved the vote of thanks to him. He was exceptionally nice to me. Advice—the soundest advice. You see, he knew about—er—everything except, yes, golf. He had to come down here to learn that. I only dared go round with him once. I enjoyed it too much. Little runny-nosed Northam caddies told him where to put his horrible feet. Ah! When he came down here, you see, his evenings were quite free, and he could drop in on me at any time, and —er—offer a few suggestions.'

Pussy shuddered all over; and he was not of the smaller makes.

'Yes,' the Head mused. 'It's a shameful story. *That* evening, he dropped in complaining that one of us—you—a boy—had nearly knocked him over in a bunker, and then used filthy language. . . . No. I never found out who the boy was. I could only envy. But the shock and the language—he was, of course, a churchwarden—made him a little—excessive, perhaps. He gave me an hour's sound advice—with a tang to it. Then I walked with him to the old Fives Court to see him off, but he sniffed like a hound opposite Number Five, and said he smelt gas escaping. (You *can't* smell it any other way, can you?) Then he began all over again, Pussy—on economics in the abstract. An eye like a lizard's. That type have the lust of detail. Yes! After one hour, he began again. Then I lied—as overworked children do.'

'By Jove! I remember your warning me about that, when I worked Lower School too hard at footer. It's true of men, too.'

'It is. I lied like a scullion—like the hireling that I was! I told him the gas was always shut off from the studies when not required. I think I told him I kept the key of the meter in my —bath-room. I don't want to think *what* I told him. He was good enough to say he took my word for it, but——'

'Did he? Wish I'd been there. Well?'

'He tracked the stink upstairs foot by foot—like Prout on a moral trail. It was I—I—who threw open the study door to show his suspicions were wrong. And there was that glorious brew laid out on the table, and the tube from the gas-jet to the stove! A tiny, little, bright, blue flame, Pussy. It went *wheee-whee*, like a toy balloon deflating. That was *me*! I deflated. He inflated for ten minutes. I am a wicked old man—as you know. I have terrorised infants and perjured myself to mothers, and intrigued with and against my Staff; but I paid for my sins then, Pussy. You'd have loved it.'

'But I'd have dropped him out of the window first,' said Pussy.

'Why? He had the obvious right of it. There *was* the smell. There *was* the waste. (As a matter of fact, it was traced to the basement.) And, I suppose, there *was* a chance of burning down the Coll. Then he was shocked at the brew. He said it showed you didn't appreciate your lawful food. Yes! He sawed at me with his voice, Pussy, till I fell. I connived—I confederated with him. I suggested that he should eavesdrop in my private study—yes, here—and listen to what I should say when I sacrificed those innocent children. Thank goodness, I have forgotten my discourse, but I know that I addressed them— him, next door, I mean—out of his own Philistine vocabulary. And you say they noticed the falling-off in my style? Aha! *Non omnis moriar!*' The Head purred.

'They couldn't make any sense of it. And did you count the cuts aloud?'

'Very like. Why should I have stopped at any crime? I was playing up to the Board—to appearances—to expediency—to fear of consequences—to all those little dirty things that I brought you children up to spit upon. Except that I didn't kneel and pray with them—Heavens! he might have exacted *that!*—there was only one redeeming feature. When it came to the execution, that little red cupboard-door stuck.'

'The rope breaking on the gallows,' Pussy amplified. 'It never did with me!'

'And I saw my face in the glass, like an ape's—a frightened, revengeful ape's. (And, so far as I *have* a gospel, it is never to carry things to the sweating-point.) That saved a remnant of

my integrity. Saved them something, as well. The licking was
a noisy one—for his benefit—but artistically, my dear boy,
you understand, a sketch—the merest outline.'

'That squares with the evidence, too. And you didn't con-
fiscate the grub. I know, because I helped eat it.'

'There are limits to my brutality. Besides, he'd gone to gorge
at his dreadful Golf Club; and I could have eaten a horse.
But it was all abject—paltry—time-serving—unjust. Not that
I believe in Justice, but I don't like to think that I ever licked
out of personal mortification and revenge.'

'Don't you worry, Bates dear. Those young devils had been
out duellin' in the Bunkers the whole afternoon. Every one of
'em was a casualty as he stood to you. What was our allowance
for that?'

'Threats of expulsion—followed by twelve of the best. The
young scoundrels! But you've taken a load off my mind,
Pussy. If I'd known that, I could have paid 'em honourably!'

'Beetle was the chap who attended to your Colonel, too.
Stalky plugged him—bending—on the edge of The Pit, and he
fell into it, cursing Stalky for all he was worth. The Colonel
was bunkered at the bottom. You see?'

'*I* see. Never again will I hear a word against Beetle—
unless I say it myself.' The Head spoke with genuine gratitude. 'But how did they hound him into the fray? Was he—
er—"decreed a rabbit"?'

'Bates, dear, is there one single dam' thing about us that
you don't know?' Pussy spoke after an admiring pause.

'We-ell! It's a shameful confession, but, you see, I loved you
all. The rest was only sending you all to bed dead-tired. . . .
You want a sheet of impot-paper? You know where it lives.
What for?'

'I'm going to restore your prestige an' give Stalky pain. He needs a tonic where he is now, poor devil! . . . Please, sir, what are common nouns in *io* called?'

What Pussy sent out (as 'code,' at State expense) from the overwhelmed little Post Office ran:—

'Capitem vidi. Stop. Constat flagellatio Studii Quinti Ricardique Quarti utsi ob caenam vere propter duellum vestrum inter arenas donata fuisse. Stop. Matutinissime si Capitem decipere vis surgendum. Stop. Amorem expedit. Stop. Felis Catus.'[1]

What Stalky, doing station-master in a freezing internationalised lamp-room, received, after two or three telegraphists of the Nearer and Farther Easts had had their flying shots at it, was:—

'Captain vids. Stop. Constance plageltio studdi quinti ricandk que qualte cuts obscene very prabst duel in vestry iter arimas donala puistse. Stop. Matushima so cahutem discipere via sargentson. Stop. Amend expent. Stop. Felix Cotes.'

He had trouble enough on his own fork at the time, so, as Pussy foretold, it proved a tonic. The office of origin and 'studdi quinti' gave him a bearing, but he upset half the railway system of Cathay, as then working, to arrive at epigraphists with a College education. A Captain of Native Infantry happened to remember the catchword, 'You must get

---

[1] 'Have seen the Head. He says the licking of Number Five Study and Dick Four ostensibly for brewing was really for your duel in the Bunkers. You've got to get up very early to take in the Head. He sends love. The Cat.'

up pretty early to take in the Head.' The rest was combined deductive scholarship. In due time a cable went back, not to F. Cotes, but to the Head:—

'These from Sinim. Stop. Knew it all along. Delighted your character for downiness cleared. Stop. Ours nationally and personally more than indifferent here. Stop. Best loves for birthday.'

Four or five names out of an Army Class followed in school order.

Not till several years later did Pussy tell Stalky and the others how they had been deceived; and cruelly rubbed in that 'Knew it all along.' As they were, then, far too senior to go to war in the ancient formation, they passed the docket over to Beetle, with instructions to 'report and revenge.'

Which had to be done!

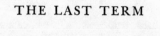

THE LAST TERM

THE LAST TERM

IT WAS WITHIN A FEW DAYS of the holidays, the term-end examinations, and, more important still, the issue of the College paper which Beetle edited. He had been cajoled into that office by the blandishments of Stalky and M'Turk and the extreme rigour of study law. Once installed, he discovered, as others have done before him, that his duty was to do the work while his friends criticised. Stalky christened it the *Swillingford Patriot*, in pious memory of Sponge—and M'Turk compared the output unfavourably with Ruskin and De Quincey. Only the Head took an interest in the publication, and his methods were peculiar. He gave Beetle the run of his brown-bound, tobacco-scented library; prohibiting nothing, recommending nothing. There Beetle found a fat armchair, a silver inkstand, and unlimited pens and paper. There were scores and scores of ancient dramatists; there were Hakluyt, his Voyages; French translations of Muscovite authors called Pushkin and Lermontoff; little tales of a heady and bewildering nature, interspersed with unusual songs—Peacock was that writer's name; there was Borrow's *Lavengro*; an odd theme, purporting to be a translation of something called a 'Rubáiyát,' which the Head said was a poem not yet come to its own; there were hundreds of volumes of verse—Crashaw; Dryden; Alexander Smith; L.E.L.; Lydia Sigourney; Fletcher and a purple island; Donne; Marlowe's *Faust*; and—this made M'Turk (to whom Beetle conveyed it) sheer drunk for three days—Ossian; *The Earthly Paradise; Atalanta in Calydon;* and Rossetti—to name only a few. Then the Head, drifting

in under pretence of playing censor to the paper, would read
here a verse and here another of these poets; opening up avenues. And, slow breathing, with half-shut eyes above his
cigar, would he speak of great men living, and journals, long
dead, founded in their riotous youth; of years when all the
planets were little new-lit stars trying to find their places in
the uncaring void, and he, the Head, knew them as young
men know one another. So the regular work went to the dogs,
Beetle being full of other matters and metres, hoarded in
secret and only told to M'Turk of an afternoon, on the sands,
walking high and disposedly round the wreck of the Armada
galleon, shouting and declaiming against the long-ridged seas.

Thanks in large part to their House-master's experienced
distrust, the three for three consecutive terms had been passed
over for promotion to the rank of prefect—an office that went
by merit, and carried with it the honour of the ground-ash,
and liberty, under restrictions, to use it.

'*But,*' said Stalky, 'come to think of it, we've done more
giddy jesting with the Sixth since we've been passed over than
any one else in the last seven years.'

He touched his neck proudly. It was encircled by the stiffest
of stick-up collars, which custom decreed could be worn only
by the Sixth. And the Sixth saw those collars and said no word.
'Pussy' Abanazar or Dick Four of a year ago would have seen
them discarded in five minutes or . . . But the Sixth of that
term was made up mostly of young but brilliantly clever boys,
pets of the House-masters, too anxious for their dignity to care
to come to open odds with the resourceful three. So they
crammed their caps at the extreme back of their heads, instead
of a trifle over one eye as the Fifth should, and rejoiced in
patent-leather boots on week-days, and marvellous made-up
ties on Sundays—no man rebuking. M'Turk was going up for
Cooper's Hill, and Stalky for Sandhurst, in the spring; and the

Head had told them both that, unless they absolutely collapsed during the holidays, they were safe. As a trainer of colts, the Head seldom erred in an estimate of form.

He had taken Beetle aside that day and given him much good advice, not one word of which did Beetle remember when he dashed up to the study, white with excitement, and poured out the wondrous tale. It demanded a great belief.

'You begin on a hundred a year?' said M'Turk unsympathetically. 'Rot!'

'And my passage out! It's all settled. The Head says he's been breaking me in for this for ever so long, and I never knew—I never knew. One don't begin with writing straight off, y'know. Begin by filling in telegrams and cutting things out o' papers with scissors.'

'Oh, Scissors! What an ungodly mess you'll make of it!' said Stalky. 'But, anyhow, this will be your last term, too. Seven years, my dearly beloved 'earers,—though not prefects.'

'Not half bad years, either,' said M'Turk. 'I shall be sorry to leave the old Coll.; shan't you?'

They looked out over the sea creaming along the Pebble Ridge in the clear winter light. 'Wonder where we shall all be this time next year?' said Stalky absently.

'This time five years,' said M'Turk.

'Oh,' said Beetle, 'my leavin's between ourselves. The Head hasn't told any one. I know he hasn't, because Prout grunted at me to-day that if I were more reasonable—yah!—I might be a prefect next term. I suppose he's hard up for his prefects.'

'Let's finish up with a row with the Sixth,' suggested M'Turk.

'Dirty little schoolboys!' said Stalky, who already saw himself a Sandhurst cadet. 'What's the use?'

'Moral effect,' quoth M'Turk. 'Leave an imperishable tradition, and all the rest of it.'

'Better go into Bideford an' pay up our debts,' said Stalky. 'I've got three quid out of my father—*ad hoc*. Don't owe more than thirty bob, either. Cut along, Beetle, and ask the Head for leave. Say you want to correct the *Swillingford Patriot*.'

'Well, I do,' said Beetle. 'It'll be my last issue, and I'd like it to look decent. I'll catch him before he goes to his lunch.'

Ten minutes later they wheeled out in line, by grace released from five o'clock call-over, and all the afternoon lay before them. So also unluckily did King, who never passed without witticisms. But brigades of Kings could not have ruffled Beetle that day.

'Aha! Enjoying the study of light literature, my friend?' said he, rubbing his hands. 'Common mathematics are not for such soaring minds as yours, are they?'

('One hundred a year,' thought Beetle, smiling into vacancy.)

'Our open incompetence takes refuge in the flowery paths of inaccurate fiction. But a day of reckoning approaches, Beetle mine. I myself have prepared a few trifling foolish questions in Latin prose which can hardly be evaded even by your practised arts of deception. Ye-es, Latin prose. I think, if I may say so—but we shall see when the papers are set—"Ulpian serves *your* need." "Aha! *Elucescebat*, quoth our friend." We shall see! We shall see!'

Still no sign from Beetle. He was on a steamer, his passage paid into the wide and wonderful world—a thousand leagues beyond Lundy Island.

King dropped him with a snarl.

'He doesn't know. He'll go on correctin' exercises an' jawin' an' showin' off before the little boys next term—an' next.' Beetle hurried after his companions up the steep path of the furze-clad hill behind the College.

They were throwing pebbles on the top of the gasometer,

and the grimy gas-man in charge bade them desist. They watched him oil a turncock sunk in the ground between two furze-bushes.

'Cokey, what's that for?' said Stalky.

'To turn the gas on to the kitchens,' said Cokey. 'If so be I didn't turn her on, yeou young gen'elmen 'ud be larnin' yeour book by candlelight.'

'Um!' said Stalky, and was silent for at least a minute . . .

'Hullo! Where are you chaps going?'

A bend of the lane brought them face to face with Tulke, senior prefect of King's House—a smallish, white-haired boy, of the type that must be promoted on account of its intellect, and ever afterwards appeals to the Head to support its authority when zeal has outrun discretion.

The three took no sort of notice. They were on lawful pass. Tulke repeated his question hotly, for he had suffered many slights from Number Five study, and fancied that he had at last caught them tripping.

'What the devil is that to you?' Stalky replied, with his sweetest smile.

'Look here, I'm not goin'—I'm not goin' to be sworn at by the Fifth!' sputtered Tulke.

'Then cut along and call a prefects' meeting,' said M'Turk, knowing Tulke's weakness.

The prefect became inarticulate with rage.

'Mustn't yell at the Fifth that way,' said Stalky. 'It's vile bad form.'

'Cough it up, ducky!' M'Turk said calmly.

'I—I want to know what you chaps are doing out of bounds?' This with an important flourish of his ground-ash.

'Ah!' said Stalky. 'Now we're gettin' at it. Why didn't you ask that before?'

'Well, I ask it now. What are you doing?'

'We're admirin' you, Tulke,' said Stalky. 'We think you're no end of a fine chap, don't we?'

'We do! We do!' A dog-cart with some girls in it swept round the corner, and Stalky promptly kneeled before Tulke in the attitude of prayer; so Tulke turned a colour.

'I've reason to believe——' he began.

'Oyez! Oyez! Oyez! shouted Beetle, after the manner of Bideford's town-crier. 'Tulke has reason to believe! Three cheers for Tulke!'

They were given. 'It's all our giddy admiration,' said Stalky. 'You know how we love you, Tulke. We love you so much we think you ought to go home and die. You're too good to live, Tulke.'

'Yes,' said M'Turk. '*Do* oblige us by dyin'. Think how lovely you'd look stuffed!'

Tulke swept up the road with an unpleasant glare in his eye.

'That means a prefects' meeting—sure pop,' said. Stalky. 'Honour of the Sixth involved, an' all the rest of it. Tulke'll write notes all this afternoon, an' Carson will call us up after tea. They daren't overlook that.'

'Bet you a bob he follows us!' said M'Turk. 'He's King's pet, and it's scalps to both of 'em if we're caught out. We must be virtuous.'

'Then I move we go to Mother Yeo's for a last gorge. We owe her about ten bob. Mary'll weep sore when she knows we're leavin',' said Beetle.

'She gave me an awful wipe on the head last time—Mary,' said Stalky.

'She does if you don't duck,' said M'Turk. 'But she generally kisses one back. Let's try Mother Yeo.'

They sought a little bottle-windowed half-dairy, half-restaurant, a dark-browed, two-hundred-year-old house, at the head of a narrow side street. They had patronised it from the days of their fagdom, and were very much friends at home.

'We've come to pay our debts, mother,' said Stalky, sliding his arm round the fifty-six-inch waist of the mistress of the establishment. 'To pay our debts and say good-bye—and—and we're awf'ly hungry.'

'Aie!' said Mother Yeo, 'makkin' love to me! I'm shaamed of 'ee.'

'Rackon us wouldn't du no such thing if Mary was here,' said M'Turk, lapsing into the broad North Devon that the boys used on their campaigns.

'Who'm takin' my name in vain?' The inner door opened, and Mary, fair-haired, blue-eyed, and apple-cheeked, entered with a bowl of cream in her hands. M'Turk kissed her. Beetle followed suit, with exemplary calm. Both boys were promptly cuffed.

'Niver kiss the maid when 'ee can kiss the mistress,' said Stalky, shamelessly winking at Mother Yeo, as he investigated a shelf of jams.

'Glad to see one of 'ee don't want his head slapped no more,' said Mary invitingly, in that direction.

'Neu! Rackon I can get 'em give me,' said Stalky, his back turned.

'Not by me—yeou little masterpiece!'

'Niver asked 'ee. There's maids to Northam. Yiss—an' Appledore.' An unreproducible sniff, half contempt, half reminiscence, rounded the retort.

'Aie! Yeou won't niver come to no good end. Whutt be 'bout, smellin' the cream?'

' 'Tes bad,' said Stalky. 'Zmell un.'

Incautiously Mary did as she was bid.

'Bidevoor kiss

Niver amiss,' said Stalky, taking it without injury.

'Yeou—yeou—yeou——' Mary began, bubbling with mirth.

'They'm better to Northam—more rich, laike—an' us gets them give back again,' he said, while M'Turk solemnly waltzed Mother Yeo out of breath, and Beetle told Mary the sad news, as they sat down to clotted cream, jam, and hot bread.

'Yiss. Yeou'll niver zee us no more, Mary. We'm goin' to be passons an' missioners.'

'Steady the Buffs!' said M'Turk, looking through the blind. 'Tulke has followed us. He's comin' up the street now.'

'They've niver put us out o' bounds,' said Mother Yeo. 'Bide yeou still, my little dearrs.' She rolled into the inner room to make the score.

'Mary,' said Stalky suddenly, with tragic intensity. 'Do 'ee lov' me, Mary?'

'Iss—fai! Talled 'ee zo since yeou was zo high!' the damsel replied.

'Zee un comin' up street, then?' Stalky pointed to the unconscious Tulke. 'He've niver been kissed by no sort or manner o' maid in hees borned laife, Mary. Oh, 'tes shaamful!'

'Whutt's to do with me? 'Twill come to un in the way o' nature, I rackon.' She nodded her head sagaciously. 'Yeou niver want me to kiss un—sure-*ly*?'

'Give 'ee half-a-crown if 'ee will,' said Stalky, exhibiting the coin.

Half-a-crown was much to Mary Yeo, and a jest was more; but——

'Yeou'm afraid,' said M'Turk, at the psychological moment.

'Aie!' Beetle echoed, knowing her weak point. 'There's not a maid to Northam 'ud think twice. An' yeou such a fine maid, tu!'

M'Turk planted one foot firmly against the inner door lest Mother Yeo should return inopportunely, for Mary's face was set. It was then that Tulke found his way blocked by a tall daughter of Devon—that county of easy kisses, the pleasantest under the sun. He dodged aside politely. She reflected a moment, and laid a vast hand upon his shoulder.

'Where be 'ee gwaine tu, my dearr?' said she.

Over the handkerchief he had crammed into his mouth Stalky could see the boy turn scarlet.

'Gie I a kiss! Don't they larn 'ee manners to College?'

Tulke gasped and wheeled. Solemnly and conscientiously Mary kissed him twice, and the luckless prefect fled.

She stepped into the shop, her eyes full of simple wonder.

'Kissed un?' said Stalky, handing over the money.

'Iss, fai! But, oh, my little body, *he*'m no Colleger. Zeemed tu-minded to cry, laike.'

'Well, *we* won't. You couldn't make us cry that way,' said M'Turk. 'Try.'

Whereupon Mary cuffed them all round.

As they went out with tingling ears, said Stalky generally, 'Don't think there'll be much of a prefects' meeting.'

'Won't there, just!' said Beetle. 'Look here. If he kissed her —which is our tack—he is a cynically immoral hog, and his conduct is blatant indecency. *Confer orationes Regis furiosissimi* when he collared me readin' "Don Juan." '

' 'Course he kissed her,' said M'Turk. 'In the middle of the street. With his House-cap on!'

'Time, 3.57 P.M. Make a note o' that. What d'you mean, Beetle?' said Stalky.

'Well! He's a truthful little beast. He may say he was kissed.'

'And then?'

'Why, then!' Beetle capered at the mere thought of it. 'Don't you see? The corollary to the giddy proposition is that the Sixth can't protect 'emselves from outrages an' ravishin's. Want nursemaids to look after 'em! We've only got to whisper that to the Coll. Jam for the Sixth! Jam for us! Either way it's jammy!'

'By Gum!' said Stalky. 'Our last term's endin' well. Now you cut along an' finish up your old rag, and Turkey an' me will help. We'll go in the back way. No need to bother Randall.'

'Don't play the giddy garden-goat, then.' Beetle knew what help meant, though he was by no means averse to showing his importance before his allies. The little loft behind Randall's printing-office was his own territory, where he saw himself already controlling *The Times*. Here, under the guidance of the inky apprentice, he had learned to find his way more or less circuitously about the case, and considered himself an expert compositor.

The school paper in its locked formes lay on a stone-topped table, a proof by the side; but not for worlds would Beetle have corrected from the mere proof. With a mallet and a pair of tweezers, he knocked out mysterious wedges of wood that released the forme, picked a letter here and inserted a letter there, reading as he went along and stopping much to chuckle over his own contributions.

'You won't show off like that,' said M'Turk, 'when you've got to do it for your livin'. Upside down and backwards, isn't it? Let's see if I can read it.'

'Get out!' said Beetle. 'Go and read those formes in the rack there, if you think you know so much.'

'Formes in a rack? What's that? Don't be so beastly professional.'

M'Turk drew off with Stalky to prowl about the office. They left little unturned.

Come here a shake, Beetle. What's this thing?' said Stalky, in a few minutes. 'Looks familiar.'

Said Beetle, after a glance: 'It's King's Latin prose exam. paper. *In—In Verrem: actio prima.* What a lark!'

'Think o' the pure-souled, high-minded boys who'd give their eyes for a squint at it!' said M'Turk.

'No, Willie dear,' said Stalky, 'that would be wrong and painful to our kind teachers. You wouldn't crib, Willie, would you?'

'Can't read the beastly stuff, anyhow,' was the reply. 'Besides, we're leavin' at the end o' the term, so it makes no difference to us.'

' 'Member what the Considerate Bloomer did to Spraggon's account of the Puffin'ton Hounds? We must sugar Mr. King's milk for him,' said Stalky, all lighted from within by a devilish joy. 'Let's see what Beetle can do with those forceps he's so proud of.'

'Don't see how you can make Latin prose much more cock-eye than it is, but we'll try,' said Beetle, transposing an *aliud* and *Asiae* from two sentences. 'Let's see! We'll put that full-stop a little further on, an' begin the sentence with the next capital. Hurroo! Here's three lines that can move up all in a lump.'

' "One of those scientific rests for which this eminent hunts-man is so justly celebrated." ' Stalky knew the Puffington run by heart.

'Hold on! Here's a *vol—voluntate quidnam* all by itself,' said M'Turk.

'I'll attend to her in a shake. *Quidnam* goes after *Dolabella.*'

'Good old Dolabella,' murmured Stalky. 'Don't break him. Vile prose Cicero wrote, didn't he? He ought to be grateful for——'

'Hullo!' said M'Turk, over another forme. 'What price a

giddy ode? *Qui—quis—*oh, it's *Quis multa gracilis,* o' course.'

'Bring it along. We've sugared the milk here,' said Stalky, after a few minutes' zealous toil. 'Never thrash your hounds unnecessarily.'

'*Quis munditiis?* I swear that's not bad,' began Beetle, plying the tweezers. 'Don't that interrogation look pretty? *Heu quoties fidem!* That sounds as if the chap were anxious an' excited. *Cui flavam religas in rosa*—Whose flavour is relegated to a rose. *Mutatosque Deos flebit in antro.*'

'Mute gods weepin' in a cave,' suggested Stalky. ' 'Pon my Sam, Horace needs as much lookin' after as—Tulke.'

They edited him faithfully till it was too dark to see.

' "Aha! *Elucescebat,* quoth our friend." Ulpian serves my need, does it? If King can make anything out of *that,* I'm a blue-eyed squatteroo,' said Beetle, as they slid out of the loft window into a back alley of old acquaintance and started on a three-mile trot to the College. But the revision of the classics had detained them over long. They halted, blown and breathless, in the furze at the back of the gasometer, the College lights twinkling below, ten minutes at least, late for tea and lock-up.

'It's no good,' puffed M'Turk. 'Bet a bob Foxy is waiting for defaulters under the lamp by the Fives Court. It's a nuisance, too, because the Head gave us long leave, and one doesn't like to break it.'

' "Let me now from the bonded ware'ouse of my knowledge," ' began Stalky.

'Oh, rot! Don't Jorrock. Can we make a run for it?' snapped M'Turk.

' "Bishops' boots Mr. Radcliffe also condemned, an' spoke 'ighly in favour of tops cleaned with champagne an' abricot jam." Where's that thing Cokey was twiddlin' this afternoon?'

They heard him groping in the wet, and presently beheld a great miracle. The lights of the Coastguard cottages near the sea went out; the brilliantly illuminated windows of the Golf Club disappeared, and were followed by the frontages of the two hotels. Scattered villas dulled, twinkled, and vanished. Last of all, the Coll. lights died also. They were left in the pitchy darkness of a windy winter's night.

' "Blister my kidneys. It *is* a frost. The dahlias are dead!" ' said Stalky. 'Bunk!'

They squattered through the dripping gorse as the College hummed like an angry hive and the dining-rooms chorussed, 'Gas! gas! gas!' till they came to the edge of the sunk path that divided them from their study. Dropping that ha-ha like bullets, and rebounding like boys, they dashed to their study; in less than two minutes had changed into dry trousers and coat, and, ostentatiously slippered, joined the mob in the dining-hall, which resembled the storm-centre of a South American revolution.

' "Hellish dark and smells of cheese." ' Stalky elbowed his way into the press, howling lustily for gas. 'Cokey must have gone for a walk. Foxy'll have to find him.'

Prout, as the nearest House-master, was trying to restore order, for rude boys were flicking butter-pats across chaos, and M'Turk had turned on the fags' tea-urn, so that many were parboiled and wept with an unfeigned dolour. The Fourth and Upper Third broke into the school song, the *'Vive la Compagnie,'* to the accompaniment of drumming knife-handles; and the junior forms shrilled batlike shrieks and raided one another's victuals. Two hundred and fifty boys in high condition, seeking for more light, are truly earnest inquirers.

When a most vile smell of gas told them that supplies had been renewed, Stalky, waistcoat unbuttoned, sat gorgedly over what might have been his fourth cup of tea. 'And that's all right,' he said. 'Hullo! 'Ere's Pomponius Ego!'

It was Carson, the head of the school, a simple, straight-minded soul, and a pillar of the First Fifteen, who crossed over from the prefects' table and in a husky, official voice invited the three to attend in his study in half an hour.

'Prefects' meetin'!' 'Prefects' meetin'!' hissed the tables, and they imitated barbarically the actions and effects of the ground-ash.

'How are we goin' to jest with 'em?' said Stalky, turning half-face to Beetle. 'It's your play this time!'

'Look here,' was the answer, 'all I want you to do is not to laugh. I'm goin' to take charge o' young Tulke's immorality—*à la* King, an' it's goin' to be serious. If you can't help laughin' don't look at me, or I'll go pop.'

'I see. All right,' said Stalky.

M'Turk's lank frame stiffened in every muscle and his eyelids dropped half over his eyes. That last was a war-signal.

The eight or nine seniors, their faces very set and sober, were ranged in chairs round Carson's severely Philistine study. Tulke was not popular among them, and a few who had had experience of Stalky and Company doubted that he might, perhaps, have made an ass of himself. But the dignity of the Sixth was to be upheld. So Carson began hurriedly:—

'Look here, you chaps, I've—we've sent for you to tell you you're a good deal too cheeky to the Sixth—have been for some time—and—and we've stood about as much as we're goin' to, and it seems you've been cursin' and swearin' at Tulke on the Bideford road this afternoon, and we're goin' to show you you can't do it. That's all.'

'Well, that's awfully good of you,' said Stalky, 'but we happen to have a few rights of our own, too. You can't, just because you happen to be made prefects, haul up seniors and jaw 'em on spec, like a House-master. *We* aren't fags, Carson. This kind of thing may do for Davies tertius, but it won't do for us.'

'It's only old Prout's lunacy that we weren't prefects long ago. You know that,' said M'Turk. 'You haven't any tact.'

'Hold on,' said Beetle. 'A prefects' meetin' has to be reported to the Head. I want to know if the Head backs Tulke in this business?'

'Well—well, it isn't exactly a prefects' meeting,' said Carson. 'We only called you in to warn you.'

'But all the prefects are here,' Beetle insisted. 'Where's the difference?'

'My Gum!' said Stalky. 'Do you mean to say you've just called us in for a jaw—after comin' to us before the whole school at tea an' givin' 'em the impression it was a prefects' meetin'? 'Pon my Sam, Carson, you'll get into trouble, you will.'

'Hole-an'-corner business—hole-an'-corner business,' said M'Turk, wagging his head. 'Beastly suspicious.'

The Sixth looked at each other uneasily. Tulke had called three prefects' meetings in two terms, till the Head had informed the Sixth that they were expected to maintain discipline without the recurrent menace of his authority. Now, it seemed that they had made a blunder at the outset; but any right-minded boy would have sunk the legality and been properly impressed by the Court. Beetle's protest was distinct 'cheek.'

'Well, you chaps deserve a lickin',' cried one Naughten incautiously. Then was Beetle filled with a noble inspiration.

'For interferin' with Tulke's amours, eh?' Tulke turned a rich sloe colour. 'Oh no, you don't!' Beetle went on. 'You've had your innin's. We've been sent up for cursing an' swearing at you, an' we're goin' to be let off with a warnin'! *Are* we? Now then, you're going to catch it.'

'I—I—I——' Tulke began. 'Don't let that young devil start jawing.'

'If you've anything to say, you must say it decently,' said Carson.

'Decently? I will. Now look here. When we went into Bideford we met this ornament of the Sixth—is that decent enough?—hangin' about on the road with a nasty look in his eye. We didn't know *then* why he was so anxious to stop us, *but* at five minutes to four, when we were in Yeo's shop, we saw Tulke *in* broad daylight, *with* his House-cap on, kissin' an' huggin' a woman *on* the pavement. Is that decent enough for you?'

'I didn't—I wasn't.'

'We saw you!' said Beetle. 'And now—I'll be decent, Carson—you sneak back with her kisses' (not for nothing had Beetle perused the later poets) 'hot on your lips an' call prefects' meetings, which aren't prefects' meetings, to uphold the honour of the Sixth.' A new and heaven-cleft path opened before him that instant. 'And how do we know,' he shouted—'how do we know how many of the Sixth are mixed up in this abominable affair?'

'Yes, that's what we want to know,' said M'Turk, with simple dignity.

'We meant to come to you about it quietly, Carson, but you *would* have the meetin',' said Stalky sympathetically.

The Sixth were too taken aback to reply. So, carefully modelling his rhetoric on King, Beetle followed up the attack, surpassing and surprising himself.

'It—it isn't so much the cynical immorality of the biznai, as the blatant indecency of it, that's so awful. As far as we can see, it's impossible for us to go into Bideford without runnin' up against some prefect's unwholesome amours. There's nothing to snigger over, Naughten. *I* don't pretend to know much about these things—but it seems to me a chap must be pretty far dead in sin' (that was a quotation from the school Chaplain) 'when he takes to embracing his paramours' (that was Hakluyt) 'before all the city' (a reminiscence of Milton). 'He might at least have the decency—you're authorities on decency, I believe—to wait till dark. But he didn't. You didn't! Oh, Tulke. You—you incontinent little animal!'

'Here, shut up a minute. What's all this about, Tulke?' said Carson.

'I—look here. I'm awfully sorry. I never thought Beetle would take this line.'

'Because—you've—no decency—you—thought—I hadn't,' cried Beetle all in one breath.

'Tried to cover it all up with a conspiracy, did you?' said Stalky.

'Direct insult to all three of us,' said M'Turk. 'A most filthy mind you have, Tulke.'

'I'll shove you fellows outside the door if you go on like this,' said Carson angrily.

'That proves it's a conspiracy,' said Stalky, with the air of a virgin martyr.

'I—I was goin' along the street—I swear I was,' cried Tulke, 'and—and I'm awfully sorry about it—a woman came up and kissed me. I swear I didn't kiss *her*.'

There was a pause, filled by Stalky's long, liquid whistle of contempt, amazement, and derision.

'On my honour,' gulped the persecuted one. 'Oh, do stop him jawing.'

'Very good,' M'Turk interjected. 'We are compelled, of course, to accept your statement.'

'Confound it!' roared Naughten. 'You aren't head-prefect here, M'Turk.'

'Oh, well,' returned the Irishman, 'you know Tulke better than we do. I am only speaking for ourselves. *We* accept Tulke's word. But all I can say is that if I'd been collared in a similarly disgustin' situation, and had offered the same explanation Tulke has, I—I wonder what you'd have said. However, it seems on Tulke's word of honour——'

'And Tulkus—beg pardon—*kiss,* of course—Tulkiss is an honourable man,' put in Stalky.

'——that the Sixth can't protect 'emselves from bein' kissed when they go for a walk!' cried Beetle, taking up the running with a rush. 'Sweet business, isn't it? Cheerful thing to tell the fags, ain't it? We aren't prefects, of course, but we aren't kissed very much. Don't think that sort of thing ever enters our heads. Does it, Stalky?'

'Oh no!' said Stalky, turning aside to hide his emotions. M'Turk's face merely expressed lofty contempt and a little weariness.

'Well, you seem to know a lot about it,' interposed a prefect.

'Can't help it—when you chaps shove it under our noses.' Beetle dropped into a drawling parody of King's most biting colloquial style—the gentle rain after the thunderstorm. 'Well, it's all very sufficiently vile an' disgraceful, isn't it? I don't know who comes out of it worst: Tulke, who happens to have been caught; or the other fellows who haven't. And we'—here he wheeled fiercely on the other two—'we've got to stand up and be jawed by them because we've disturbed their intrigues.'

'Hang it! I only wanted to give you a word of warning,' said Carson, thereby handing himself bound to the enemy.

'Warn? You?' This with the air of one who finds loathsome gifts in his locker. 'Carson, *would* you be good enough to tell us what conceivable thing there is that you are entitled to warn us about after this exposure? Warn? Oh, it's a little too much! Let's go somewhere where it's clean.'

The door banged behind their outraged innocence.

'Oh, Beetle! Beetle! Beetle! Golden Beetle!' sobbed Stalky, hurling himself on Beetle's panting bosom as soon as they reached the study. 'How ever did you do it?'

'Dear-r man!' said M'Turk, embracing Beetle's head with both arms, while he swayed it to and fro on the neck, in time to this ancient burden:—

> *'Pretty lips—sweeter than—cherry or plum,*
> *Always look—jolly and—never look glum;*
> *Seem to say—Come away. Kissy!—come, come!*
> *Yummy-yum! Yummy-yum! Yummy-yum-yum!'*

'Look out. You'll smash my gig-lamps,' puffed Beetle, emerging. 'Wasn't it glorious? Didn't I "Eric" 'em splendidly? Did you spot my cribs from King? Oh, blow!' His countenance clouded. 'There's one adjective I didn't use—obscene. Don't know how I forgot that. It's one of King's pet ones, too.'

'Never mind. They'll be sendin' ambassadors round in half a shake to beg us not to tell the Coll. It's a deuced serious business for them,' said M'Turk. 'Poor Sixth—poor old Sixth!'

'Immoral young rips,' Stalky snorted. 'What an example to pure-souled boys like you and me!'

And the Sixth in Carson's study stood aghast, glowering at Tulke, who was on the edge of tears.

'Well!' said the head-prefect acidly. 'You've made a pretty average ghastly mess of it, Tulke.'

'Why—why didn't you lick that young devil Beetle before he began jawing?' Tulke wailed.

'I knew there'd be a row,' said a prefect of Prout's House. 'But you would insist on the meeting, Tulke.'

'Yes, and a fat lot of good it's done us,' said Naughten. 'They come in here and jaw our heads off when we ought to be jawin' them. Beetle talks to us as if we were a lot of black-guards and—and all that. And when they've hung us up to dry, they go out and slam the door like a House-master. All your fault, Tulke.'

'But I didn't kiss her.'

'You ass! If you'd said you *had* and stuck to it, it would have been ten times better than what you did,' Naughten retorted. 'Now they'll tell the whole Coll.—and Beetle'll make up a lot of beastly rhymes and nicknames.'

'But, hang it, *she* kissed *me*!' Outside his work, Tulke's mind moved slowly.

'I'm not thinking of you. I'm thinking of us. I'll go up to their study and see if I can make 'em keep quiet!' . . .

'Tulke's awf'ly cut up about this business,' Naughten began, ingratiatingly, when he found Beetle.

'Who's kissed him this time?'

'——and I've come to ask you chaps, and especially you, Beetle, not to let the thing be known all over the Coll. Of course, fellows as senior as you are can easily see why.'

'Um!' said Beetle, with the cold reluctance of one who faces an unpleasant public duty. 'I suppose I must go and talk to the Sixth again.'

'Not the least need, my dear chap, I assure you,' said Naughten hastily. 'I'll take any message you care to send.'

But the chance of supplying the missing adjective was too tempting. So Naughten returned to that still undissolved meeting, Beetle, white, icy, and aloof, at his heels.

'There seems,' he began, with laboriously crisp articulation, 'there seems to be a certain amount of uneasiness among you

as to the steps we may think fit to take in regard to this last
revelation of the—ah—obscene. If it is any consolation to you
to know that we have decided—for the honour of the school,
you understand—to keep our mouths shut as to these—ah—
obscenities, you—ah—have it.'

He wheeled, his head among the stars, and strode statelily
back to his study, where Stalky and M'Turk lay side by side
upon the table wiping their tearful eyes—too weak to move.

The Latin prose paper was a success beyond their wildest
dreams. Stalky and M'Turk were, of course, out of all examinations (they did extra-tuition with the Head), but Beetle
attended with zeal.

'This, I presume, is a par-ergon on your part,' said King,
as he dealt out the papers. 'One final exhibition ere you are
translated to loftier spheres? A last attack on the classics? It
seems to confound you already.'

Beetle studied the print with knit brows. 'I can't make head
or tail of it,' he murmured. 'What does it mean?'

'No, no!' said King, with scholastic coquetry. 'We depend
upon *you* to give us the meaning. This is an examination,
Beetle mine, not a guessing-competition. You will find your
associates have no difficulty in——'

Tulke left his place and laid the paper on the desk. King
looked, read, and turned a ghastly green.

'Stalky's missing a heap,' thought Beetle. 'Wonder how
King'll get out of it?'

'There seems,' King began with a gulp, 'a certain modicum
of truth in our Beetle's remark. I am—er—inclined to believe
that the worthy Randall must have dropped this in forme—
if you know what that means. Beetle, you purport to be an
editor. Perhaps you can enlighten the Form as to formes.'

'What, sir? Whose form? I don't see that there's any verb in this sentence at all, an'—an'—the Ode is all different, some-how.'

'I was about to say, before you volunteered your criticism, that an accident must have befallen the paper in type, and that the printer reset it by the light of nature. No—' he held the thing at arm's length—'our Randall is not an authority on Cicero or Horace.'

'Rather mean to shove it off on Randall,' whispered Beetle to his neighbour. 'King must ha' been as screwed as an owl when he wrote it out.'

'But we can amend the error by dictating it.'

'No, sir.' The answer came pat from a dozen throats at once. 'That cuts the time for the exam. Only two hours al-lowed, sir. 'Tisn't fair. It's a printed-paper exam. How're we goin' to be marked for it? It's all Randall's fault. It isn't *our* fault, anyhow. An exam.'s an exam.,' etc., etc.

Naturally Mr. King considered this was an attempt to un-dermine his authority, and, instead of beginning dictation at once, delivered a lecture on the spirit in which examinations should be approached. As the storm subsided, Beetle fanned it afresh.

'Eh? What? What was that you were saying to MacLagan?'

'I only said I thought the papers ought to have been looked at before they were given out, sir.'

'Hear, hear!' from a back bench.

Mr. King wished to know whether Beetle took it upon him-self personally to conduct the traditions of the school. His zeal for knowledge ate up another fifteen minutes, during which the prefects showed unmistakable signs of boredom.

'Oh, it was a giddy time,' said Beetle, afterwards, in dis-mantled Number Five. 'He gibbered a bit, and I kept him on the gibber, and then he dictated about a half of Dolabella & Co.'

'Good old Dolabella! Friend of mine. Yes?' said Stalky tenderly.

'Then we had to ask him how every other word was spelt, of course, an' he gibbered a lot more. He cursed me and Mac-Lagan (Mac played up like a trump) and Randall, and the "materialised ignorance of the unscholarly middle classes," "lust for mere marks," and all the rest. It was what you might call a final exhibition—a last attack—a giddy par-ergon.'

'But of course he was blind squiffy when he wrote the paper. I hope you explained *that*?' said Stalky.

'Oh yes. I told Tulke so. I said an immoral prefect an' a drunken House-master were legitimate inferences. Tulke nearly blubbed. He's awfully shy of us since Mary's time.'

Tulke preserved that modesty till the last moment—till the journey-money had been paid, and the boys were filling the brakes that took them to the station. Then the three happily constrained him to wait awhile.

'You see, Tulke, you may be a prefect,' said Stalky, 'but I've left the Coll. Do you see, Tulke, dear?'

'Yes, I see. Don't bear malice, Stalky.'

'Stalky? Curse your impudence, you young cub,' shouted Stalky, magnificent in top-hat, stiff collar, spats, and high-waisted, snuff-coloured ulster. 'I want you to understand that *I*'m Mister Corkran, an' you're a dirty little schoolboy.'

'Besides bein' frabjously immoral,' said M'Turk. 'Wonder you aren't ashamed to foist your company on pure-minded boys like us!'

'Come on, Tulke,' cried Naughten, from the prefects' brake.

'Yes, we're comin'. Shove up and make room, you Collegers. You've all got to be back next term, with your "Yes, sir," and "Oh, sir," an' "No, sir," an' "Please, sir"; but before we say good-bye we're goin' to tell you a little story. Go on, Dickie' (this to the driver); 'we're quite ready. Kick that hat-box under the seat, an' don't crowd your Uncle Stalky.'

'As nice a lot of high-minded youngsters as you'd wish to see,' said M'Turk, gazing round with bland patronage. 'A trifle immoral, but then—boys will be boys. It's no good tryin' to look stuffy, Carson. Mister Corkran will now oblige with the story of Tulke an' Mary Yeo!'

SLAVES OF THE LAMP

PART II

SLAVES OF THE LAMP

Part II

THAT VERY INFANT who told the story of the capture of Boh Na-ghee[1] to Eustace Cleever, novelist, inherited an estateful baronetcy, with vast revenues, resigned the Service, and became a landholder, while his mother stood guard over him to see that he married the right girl. But, new to his position, he presented the local Volunteers with a full-sized magazine-rifle range, two miles long, across the heart of his estate, and the surrounding families, who lived in savage seclusion among woods full of pheasants, regarded him as an erring maniac. The noise of the firing disturbed their poultry, and Infant was cast out from the society of J.P.'s and decent men till such time as a daughter of the county might lure him back to right thinking. He took his revenge by filling the house with choice selections of old schoolmates home on leave—affable detrimentals, at whom the bicycle-riding maidens of the surrounding families were allowed to look from afar. I knew when a troopship was in port by The Infant's invitations. Sometimes he would produce old friends of equal seniority; at others, young and blushing giants whom I had left small fags far down in the Lower Second; and to these Infant and the elders expounded the whole duty of Man in the Army.

'I've had to cut the Service,' said The Infant; 'but that's no reason why my vast stores of experience should be lost to

---

[1] 'A Conference of the Powers': *Many Inventions*.

posterity.' He was just thirty, and in that same summer an imperious wire drew me to his baronial castle: 'Got good haul; ex *Tamar*. Come along.'

It was an unusually good haul, arranged with a single eye to my benefit. There was a baldish, broken-down captain of Native Infantry, shivering with ague behind an indomitable red nose—and they called him Captain Dickson. There was another captain, also of Native Infantry, with a fair moustache; his face was like white glass, and his hands were fragile, but he answered joyfully to the cry of Tertius. There was an enormously big and well-kept man, who had evidently not campaigned for years, clean-shaved, soft-voiced, and cat-like, but still Abanazar for all that he adorned the Indian Political Service; and there was a lean Irishman, his face tanned blue-black with the suns of the Telegraph Department. Luckily the baize doors of the bachelors' wing fitted tight, for we dressed promiscuously in the corridor or in each other's rooms, talking, calling, shouting, and anon waltzing by pairs to songs of Dick Four's own devising.

There were sixty years of mixed work to be sifted out between us, and since we had met one another from time to time in the quick scene-shifting of India—a dinner, camp, or a race-meeting here; a *dâk*-bungalow or railway station up country somewhere else—we had never quite lost touch. Infant sat on the banisters, hungrily and enviously drinking it in. He enjoyed his baronetcy, but his heart yearned for the old days.

It was a cheerful babel of matters personal, provincial, and imperial, pieces of old call-over lists, and new policies, cut short by the roar of a Burmese gong, and we went down not less than a quarter of a mile of stairs to meet Infant's mother, who had known us all in our school-days and greeted us as if those had ended a week ago. But it was fifteen years since, with tears of laughter, she had lent me a grey princess-skirt for amateur theatricals.

That was a dinner from the *Arabian Nights* served in an eighty-foot hall full of ancestors and pots of flowering roses, and (this was more impressive) heated by steam. When it was ended and the little mother had gone away—('You boys want to talk, so I shall say good-night now')—we gathered about an apple-wood fire, in a gigantic polished steel grate, under a mantelpiece ten feet high, and The Infant compassed us about with curious liqueurs and that kind of cigarette which serves best to introduce your own pipe.

'Oh, bliss!' grunted Dick Four from a sofa, where he had been packed with a rug over him. 'First time I've been warm since I came Home.'

We were all nearly on top of the fire, except Infant, who had been long enough at Home to take exercise when he felt chilled. This is a grisly diversion, but one much affected by the English of the Island.

'If you say a word about cold tubs and brisk walks,' drawled M'Turk, 'I'll kill you, Infant. I've got a liver, too. 'Member when we used to think it a treat to turn out of our beds on a Sunday morning—thermometer fifty-seven degrees if it was summer—and bathe off the Pebble Ridge? Ugh!'

'Thing I don't understand,' said Tertius, 'was the way we chaps used to go down into the lavatories, boil ourselves pink, and then come up with all our pores open into a young snow-storm or a black frost. Yet none of our chaps died, that I can remember.'

'Talkin' of baths,' said M'Turk, with a chuckle, ' 'member our bath in Number Five, Beetle, the night Rabbits-Eggs rocked King? What wouldn't I give to see old Stalky now! He is the only one of the two studies not here.'

'Stalky is the Great Man of his Century,' said Dick Four.

'How d'you know?' I asked.

'How do I know?' said Dick Four scornfully. 'If you've ever been in a tight place with Stalky you wouldn't ask.'

'I haven't seen him since the camp at Pindi in '87,' I said. 'He was goin' strong then—about seven feet high and four feet thick.'

'Adequate chap. Infernally adequate,' said Tertius, pulling his moustache and staring into the fire.

'Got dam' near court-martialled and broke in Egypt in '84,' The Infant volunteered. 'I went out in the same trooper with him—as raw as he was. Only *I* showed it, and Stalky didn't.'

'What was the trouble?' said M'Turk, reaching forward absently to twitch my dress-tie into position.

'Oh, nothing. His Colonel trusted him to take twenty Tommies out to wash, or groom camels, or something at the back of Suakin, and Stalky got embroiled with Fuzzies five miles in the interior. He conducted a masterly retreat and wiped up eight of 'em. He knew jolly well he'd no right to go out so far, so he took the initiative and pitched in a letter to his Colonel, who was frothing at the mouth, complaining of the "paucity of support accorded to him in his operations." Gad, it might have been one fat brigadier slangin' another! Then he went into the Staff Corps.'

'That—is—entirely—Stalky,' said Abanazar from his arm-chair.

'You've come across him, too?' I said.

'Oh yes,' he replied in his softest tones. 'I was at the tail of that—that epic. Don't you chaps know?'

We did not—Infant, M'Turk, and I; and we called for information very politely.

' 'Twasn't anything,' said Tertius. 'We got into a mess up

in the Khye-Kheen Hills a couple o' years ago, and Stalky pulled us through. That's all.'

M'Turk gazed at Tertius with all an Irishman's contempt for the tongue-tied Saxon.

'Heavens!' he said. 'And it's you and your likes govern Ireland. Tertius, aren't you ashamed?'

'Well, I can't tell a yarn. I can chip in when the other fellow starts. Ask him.' He pointed to Dick Four, whose nose gleamed scornfully over the rug.

'I knew you couldn't,' said Dick Four. 'Give me a whisky and soda. I've been drinking lemon-squash and ammoniated quinine while you chaps were bathin' in champagne, and my head's singin' like a top.'

He wiped his ragged moustache above the drink; and, his teeth chattering in his head, began:—

'You know the Khye-Kheen-Malôt expedition when we scared the souls out of 'em with a field force they daren't fight against? Well, both tribes—there was a coalition against us—came in without firing a shot: and a lot of hairy villains, who had no more power over their men than I had, promised and vowed all sorts of things. On that very slender evidence, Pussy dear——'

'I was at Simla,' said Abanazar hastily.

'Never mind, you're tarred with the same brush. On the strength of those tupenny-ha'penny treaties, your asses of Politicals reported the country as pacified, and the Government, being a fool, as usual, began road-makin'—dependin' on local supply for labour. 'Member *that*, Pussy? Rest of our chaps who'd had no look-in during the campaign didn't think there'd be any more of it, and were anxious to get back to India. But I'd been in two of these little rows before, and I had my suspicions. I engineered myself, *summo ingenio*, into

command of a road-patrol—no shovellin', only marching up
and down genteelly with a guard. They'd withdrawn all the
troops they could, but I nucleused about forty Pathans, recruits chiefly, of my Regiment, and sat tight at the base-camp
while the road-parties went to work, as per Political survey.'

'Had some rippin' sing-songs in camp, too,' said Tertius.

'My pup'—thus did Dick Four refer to his subaltern—'was
a pious little beast. He didn't like the sing-songs, and so he
went down with pneumonia. I rootled round the camp, and
found Tertius gassing about as a D.A.Q.M.G., which, God
knows, he isn't cut out for. There were six or eight of the old
Coll. at base-camp (we're always in force for a Frontier row),
but I'd heard of Tertius as a steady old hack, and I told him
he had to shake off his D.A.Q.M.G. breeches and help *me*.
Tertius volunteered like a shot, and we settled it with the
authorities, and out we went—forty Pathans, Tertius, and me,
looking up the road-parties. Macnamara's—'member old Mac,
the Sapper, who played the fiddle so damnably at Umballa?—
Mac's party was the last but one. The last was Stalky's. He was
at the head of the road with some of his pet Sikhs. Mac said
he believed he was all right.'

'Stalky *is* a Sikh,' said Tertius. 'He takes his men to pray at
the Durbar Sahib at Amritzar, regular as clockwork, when he
can.'

'Don't interrupt, Tertius. It was about forty miles beyond
Mac's before I found him; and my men pointed out gently,
but firmly, that the country was risin'. What kind o' country,
Beetle? Well, I'm no word-painter, thank goodness, but *you*
might call it a hellish country! When we weren't up to our
necks in snow, we were rolling down the khud. The well-
disposed inhabitants, who were to supply labour for the road-
making (don't forget that, Pussy dear), sat behind rocks and

took pot-shots at us. Old, old story! We all legged it in search of Stalky. I had a feeling that he'd be in good cover, and about dusk we found him and his road-party, as snug as a bug in a rug, in an old Malôt stone fort, with a watch-tower at one corner. It overhung the road they had blasted out of the cliff fifty feet below; and under the road things went down pretty sheer, for five or six hundred feet, into a gorge about half a mile wide and two or three miles long. There were chaps on the other side of the gorge scientifically gettin' our range. So I hammered on the gate and nipped in, and tripped over Stalky in a greasy, bloody old poshteen, squatting on the ground, eating with his men. I'd only seen him for half a minute about three months before, but I might have met him yesterday. He waved his hand all sereno.

' "Hullo, Aladdin! Hullo, Emperor!" he said. "You're just in time for the performance."

'I saw his Sikhs looked a bit battered. "Where's your command? Where's your subaltern?" I said.

' "Here—all there is of it," said Stalky. "If you want young Everett, he's dead, and his body's in the watch-tower. They rushed our road-party last week, and got him and seven men. We've been besieged for five days. I suppose they let you through to make sure of you. The whole country's up. Strikes me you walked into a first-class trap." He grinned, but neither Tertius nor I could see where the deuce the fun was. We hadn't any grub for our men, and Stalky had only four days' whack for his. That came of dependin' upon your asinine Politicals, Pussy dear, who told us that the inhabitants were friendly.

'To make us quite comfy, Stalky took us up to the watch-tower to see poor Everett's body, lyin' in a foot o' drifted snow. It looked like a girl of fifteen—not a hair on the little fellow's face. He'd been shot through the temple, but the Malôts had left their mark on him. Stalky unbuttoned the tunic, and showed it to us—a rummy sickle-shaped cut on the chest. 'Member the snow all white on his eyebrows, Tertius? 'Member when Stalky moved the lamp and it looked as if he was alive?'

'Ye-es,' said Tertius, with a shudder. ''Member the beastly look on Stalky's face, though, with his nostrils all blown out, same as he used to look when he was bullyin' a fag? That was a lovely evening.'

'We held a council of war up there over Everett's body. Stalky said the Malôts and Khye-Kheens were up together; havin' sunk their blood-feuds to settle us. The chaps we'd seen across the gorge were Khye-Kheens. It was about half a mile from them to us as a bullet flies, and they'd made a line of sungars under the brow of the hill to sleep in and starve us out. The Malôts, he said, were in front of us promiscuous. There wasn't good cover behind the fort, or they'd have been there, too. Stalky didn't mind the Malôts half as much as he did the Khye-Kheens. He said the Malôts were treacherous curs. What I couldn't understand was, why in the world the two gangs didn't join in and rush us. There must have been at least five hundred of 'em. Stalky said they didn't trust each other very well, because they were ancestral enemies when they were at home; and the only time they'd tried a rush he'd hove a couple of blasting-charges among 'em, and that had sickened 'em a bit.

'It was dark by the time we finished, and Stalky, always sereno, said: "You command now. I don't suppose you mind my taking any action I may consider necessary to reprovision the fort?" I said "Of course not," and then the lamp blew out. So Tertius and I had to climb down the tower steps (we didn't want to stay with Everett) and got back to our men. Stalky had gone off—to count the stores, I supposed. Anyhow, Tertius and I sat up in case of a rush (they were plugging at us pretty generally, you know), relieving each other till the mornin'.

'Mornin' came. No Stalky. Not a sign of him. I took counsel with his senior native officer—a grand, white-whiskered old chap—Rutton Singh, from Jullunder way. He only grinned, and said it was all right. Stalky had been out of the fort twice before, somewhere or other, accordin' to him. He said Stalky 'ud come back unchipped, and gave me to understand that Stalky was an invulnerable *Guru* of sorts. All the same, I put the whole command on half rations, and set 'em to pickin' out loop-holes.

'About noon there was no end of a snowstorm, and the enemy stopped firing. We replied gingerly, because we were awfully short of ammunition. Don't suppose we fired five shots an hour, but we generally got our man. Well, while I was talking with Rutton Singh I saw Stalky coming down from the watch-tower, rather puffy about the eyes, his poshteen coated with claret-coloured ice.

' "No trustin' these snowstorms," he said. "Nip out quick and snaffle what you can get. There's a certain amount of friction between the Khye-Kheens and the Malôts just now."

'I turned Tertius out with twenty Pathans, and they bucked about in the snow for a bit till they came on to a sort of camp about eight hundred yards away, with only a few men in charge and half-a-dozen sheep by the fire. They finished off the men, and snaffled the sheep and as much grain as they could carry, and came back. No one fired a shot at 'em. There didn't seem to be anybody about, but the snow was falling pretty thick.

' "That's good enough," said Stalky when we got dinner ready and he was chewin' mutton-kababs off a cleanin'-rod. "There's no sense riskin' men. They're holding a pow-wow between the Khye-Kheens and the Malôts at the head of the gorge. I don't think these so-called coalitions are much good."

'Do you know what that maniac had done? Tertius and I shook it out of him by instalments. There was an underground granary cellar-room below the watch-tower, and in blasting the road Stalky had blown a hole into one side of it. Being no one else *but* Stalky, he'd kept the hole open for his own ends; and laid poor Everett's body slap over the well of the stairs that led down to it from the watch-tower. He'd had to remove and replace the corpse every time he used the passage. The Sikhs wouldn't go near the place, of course. Well, he'd got out of this hole, and dropped on to the road. Then, in the night *and* a howling snowstorm, he'd dropped over the edge of the khud, made his way down to the bottom of the gorge, forded the nullah, which was half frozen, climbed up on the other side along a track he'd discovered, and come out on the right flank of the Khye-Kheens. He had then—listen to this!— crossed over a ridge that paralleled their rear, walked half a mile behind that, and come out on the left of their line where the gorge gets shallow and where there was a regular track between the Malôt and the Khye-Kheen camps. That was about two in the morning, and, as it turned out, a man spotted him—a Khye-Kheen. So Stalky abolished him quietly, and left him—*with* the Malôt mark on his chest, same as Everett had.

' "I was just as economical as I could be," Stalky said to us. "If he'd shouted I should have been slain. I'd never had to do that kind of thing but once before, and that was the first time I tried that path. It's perfectly practicable for infantry, you know."

' "What about your first man?" I said.

' "Oh, that was the night after they killed Everett, and I went out lookin' for a line of retreat for my men. A man found me. I abolished him—*privatim*—scragged him. But on thinkin' it over it occurred to me that if I could find the body (I'd hove it down some rocks) I might decorate it with the Malôt mark and leave it to the Khye-Kheens to draw inferences. So I went out again the next night and did. The Khye-Kheens are shocked at the Malôts perpetratin' these two dastardly outrages after they'd sworn to sink all blood-feuds. I lay up behind their sungars early this morning and watched 'em. They all went to confer about it at the head of the gorge. Awf'ly annoyed they are. Don't wonder." You know the way Stalky drops out his words, one by one.'

'My God!' said The Infant explosively, as the full depth of the strategy dawned on him.

'Dear-r man!' said M'Turk, purring rapturously.

'Stalky stalked,' said Tertius. 'That's all there is to it.'

'No, he didn't,' said Dick Four. 'Don't you remember how he insisted that he had only applied his luck? Don't you remember how Rutton Singh grabbed his boots and grovelled in the snow, and how our men shouted?'

'None of our Pathans believed that was luck,' said Tertius. 'They swore Stalky ought to have been born a Pathan, and—'member we nearly had a row in the fort when Rutton Singh said Stalky was a Sikh? Gad, how furious the old chap was with my Pathan Jemadar! But Stalky just waggled his finger and they shut up.'

'Old Rutton Singh's sword was half out, though, and he swore he'd cremate every Khye-Kheen and Malôt he killed. That made the Jemadar pretty wild, because he didn't mind fighting against his own creed, but he wasn't going to crab a fellow-Mussulman's chances of Paradise. Then Stalky jabbered

Pushtu and Punjabi in alternate streaks. Where the deuce did he pick up his .Pushtu from, Beetle?'

'Never mind his language, Dick,' said I. 'Give us the gist of it.'

'I flatter myself I can address the wily Pathan on occasion, but, hang it all, I can't make puns in Pushtu, or top off my arguments with a smutty story, as he did. He played on those two old dogs o' war like a—like a concertina. Stalky said—and the other two backed up his knowledge of Oriental nature—that the Khye-Kheens and the Malôts between 'em would organise a combined attack on us that night, as a proof of good faith. They wouldn't drive it home, though, because neither side would trust the other, on account, as Rutton Singh put it, of the little accidents. Stalky's notion was to crawl out at dusk with his Sikhs, manœuvre 'em along this ungodly goat-track that he'd found, to the back of the Khye-Kheen position, and then lob in a few long shots at the Malôts when the attack was well on. "That'll divert their minds and help to agitate 'em," he said. "Then you chaps can come out and sweep up the pieces, and we'll rendezvous at the head of the gorge. After that, I move we get back to Mac's camp and have something to eat." '

'*You* were commandin'?' The Infant suggested.

'I was about three months senior to Stalky, and two months Tertius's senior,' Dick Four replied. '*But* we were all from the same old Coll. I should say ours was the only little affair on record where some one wasn't jealous of some one else.'

'We weren't,' Tertius broke in, 'but there was another row between Gul Sher Khan and Rutton Singh. Our Jemadar said —he was quite right—that no Sikh living could stalk worth a damn; and that Koran Sahib had better take out the Pathans, who understood that kind of mountain work. Rutton

SLAVES OF THE LAMP, II

Singh said that Koran Sahib jolly well knew every Pathan was a born deserter, and every Sikh was a gentleman, even if he couldn't crawl on his belly. Stalky struck in with some woman's proverb or other, that had the effect of doublin' both men up with a grin. He said the Sikhs and the Pathans could settle their claims on the Khye-Kheens and Malôts later on, but he was going to take his Sikhs along for this mountain-climbing job, because Sikhs could shoot. They can too. Give 'em a mule-load of ammunition apiece, and they're perfectly happy.'

'And out he gat,' said Dick Four. 'As soon as it was dark, and he'd had a bit of a snooze, him and thirty Sikhs went down through the staircase in the tower, every mother's son of 'em salutin' little Everett where It stood propped up against the wall. The last I heard him say was, "Kubbadar! tumbleinga!"[1] and they tumbleingaed over the black edge of nothing. Close upon 9 P.M. the combined attack developed; Khye-Kheens across the valley, and Malôts in front of us, pluggin' at long range and yellin' to each other to come along and cut our infidel throats. Then they skirmished up to the gate, and began the old game of calling our Pathans renegades, and invitin' 'em to join the holy war. One of our men, a young fellow from Dera Ismail, jumped on the wall to slang 'em back, and jumped down, blubbing like a child. He'd been hit smack in the middle of the hand. Never saw a man yet who could stand a hit in the hand without weepin' bitterly. It tickles up all the nerves. So Tertius took his rifle and smote the others on the head to keep them quiet at the loopholes. The dear children wanted to open the gate and go in at 'em generally, but that didn't suit our book.

'At last, near midnight, I heard the wop, wop, wop, of

[1] 'Look out; you'll fall!'

367

Stalky's Martinis across the valley, and some general cursing among the Malôts, whose main body was hid from us by a fold in the hillside. Stalky was brownin' 'em at a great rate, and very naturally they turned half right and began to blaze at their faithless allies, the Khye-Kheens—regular volley firin'. In less than ten minutes after Stalky opened the diversion they were going it hammer and tongs, both sides the valley. When we could see, the valley was rather a mixed-up affair. The Khye-Kheens had streamed out of their sungars above the gorge to chastise the Malôts, and Stalky—I was watching him through my glasses—had slipped in behind 'em. Very good. The Khye-Kheens had to leg it along the hillside up to where the gorge got shallow and they could cross over to the Malôts, who were awfully cheered to see the Khye-Kheens taken in the rear.

'Then it occurred to me to comfort the Khye-Kheens. So I turned out the whole command, and we advanced *à la pas de charge*, doublin' up what, for the sake of argument, we'll call the Malôts' left flank. Even then, if they'd sunk their differences, they could have eaten us alive; but they'd been firin' at each other half the night, and they went on firin'. Queerest thing you ever saw in your born days! As soon as our men doubled up to the Malôts, they'd blaze at the Khye-Kheens more zealously than ever, to show they were on our side, run up the valley a few hundred yards, and halt to fire again. The moment Stalky saw our game he duplicated it his side the gorge; and, by Jove! the Khye-Kheens did just the same thing.'

'Yes, but,' said Tertius, 'you've forgot him playin' "Arrah, Patsy, mind the baby" on the bugle to hurry us up.'

'Did he?' roared M'Turk. Somehow we all began to sing it, and there was an interruption.

'Rather,' said Tertius, when we were quiet. No one of the

Aladdin Company could forget that tune. 'Yes, he played "Patsy." Go on, Dick.'

'Finally,' said Dick Four, 'we drove both mobs into each other's arms on a bit of level ground at the head of the valley, and saw the whole crew whirl off, fightin' and stabbin' and swearin' in a blinding snowstorm. They were a heavy, hairy lot, and we didn't follow 'em.

'Stalky had captured one prisoner—an old pensioned Sepoy of twenty-five years' service, who produced his discharge—an awf'ly sportin' old card. He had been tryin' to make his men rush us early in the day. He was sulky—angry with his own side for their cowardice, and Rutton Singh wanted to bayonet him—Sikhs don't understand fightin' against the Government after you've served it honestly—But Stalky rescued him, and froze on to him tight—with ulterior motives, I believe. When we got back to the fort, we buried young Everett—Stalky wouldn't hear of blowin' up the place—and bunked. We'd only lost ten men, all told.'

'Only ten, out of seventy. How did you lose 'em?' I asked.

'Oh, there was a rush on the fort early in the night, and a few Malôts got over the gate. It was rather a tight thing for a minute or two, but the recruits took it beautifully. Lucky job we hadn't any badly wounded men to carry, because we had forty miles to Macnamara's camp. By Jove, how we legged it! Half way in, old Rutton Singh collapsed, so we slung him across four rifles and Stalky's overcoat; and Stalky, his prisoner, and a couple of Sikhs were his bearers. After that I went to sleep. You can, you know, on the march, when your legs get properly numbed. Mac swears we all marched into his camp snoring, and dropped where we halted. His men lugged us into the tents like gram-bags. I remember wakin' up and seeing Stalky asleep with his head on old Rutton Singh's chest.

He slept twenty-four hours. I only slept seventeen, but then I was coming down with dysentery.'

'Coming down! What rot! He had it on him before we joined Stalky in the fort,' said Tertius.

'Well, *you* needn't talk! You hove your sword at Macnamara and demanded a drum-head court-martial every time you saw him. The only thing that soothed you was putting you under arrest every half-hour. You were off your head for three days.'

'Don't remember a word of it,' said Tertius placidly. 'I remember my orderly giving me milk, though.'

'How did Stalky come out?' M'Turk demanded, puffing hard over his pipe.

'Stalky? Like a serene Brahmini bull. Poor old Mac was at his Royal Engineer's wits' end to know what to do. You see, I was putrid with dysentery, Tertius was ravin', half the men had frost-bite, and Macnamara's orders were to break camp and come in before winter. So Stalky, who hadn't turned a hair, took half his supplies to save him the bother o' luggin' 'em back to the Plains, and all the ammunition he could get at, and, *consilio et auxilio* Rutton Singhi, tramped back to his fort with all his Sikhs and his precious prisoner, *and* a lot of dissolute hangers-on that he and the prisoner had seduced into service. He had sixty men of sorts—and his brazen cheek. Mac nearly wept with joy when he went. You see, there weren't any explicit orders to Stalky to come in before the passes were blocked: Mac is a great man for orders, and Stalky's a great man for orders—when they suit his book.'

'He told me he was goin' to the Engadine,' said Tertius. 'Sat on my cot smokin' a cigarette, and makin' me laugh till I cried. Macnamara bundled the whole lot of us down to the Plains next day. We were a walkin' hospital.'

'Stalky told me that Macnamara was a simple god-send to him,' said Dick Four. 'I used to see him in Mac's tent listenin' to Mac playin' the fiddle, and, between the pieces, wheedlin' Mac out of picks and shovels and dynamite cartridges hand-over-fist. Well, that was the last we saw of Stalky. A week or so later the passes were shut with snow, and I don't think Stalky wanted to be found particularly just then.'

'He didn't,' said the fair and fat Abanazar. 'He didn't. Ho, ho!'

Dick Four threw up his thin, dry hand with the blue veins at the back of it. 'Hold on a minute, Pussy. I'll let you in at the proper time. I went down to my Regiment, and that spring, five months later, I got off with a couple of companies on detachment: nominally to look after some friends of ours across the Border; actually, of course, to recruit. It was a bit unfortunate, because an ass of a young Naik carried a frivolous blood-feud he'd inherited from his aunt into those hills, and the local gentry wouldn't volunteer into my corps. Of course, the Naik had taken short leave to manage the business; that was all regular enough; *but* he'd stalked my pet orderly's uncle. It was an infernal shame, because I knew Harris of the Ghuznees would be covering that ground three months later, and he'd snaffle all the chaps I had my eyes on. Everybody was down on the Naik, because they felt he ought to have had the decency to postpone his—his disgustful amours till our companies were full strength.

'Still, the beast had a certain amount of professional feeling left. He sent one of his aunt's clan by night to tell me that, if I'd take safeguard, he'd put me on to a batch of beauties. I nipped over the Border like a shot, and about ten miles the other side, in a nullah, my rapparee-in-charge showed me about seventy men variously armed, but standing up like a Queen's Company. Then one of 'em stepped out and lugged round an old bugle, just like—who's the man?—Bancroft, ain't it?—feeling for his eyeglass in a farce, and played "Arrah, Patsy, mind the baby. Arrah, Patsy, mind"—that was as far as he could get.'

That also was as far as Dick Four could get, because we had to sing the old song through twice, again and once more, and subsequently, in order to repeat it.

'He explained that if I knew the rest of the song he had a note for me from the man the song belonged to. Whereupon, my children, I finished that old tune on that bugle, and *this* is what I got. I knew you'd like to look at it. Don't grab.' (We were all struggling for a sight of the well-known unformed handwriting.) 'I'll read it aloud:—

"FORT EVERETT, *February* 19.

"DEAR DICK, OR TERTIUS: The bearer of this is in charge of seventy-five recruits, all pukka devils, but desirous of leading new lives. They have been slightly polished, and after being boiled may shape well. I want you to give thirty of them to my Adjutant, who, though God's Own ass, will need men this spring. The rest you can keep. You will be interested to learn that I have extended my road to the end of the Malôt country. All headmen and priests concerned in last September's affair worked one month each, supplying road-metal from their own houses. Everett's grave is covered by a forty-foot mound, which should serve well as a base for future triangulations. Rutton Singh sends his best salaams. I am making some treaties, and have given my prisoner—who also sends his salaams—local rank of Khan Bahadur.

"A. L. CORKRAN."

'Well, that was all,' said Dick Four, when the roaring, the shouting, the laughter, and, I think, the tears, had subsided. 'I chaperoned the gang across the Border as quick as I could. They were rather homesick, but they cheered up when they recognised some of my chaps, who had been in the Khye-Kheen row, and they made a rippin' good lot. It's rather more than three hundred miles from Fort Everett to where I picked 'em up. Now, Pussy, tell 'em the latter end o' Stalky as you saw it.'

Abanazar laughed a little nervous, misleading, official laugh.

'Oh, it wasn't much. I was at Simla in the spring, when our Stalky, out of his snows, began corresponding direct with the Government.'

'After the manner of a king,' suggested Dick Four.

'My turn now, Dick. He'd done a whole lot of things he shouldn't have done, and constructively pledged the Government to all sorts of action.'

'Pledged the State's ticker, eh?' said M'Turk, with a nod to me.

'About that; but the embarrassin' part was that it was all so thunderin' convenient, so well reasoned, don't you know. Came in as pat as if he'd had access to all sorts of information—which he couldn't, of course.'

'Pooh!' said Tertius, 'I back Stalky against the Foreign Office any day.'

'He'd done pretty nearly everything he could think of, except strikin' coins in his own image and superscription, all under cover of buildin' this infernal road and bein' blocked by the snow. His report was simply amazin'. Von Lennaert tore his hair over it at first, and then he gasped, "Who the dooce is this unknown Warren Hastings? He must be slain. He must be slain officially! The Viceroy'll never stand it. It's unheard-of. He must be slain by His Excellency in person. Order him up here and pitch in a stinger." Well, I sent him no end of an official stinger, and I pitched in an unofficial telegram at the same time.'

'You!' This with amazement from The Infant, for Abanazar resembled nothing so much as a fluffy Persian cat.

'Yes—me,' said Abanazar. ' 'Twasn't much, but after what you've said, Dicky, it was rather a coincidence, because I wired:—

> *"Aladdin now has won his wife,*
> *Your Emperor is appeased.*
> *I think you'd better come to life:*
> *We hope you've all been pleased."*

Funny how that old song came up in my head. That was fairly non-committal and encouragin'. The only flaw was that his Emperor wasn't appeased by very long chalks. Stalky extricated himself from his mountain fastnesses and loafed up to Simla at his leisure, to be offered up on the horns of the altar.'

'But,' I began, 'surely the Commander-in-Chief is the proper——'

'His Excellency had an idea that if he blew up one single junior captain—same as King used to blow us up—he was holdin' the reins of Empire, and, of course, as long as he had that idea, Von Lennaert encouraged him. I'm not sure Von Lennaert didn't put that notion into his head.'

'They've changed the breed, then, since my time,' I said.

'P'r'aps. Stalky was sent up for his wiggin' like a bad little boy. I've reason to believe that His Excellency's hair stood on end. He walked into Stalky for one hour—Stalky at attention in the middle of the floor, and (so he vowed) Von Lennaert pretending to soothe down His Excellency's top-knot in dumb show in the background. Stalky didn't dare to look up, or he'd have laughed.'

'Now, wherefore was Stalky not broken publicly?' said The Infant, with a large and luminous leer.

'Ah, wherefore?' said Abanazar. 'To give him a chance to retrieve his blasted career, and not to break his father's heart. Stalky hadn't a father, but that didn't matter. He behaved like a—like the Sanawar Orphan Asylum, and His Excellency graciously spared him. Then he came round to my office and sat opposite me for ten minutes, puffing out his nostrils. Then he said, "Pussy, if I thought that basket-hanger——" '

'Hah! He remembered *that*,' said M'Turk.

' "That two-anna basket-hanger governed India, I swear I'd become a naturalised Muscovite to-morrow. I'm a *femme incomprise*. This thing's broken my heart. It'll take six months' shootin'-leave in India to mend it. Do you think I can get it, Pussy?"

'He got it in about three minutes and a half, and seventeen days later he was back in the arms of Rutton Singh—horrid disgraced—with orders to hand over his command, etc., to Cathcart MacMonnie.'

'Observe!' said Dick Four. 'One Colonel of the Political Department in charge of thirty Sikhs on a hilltop. Observe, my children!'

'Naturally, Cathcart, not being a fool, even if he *is* a Political, let Stalky do his shooting within fifteen miles of Fort Everett for the next six months; and I always understood they and Rutton Singh *and* the prisoner were as thick as thieves. Then Stalky loafed back to his Regiment, I believe. I've never seen him since.'

'I have, though,' said M'Turk, swelling with pride.

We all turned as one man.

'It was at the beginning of this hot weather. I was in camp in the Jullunder doab and stumbled slap on Stalky in a Sikh village; sitting on the one chair of state, with half the population grovellin' before him, a dozen Sikh babies on his knees, an old harridan clappin' him on the shoulder, and a garland o' flowers round his neck. Told me he was recruitin'. We dined together that night, but he never said a word of the business of the Fort. Told me, though, that if I wanted any supplies I'd better say I was Koran Sahib's *bhai*; and I did, and the Sikhs wouldn't take my money.'

'Ah! That must have been one of Rutton Singh's villages,' said Dick Four; and we smoked for some time in silence.

'I say,' said M'Turk, casting back through the years. 'Did Stalky ever tell you *how* Rabbits-Eggs came to rock King that night?'

'No,' said Dick Four.

Then M'Turk told.

'I see,' said Dick Four, nodding. 'Practically he duplicated that trick over again. There's nobody like Stalky.'

'That's just where you make the mistake,' I said. 'India's full of Stalkies—Cheltenham and Haileybury and Marlborough chaps—that we don't know anything about, and the surprises will begin when there is really a big row on.'

'Who will be surprised?' said Dick Four.

'The other side. The gentlemen who go to the Front in first-class carriages. Just imagine Stalky let loose on the south side of Europe with a sufficiency of Sikhs and a reasonable prospect of loot. Consider it quietly.'

'There's something in that, but you're too much of an optimist, Beetle,' said The Infant.

'Well, I've a right to be. Ain't I responsible for the whole thing? You needn't laugh. Who wrote "Aladdin now has won his wife"—eh?'

'What's that got to do with it?' said Tertius.

'Everything,' said I.

'Prove it,' said The Infant.

And I have!

LAND AND SEA TALES

PREFACE

To all to whom this little book may come—
  Health for yourselves and those you hold most dear!
Content abroad, and happiness at home,
  And—one grand secret in your private ear:—
Nations have passed away and left no traces,
And History gives the naked cause of it—
  One single, simple reason in all cases;
They fell because their peoples were not fit.

Now, though your Body be mis-shapen, blind,
  Lame, feverish, lacking substance, power or skill,
Certain it is that men can school the Mind
  To school the sickliest Body to her will—
  As many have done, whose glory blazes still
Like mighty flames in meanest lanterns lit:
  Wherefore, we pray the crippled, weak and ill—
Be fit—be fit! In mind at first be fit!

And, though your Spirit seem uncouth or small,
  Stubborn as clay or shifting as the sand,
Strengthen the Body, and the Body shall
  Strengthen the Spirit till she take command;
  As a bold rider brings his horse in hand

At the tall fence, with voice and heel and bit,
And leaps while all the field are at a stand.
Be fit—be`fit! In body next be fit!

Nothing on earth—no Arts, no Gifts, nor Graces—
   No Fame, no Wealth—outweighs the want of it.
This is the Law which every law embraces—
   Be fit—be fit! In mind and body be fit!

The even heart that seldom slurs its beat— .
   The cool head weighing what that heart desires—
The measuring eye that guides the hands and feet—
   The Soul unbroken when the Body tires—
   These are the things our weary world requires
Far more than superfluities of wit;
   Wherefore we pray you, sons of generous sires,
Be fit—be fit! For Honour's sake be fit.

There is one lesson at all Times and Places—
   One changeless Truth on all things changing writ,
For boys and girls, men, women, nations, races—
   Be fit—be fit! And once again, be fit!

CONTENTS

Land and Sea Tales was first published in 1923

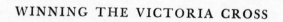

WINNING THE VICTORIA CROSS

WINNING THE VICTORIA CROSS

THE HISTORY of the Victoria Cross has been told so often that it is only necessary to say that the Order was created by Queen Victoria on January 29th, 1856, in the year of the peace with Russia, when the new racing Cunard paddle-steamer *Persia* of three thousand tons was making thirteen knots between England and America, and all the world wondered at the advance of Civilisation and Progress.

Any rank of the English Army, Navy, Reserve or Volunteer forces, from a duke to a negro, can wear on his left breast the little ugly bronze Maltese cross with the crowned lion atop and the inscription 'For Valour' below, if he has only 'performed some signal act of valour' or devotion to his country 'in the presence of the enemy.' Nothing else makes any difference; for it is explicitly laid down in the warrant that 'neither rank, nor long service, nor wounds, nor any other circumstance whatsoever, save the merit of conspicuous bravery, shall be held to establish a sufficient claim to this Order.'

There are many kinds of bravery, and if one looks through the records of the four hundred and eleven men, living and dead, that held the Victoria Cross before the Great War, one finds instances of every imaginable variety of heroism.

There is bravery in the early morning, when it takes great courage even to leave warm blankets, let alone to walk into dirt, cold, and death; on foot and on horse; empty or fed; sick or well; coolness of brain that thinks out a plan at dawn and holds to it all through the long, murderous day; bravery of the mind that makes the jerking nerves hold still and do nothing except show a good example; sheer reckless strength that hacks through a crowd of amazed men and comes out grinning on the other side; enduring spirit that wears through a long siege, never losing heart or manners or temper; quick, flashing bravery that heaves a lighted shell overboard or rushes the stockade while others are gaping at it; and the calculated craftmanship that camps alone before the angry rifle-pit or shell-hole, and cleanly and methodically wipes out every soul in it.

Before the Great War, England dealt with many different peoples, and, generally speaking, all of them, Zulu, Malay, Maori, Burman, Boer, the little hillman of the North-East Indian Frontier, Afridi, Pathan, Biluch, the Arab of East Africa and the Sudanese of the North of Africa, and the rest, played a thoroughly good game. For this we owe them many thanks; since they showed us every variety of climate and almost every variety of attack, from long-range fire to hand-to-hand scrimmage; except, of course, the ordered movements of Continental armies and the scientific ruin of towns. . . . That came later and on the largest scale.

It is rather the fashion to look down on these little wars and to call them 'military promenades' and so forth, but in reality no enemy can do much more than poison your wells, rush your camp, ambuscade you, kill you with his climate, fight you body to body, make you build your own means of communication under his fire, and horribly cut up your wounded. He may do this on a large or small scale, but the value of the teaching is the same.

It was in these rough-and-tumble affairs that many of the first Crosses were won; and some of the records for the far-away Crimea and the India Mutiny are well worth remembering, if only to show that valour never varies.

WINNING THE VICTORIA CROSS

The Crimea was clean fighting as far as the enemy were concerned,—for the very old men say that no one could wish for better troops than the Russians of Inkerman and Alma,— but our own War Office then, as two generations later, helped the enemy with ignorant mismanagement and neglect. In the Mutiny of 1857 all India, Bengal and the North-West Provinces, seemed to be crumbling like sand-bag walls in flood, and wherever there were three or four Englishmen left, they had to kill or be killed till help came. Hundreds of Crosses must have been won then, had anybody had time to notice; for the average of the work, allowing for the improvements in man-killing machinery, was as high as in the Great War.

For instance—this is a rather extensive and varied record— one man shut up in the Residency at Lucknow stole out three times at the risk of his life to get cattle for the besieged to eat. Later, he extinguished a fire near a powder-magazine and a month afterwards put out another fire. Then he led twelve men to capture two guns which were wrecking the Residency at close range. Next day, he captured an outlying position full of mutineers. Three days later he captured another gun, and finished up by capturing a fourth. So he got his Cross.

Another young man was a Lieutenant in the Southern Mahratta Horse, and a full regiment of mutineers broke into his part of the world, upsetting the minds of the people. He collected some loyal troopers, chased the regiment eighty miles, stormed the fort they had taken refuge in, and killed, captured, or wounded every soul there.

Then there was a lance-corporal who afterwards rose to be Lieutenant-Colonel. He was the enduring type of man, for he won his Cross merely for taking a hand in every fight that came along through nearly seventy consecutive days.

There were also two brothers who earned the Cross about

six times between them for leading forlorn hopes and such-like. Likewise there was a private of 'persuasive powers and cheerful disposition,' so the record says, who was cut off with nine companions in a burning house while the mutineers were firing in at the windows. He, however, cheerfully persuaded the enemy to retire, and in the end all his party were saved through his practical 'cheerfulness.' He must have been a man worth knowing.

And there was a little man in the Sutherland Highlanders—a private who eventually became a Major-General. In one attack near Lucknow he killed eleven men with his claymore, which is a heating sort of weapon to handle.

Even he was not more thorough than two troopers who rode to the rescue of their Colonel, cut off and knocked down by mutineers. They helped him to rise, and they must have been annoyed, for the three of them killed all the mutineers—about fifty.

Then there was a negro captain of the foretop, William Hall, R.N., who with two other negroes, Samuel Hodge and W. J. Gordon of the 4th and 1st West Indian Infantry, came up the river with the Naval Brigade from Calcutta to work big guns. They worked them so thoroughly that each got a Cross. They must have done a good deal, for no one is quite so crazy-reckless as a West Indian negro when he is really excited.

There was a man in the Mounted Police who with sixty horsemen charged one thousand mutineers and broke them up. And so the tale runs on.

Three Bengal Civilian Government officers were, I believe, the only strict non-combatants who ever received the Cross. As a matter of fact they had to fight with the rest, but the story of 'Lucknow' Kavanagh's adventures in disguise, of Ross

Mangle's heroism after the first attempt to relieve the Little
House at Arrah had failed (Arrah was a place where ten white
men and fifty-six loyal natives barricaded themselves in a bil-
liard-room in a garden and stood a siege of three regiments of
mutineers for three weeks), and of McDonell's cool-headedness
in the retreat down the river, are things that ought to be told
by themselves. Almost any one can fight well on the winning
side, but those men who can patch up a thoroughly bad
business and pull it off in some sort of shape, are most to be
respected.

Army Chaplains and Doctors are officially supposed to be
non-combatants—they are not really so—but about twenty
years after the Mutiny a Chaplain was decorated under circumstances that made it impossible to overlook his bravery.
Still, I do not think he quite cared for the publicity. He was
a regimental Chaplain—in action a Chaplain is generally
supposed to stay with or near the Doctor—and he seems to
have drifted up close to a cavalry charge, for he helped a
wounded officer of the Ninth Lancers into an ambulance. He
was then going about his business when he found two troopers who had tumbled into a watercourse all mixed with their
horses, and a knot of Afghans were hurrying to attend to
them. The record says that he rescued both men, but the tale,
as I heard it unofficially, declares that he found a revolver
somewhere with which he did excellent work while the troopers were struggling out of the ditch. This seems very possible,
for the Afghans do not leave disabled men without the strongest hint, and I know that in nine cases out of ten if you want
a coherent account of what happened in an action you had
better ask the Chaplain or the Roman Catholic priest of a
battalion.

But it is difficult to get details. I have met perhaps a dozen or so of V.C.'s, and in every case they explained that they did the first thing that came to their hand without worrying about alternatives. One man headed a charge into a mass of Afghans, who are very good fighters so long as they stay interested in their work, and cut down five of them. All he said was: 'Well, they were there, and they wouldn't go away. What was a man to do? Write 'em a note and ask 'em to shift?'

Another man I questioned was a doctor. Army doctors, by the way, have special opportunities for getting Crosses. Their duty compels them to stay somewhere within touch of the firing-line, and most of them run right up and lie down, to keep an eye on the wounded.

It is a heart-breaking thing for a doctor who has pulled a likely young private of twenty-three through typhoid fever and set him on his feet and watched him develop, to see the youngster wasted with a casual bullet. It must have been this feeling that made my friend do the old, splendid thing that never grows stale—rescue a wounded man under fire. He won this Cross, but all he said was: '*I* didn't want any unauthorised consultations—*or* amputations—while I was Medical Officer in charge. 'Tisn't etiquette.'

His own head was very nearly blown off as he was tying up an artery—for it was blind, bad bush-fighting with puffs of smoke popping in and out among the high grass and never a man visible—but he only grunted when his helmet was cracked across by a bullet, and went on tightening the tourniquet.

As I have hinted, in most of our little affairs before the War, the enemy knew nothing about the Geneva Convention or the treatment of wounded, but fired at a doctor on his face value as a white man. One cannot blame them—it was their custom—but it was exceedingly awkward when our doctors took care of their wounded who did not understand these things and tried to go on fighting in hospital.

There is an interesting tale of a wounded Sudanese—what our soldiers used to call a 'Fuzzy'—who was carefully attended to in a hospital after a fight. As soon as he had any strength again, he proposed to a native orderly that they two should massacre all the infidel wounded in the other beds. The orderly did not see it; so when the doctor came in he found the 'Fuzzy' was trying to work out his plan single-handed. The doctor had a very unpleasant scuffle with that simple-minded man, but, at last, he slipped the chloroform-bag over his nose. The man understood bullets and was not afraid of them; but this magic smelly stuff that sent him to sleep cowed him altogether, and he gave no more trouble in the ward.

So a doctor's life is always a little hazardous and, besides his professional duties, he may find himself senior officer in charge of what is left of the command, if the others have been shot down. As doctors are always full of theories, I believe they rather like this chance of testing them. Sometimes doctors have run out to help a mortally wounded man of their battalion, because they know that he may have last messages to give, and it eases him to die with some human being holding his hand. This is a most noble thing to do under fire, because it means sitting still among bullets. Chaplains have done it also, but it is part of what they reckon as their regular duty.

Another V.C. of my acquaintance—he was anything but a doctor or a chaplain—once saved a trooper whose horse had been killed. His method was rather original. The man was on foot and the enemy—Zulus this time—were coming down at a run, and the trooper said, very decently, that he did not see his way to periling his officer's life by double-weighting the only available horse.

To this his officer replied: 'If you don't get up behind me, I'll get off and give you such a licking as you've never had in your life.' The man was more afraid of fists than of assegais, and the good horse pulled them both out of the scrape. Now by our Regulations an officer who insults or 'threatens with violence' a subordinate in the Service is liable to lose his commission and to be declared 'incapable of serving the King in any capacity.' But for some reason or other the trooper never reported his superior.

The humour and the honour of fighting are by no means all on one side. A good many years ago there was a war in New Zealand against the Maoris, who, though they tortured prisoners and occasionally ate a man, liked fighting for its own sake. One of their chiefs cut off a detachment of our men in a stockade where he might have starved them out, and eaten them at leisure later. But word reached him that they were short of provisions, and so he sent in a canoeful of pig and potatoes with the message that it was no fun to play war-games with weak men, and he would be happy to meet them after rest and a full meal. There are many cases in which men, very young as a rule, have forced their way through a stockade of thorns that hook or bamboos that cut, and held on in the face of heavy fire or just so long as served to bring up their comrades. Those who have done this say that getting in is exciting enough, but the bad time, when the minutes drag like hours, lies between the first scuffle with the angry faces in the smoke, and the 'Hi, get out o' this!' that shows that the others of our side are tumbling up behind. They say it is as bad as football when you get off the ball just as slowly as you dare, so that your own side may have time to come up.

WINNING THE VICTORIA CROSS

Most men, after they have been shot over a little, only want a lead to do good work; so the result of a young man's daring is often out of all proportion to his actual performances.

Here is a case which never won notice because very few people talked about it—a case of the courage of Ulysses, one might say.

A column of troops, heavily weighted with sick and wounded, had drifted into a bad place—a pass where an enemy, hidden behind rocks, were picking them off at known ranges, as they retreated. Half a battalion was acting as rear-guard —company after company facing about on the narrow road and trying to keep down the wicked, flickering fire from the hillsides. And it was twilight; and it was cold and raining; and it was altogether horrible for every one.

Presently, the rear-guard began to fire a little too quickly and to hurry back to the main body a little too soon, and the bearers put down the ambulances a little too often, and looked on each side of the road for possible cover. Altogether, there were the makings of a nasty little breakdown—and after that would come primitive slaughter.

A boy whom I knew was acting in command of one company that was specially bored and sulky, and there were shouts from the column of 'Hurry up! Hurry there!' neither necessary or soothing. He kept his men in hand as well as he could, hitting down rifles when they fired wild, till some one along the line shouted: 'What on earth are you fellows waiting so long for?'

Then my friend—I am rather proud that he was my friend —hunted for his pipe and tobacco, filled the bowl *in* his pocket because, he said afterwards, he didn't want any one to see how his hand shook, lit a fuzee, and shouted back between very short puffs: 'Hold on a minute. I'm lighting my pipe.'

395

There was a roar of rather crackly laughter and the company joker said: 'Since you *are* so pressin', I think I'll 'ave a draw meself.'

I don't believe either pipe was smoked out, but—and this is a very big but—the little bit of acting steadied the company, and the news of it ran down the line, and even the wounded in the litters laughed, and every one felt better. Whether the enemy heard the laughing, or were impressed by the even 'one-two-three-four' firing that followed it, will never be known, but the column came to camp at the regulation step and not at a run, with very few casualties. That is what one may call the courage of the much-enduring Ulysses, but the only comment that I ever heard on the affair was the boy's own, and all *he* said was: 'It was transpontine [which means theatrical], but necessary.'

Of course he must have been a good boy from the beginning, for little bits of pure inspiration seldom come to or are acted upon by slovens, self-indulgent or undisciplined people. I have not yet met one V.C. who had not strict notions about washing and shaving and keeping himself decent on his way through the civilised world, whatever he may have done outside it.

Indeed, it is very curious, after one has known hundreds of young men and young officers, to sit still at a distance and watch them come forward to success in their profession. Somehow, the clean and considerate man mostly seems to take hold of circumstances at the right end.

One of the youngest of the V.C.'s of his time I used to know distantly as a beautiful being whom they called Aide-de-Camp to a big official in India. So far as strangers could judge, his duties consisted in wearing a uniform faced with blue satin, and in seeing that every one was looked after at the dances and dinners. He would wander about smiling, with eyes at the back of his head, introducing men who were strangers and a little out of it, to girls whose dance-cards were rather empty; taking old and uninteresting women in to supper, and tucking them into their carriages afterwards; or pleasantly steering white-whiskered native officers all covered with medals and half-blind with confusion through the maze of a big levee into the presence of the Viceroy or Commander-in-Chief, or whoever it was they were being presented to.

After a few years of this work, his chance came, and he made the most of it. We were then smoking out a nest of caravan-raiders, slave-dealers, and general thieves who lived somewhere under the Karakoram Mountains among glaciers about sixteen thousand feet above sea-level. The mere road to the place was too much for many mules, for it ran by precipices and round rock-curves and over roaring, snow-fed rivers.

The enemy—they were called Kanjuts—had fortified themselves in a place nearly as impregnable as nature and man could make it. One position was on the top of a cliff about twelve hundred feet high, whence they could roll stones directly on the head of any attacking force. Our men objected to the stones much more than to the rifle-fire. They were camped in a river-bed at the bottom of an icy pass with some three tiers of these cliff-like defences above them, and the Kanjuts on each tier were very well armed. To make all specially pleasant, it was December.

This ex-Aide-de-Camp happened to be a good mountaineer, and he was told off with a hundred native troops, Gurkhas and Dogra Sikhs, to climb up into the top tier of the fortifications. The only way of arriving was to follow a sort of shoot in the cliff-face which the enemy had worn smooth by throwing rocks down. Even in daylight, in peace, and with good guides, it would have been fair mountaineering.

He went up in the dark, by eye and guess, against some two thousand Kanjuts very much at war with him. When he had climbed eight hundred feet almost perpendicular he found he had to come back, because even he and his Gurkha cragsmen could find no way.

He returned to the river-bed and tried again in a new place, working his men up between avalanches of stones that slid along and knocked people over. When he struggled to the top he had to take his men into the forts with the bayonet and the *kukri*, the little Gurkha knife. The attack was so utterly bold and unexpected that it broke the hearts of the enemy and practically ended the campaign. If you could see the photograph of the place you would understand why.

It was hard toe-nail and finger-nail crag-climbing under fire, and the men behind him were not regulars, but what are called Imperial Service troops—men raised by the semi-independent kings and used to defend the frontier. They enjoyed themselves immensely and the little Aide-de-Camp got a deserved Victoria Cross. The courage of Ulysses again; for he had to think as he climbed, and until he was directly underneath the fortifications, one chance-hopping boulder might just have planed his men off all along the line.

But there is a heroism beyond all, for which no Victoria Cross is ever given, because there is no official enemy nor any sort of firing, except one volley in the early morning at some spot where the noise does not echo into the newspapers.

It is necessary from time to time to send unarmed men into No Man's Land and the Back of Beyond across the Khudajanta Khan (The Lord-knows-where) Mountains, merely to find out what is going on there among people who some day or other may become dangerous enemies.

The understanding is that if the men return with their reports so much the better for them. They may then receive some sort of decoration, given, so far as the public can make out, for no real reason. If they do not come back—and people disappear very mysteriously at the Back of Beyond—that is their own concern, and no questions will be asked, and no inquiries made.

They tell a tale of one man who, some years ago, strayed into No Man's Land to see how things were, and met a very amiable set of people, who asked him to a round of dinners and lunches and dances. And all that time he knew, and they knew that he knew, that his hosts were debating between themselves whether they should suffer him to live till next morning, and if they decided not to let him live, in what way they should wipe him out most quietly.

The only consideration that made them hesitate was that they could not tell from his manner whether there were five hundred Englishmen within a few miles of him or no Englishmen at all within five hundred miles of him; and, as matters stood at that moment, they could not very well go out to look and make sure.

So he danced and dined with those pleasant, merry folk,—all good friends,—and talked about hunting and shooting and so forth, never knowing when the polite servants behind his chair would turn into the firing-party. At last his hosts decided, without rude words said, to let him go; and when they made up their minds they did it very handsomely, for, you must remember, there is no malice borne on either side in that game.

They gave him a farewell banquet and drank his health, and he thanked them for his delightful visit, and they said: 'So glad you're glad. *Au revoir*,' and he came away looking a little bored.

Later on, so the tale runs, his hosts discovered that their guest had been given up for lost by his friends in England, where no one ever expected to see him again. Then they were sorry that they had not put him against a wall and shot him.

That is a case of the cold-blooded courage worked up to after years of training—courage of mind forcing the body through an unpleasant situation for the sake of the game.

When all is said and done, courage of mind is the finest thing any one can hope to attain to. A weak or undisciplined soul is apt to become reckless under strain (which is only being afraid the wrong way about), or to act for its own immediate advantage. For this reason the Victoria Cross is jealously guarded, and if there be suspicion that the man is playing to the gallery or pot-hunting for medals, as they call it, he is often left to head his charges and rescue his wounded all over again as a guarantee of good faith.

In the Great War there was very little suspicion, or chance, of gallery-play for the V.C., because there was ample opportunity and, very often, strong necessity for a man to repeat his performances several times over. Moreover, he was generally facing much deadlier weapons than mere single rifles or edged tools, and the rescue of wounded under fire was, by so much, a more serious business. But one or two War V.C.'s of my acquaintance have told me that if you can manage the little matter of keeping your head, it is not as difficult as it sounds to get on the blind side of a machine-gun, or to lie out under its lowest line of fire, where, they say, you are 'quite comfortable if you don't fuss.' Also, every V.C. of the Great War I have spoken to has been rather careful to explain that he won his Cross because what he did happened to be done when and where some one could notice it. Thousands of men, they said, did just the same, but in places where there were no observers. And that is true; for the real spirit of the Army changes very little through the years.

Men are taught to volunteer for anything and everything; going out quietly after, not before, the authorities have filled their place. They are also instructed that it is cowardly, it is childish, and it is cheating to neglect or scamp the plain work immediately in front of them—the duties they are trusted to do—for the sake of stepping aside to snatch at what to an outsider may resemble fame or distinction. Above all, their own hard equals, whose opinion is the sole opinion worth having, are always sitting unofficially in judgment on them.

The Order itself is a personal decoration, and the honour and glory of it belongs to the wearer; but he can only win it by forgetting himself, his own honour and glory, and by working for something beyond and outside and apart from his own self. And there seems to be no other way in which you get anything in this world worth the keeping.

THE WAY THAT HE TOOK

1900

THE WAY THAT HE TOOK

Almost every word of this story is based on fact. The Boer War of 1899–1902 was a very small one as wars were reckoned, and was fought without any particular malice, but it taught our men the practical value of scouting in the field. They were slow to learn at the outset, and it cost them many unnecessary losses, as is always the case when men think they can do their work without taking trouble beforehand.

THE GUNS OF THE FIELD-BATTERY were ambushed behind white-thorned mimosas, scarcely taller than their wheels, that marked the line of a dry nullah; and the camp pretended to find shade under a clump of gums planted as an experiment by some Minister of Agriculture. One small hut, reddish stone with a tin roof, stood where the single track of the railway split into a siding. A rolling plain of red earth, speckled with loose stones and sugar-bush, ran northward to the scarps and spurs of a range of little hills—all barren and exaggerated in the heat-haze. Southward, the level lost itself in a tangle of scrub-furred hillocks, upheaved without purpose or order, seared and blackened by the strokes of the careless lightning, seamed down their sides with spent watercourses, and peppered from base to summit with stones—riven, piled, scattered stones. Far away, to the eastward, a line of blue-grey mountains, peaked and horned, lifted itself over the huddle of the tortured earth. It was the only thing that held steady through the liquid mirage. The nearer hills detached themselves from the plain,

and swam forward like islands in a milky ocean. While the
Major stared through puckered eyelids, Leviathan himself
waded through the far shallows of it—a black and formless
beast.

'That,' said the Major, 'must be the Guns coming back.' He
had sent out two guns, nominally for exercise—actually to
show the loyal Dutch that there was artillery near the railway
if any patriot thought fit to tamper with it. Chocolate smears,
looking as though they had been swept with a besom through
the raffle of stones, wandered across the earth—unbridged, un-
graded, unmetalled. They were the roads to the brown mud
huts, one in each valley, that were officially styled farm-houses.
At very long intervals a dusty Cape-cart or a tilted wagon
would move along them, and men, dirtier than the dirt, would
come to sell fruit or scraggy sheep. At night the farm-houses
were lighted up in a style out of all keeping with Dutch
economy; the scrub would light itself on some far headland,
and the house-lights twinkled in reply. Three or four days later
the Major would read bad news in the Cape Town papers
thrown to him from the passing troop trains.

The guns and their escort changed from Leviathan to the
likeness of wrecked boats, their crews struggling beside them.
Presently they took on their true shape, and lurched into camp
amid clouds of dust.

The Mounted Infantry escort set about its evening meal;
the hot air filled with the scent of burning wood; sweating
men rough-dried sweating horses with wisps of precious
forage; the sun dipped behind the hills, and they heard the
whistle of a train from the south.

'What's that?' said the Major, slipping into his coat. The
decencies had not yet left him.

'Ambulance train,' said the Captain of Mounted Infantry,

raising his glasses. 'I'd like to talk to a woman again, but it won't stop here. . . . It *is* stopping, though, and making a beastly noise. Let's look.'

The engine had sprung a leaky tube, and ran lamely into the siding. It would be two or three hours at least before she could be patched up.

Two doctors and a couple of Nursing Sisters stood on the rear platform of a carriage. The Major explained the situation, and invited them to tea.

'We were just going to ask *you*,' said the medical Major of the ambulance train.

'No, come to our camp. Let the men see a woman again!' he pleaded.

Sister Dorothy, old in the needs of war, for all her twenty-four years, gathered up a tin of biscuits and some bread and butter new cut by the orderlies. Sister Margaret picked up the teapot, the spirit-lamp, and a water-bottle.

'Cape Town water,' she said, with a nod. 'Filtered too. *I* know Karroo water.' She jumped down lightly on to the ballast.

'What do you know about the Karroo, Sister?' said the Captain of Mounted Infantry, indulgently, as a veteran of a month's standing. He understood that all that desert as it seemed to him was called by that name.

She laughed. 'This is my home. I was born out they-ah—just behind that big range of hills—out Oudtshorn way. It's only sixty miles from here. Oh, how good it is!'

She slipped the Nurse's cap from her head, tossed it through the open car-window, and drew a breath of deep content. With the sinking of the sun the dry hills had taken life and glowed against the green of the horizon. They rose up like jewels in the utterly lucid air, while the valleys between flooded with purple shadow. A mile away, stark-clear, with-ered rocks showed as though one could touch them with the hand, and the voice of a native herd-boy in charge of a flock of sheep came in clear and sharp over twice that distance. Sister Margaret devoured the huge spaces with eyes unused to shorter ranges, snuffed again the air that has no equal under God's skies, and, turning to her companion, said: 'What do *you* think of it?'

'I am afraid I'm rather singular,' he replied. 'Most of us hate the Karroo. I used to, but it grows on one somehow. I suppose it's the lack of fences and roads that's so fascinating. And when one gets back from the railway——'

'You're quite right,' she said, with an emphatic stamp of her foot. 'People come to Matjesfontein—ugh!—with their lungs, and they live opposite the railway station and that new hotel, and they think *that*'s the Karroo. They say there isn't anything in it. It's *full* of life when you really get into it. You see that? I'm *so* glad. D'you know, you're the first English officer I've heard who has spoken a good word for my country.'

'I'm glad I pleased you,' said the Captain, looking into Sister Margaret's black-lashed grey eyes under the heavy brown hair shot with grey where it rolled back from the tanned forehead. This kind of nurse was new in his experience. The average Sister did not lightly stride over rolling stones, and—was it possible that her easy pace uphill was beginning to pump him? As she walked, she hummed joyously to herself, a queer catchy tune of one line several times repeated:

> *'Vat jou goed en trek, Ferreira,*
> *Vat jou goed en trek.'*

It ran off with a little trill that sounded like:

THE WAY THAT HE TOOK

'Swaar draa, alle en die ein kant;
Jannie met die hoepelbeen!'[1]

'Listen!' she said suddenly. 'What was that?'

'It must be a wagon on the road. I heard the whip, I think.'

'Yes, but you didn't hear the wheels, did you? It's a little bird that makes just that noise, "Whe-ew"!' She duplicated it perfectly. 'We call it'—she gave the Dutch name, which did not, of course, abide with the Captain. 'We must have given him a scare! You hear him in the early mornings when you are sleeping in the wagons. It's just like the noise of a whip-lash, isn't it?'

They entered the Major's tent a little behind the others, who were discussing the scanty news of the campaign.

'Oh no,' said Sister Margaret coolly, bending over the spirit-lamp, 'the Transvaalers will stay round Kimberley and try to put Rhodes in a cage. But, of course, if a commando gets through to De Aar they will all rise——'

'You think so, Sister?' said the medical Major deferentially.

'I know so. They will rise anywhere in the Colony if a commando comes actually to them. Presently they will rise in Prieska—if it is only to steal the forage at Van Wyk's Vlei. Why not?'

'We get most of our opinions of the war from Sister Margaret,' said the civilian doctor of the train. 'It's all new to me, but, so far, her prophecies have come true.'

A few months ago that doctor had retired from practice to a country house in rainy England, his fortune made and, as he tried to believe, his life-work done. Then the bugles blew,

[1] *Pack your kit and trek, Ferreira,*
Pack your kit and trek.
A long pull, all on one side,
Johnnie with the lame leg.

and, rejoicing at the change, he found himself, his experience, and his fine bedside manner, buttoned up in a black-tabbed khaki coat, on a hospital train that covered eleven hundred miles a week, carried a hundred wounded each trip and dealt him more experience in a month than he had ever gained in a year of Home practice.

Sister Margaret and the Captain of Mounted Infantry took their cups outside the tent. The Captain wished to know something more about her. Till that day he had believed South Africa to be populated by sullen Dutchmen and slack-waisted women; and in some clumsy fashion had betrayed the belief.

'Of course, you don't see any others where you are,' said Sister Margaret, leniently, from her camp-chair. 'They are all at the war. I have two brothers, and a nephew, my sister's son, and—oh, I can't count my cousins.' She flung her hands outward with a curiously un-English gesture. 'And then, too, you have never been off the railway. You have only seen Cape Town? All the schel—all the useless people are there. You should see *our* country beyond the ranges—out Oudtshorn way. We grow fruit and vines. It is much prettier, *I* think, than Paarl.'

'I'd like to very much. I may be stationed in Africa after the war is over.'

'Ah, but we know the English officers. They say that this is a "beastly country," and they do not know how to—to be nice to people. Shall I tell you? There was an aide-de-camp at Government House three years ago. He sent out invitations to dinner to Piet—to Mr. Van der Hooven's wife. *And* she had been dead eight years, and Van der Hooven—he has the big farms round Craddock—just then was thinking of changing his politics, you see—he was against the Government,—

and taking a house in Cape Town, because of the Army meat contracts. That was why, you see?'

'I see,' said the Captain, to whom this was all Greek.

'Piet was a little angry—not much—but he went to Cape Town, and that aide-de-camp had made a joke about it—about inviting the dead woman—in the Civil Service Club. You see? So of *course* the opposition there told Van der Hooven that the aide-de-camp had said he could not remember all the old Dutch vrouws that had died, and so Piet van der Hooven went away angry, and now he is more hot than ever against the Government. If you stay with us you must not be like *that*. You see?'

'I won't,' said the Captain seriously. 'What a night it is, Sister!' He dwelt lovingly on the last word, as men did in South Africa.

The soft darkness had shut upon them unawares and the world had vanished. There was not so much breeze as a slow motion of the whole dry air under the vault of the immeasurably deep heavens. 'Look up,' said the Captain. 'Doesn't it make you feel as if we were tumbling down into the stars— all upside down?'

'Yes,' said Sister Margaret, tilting her head back. 'It is always like that. I know. And those are *our* stars.'

They burned with a great glory, large as the eyes of cattle by lamp-light; planet after planet of the mild Southern sky. As the Captain said, one seemed to be falling from out the hidden earth sheer through space, between them.

'Now, when I was little,' Sister Margaret began very softly, 'there was one day in the week at home that was all our own. We could get up as soon as we liked after midnight, and there was the basket in the kitchen—our food. We used to go out at three o'clock sometimes, my two brothers, my sisters, and the two little ones—out into the Karroo for all the day. All—the—long—day. First we built a fire, and then we made a kraal for the two little ones—a kraal of thorn bushes so that they should not be bitten by anything. You see? Often we made the kraal before morning—when those'—she jerked her firm chin at the stars—'were just going out. Then we old ones went hunting lizards—and snakes and birds and centipedes, and all that sort of nice thing. Our father collected them. He gave us half-a-crown for a spuugh—slange—a kind of snake. You see?'

'How old were you?' Snake-hunting did not strike the Captain as a safe amusement for the young.

'I was eleven then—or ten, perhaps, and the little ones were two and three. Why? Then we came back to eat, and we sat under a rock all afternoon. It was hot, you see, and we played —we played with the stones and the flowers. You should see our Karroo in spring! All flowers! All our flowers! Then we came home, carrying the little ones on our backs asleep—came home through the dark—just like this night. That was our own day! Oh, the good days! We used to watch the meer-cats playing, too, and the little buck. When I was at Guy's learning to nurse, how home-sick that made me!'

'But what a splendid open-air life!' said the Captain.

'Where else *is* there to live except the open air?' said Sister Margaret, looking off into twenty thousand square miles of it with eyes that burned.

'You're quite right.'

'I'm sorry to interrupt you two,' said Sister Dorothy, who had been talking to the Gunner Major; 'but the guard says we shall be ready to go in a few minutes. Major Devine and Dr. Johnson have gone down already.'

'Very good, Sister. We'll follow.' The Captain rose unwillingly and made for the worn path from the camp to the rail.

'Isn't there another way?' said Sister Margaret. Her grey nursing gown glimmered like some big moth's wing.

'No. I'll bring a lantern. It's quite safe.'

'I did not think of *that*,' she said, with a laugh; 'only *we* never come home by the way we left it when we live in the Karroo. If any one—suppose you had dismissed a Kaffir, or got him sjamboked,[1] and he saw you go out? He would wait for you to come back on a tired horse, and then. . . . You see? But, of course, in England, where the road is all walled, it is different. How funny! Even when we were little we learned never to come home by the way we went out.'

'Very good,' said the Captain obediently. It made the walk longer, and he approved of that.

'That's a curious sort of woman,' said the Captain to the Major, as they smoked a lonely pipe together when the train had gone.

'*You* seemed to think so.'

'Well,—I couldn't monopolise Sister Dorothy in the presence of my senior officer. What was she like?'

'Oh, it came out that she knew a lot of my people in London. She's the daughter of a chap in the next county to us, too.'

The General's flag still flew before his unstruck tent to amuse Boer binoculars, and loyal lying correspondents still telegraphed accounts of his daily work. But the General himself had gone to join an army a hundred miles away; drawing off, from time to time, every squadron, gun, and company that he dared. His last words to the few troops he left behind covered the entire situation.

---

[1] Beaten.

'If you can bluff 'em till we get round 'em up North to tread on their tails, it's all right. If you can't, they'll probably eat you up. Hold 'em as long as you can.'

So the skeleton remnant of the brigade lay close among the kopjes till the Boers, not seeing them in force on the skyline, feared that they might have learned the rudiments of war. They rarely disclosed a gun, for the reason that they had so few; they scouted by fours and fives instead of clattering troops and chattering companies, and where they saw a too obvious way opened to attack, they, lacking force to drive it home, looked elsewhere. Great was the anger in the Boer commando across the river—the anger and unease.

'The reason is they have so few men,' the loyal farmers reported, all fresh from selling melons to the camp, and drinking Queen Victoria's health in good whiskey. 'They have no horses—only what they call Mounted Infantry. They are afraid of us. They try to make us friends by giving us brandy. Come on and shoot them. Then they will see us rise and cut the line.'

'Yes, we know how you rise, you Colonials,' said the Boer commandant above his pipe. 'We know what has come to all your promises from Beaufort West, and even from De Aar. *We* do the work—all the work,—and you kneel down with your parsons and pray for our success. What good is that? The President has told you a hundred times God is on our side. Why do you worry *Him*? We did not send you Mausers and ammunition for that.'

'We kept our commando-horses ready for six months—and forage is very dear. We sent all our young men,' said an honoured member of local society.

'A few here and a few servants there. What is that? You should have risen down to the sea all together.'

'But you were so quick. Why did not you wait the year? We were not ready, Jan.'

'That is a lie. All you Cape people lie. You want to save your cattle and your farms. Wait till *our* flag flies from here to Port Elizabeth, and you shall see what you will save when the President learns how you have risen—you clever Cape people.'

The saddle-coloured sons of the soil looked down their noses. 'Yes—it is true. Some of our farms are close to the line. They say at Worcester and in the Paarl that many soldiers are always coming in from the sea. One must think of that—at least till they are shot. But we know there are very few in front of you here. Give them what you gave the fools at Stormberg, and you will see how we can shoot rooineks.'[1]

'Yes. I know that cow. She is always going to calve. Get away. I am answerable to the President—not to the Cape.'

But the information stayed in his mind, and, not being a student of military works, he made a plan to suit. The tall kopje on which the English had planted their helio-station commanded the more or less open plain to the northward, but did not command the five-mile belt of broken country between that and the outmost English pickets, some three miles from camp. The Boers had established themselves very comfortably among these rock-ridges and scrub-patches, and the 'great war' drizzled down to long shots and longer stalking. The young bloods wanted rooineks to shoot, and said so.

'See here,' quoth the experienced Jan van Staden that evening to as many of his commando as cared to listen. 'You youngsters from the Colony talk a lot. Go and turn the rooineks out of their kopjes to-night. Eh? Go and take their bayonets from them and stick them into them. Eh? You don't go!' He laughed at the silence round the fire.

[1] Red necks—English soldiers.

'Jan—Jan,' said one young man appealingly, 'don't make a mock of us.'

'I thought that was what you wanted so badly. No? Then listen to me. Behind us the grazing is bad. We have too many cattle here.' (They had been stolen from farmers who had been heard to express fears of defeat.) 'To-morrow, by the sky's look, it will blow a good wind. So to-morrow early I shall send all our cattle north to the new grazing. That will make a great dust for the English to see from their helio yonder.' He pointed to a winking night-lamp stabbing the darkness with orders to an outlying picket. 'With the cattle we will send all our women. Yes, all the women and the wagons we can spare, and the lame ponies and the broken carts we took from Andersen's farm. That will make a big dust—the dust of our retreat. Do you see?'

They saw and approved, and said so.

'Good. There are many men here who want to go home to their wives. I shall let thirty of them away for a week. Men who wish to do this will speak to me to-night.' (This meant that Jan needed money, and furlough would be granted on strictly business lines.) 'These men will look after the cattle and see that they make a great dust for a long way. They will run about behind the cattle showing their guns, too. So *that*, if the wind blows well, will be our retreat. The cattle will feed beyond Koopman's Kop.'

'No good water there,' growled a farmer who knew that section. 'Better go on to Zwartpan. It is always sweet at Zwartpan.'

The commando discussed the point for twenty minutes. It was much more serious than shooting rooineks. Then Jan went on:

'When the rooineks see our retreat they may all come into our kopjes together. If so, good. But it is tempting God to expect such a favour. *I* think they will first send some men to scout.' He grinned broadly, twisting the English word. 'Almighty! To scoot! They have none of that new sort of rooinek that they used at Sunnyside.' (Jan meant an incomprehensible animal from a place called Australia across the Southern seas who played what they knew of the war-game to kill.) 'They have only some Mounted Infantry,'—again he used the English words. 'They were once a Red-jacket regiment, so their scoots will stand up bravely to be shot at.'

'Good—good, we will shoot them,' said a youngster from Stellenbosch, who had come up on free pass as a Cape Town excursionist just before the war to a farm on the border, where his aunt was taking care of his horse and rifle.

'But if you shoot their scoots I will sjambok you myself,' said Jan, amid roars of laughter. 'We must let them *all* come into the kopjes to look for us; and I pray God will not allow any of us to be tempted to shoot them. They will cross the ford in front of their camp. They will come along the road— so!' He imitated with ponderous arms the Army style of riding. 'They will trot up the road this way and that way'—here he snaked his hard finger in the dust—'between kopjes, till they come here, where they can see the plain and all our cattle going away. Then they will *all* come in close together. Perhaps they will even fix their bayonets. *We* shall be up here behind the rock—there and there.' He pointed to two flat-topped kopjes, one on either side of the road, some eight hundred yards away. 'That is our place. We will go there before sunrise. Remember we must be careful to let the very last of the rooineks pass before we begin shooting. They will come along a little careful at first. But we do not shoot. Then they will see our fires and the fresh horse-dung, so they will know we have gone on. They will run together and talk and point and shout in this nice open place. Then we begin shooting them from above.'

'Yes, uncle, but if the scoots see nothing and there are no shots and we let them go back quite quiet, they will think it was a trick. Perhaps the main body may never come here at all. Even rooineks learn in time—and so we may lose even the scoots.'

'I have thought of that too,' said Jan, with slow contempt, as the Stellenbosch boy delivered his shot. 'If you had been *my* son I should have sjamboked you more when you were a youngster. I shall put *you* and four or five more on the Nek [the pass], where the road comes from their camp into these kopjes. You go there before it is light. Let the scoots pass in or I will sjambok you myself. When the scoots come back after seeing nothing here, then you may shoot them, but *not* till they have passed the Nek and are on the straight road back to their camp again. Do you understand? Repeat what I have said, so that I shall know.'

The youth obediently repeated his orders.

'Kill their officers if you can. If not, no great matter, because the scoots will run to camp with the news that our kopjes are empty. Their helio-station will see your party trying to hold the Nek so hard—and all that time they will see our dust out yonder, and they will think you are the rear-guard, and they will think *we* are escaping. They will be angry.'

'Yes—yes, uncle, we see,' from a dozen elderly voices.

'But this calf does not. Be silent! They will shoot at you, Niclaus, on the Nek, because they will think you are to cover our getting away. They will shell the Nek. They will miss. You will then ride away. All the rooineks will come after you, hot and in a hurry—perhaps, even, with their cannon. They will pass our fires and our fresh horse-dung. They will come

here as their scoots came. They will see the plain so full of
our dust. They will say, "The scoots spoke truth. It is a full
retreat." *Then* we up there on the rocks will shoot, and it will
be like the fight at Stormberg in daytime. Do you understand
now?'

Those of the commando directly interested lit new pipes
and discussed the matter in detail till midnight.

Next morning the operations began with—if one may borrow the language of some official despatches—'the precision of
well-oiled machinery.'

The helio-station reported the dust of the wagons and the
movements of armed men in full flight across the plain beyond
the kopjes. A Colonel, newly appointed from England, by reason of his seniority, sent forth a dozen Mounted Infantry
under command of a Captain. Till a month ago they had been
drilled by a cavalry instructor, who taught them 'shock' tactics
to the music of trumpets. They knew how to advance in
echelon of squadrons, by cat's-cradle of troops, in quarter
column of stable-litter, how to trot, to gallop, and above all
to charge. They knew how to sit their horses unremittingly,
so that at the day's end they might boast how many hours they
had been in the saddle without relief, and they learned to
rejoice in the clatter and stamp of a troop moving as such, and
therefore audible five miles away.

They trotted out two and two along the farm road, that
trailed lazily through the wind-driven dust; across the half-
dried ford to a nek between low stony hills leading into the
debatable land. (Vrooman of Emmaus from his neatly bushed
hole noted that one man carried a sporting Lee-Enfield rifle
with a short fore-end. Vrooman of Emmaus argued that the
owner of it was the officer to be killed on his return, and went
to sleep.) They saw nothing except a small flock of sheep and

a Kaffir herdsman who spoke broken English with curious fluency. He had heard that the Boers had decided to retreat on account of their sick and wounded. The Captain in charge of the detachment turned to look at the helio-station four miles away. 'Hurry up,' said the dazzling flash. 'Retreat apparently continues, but suggest you make sure. Quick.'

'Ye-es,' said the Captain, a shade bitterly, as he wiped the sweat from a sun-skinned nose. 'You want me to come back and report all clear. If anything happens it will be my fault. If they get away it will be my fault for disregarding the signal. I love officers who suggest and advise, and want to make their reputations in twenty minutes.'

'Don't see much 'ere, sir,' said the sergeant, scanning the bare cup of the hollow where a dust-devil danced alone.

'No? We'll go on.'

'If we get among these steep 'ills we lose touch of the 'elio.'

'Very likely. Trot.'

The rounded mounds grew to spiked kopjes, heart-breaking to climb under a hot sun at four thousand feet above sea-level. This is where the scouts found their spurs peculiarly useful.

Jan van Staden had thoughtfully allowed the invading force a front of two rifle-shots or four thousand yards, and they kept a thousand yards within his estimate. Ten men strung over two miles feel that they have explored all the round earth.

They saw stony slopes combing over in scrub, narrow valleys clothed with stone, low ridges of splintered stone, and tufts of brittle-stemmed bush. An irritating wind, split up by many rocky barriers, cuffed them over the ears and slapped them in the face at every turn. They came upon an abandoned campfire, a little fresh horse-dung, and an empty ammunition-box splintered up for firewood, an old boot, and a stale bandage.

A few hundred yards farther along the road a battered

Mauser had been thrown into a bush. The glimmer of its barrel drew the scouts from the hillside, and here the road after passing between two flat-topped kopjes entered a valley nearly half a mile wide, rose slightly, and over the nek of a ridge gave clear view across the windy plain northward.

'They're on the dead run, for sure,' said a trooper. 'Here's their fires and their litter and their guns, and that's where they're bolting to.' He pointed over the ridge to the bellying dust-cloud a mile long. A vulture high overhead flickered down, steadied herself, and hung motionless.

'See!' said Jan van Staden from the rocks above the road, to his waiting commando. 'It turns like a well-oiled wheel. They look where they need not look, but *here*, where they should look on both sides, they look at our retreat—straight before them. It is tempting our people too much. I pray God no one will shoot them.'

'That's about the size of it,' said the Captain, rubbing the dust from his binoculars. 'Boers on the run. I expect they find their main line of retreat to the north is threatened. We'll get back and tell the camp.' He wheeled his pony, and his eye traversed the flat-topped kopje commanding the road. The stones at its edge seemed to be piled with less than Nature's carelessness.

'That 'ud be a dashed ugly place if it were occupied—and that other one, too. Those rocks aren't five hundred yards from the road, either of 'em. Hold on, sergeant, I'll light a pipe.' He bent over the bowl, and above his lighted match squinted at the kopje. A stone, a small roundish brown boulder on the lip of another one, seemed to move very slightly. The short hairs of his neck grated his collar. 'I'll have another squint at their retreat,' he cried to the sergeant, astonished at the steadiness of his own voice. He swept the

plain, and, wheeling, let the glass rest for a moment on the
kopje's top. One cranny between the rocks was pinkish, where
blue sky should have shown. His men, dotted down the valley,
sat heavily on their horses—it never occurred to them to dis-
mount. He could hear the squeak of the leathers as a man
shifted. An impatient gust blew through the valley and rattled
the bushes. On all sides the expectant hills stood still under
the pale blue.

'And we passed within a quarter of a mile of 'em! We're
done!' The thumping heart slowed down, and the Captain
began to think clearly—so clearly that the thoughts seemed
solid things. 'It's Pretoria jail for us all. Perhaps that man's
only a look-out, though. We'll have to bolt! And I led 'em
into it! . . . You fool!' said his other self, above the beat of
the blood in his ear-drums. 'If they could snipe you all from
up there, why haven't they begun already? Because you're the
bait for the rest of the attack. They don't want you *now*.
You're to go back and bring up the others to be killed. Go
back! Don't detach a man or they'll suspect. Go back all together. Tell the sergeant you're going. Some of them up there
will understand English. Tell it aloud! Then back you go with
the news—the real news.'

'The country's all clear, sergeant,' he shouted. 'We'll go
back and tell the Colonel.' With an idiotic giggle he added,
'It's a good road for guns, don't you think?'

'Hear you that?' said Jan van Staden, gripping a burgher's
arm. 'God is on our side to-day. They *will* bring their little
cannons after all!'

'Go easy. No good bucketing the horses to pieces. We'll need
'em for the pursuit later,' said the Captain. 'Hullo, there's a
vulture! How far would you make him?'

'Can't tell, sir, in this dry air.'

The bird swooped towards the second flat-topped kopje, but suddenly shivered sideways, and wheeled off again, followed intently by the Captain's glance.

'And that kopje's simply full of 'em, too,' he said, flushing. 'Perfectly confident they are, that we'll take this road—and then they'll scupper the whole boiling of us! They'll let us through to fetch up the others. But I mustn't let 'em know we know. By Jove, they do *not* think much of us! Don't blame 'em.'

The cunning of the trap did not impress him until later.

Down the track jolted a dozen well-equipped men, laughing and talking—a mark to make a pious burgher's mouth water. Thrice had their Captain explicitly said they were to march easy, so a trooper began to hum a tune that he had picked up in Cape Town streets:

> *'Vat jou goed en trek, Ferreira,*
> *Vat jou goed en trek;*
> *Jannie met die hoepelbeen, Ferreira,*
> *Jannie met die hoepelbeen!'*

Then, with a whistle:

> *'Swaar draa—alle en die ein kant—'*

The Captain, thinking furiously, found his mind turn to a camp in the Karroo, months before; an engine that had halted in that waste, and a woman with brown hair, early grizzled—an extraordinary woman. . . . Yes, but as soon as they had dropped the flat-topped kopje behind its neighbour he must hurry back and report. . . . A woman with grey eyes and black eyelashes. . . . The Boers would probably be massed on

those two kopjes. How soon dare he break into a canter? . . .
A woman with a queer cadence in her speech. . . . It was not
more than five miles home by the straight road—

*'Even when we were children we learned not to go back by
the way we had come.'*

The sentence came back to him, self-shouted, so clearly that
he almost turned to see if the scouts had heard. The two flat-
topped kopjes behind him were covered by a long ridge. The
camp lay due south. He had only to follow the road to the
Nek—a notch, unscouted as he recalled now, between the two
hills.

He wheeled his men up a long valley.

'Excuse me, sir, that ain't our road!' said the sergeant. 'Once
we get over this rise, straight on, we come into direct touch
with the 'elio, on that flat bit o' road where they 'elioed us
goin' out.'

'But we aren't going to get in touch with them just now.
Come along, and come quick.'

'What's the meaning of this?' said a private in the rear.
'What's 'e doin' this detour for? We shan't get in for hours
an' hours.'

'Come on, men. Flog a canter out of your brutes, somehow,'
the Captain called back.

For two throat-parched hours he held west by south, away
from the Nek, puzzling over a compass already demented by
the ironstone in the hills, and then turned south-east through
an eruption of low hills that ran far into the re-entering bend
of the river that circled the left bank of the camp.

Eight miles to eastward that student from Stellenbosch had
wriggled out on the rocks above the Nek to have a word with
Vrooman of Emmaus. The bottom seemed to have dropped
out of at least one portion of their programme; for the scouting party were not to be seen.

'Jan is a clever man,' he said to his companion, 'but he does not think that even rooineks may learn. Perhaps those scouts will have seen Jan's commando, and perhaps they will come back to warn the rooineks. That is why I think he should have shot them *before* they came to the Nek, and made quite sure that only one or two got away. It would have made the English angry, and they would have come out across the open in hundreds to be shot. Then when we ran away they would have come after us without thinking. If you can make the English hurry, they never think. Jan is wrong this time.'

'Lie down, and pray you have not shown yourself to their helio-station,' growled Vrooman of Emmaus. 'You throw with your arms and kick with your legs like a rooinek. When we get back I will tell Jan and he will sjambok you. All will yet come right. They will go and warn the rest, and the rest will hurry out by this very Nek. Then we can shoot. Now you lie still and wait.'

' 'Ere's a rummy picnic. We left camp, as it were, by the front door. 'E *as* given us a giddy-go-round, an' no mistake,' said a dripping private as he dismounted behind the infantry lines.

'Did you see our helio?' This was the Colonel, hot from racing down from the helio-station. 'There were a lot of Boers waiting for you on the Nek. We saw 'em. We tried to get at you with the helio, and tell you we were coming out to help you. Then we saw you didn't come over that flat bit of road where we had signalled you going out, and we wondered why. We didn't hear any shots.'

'I turned off, sir, and came in by another road,' said the Captain.

'By another road!' The Colonel lifted his eyebrows. 'Perhaps you're not aware, sir, that the Boers have been in full retreat for the last three hours, and that those men on the

Nek were simply a rear-guard put out to delay us for a little. We could see that much from here. Your duty, sir, was to have taken them in the rear, and then we could have brushed them aside. The Boer retreat has been going on all morning, sir— all morning. You were despatched to see the front clear and to return at once. The whole camp has been under arms for three hours; and instead of doing your work you wander all about Africa with your scouts to avoid a handful of skulking Boers! You should have sent a man back at once—you should have——'

The Captain got off his horse stiffly.

'As a matter of fact,' said he, 'I didn't know for sure that there were any Boers on the Nek, but I went round it in case it was so. But I *do* know that the kopjes beyond the Nek are simply crawling with Boers.'

'Nonsense. We can see the whole lot of 'em retreating out yonder.'

'Of course you can. That's part of their game, sir. I saw 'em lying on the top of a couple of kopjes commanding the road, where it goes into the plain on the far side. They let us come in to see, and they let us go out to report the country clear and bring you up. Now they are waiting for *you*. The whole thing is a trap.'

'D'you expect any officer of my experience to believe that?'

'As you please, sir,' said the Captain hopelessly. 'My responsibility ends with my report.'

AN UNQUALIFIED PILOT

1895

AN UNQUALIFIED PILOT

This tale is founded on something that happened a good many years ago in the Port of Calcutta, before wireless telegraphy was used on ships, and men and boys were less easy to catch when once they were in a ship. It is not meant to show that anybody who thinks he would like to become eminent in his business can do so at a moment's notice; but it proves the old saying that if you want anything badly enough and are willing to pay the price for it, you generally get it. If you don't get what you want, it is a sign either that you did not seriously want it, or that you tried to bargain over the price.

ALMOST ANY PILOT WILL TELL YOU that his work is much more difficult than you imagine; but the Pilots of the Hugli know that they have one hundred miles of the most dangerous river on earth running through their hands—the Hugli between Calcutta and the Bay of Bengal—and they say nothing. Their Service is picked and sifted as carefully as the Bench of the Supreme Court, for a judge can only hang the wrong man, or pass a bad law; but a careless pilot can lose a ten-thousand-ton ship with crew and cargo in less time than it takes to reverse her engines.

There is very little chance of anything getting off again when once she touches in the furious Hugli current, loaded with all the fat silt of the fields of Bengal, where the soundings change two feet between tides, and new channels make and unmake themselves in one rainy season. Men have fought the

Hugli for two hundred years, till now the river owns a huge building, with drawing, survey, and telegraph departments, devoted to its private service, as well as a body of wardens, who are called the Port Commissioners.

They and their officers govern everything that floats from the Hugli Bridge to the last buoy at Pilots' Ridge, one hundred and forty miles away, far out in the Bay of Bengal, where the steamers first pick up the pilots from the pilot brig.

A Hugli pilot does not kindly bring papers aboard for the passengers, or scramble up the ship's side by wet, swaying rope-ladders. He arrives in his best clothes, with a native servant or an assistant pilot to wait on him, and he behaves as a man should who can earn two or three thousand pounds a year after twenty years' apprenticeship. He has beautiful rooms in the Port Office at Calcutta, and generally keeps himself to the society of his own profession, for though the telegraph reports the more important soundings of the river daily, there is much to be learned from brother pilots between each trip.

Some million tons of shipping must find their way to and from Calcutta each twelvemonth, and unless the Hugli were watched as closely as his keeper watches an elephant, there is a fear that it might silt up, as it has silted up round the old Dutch and Portuguese ports twenty and thirty miles behind Calcutta.

So the Port Office sounds and scours and dredges the river, and builds spurs and devices for coaxing currents, and labels all the buoys with their proper letters, and attends to the semaphores and the lights and the drum, ball and cone storm signals; and the pilots of the Hugli do the rest; but, in spite of all care and the very best attention, the Hugli swallows her ship or two every year. Even the coming of wireless telegraphy does not spoil her appetite.

AN UNQUALIFIED PILOT

When Martin Trevor had waited on the river from his boyhood; when he had risen to be a Senior Pilot, entitled to bring
up to Calcutta the very biggest ships; when he had thought
and talked of nothing but Hugli pilotage all his life to nobody
except Hugli pilots, he was exceedingly surprised and indignant that his only son should decide to follow his father's
profession. Mrs. Trevor had died when the boy was a child,
and as he grew older, Trevor, in the intervals of his business,
noticed that the lad was very often by the river-side—no place,
he said, for a nice boy. But, as he was not often at home, and
as the aunt who looked after Jim naturally could not follow
him to his chosen haunts, and as Jim had not the faintest intention of giving up old friends there, nothing but ineffectual
growls came of the remark. Later, when Trevor once asked
him if he could make anything out of the shipping on the
water, Jim replied by reeling off the list of all the house-flags
in sight at the moorings, together with supplementary information about their tonnage and captains.

'You'll come to a bad end, Jim,' said Trevor. 'Boys of your
age haven't any business to waste their time on these things.'

'Oh, Pedro at the Sailors' Home says you can't begin too
early.'

'At what, please?'

'Piloting. I'm nearly fourteen now, and—and I know where
most of the shipping in the river is, and I know what there
was yesterday over the Mayapur Bar, and I've been down to
Diamond Harbour—oh, a hundred times already, and I've——'

'You'll go to school, son, and learn what they teach you,
and you'll turn out something better than a pilot,' said his
father, who wanted Jim to enter the Subordinate Civil Service.
But he might just as well have told a shovel-nosed porpoise
of the river to come ashore and begin life as a hen. Jim held

his tongue; he noticed that all the best pilots in the Port Office did that; and devoted his young attention and all his spare time to the River he loved. He had seen the nice young gentlemen in the Subordinate Civil Service, and he called them a very rude native name for 'clerks.'

He became as well known as the Bankshall itself; and the Port Police let him inspect their launches, and the tug-boat captains had always a place for him at their tables, and the mates of the big steam-dredgers used to show him how the machinery worked, and there were certain native row-boats which Jim practically owned; and he extended his patronage to the railway that runs to Diamond Harbour, forty miles down the river. In the old days nearly all the East India Company's ships used to discharge at Diamond Harbour, on account of the shoals above, but now ships go straight up to Calcutta, and they have only some moorings for vessels in distress there, and a telegraph service, and a harbour-master, who was one of Jim's most intimate friends.

He would sit in the Office listening to the soundings of the shoals as they were reported every day, and attending to the movements of the steamers up and down (Jim always felt he had lost something irretrievable if a boat got in or out of his River without his knowing about it), and when the big liners with their rows of blazing portholes tied up in Diamond Harbour for the night, Jim would row from one ship to the other through the sticky hot air and the buzzing mosquitoes and listen respectfully as the pilots conferred together about the habits of steamers.

Once, for a treat, his father took him down clear out to the Sandheads and the pilot brig there, and Jim was happily sea-sick as she tossed and pitched in the Bay. The cream of life, though, was coming up in a tug or a police-boat from Diamond

Harbour to Calcutta, over the 'James and Mary,' those terrible sands christened after a royal ship that they sunk two hundred years before. They are made by two rivers that enter the Hugli six miles apart and throw their own silt across the silt of the main stream, so that with each turn of the weather and tide the sands shift and change under water like clouds in the sky. It was here (the tales sound much worse when they are told in the rush and growl of the muddy waters) that the *Countess of Stirling*, fifteen hundred tons, touched and capsized in ten minutes, and a two-thousand-ton steamer in two, and a pilgrim ship in five, and another steamer literally in one instant, holding down her men with the masts and shrouds as she lashed over. When a ship touches on the 'James and Mary,' the river knocks her down and buries her, and the sands quiver all around her and reach out under water and take new shapes over the corpse.

Young Jim would lie up in the bows of the tug and watch the straining buoys kick and choke in the coffee-coloured current, while the semaphores and flags signalled from the bank how much water there was in the channel, till he learned that men who deal with men can afford to be careless, on the chance of their fellows being like them; but men who deal with things dare not relax for an instant. 'And that's the very reason,' old McEwan said to him once, 'that the "James and Mary" is the safest part of the river,' and he shoved the big black *Bandoorah*, that draws twenty-five feet, through the Eastern Gut, with a turban of white foam wrapped around her forefoot and her screw beating as steadily as his own heart.

If Jim could not get away to the river there was always the big, cool Port Office, where the soundings were worked out and the maps drawn; or the Pilots' room, where he could lie in a long chair and listen quietly to the talk about the Hugli.

433

There was the library, too, where if you had money you could buy charts and books of directions against the time that you would actually have to steam over the places themselves. It was exceedingly hard for Jim to hold the list of Jewish Kings in his head, and he was more than uncertain as to the end of the verb *audio* if you followed it far enough down the page, but he could keep the soundings of three channels distinct in his head, and, what is more confusing, the changes in the buoys from 'Garden Reach' down to Saugor, as well as the greater part of the *Calcutta Telegraph*, the only paper he ever read.

Unluckily, you cannot peruse about the Hugli without money, even though you are the son of the best-known pilot on the river, and as soon as Trevor understood how his son was spending his time, he cut down his pocket-money, of which Jim had a very generous allowance. In his extremity he took counsel with Pedro, the plum-coloured mulatto at the Sailors' Home, and Pedro was a bad, designing man. He introduced Jim to a Chinaman in Muchuatollah, an unpleasing place in itself, and the Chinaman, who answered to the name of Erh-Tze, when he was not smoking opium, talked business in pidgin-English to Jim for an hour. Every bit of that business from first to last was flying in the face of every law on the river, but it interested Jim.

'S'pose you takee. Can do?' Erh-Tze said at last.

Jim considered his chances. A junk, he knew, would draw about eleven feet, and the regular fee for a qualified pilot, outward to the Sandheads, would be two hundred rupees. On the one hand he was not qualified, so he dared not ask more than half. *But*, on the other hand, he was fully certain of the thrashing of his life from his father for piloting without a license, let alone what the Port Authorities might do to him. So he asked one hundred and seventy-five rupees, and Erh-Tze beat him down to a hundred and twenty. The cargo of his junk was worth anything from seventy to a hundred and fifty thousand rupees, some of which he was getting as enormous freight on the coffins of thirty or forty dead Chinamen, whom he was taking to be buried in their native country.

Rich Chinamen will pay fancy prices for this service, and they have a superstition that the iron of steamships is bad for the spiritual health of their dead. Erh-Tze's junk had crept up from Singapore, *via* Penang and Rangoon, to Calcutta, where Erh-Tze had been staggered by the Pilot dues. This time he was going out at a reduction with Jim, who, as Pedro kept telling him, was just as good as a pilot, and a heap cheaper.

Jim knew something of the manners of junks, but he was not prepared, when he went down that night with his charts, for the confusion of cargo and coolies and coffins and clay cooking-places, and other things that littered her decks. He had sense enough to haul the rudder up a few feet, for he knew that a junk's rudder goes far below the bottom, and he allowed a foot extra to Erh-Tze's estimate of the junk's depth. Then they staggered out into midstream very early, and never had the city of his birth looked so beautiful as when he feared he would not come back to see it. Going down 'Garden Reach' he discovered that the junk would answer to her helm if you put it over far enough, and that she had a fair, though Chinese, notion of sailing. He took charge of the tiller by stationing three Chinese on each side of it, and standing a little forward, gathered their pigtails into his hands, three right and three left, as though they had been the yoke-lines of a row-boat. Erh-Tze almost smiled at this; he felt he was getting good care for his money; and took a neat little polished bamboo to keep the men attentive, for he said this was no time to teach the crew pidgin-English. The more way they could get on the junk the better would she steer, and as soon as he felt a little confidence in her, Jim ordered the stiff, rustling sails to be hauled up tighter and tighter. He did not know their names —at least any name that would be likely to interest a Chinaman—but Erh-Tze had not banged about the waters of the Malay Archipelago all his life for nothing. He rolled forward with his bamboo, and the sail rose like Eastern incantations.

Early as they were on the river, a big American oil (but they called it 'kerosene' in those days) ship was ahead of them in tow, and when Jim saw her through the lifted mist he was thankful. She would draw all of seventeen feet, and if he could steer by her they would be safe. It is easier to scurry up and down the 'James and Mary' in a police-boat that some one else is handling than to cram a hard-mouthed old junk across the same sands alone, with the certainty of a thrashing if you come out alive.

Jim glued his eyes to the American, and saw that at Fultah she dropped her tug and stood down the river under sail. He all but whooped aloud, for he knew that the number of pilots who preferred to work a ship through the 'James and Mary' was strictly limited. 'If it isn't Father, it's Dearsley,' said Jim. 'And Dearsley went down yesterday with the *Bancoora*. So it's Father. If I'd gone home last night instead of going to Pedro, I'd have met him. He must have got his ship quick, but— Father *is* a very quick man.' Then Jim reflected that they kept a piece of knotted rope on the pilot brig that stung like a wasp; but this thought he dismissed as beneath the dignity of an officiating pilot, who needed only to nod his head to set Erh-Tze's bamboo to work.

As the American came round, just before the Fultah Sands, Jim raked her with his spy-glass, and saw his father on the poop, an unlighted cigar between his teeth. That cigar, Jim knew, would be smoked on the other side of the 'James and

Mary,' and Jim felt so entirely safe and happy that he lit a cigar on his own account. This kind of piloting was child's play. His father could not make a mistake if he tried; and Jim, with his six obedient pigtails in his two hands, had leisure to admire the perfect style in which the American was handled —how she would point her bowsprit jeeringly at a hidden bank, as much as to say, 'Not to-day, thank you, dear,' and bow down lovingly to a buoy, as much as to say, 'You're a gentleman, at any rate,' and come round sharp on her heel with a flutter and a rustle, and a slow, steady swing something like a well-dressed woman staring all round the theatre through opera-glasses.

It was hard work to keep the junk near her, though Erh-Tze set everything that was by any means settable, and used his bamboo most generously. When they were nearly under her counter, and a little to her left, Jim, hidden behind a sail, would feel warm and happy all over, thinking of the thousand nautical and piloting things that he knew. When they fell more than half a mile behind, he was cold and miserable thinking of all the million things he did not know or was not quite sure of. And so they went down, Jim steering by his father, turn for turn, over the Mayapur Bar, with the semaphores on each bank duly signaling the depth of water, through the Western Gut, and round Makoaputti Lumps, and in and out of twenty places, each more exciting than the last, and Jim nearly pulled the six pigtails out for pure joy when the last of the 'James and Mary' had gone astern, and they were walking through Diamond Harbour.

From there to the mouth of the Hugli things are not so bad —at least, that was what Jim thought, and held on till the swell from the Bay of Bengal made the old junk heave and snort, and the river broadened into an inland sea, with islands only a foot or two high scattered about it. The American walked away from the junk as soon as they were beyond Kedgeree, and the night came on and the river looked very big and desolate, so Jim promptly anchored somewhere in grey water, with the Saugor Light away off toward the east. He had a great respect for the Hugli to the last yard of her, and had no desire whatever to find himself on the Gaspar Sand or any other little shoal. Erh-Tze and the crew highly approved of this piece of seamanship. They set no watch, lit no lights, and at once went to sleep.

Jim lay down between a red-and-black lacquer coffin and a little live pig in a basket. As soon as it was light he began studying his chart of the Hugli mouth, and trying to find out where in the river he might be. He decided to be on the safe side and wait for another sailing-ship and follow her out. So he made an enormous breakfast of rice and boiled fish, while Erh-Tze lit fire-crackers and burned gilt paper to the Joss who had saved them so far. Then they heaved up their rough-and-tumble anchor, and made after a big, fat, iron four-masted sailing ship, heavy as a hay-wain.

The junk, which was really a very weatherly boat, and might have begun life as a private pirate in Annam forty years before, followed under easy sail; for the four-master would run no risks. She was in old McEwan's hands, and she waddled about like a broody hen, giving each shoal wide allowances. All this happened near the outer Floating Light, some hundred and twenty miles from Calcutta, and apparently in the open sea.

Jim knew old McEwan's appetite, and often heard him pride himself on getting his ship to the pilot brig close upon meal hours, so he argued that if the pilot brig was get-at-able (and Jim himself had not the ghost of a notion where she would lie), McEwan would find her before one o'clock.

AN UNQUALIFIED PILOT

It was a blazing hot day, and McEwan fidgeted the four-master down to Pilots' Ridge with what little wind remained, and, sure enough, there lay the pilot brig, and Jim felt shivers up his back as Erh-Tze paid him his hundred and twenty rupees and he went overside in the junk's one crazy dinghy. McEwan was leaving the four-master in a long, slashing whale-boat that looked very spruce and pretty, and Jim could see that there was a certain amount of excitement among the pilots on the brig. There was his father too. The ragged Chinese boatmen gave way in a most ragged fashion, and Jim felt very unwashed and disreputable when he heard the click of McEwan's oars alongside, and McEwan saying, 'James Trevor, I'll trouble you to lay alongside me.'

Jim obeyed, and from the corner of one eye watched McEwan's angry whiskers stand up all round his face, which turned purple.

'An' how is it you break the regulations o' the Porrt o' Calcutta? Are ye aware o' the penalties and impreesonments ye've laid yourself open to?' McEwan began.

Jim said nothing; there was not very much to say just then; and McEwan roared aloud: 'Man, ye've perrsonated a Hugli pilot, an' that's as much as to say ye've perrsonated *ME*! What did yon heathen give ye for honorarium?'

'Hundred and twenty,' said Jim.

'An' by what manner o' means did ye get through the "James and Mary"?'

'Father,' was the answer. 'He went down the same tide and I—we—steered by him.'

McEwan whistled and choked, perhaps it was with anger. 'Ye've made a stalkin'-horse o' your father, then? Jim, laddie, he'll make an example o' you.'

The boat hooked on to the brig's chains, and McEwan said,

as he set foot on deck before Jim could speak: 'Yon's an enterprisin' cub o' yours, Trevor. Ye'd better enter him in the regular business, or one o' these fine days he'll be actin' as pilot before he's qualified, and sinkin' junks in the fairway. He fetched yon junk down last night. If ye've no other designs I'm thinkin' I'll take him as my cub, for there's no denyin' he's a resourceful lad—for all he's an unlicked whelp.'

'That,' said Trevor, reaching for Jim's left ear, 'is something we can remedy,' and he led Jim below.

The little knotted rope that they keep for general purposes on the pilot brig did its duty, but when it was all over Jim was unlicked no longer. He was McEwan's property to be registered under the laws of the Port of Calcutta, and a week later, when the *Ellora* came along, he bundled over the pilot brig's side with McEwan's enamelled leather hand-bag and a roll of charts and a little bag of his own, and he dropped into the stern sheets of the pilot gig with a very creditable imitation of McEwan's slow, swaying sit-down and hump of the shoulders.

THE JUNK AND THE DHOW

Once a pair of savages found a stranded tree.
  (One-piecee stick-pidgin—two-piecee man.
Straddle-um—paddle-um—push-um off to sea.
  That way Foleign Debbil-boat began.[1])
But before, and before, and ever so long before
  Any shape of sailing-craft was known,
The Junk and the Dhow had a stern and a bow,
  And a mast and a sail of their own—ahoy, alone!
  As they crashed across the Oceans on their own!

Once there was a pirate-ship, being blown ashore—
  (Plitty soon pilum up, s'posee no can tack.
Seven-piecee stlong man pullum sta'boa'd oar.
  That way bling her head alound and sail-o back.)
But before, and before, and ever so long before
  Grand Commander Noah took the wheel,
The Junk and the Dhow, though they look like anyhow,
  Had rudders reaching deep below their keel—akeel—
    akeel!
  As they laid the Eastern Seas beneath their keel!

Once there was a galliot yawing in a tide.
  (Too much foolee side-slip. How can stop?
Man catchee tea-box lid—lasha longaside.
  That way make her plenty glip and sail first-chop.)
But before, and before, and ever so long before
  Any such contrivances were used,

[1] Remember, the Chinaman generally says 'l' for 'r.'

441

The whole Confucian sea-board had standardized the lee-board,
  And hauled it up or dropped it as they choosed—or chose
    —or chused!
  According to the weather, when they cruised!

Once there was a caravel in a beam-sea roll—
  (Ca'go shiftee—all adliftee—no can livee long.
S'posum nail-o boa'd acloss—makee ploper hol'?
  That way, ca'go sittum still, an' ship mo' stlong.)
But before, and before, and ever so long before
  Any square-rigged vessel hove in sight,
The Canton deep-sea craft carried bulkheads fore and aft,
  And took good care to keep 'em water-tight—atite—atite!
  From Amboyna to the Great Australian Bight!

Once there was a sailor-man singing just this way—
  (Too muchee yowl-o, sickum best flend!
Singee all-same pullee lope—haul and belay.
  Hully up and coilum down an'—bite off end!)
But before, and before, and ever so long before
  Any sort of chanty crossed our lips,
The Junk and the Dhow, though they look like anyhow,
  Were the Mother and the Father of all Ships—ahoy!—a'
    ships!
  And of half the new inventions in our Ships!
  From Tarifa to Formosa in our Ships!
    From Socotra to Selankhor of the windlass and the anchor,
  And the Navigator's Compass in our Ships—ahoy!—our
    Ships!
(O, hully up and coilum down an'—bite—off—end!)

HIS GIFT

1922

HIS GIFT

His scoutmaster and his comrades, who disagreed on several points, were united in one conviction—that William Glasse Sawyer was, without exception, the most unprofitable person, not merely in the Pelican Troop, who lived in the wilderness of the 47th Postal District, London, S.E., but in the whole body of Boy Scouts throughout the world.

No one, except a ferocious uncle who was also a French-polisher, seemed responsible for his beginnings. There was a legend that he had been entered as a Wolf-Cub at the age of eight, under Miss Doughty, whom the uncle had either bribed or terrorised to accept him; and that after six months Miss Doughty confessed that she could make nothing of him and retired to teach school in the Yorkshire moors. There is also a red-headed ex-cub of that Troop (he is now in a shipping-office) who asserts proudly that he used to bite William Glasse Sawyer on the leg in the hope of waking him up, and takes most of the credit for William's present success. But when William moved into the larger life of the Pelicans, who were gay birds, he was not what you might call alert. In shape he resembled the ace of diamonds; in colour he was an oily sallow.

He could accomplish nothing that required one glimmer of reason, thought, or common sense. He cleaned himself only under bitter compulsion. He lost his bearings equally in town or country after a five-minutes' stroll. He could track nothing smaller than a tram-car on a single line, and that only if there were no traffic. He could neither hammer a nail, carry an order, tie a knot, light a fire, notice any natural object, except food, nor use any edged tool except a table-knife. To crown all, his innumerable errors and omissions were not even funny.

But it is an old law of human nature that if you hold to one known course of conduct—good or evil—you end by becoming an institution; and when he was fifteen or thereabouts William achieved that position. The Pelicans gradually took pride in the notorious fact that they possessed the only Sealed Pattern, Mark A, Ass—an unique jewel, so to speak, of Absolute, Unalterable Incapacity. The poet of a neighbouring Troop used to write verses about him, and recite them from public places, such as the tops of passing trams. William made no comment, but wrapped himself up in long silences that he seldom broke till the juniors of the Troop (the elders had given it up long before) tried to do him good turns with their Scout-staves.

In private life he assisted his uncle at the mystery of French-polishing, which, he said, was 'boiling up things in pots and rubbing down bits of wood.' The boiling-up, he said, he did not mind so much. The rubbing-down he hated. Once, too, he volunteered that his uncle and only relative had been in the Navy, and 'did not like to be played with'; and the vision of William playing with any human being upset even his Scoutmaster.

Now it happened, upon a certain summer that was really a summer with heat to it, the Pelicans had been lent a dream of a summer camp in a dream of a park, which offered opportunities for every form of diversion, including bridging muddy-banked streams and unlimited cutting into young alders and undergrowth at large. A convenient village lay just outside the Park wall, and the ferny slopes round the camp were rich in rabbits, not to mention hedgehogs and other fascinating vermin. It was reached—Mr. Hale their Scoutmaster saw to that —after two days' hard labour, with the Troop trek-cart, along sunny roads.

William's share in the affair was—what it had always been. First he lost most of his kit; next his uncle talked to him after the fashion of the Navy of '96 before refitting him; thirdly he went lame behind the trek-cart by reason of a stone in his shoe, and on arrival in camp dropped—not for the first, second, or third time—into his unhonoured office as Camp Orderly, and was placed at the disposal of The Prawn, whose light blue eyes stuck out from his freckled face, and whose long skinny arm was covered with badges. From that point on, the procedure was as usual. Once again did The Prawn assure his Scoutmaster that he would take enormous care of William and give him work suited to his capacity and intelligence. Once again did William grunt and wriggle at the news, and once again in the silence of the deserted camp next morning, while the rest of the Pelicans were joyously mucking themselves up to their young bills at bridging brooks, did he bow his neck to The Prawn's many orders. For The Prawn was a born organiser. He set William to unpack the trek-cart and then to neatly and exactly replace all parcels, bags, tins, and boxes. He despatched him thrice in the forenoon across the hot Park to fetch water from a distant well equipped with a stiff-necked windlass and a split handle that pinched William's fat palms. He bade him collect sticks, thorny for choice, out of the flanks of a hedge full of ripe nettles against which Scout uniforms offer small protection. He then made him lay them in the camp cooking-place, carefully rejecting the green ones, for most sticks were alike to William; and when everything else failed, he set him to pick up stray papers and rubbish the length and breadth of the camp. All that while, he not only chased him with comments but expected that William would show gratitude to him for forming his young mind.

' 'Tisn't every one 'ud take this amount o' trouble with you, Mug,' said The Prawn virtuously, when even his energetic soul could make no further work for his vassal. 'Now you open that bully-beef tin and we'll have something to eat, and then you're off duty—for a bit. I shall try my hand at a little camp-cooking.'

William found the tin—at the very bottom, of course, of the trek-cart; cut himself generously over the knuckles in opening it (till The Prawn showed him how this should be done), and in due course, being full of bread and bully, withdrew towards a grateful clump of high fern that he had had his eye on for some time, wriggled deep into it, and on a little rabbit-browsed clearing of turf stretched out and slept the sleep of the weary who have been up and under strict orders since six A.M. Till that hour of that day, be it remembered, William had given no proof either of intelligence or initiative in any direction.

He waked, slowly as was his habit, and noticed that the shadows were stretching a little, even as he stretched himself. Then he heard The Prawn clanking pot-lids, between soft bursts of song. William sniffed. The Prawn was cooking—was probably qualifying for something or other. The Prawn did nothing but qualify for badges. On reflection William discovered that he loved The Prawn even less this camp than the last, or the one before that. Then he heard the voice of a stranger.

'Yes,' was The Prawn's reply. 'I'm in charge of the camp. Would you like to look at it, sir?'

'Seen 'em—seen heaps of 'em,' said the unknown. 'My son

was in 'em once—Buffaloes, out Hendon way. What are *you?*'

'Well, just now I'm sort of temporary Cook,' said The Prawn, whose manners were far better than William's.

'Temp'ry! Temp'ry!' the stranger puffed. 'Can't be a temp'ry Cook any more'n you can be a temp'ry Parson. Not so much. Cookin's cookin'! Let's see *your* notions of cookin'.'

William had never heard any one address The Prawn in these tones, and somehow it cheered him. In the silence that followed he turned on his face and wriggled unostentatiously through the fern, as a Scout should, till he could see that bold man without attracting The Prawn's notice. And this, too, was the first time that William had ever profited by the instruction of his Scoutmaster or the example of his comrades.

Heavenly sights rewarded him. The Prawn, visibly ill at ease, was shifting from one sinewy leg to the other, while an enormously fat little man with a pointed grey beard and arms like the fins of a fish investigated a couple of pots that hung on properly crutched sticks over the small fire that William had lighted in the cooking-place. He did not seem to approve of what he saw or smelt. And yet it was the impeccable Prawn's own cookery!

'Lor'!' said he at last after more sniffs of contempt, as he replaced the lid. 'If you hot up things in tins, *that* ain't cookery. That's vittles—mere vittles! And the way you've set that pot on, you're drawing all the nesty wood-smoke into the water. The spuds won't take much harm of it, but you've ruined the meat. That *is* meat, ain't it? Get me a fork.'

William hugged himself. The Prawn, looking exactly like his namesake well boiled, fetched a big fork. The little man prodded into the pot.

'It's stew!' The Prawn explained, but his voice shook.

'Lor'!' said the man again. 'It's boilin'! It's boilin'! You don't boil when you stew, my son; an' as for *this*'—up came a grey slab of mutton—'there's no odds between this and motor-tyres. Well! Well! As I was sayin'——' He joined his hands behind his globular back and shook his head in silence. After a while, The Prawn tried to assert himself.

'Cookin' isn't my strong point,' began The Prawn, 'but——'

'Pore boys! Pore boys!' the stranger soliloquised, looking straight in front of him. '*Pore* little boys! Wicked, *I* call it. They don't ever let you make bread, do they, my son?'

The Prawn said they generally bought their bread at a shop.

'Ah! I'm a shopkeeper meself. Marsh, the Baker here, is me. *Pore* boys! Well! Well! . . . Though it's against me own interest to say so, *I* think shops are wicked. They sell people things out o' tins which save 'em trouble, an' fill the 'ospitals with stummick-cases afterwards. An' the muck that's sold for flour. . . .' His voice faded away and he meditated again. 'Well! Well! *As* I was sayin'—— Pore boys! *Pore* boys! I'm glad you ain't askin' me to dinner. Good-bye.'

He rolled away across the fern, leaving The Prawn dumb behind him.

It seemed to William best to wriggle back in his cover as far as he could, ere The Prawn should call him to work again. He was not a Scout by instinct, but his uncle had shown him that when things went wrong in the world, some one generally passed it on to some one else. Very soon he heard his name called, acidly, several times. He crawled out from the far end of the fern-patch, rubbing his eyes, and The Prawn re-enslaved him on the spot. For once in his life William was alert and intelligent, but The Prawn paid him no compliments, nor when the very muddy Pelicans came back from the bridging did The Prawn refer in any way to the visit of Messrs. E. M. Marsh & Son, Bakers and Confectioners in the village street just outside the Park wall. Nor, for that matter, did he serve the Pelicans much besides tinned meats for their evening meal.

To say that William did not sleep a wink that night would be what has been called 'nature-faking'; which is a sin. His system demanded at least nine hours' rest, but he lay awake for quite twenty minutes, during which he thought intensely, rapidly, and joyously. Had he been asked he would have said that his thoughts dealt solely with The Prawn and the judgment that had fallen upon him; but William was no psychologist. He did not know that hate—raging hate against a too-badged, too-virtuous senior—had shot him into a new world, exactly as the large blunt shell is heaved through space and dropped into a factory, a garden, or a barracks by the charge behind it. And, as the shell, which is but metal and mixed chemicals, needs the mere graze on the fuse to spread itself all over the landscape, so did his mind need but the touch of that hate to flare up and illuminate not only all his world, but his own way through it.

Next morning, something sang in his ear that it was long since he had done good turns to any one except his uncle, who was slow to appreciate them. He would amend that error; and the more safely since The Prawn would be off all that day with the Troop on a tramp in the natural history line, and his place as Camp Warden and Provost-Marshal would be filled by the placid and easy-going Walrus, whose proper name was Carpenter, who never tried for badges, but who could not see a rabbit without going after him. And the owner of the Park had given full leave to the Pelicans to slay by any means, except by gun, any rabbits they could. So William ingratiated himself with his Superior Officer as soon as the Pelicans had left. . . .

No, the excellent Carpenter did not see that he needed William by his side all day. He might take himself and his bruised foot pretty much where he chose. He went, and this new and active mind of his that he did not realise, accompanied him—straight up the path of duty which, poetry tells us, is so often the road to glory.

He began by cleaning himself and his kit at seven o'clock in the morning, long before the village shops were open. This he did near a postern gate with a crack in it, in the Park wall, commanding a limited but quite sufficient view of the establishment of E. M. Marsh & Son across the street. It was perfect weather, and about eight o'clock Mr. Marsh himself in his shirt-sleeves rolled out to enjoy it before he took down the shutters. Hardly had he shifted the first of them when a fattish Boy Scout with a flat face and a slight limp laid hold of the second and began to slide it towards him.

'Well! Well!' said Mr. Marsh. 'Ah! Your good turn, eh?'

'Yes,' said William briefly.

'That's right! Handsomely now, handsomely,' for the shutter was jamming in its groove. William knew from his uncle that 'handsomely' meant slowly and with care. The shutter responded to the coaxing. The others followed.

'Belay!' said Mr. Marsh, wiping his forehead, for, like William, he perspired easily. When he turned round William had gone. The Movies had taught him, though he knew it not, the value of dramatic effect. He continued to watch Mr. Marsh through the crack in the postern—it was the little wooden door at the end of the right of way through the Park—and when, an hour or so later, Mr. Marsh came out of his shop and headed towards it, William retired backwards into the high fern and brambles. The manœuvre would have rejoiced Mr. Hale's heart, for generally William moved like an elephant with her young. He turned up, quite casually, when Mr. Marsh had puffed his way again into the empty camp. Carpenter was off in pursuit of rabbits, with a pocket full of fine picture-wire.

HIS GIFT

It was the first time William had ever done the honours of any establishment. He came to attention and smiled.

'Well! Well!' Mr. Marsh nodded friendlily. 'What are *you?*'

'Camp-Guard,' said William, improvising for the first time in his life. 'Can I show you anything, sir?'

'No, thank'ee. My son was a Scout once. I've just come to look round at things. No one tryin' any cookin' to-day?'

'No, sir.'

' 'Bout's well. *Pore* boys! What you goin' to have for dinner? Tinned stuff?'

'I expect so, sir.'

'D'you like it?'

'Used to it.' William rather approved of this round person who wasted no time on abstract ideas.

'*Pore* boys! Well! Well! It saves trouble—for the present. Knots and splices in your stummick afterwards—in 'ospital.' Mr. Marsh looked at the cold camp cooking-place and its three big stones, and sniffed.

'Would you like it lit?' said William suddenly.

'What for?'

'To cook with.'

'What d'*you* know about cookin'?' Mr. Marsh's little eyes opened wide.

'Nothing, sir.'

'What makes you think *I'm* a cook?'

'By the way you looked at our cooking-place,' the mendacious William answered. The Prawn had always urged him to cultivate habits of observation. They seemed easy—after you had observed the things.

'Well! Well! Quite a young Sherlock, you are. Don't think much o' *this*, though.' Mr. Marsh began to stoop to rearrange the open-air hearth to his liking.

'Show me how and I'll do it,' said William.

'Shove that stone a little more to the left then. Steady—So! That'll do! Got any wood? No? You slip across to the shop and ask them to give you some small brush-stuff from the oven. Stop! *And* my apron, too. Marsh is the name.'

William left him chuckling wheezily. When he returned Mr. Marsh clad himself in a long white apron of office which showed so clearly that Carpenter from far off returned at once.

'H'sh! H'sh!' said Mr. Marsh before he could speak. 'You carry on with what you're doing. Marsh is my name. My son was a Scout once. Buffaloes—Hendon way. It's all right. Don't you grudge an old man enjoying himself.'

The Walrus looked amazedly at William moving in three directions at once with his face aflame.

'It's all right,' said William. 'He's giving us cooking-lessons.' Then—the words came into his mouth by themselves—'I'll take the responsibility.'

'Yes, yes! He knew I could cook. Quite a young Sherlock he is! *You* carry on.' Mr. Marsh turned his back on The Walrus and despatched William again with some orders to his shop across the road. 'And you'd better tell 'em to put 'em all in a basket,' he cried after him.

William returned with a fair assortment of mixed material, including eggs, two rashers of bacon, and a packet of patent flour, concerning which last Mr. Marsh said things no baker should say about his own goods. The frying-pan came out of the trek-cart, with some other oddments, and it was not till after it was greased that Mr. Marsh demanded William's name. He got it in full, and it produced strange effects on the little fat man.

'An' 'ow do you spell your middle name?' he asked.

'G-l-a-double-s-e,' said William.

'Might that be your mother's?' William nodded. 'Well!

454

HIS GIFT

Well! I wonder now! I *do* wonder. It's a great name. There was a Sawyer in the cooking line once, but 'e was a Frenchman and spelt it different. Glasse is serious though. And you say it was your ma's?' He fell into an abstraction, frying-pan in hand. Anon, as he cracked an egg miraculously on its edge: 'Whether you're a descendant or not, it's worth livin' up to, a name like that.'

'Why?' said William, as the egg slid into the pan and spread as evenly as paint under an expert's hand.

'I'll tell you some day. She was a very great cook—but she'd have come expensive at to-day's prices. Now, you take the pan an' I'll draw me own conclusions.'

The boy worked the pan over the level red fire with a motion that he had learned somehow or other while 'boiling up' things for his uncle. It seemed to him natural and easy. Mr. Marsh watched in unbroken silence for at least two minutes.

'It's early to say—yet,' was his verdict. 'But I 'ave 'opes. You 'ave good 'ands, an' your knowin' I was a cook shows you 'ave the instinck. *If* you 'ave got the Touch—mark you, I only say if—but *if* you 'ave anything like the Genuine Touch, you're provided for for life. *An'* further—don't tilt her that way!— you 'old your neighbours, friends, and employers in the 'ollow of your 'and.'

'How do you mean?' said William, intent on his egg.

'Everything which a man *is* depends on what 'e puts inside 'im,' was the reply. 'A good cook's a King of men—besides being thunderin' well off if 'e don't drink. It's the only sure business in the whole round world; and *I*'ve been round it eight times, in the Mercantile Marine, before I married the second Mrs. M.'

William, more interested in the pan than Mr. Marsh's marriages, made no reply. 'Yes, a good cook,' Mr. Marsh went on reminiscently, 'even on Board o' Trade allowance, 'as brought many a ship to port that 'ud otherwise 'ave mut'nied on the 'igh seas.'

The eggs and bacon mellowed together. Mr. Marsh supplied some wonderful last touches and the result was eaten, with The Walrus's help, sizzling out of the pan and washed down with some stone ginger-beer from the convenient establishment of Mr. E. M. Marsh outside the Park wall.

'I've ruined me dinner,' Mr. Marsh confided to the boys, 'but I 'aven't enjoyed myself like this, not since Noah was an able seaman. You wash up, young Sherlock, an' I'll tell you something.'

He filled an ancient pipe with eloquent tobacco, and while William scoured the pan, he held forth on the art and science and mystery of cooking as inspiredly as Mr. Jorrocks, Master of Foxhounds, had lectured upon the Chase. The burden of his song was Power—power which, striking directly at the stomach of man, makes the rudest polite, not to say sycophantic, towards a good cook, whether at sea, in camp, in the face of war, or (here he embellished his text with personal experiences) the crowded competitive cities where a good meal was as rare, he declared, as silk pyjamas in a pig-sty. 'An' mark you,' he concluded, 'three times a day the 'aughtiest and most overbearin' of 'em all 'ave to come crawling to you for a round belly-full. Put *that* in your pipe and smoke it out, young Sherlock!'

He unloosed his sacrificial apron and rolled away.

The Boy Scout is used to strangers who give him good advice on the smallest provocation; but strangers who fill you up with bacon and eggs and ginger-beer are few.

'What started it all?' The Walrus demanded.

'Well, I can't exactly say,' William answered, and as he had never been known to give a coherent account of anything, The Walrus returned to his wires, and William lay out and dreamed in the fern among the cattle-flies. He had dismissed The Prawn altogether from his miraculously enlarging mind. Very soon he was on the High Seas, a locality which till that instant had never appealed to him, in a gale, issuing bacon and eggs to crews on the edge of mutiny. Next, he was at war, turning the tides of it to victory for his own land by meals of bacon and eggs that brought bemedalled Generals in troops like Pelicans, to his fireplace. Then he was sustaining his uncle, at the door of an enormous restaurant, with plates of bacon and eggs sent out by gilded commissionaries such as guard the cinemas, while his uncle wept with gratitude and remorse, and The Prawn, badges and all, begged for the scraps.

His chin struck his chest and half waked him to fresh flights of glory. He might have the Genuine Touch, Mr. Marsh had said it. Moreover, he, The Mug, had a middle name which had filled that great man with respect. All the 47th Postal District should ring with that name, even to the exclusion of the racing-news, in its evening papers. And on his return from camp, or perhaps a day or two later, he would defy his very uncle and escape for ever from the foul business of French-polishing.

Here he slept generously and dreamlessly till evening, when the Pelicans returned, their pouches full of samples of uncookable vegetables and insects, and The Walrus made his report of the day's Camp doings to the Scoutmaster.

'Wait a minute, Walrus. You say The Mug actually *did* the cooking.'

'Mr. Marsh had him under instruction, sir. But The Mug did a lot of it—he held the pan over the fire. I saw him, sir. And he washed up afterwards.'

'Did he?' said the Scoutmaster lightly. 'Well, that's something.' But when The Walrus had gone Mr. Hale smote thrice upon his bare knees and laughed, as a Scout should, without noise.

He thanked Mr. Marsh next morning for the interest he had shown in the camp, and suggested (this was while he was buying many very solid buns for a route-march) that nothing would delight the Pelicans more than a few words from Mr. Marsh on the subject of cookery, if he could see his way to it.

'Quite so,' said Mr. Marsh. '*I'm* worth listenin' to. Well! Well! I'll be along this evening, and, maybe, I'll bring some odds an' ends with me. Send over young Sherlock-Glasse to 'elp me fetch 'em. *That's* a boy with 'is stummick in the proper place. Know anything about 'im?'

Mr. Hale knew a good deal, but he did not tell it all. He suggested that William himself should be approached, and would excuse him from the route-march for that purpose.

'Route-march!' said Mr. Marsh in horror. 'Lor'! The very worst use you can make of your feet is walkin' on 'em. Gives you bunions. Besides, 'e ain't got the figure for marches. 'E's a cook by build as well as instinck. 'Eavy in the run, oily in the skin, broad in the beam, short in the arm, *but,* mark you, light on the feet. That's the way cooks ought to be issued. You never 'eard of a really good *thin* cook yet, did you? No. Nor me. An' I've known millions that called 'emselves cooks.'

Mr. Hale regretted that he had not studied the natural history of cooks, and sent William over early in the day.

Mr. Marsh spoke to the Pelicans for an hour that evening beside an open wood fire, from the ashes of which he drew forth (talking all the while) wonderful hot cakes called 'dampers'; while from its top he drew off pans full of 'lobscouse,' which he said was not to be confounded with 'salmagundi,' and a hair-raising compound of bacon, cheese, and onions all

458

melted together. And while the Pelicans ate, he convulsed them with mirth or held them breathless with anecdotes of the High Seas and the World, so that the vote of thanks they passed him at the end waked all the cows in the Park. But William sat wrapped in visions, his hands twitching sympathetically to Mr. Marsh's wizardry among the pots and pans. He knew now what the name of Glasse signified; for he had spent an hour at the back of the baker's shop reading in a brown-leather book dated A.D. 1767 and called *The Art of Cookery Made Plain and Easy by a Lady*, and that lady's name, as it appeared in facsimile at the head of Chap. I., was 'H. Glasse.' Torture would not have persuaded him (or Mr. Marsh), by that time, that she was not his direct ancestress; but, as a matter of form, he intended to ask his uncle.

When The Prawn, very grateful that Mr. Marsh had made no reference to his notions of cookery, asked William what he thought of the lecture and exhibition, William came out of his dreams with a start, and 'Oh, all right, I suppose, but I wasn't listening much.' Then The Prawn, who always improved an occasion, lectured him on lack of attention; and William missed all that too. The question in his mind was whether his uncle would let him stay with Mr. Marsh for a couple of days after Camp broke up, or whether he would use the reply-paid telegram, which Mr. Marsh had sent him, for his own French-polishing concerns. When The Prawn's voice ceased, he not only promised to do better next time, but added, out of a vast and inexplicable pity that suddenly rose up inside him, 'And I'm grateful to you, Prawn. I am reelly.'

On his return to Town from that wonder-revealing visit, he found the Pelicans treating him with a new respect. For one thing, The Walrus had talked about the bacon and eggs; for another, The Prawn, who when he let himself go could be really funny, had given some artistic imitations of Mr. Marsh's comments on his cookery. Lastly, Mr. Hale had laid down that William's future employ would be to cook for the Pelicans when they camped abroad. 'And look out that you don't poison us too much,' he added.

There were occasional mistakes and some very flat failures, but the Pelicans swallowed them all loyally; no one had even a stomach-ache, and the office of Cook's mate to William was in great demand. The Prawn himself sought it next spring when the Troop stole a couple of fair May days on the out-skirts of a brick-field, and were very happy. But William set him aside in favour of a new and specially hopeless recruit; oily-skinned, fat, short-armed, but light on his feet, and with some notion of lifting pot-lids without wrecking or flooding the whole fireplace.

'You see, Prawn,' he explained, 'cookin' isn't a thing one can just pick up.'

'Yes, I could—watchin' you,' The Prawn insisted.

'No. Mr. Marsh says it's a Gift—same as a Talent.'

'D'you mean to tell me Rickworth's got it, then?'

'Dunno. It's *my* job to find that out—Mr. Marsh says. Any-way, Rickworth told me he liked cleaning out a fryin'-pan because it made him think of what it might be cookin' next time.'

'Well, if that isn't silliness, it's just greediness,' said The Prawn. 'What about those dampers you were talking of when I bought the fire-lighters for you this morning?'

William drew one out of the ashes, tapped it lightly with his small hazel-wand of office, and slid it over, puffed and perfect, towards The Prawn.

Once again the wave of pity—the Master's pity for the mere consuming Public—swept over him as he watched The Prawn wolf it down.

HIS GIFT

'I'm grateful to you. I reely *am*, Prawn,' said William Glasse Sawyer.

After all, as he was used to say in later years, if it hadn't been for The Prawn, where would he have been?

PROLOGUE TO THE MASTER-COOK'S TALE

This is what might be called a parody or imitation of the verses of Geoffrey Chaucer, one of the earliest and the greatest of our English poets. It looks difficult to read, but you will find it comes quite easily if you say it aloud, remembering that where there is an accent over the end of a word, that word is pronounced as two syllables—not one. 'Snailés,' for instance, would be spoken as 'snai-les,' and so on.

With us there rade a Maister-Cook that came
From the Rochelle which is neere Angoulême.
Littel hee was, but rounder than a topp,
And his small berd hadde dipped in manie a soppe.
His honde was smoother than beseemeth mann's,
And his discoorse was all of marzipans,[1]
Of tripes of Caen, or Burdeux snailés swote,[2]
And Seinte Menhoulde wher cooken piggés-foote.[3]
To Thoulouse and to Bress and Carcasson
For pyes and fowles and chesnottes hadde hee wonne;[4]
Of hammés of Thuringie[5] *colde hee prate,*
And well hee knew what Princes hadde on plate
At Christmas-tide, from Artois to Gascogne.
Lordinges, quod hee, manne liveth nat alone

[1] A kind of sticky sweetmeat.
[2] Bordeaux snails are specially large and sweet.
[3] They grill pigs'-feet still at St. Menehould, not far from Verdun, better than anywhere else in all the world.
[4] Gone—to get pâtés of ducks' liver at Toulouse; fatted poultry at Bourg in Bresse, on the road to Geneva; and very large chestnuts in sugar at Carcassonne, about forty miles from Toulouse.
[5] This would probably be some sort of wild-boar ham from Germany.

By bred, but meatés rost and seethed, and broth,
And purchasable¹ deinties, on mine othe.
Honey and hote gingere well liketh hee,
And Whalés-flesch mortred² with spicerie.
For, lat be all how man denie or carpe,³
Him thries a daie his honger maketh sharpe,
And setteth him at boorde⁴ with hawkés eyne,
Snuffing what dish is set beforne to deyne,
Nor, till with meate hee all-to-fill to brim,
None other matter nowher mooveth him.
Lat holie Seintés sterve⁵ as bookés boast,
Most mannés soule is in his bellie most.
For, as man thinketh in his hearte is hee,
But, as hee eateth so his thought shall bee.
And Holie Fader's self⁶ (with reveraunce)
Oweth to Cooke his port and his presaunce.
Wherbye it cometh past disputison⁷
Cookes over alle men have dominion,
Which follow them as schippe her gouvernail.⁸
Enoff of wordes—beginneth heere my tale:—

¹ Expensive. ² Beaten up. ³ Sneer or despise.
⁴ Brings him to table. ⁵ Starve.
⁶ The Pope himself, who depends on his cook for being healthy and well-fed.
⁷ Dispute or argument.
⁸ Men are influenced by their cooks as ships are steered by their rudders.

A FLIGHT OF FACT

1918

A FLIGHT OF FACT

Most of this tale actually happened during the War about the years 1916 or 1917; but it was much funnier as I heard it told by a Naval officer than it stands as I have written it from memory. It shows, what one always believed was true—that there is nothing that cannot happen in the Navy.

H.M.S. *Gardenia* (we will take her name from the Herbaceous Border which belonged to the sloops, though she was a destroyer by profession) came quietly back to her berth some time after midnight, and disturbed half-a-dozen of her sisters as she settled down. They all talked about it next morning, especially *Phlox* and *Stephanotis*, her left- and right-hand neighbours in the big basin on the East Coast of England, that was crowded with destroyers.

But the soul of the *Gardenia*—Lieutenant-in-Command H. R. Duckett—was lifted far above insults. What he had done during his last trip had been well done. Vastly more important—*Gardenia* was in for a boiler-clean, which meant four days' leave for her commanding officer.

'Where did you get that fender from, you dockyard burglar?' *Stephanotis* clamoured over his rail, for *Gardenia* was wearing a large coir-matting fender, evidently fresh from store, over her rail. It creaked with newness. 'You common thief of the beach, where did you find that new fender?'

The only craft that a destroyer will, sometimes, not steal equipment from is a destroyer; which accounts for the purity

467

of her morals and the loftiness of her conversation, and her curiosity in respect to stolen fittings.

Duckett, unmoved, went below, to return with a valise which he carried on to His Majesty's quarter-deck, and, atop of a suit of rat-catcher clothes, crammed into it a pair of ancient pigskin gaiters.

Here *Phlox*, assisted by her Dandie Dinmont, Dinah, who had been trained to howl at certain notes in her master's voice, gave a spirited and imaginative account of *Gardenia's* return the night before, which was compared to that of an ambulance with a lady-driver. Duckett retaliated by slipping on to his head for one coquettish instant a gravy-coloured soft cloth cap. It was the last straw. *Phlox* and *Stephanotis*, who had no hope of any leave for the present, pronounced it an offence, only to be wiped out by drinks.

'All things considered,' said Duckett, 'I don't care if I *do*. Come along!' and, the hour being what it was, he gave the necessary orders through the wardroom's tiny skylight. The captains came. *Phlox*—Lieutenant-Commander Jerry Marlett, a large and weather-beaten person, docked himself in the armchair by the wardroom stove with his cherished Dinah in his arms. Great possessions and much land, inherited from an uncle, had removed him from the Navy on the eve of the War. Three days after the declaration of it, he was back again, and had been very busy ever since. *Stephanotis*—Lieutenant-in-Command Augustus Holwell Rayne, *alias* 'The Damper,' because of his pessimism, spread himself out on the settee. He was small and agile, but of gloomy outlook, which a D.S.O. earned, he said, quite by mistake could not lighten. 'Horse' Duckett, *Gardenia's* skipper, was a reversion to the primitive Marryat type—a predatory, astute, resourceful pirate, too well known to all His Majesty's dockyards, a man

of easily injured innocence who could always prove an alibi,
and in whose ship, if his torpedo-coxswain had ever allowed
any one to look there, several sorts of missing Government
property might have been found. His ambition was to raise
pigs (animals he only knew as bacon) in Shropshire (a county
he had never seen) after the War, so he waged his war with
zeal to bring that happy day nearer. He sat in the arm-chair
by the door, whence he controlled the operations of 'Crippen,' the wardroom steward, late of Bolitho's Travelling Cir-
cus and Swings, who had taken to the high seas to avoid the
attentions of the Police ashore.

As usual, Duckett's character had been blackened by My
Lords of the Admiralty, and he was in the midst of a hot
campaign against them. An able-seaman's widowed mother
had sent a ham to her son, whose name was E. R. Davids.
Unfortunately, Engine-room-Artificer E. Davies, who swore
that he had both a mother and expectations of hams from
her, came across the ham first, and, misreading its address,
had had it boiled for, and at once eaten by, the Engineers'
mess. E. R. Davids, a vindictive soul, wrote to his mother,
who, it seems, wrote to the Admiralty, who, according to
Duckett, wrote to him daily every day for a month to know
what had become of E. R. Davids' ham. In the meantime the
guilty Engine-room-Artificer E. Davies had been transferred
to a sloop off the Irish coast.

'An' what the dooce *am* I to do?' Duckett asked his guests
plaintively.

'Apply for leave to go to Ireland with a stomach-pump and
heave the ham out of Davies,' Jerry suggested promptly.

'That's rather a wheeze,' said Duckett. 'I *had* thought of
marryin' Davids' mother to settle the case. Anyhow, it was
all Crippen's fault for not steerin' the ham into the wardroom

when it came aboard. Don't let it occur again, Crippen. Hams are goin' to be very scarce.'

'Well, now you've got all that off your chest'—Jerry Marlett lowered his voice—'suppose you tell us about what happened—the night before last.'

The talk became professional. Duckett produced certain evidence—still damp—in support of the claims that he had sent in concerning the fate of a German submarine, and gave a chain of facts and figures and bearings that the others duly noted.

'And how did your Acting Sub do?' asked Jerry at last.

'Oh, very fair, but I didn't tell him so, of course. They're hard enough to hold at the best of times, these makee-do officers. Have you noticed that they are always above their job—always thinkin' round the corner when they're thinkin' at all? On our way back, this young merchant o' mine—when I'd almost made up my mind to tell him he wasn't as big tripes as he looked—told me his one dream in life was to fly. Fly! He flew all right by the time I'd done with him, but— imagine one's Sub *tellin'* one a thing like that! "It must be *so* interestin' to fly," he said. The whole North Sea one bloomin' burgoo of what-come-nexts, an' this pup complainin' of lack of interest in it! Fly! Fly! When *I* was a Sub-Lootenant——'

He turned pathetically towards The Damper, who had known him in that rank in the Mediterranean.

'There wasn't much flyin' in our day,' said The Damper mournfully. 'But I can't remember anything else we didn't do.'

'Quite so; but we had some decency knocked into us. The new breed wouldn't know decency if they met it on a dungfork. *That*'s what I mean.'

A FLIGHT OF FACT

'When *I* was Actin' Sub,' Jerry opened thoughtfully, 'in the *Polycarp*—the pious *Polycarp*—Nineteen-O-Seven, I got nine cuts of the best from the Senior Sub for occupyin' the bathroom ten seconds too long. Twenty minutes later, just when the welts were beginnin' to come up, y' know, I was sent off in the gig with a Corporal o' Marines an' a private to fetch the Headman of All the Pelungas aboard. He was wanted for slavery, or barratry, or bigamy or something.'

'All the Pelungas?' Duckett repeated with interest. 'Odd you should mention that part of the world. What are the Pelungas like?'

'Very nice. Hundreds of islands and millions of coral reefs with atolls an' lagoons an' palm-trees, an' all the population scullin' round in outrigger canoes between 'em like a permanent regatta. Filthy navigation, though. *Polycarp* had to lie five miles out on account of the reefs (even then our navigator was tearin' his hair), an' I had an hour's steerin' on hot, hard thwarts. Talk o' tortures! *You* know. We landed in a white lather at the boat-steps of the Headman's island. The Headman wasn't takin' any at first. He'd drawn up his whole army—three hundred strong, with old Martini rifles an' a couple of ancestral seven-pounders—in front of his fort. *We* didn't know anything about his domestic arrangements. We just dropped in among 'em, so to say. Then my Corporal of Marines—the fattest man in the Service bar one—fell down the landin' steps. The Headman had a Prime Minister—about as fat as my Corporal—and he helped him up. Well, *that* broke the ice a bit. The Prime Minister was a statesman. He poured oil on the crisis, while the Headman cursed me and the Navy and the British Government, and I kept wrigglin' in my white ducks to keep 'em from drawin' tight on me. *You* know how it feels! I remember I told the Headman the *Polycarp* 'ud blow him an' his island out of the water if he didn't come along quick. She could have done it—in a week or two; but we were scrubbin' hammocks at the time. I forgot that little fact for the minute. I was a bit hot—all over. The Prime Minister soothed us down again, an' by and by the Headman said he'd pay us a State call—as a favour. I didn't care what he called it s'long as he came. So I lay about a quarter of a mile off-shore in the gig, in case the seven-pounders pooped off—I knew the Martinis couldn't hit us at that range—and I waited for him till he shoved off in his State barge—forty rowers a side. Would you believe it, he wanted to take precedence of the White Ensign on the way to the ship? I had to fall him in behind the gig and bring him alongside properly. I was so sore I could hardly get aboard at the finish.'

'What happened to the Headman?' said The Damper.

'Nothing. He was acquitted or condemned—I forget which —but he was a perfect gentleman. We used to go sailin' with him and his people—dancin' with 'em on the beach and all that sort of thing. *I* don't want to meet a nicer community than the Pelungaloos. They aren't used to white men—but they're first-class learners.'

'Yes, they *do* seem a cheery crowd,' Duckett commented.

'Where have *you* come across them?' said Jerry.

'Nowhere; but this Acting Sub of mine has got a cousin who's been flyin' down there.'

'Flyin' in All the Pelungas?' Jerry cried. 'That's impossible!'

'In these days? Where's your bright lexicon of youth? Nothing's impossible anywhere now,' Duckett replied. 'All the best people fly.'

'Count me out,' Jerry grunted. 'We went up once, Dinah,

little dog, and it made us both very sick, didn't it? When did it all happen, Horse?'

'Some time last year. This chap, my Sub's cousin—a man called Baxter—went adrift among All the Pelungas in his machine and failed to connect with his ship. He was reported missin' for months. Then he turned up again. That's all.'

'He was called Baxter?' said The Damper. 'Hold on a shake! I wonder if he's "Beloo" Baxter, by any chance. There was a chap of that name about five years ago on the China Station. He had himself tattooed all over, regardless, in Rangoon. Then he got as good as engaged to a woman in Hongkong—rich woman too. But the Pusser of his ship gave him away. He had a regular cinema of frogs and dragon-flies up his legs. And that was only the beginnin' of the show. So she broke off the engagement, and he half-killed the Pusser, and then he became a Buddhist, or something.'

'That couldn't have been this Baxter, or my Sub would have told me,' said Duckett. 'My Sub's a morbid-minded young animal.'

'*Maskee*[1] your Sub's mind!' said Jerry. 'What was this Baxter man—plain *or* coloured—doin' in All *my* Pelungas?'

'As far as I can make out,' said Duckett, 'Lootenant Baxter was flyin' in those parts—with an observer—out of a ship.'

'Yes, but what *for*?' Jerry insisted. 'And what ship?'

'He was flyin' for exercise, I suppose, an' his ship was the *Cormorang*. D'you feel wiser? An' he flew, an' he flew, an' he flew till, between him an' his observer and the low visibility and Providence and all that sort of thing, he lost his ship— just like some other people I know. Then he flapped about huntin' for her till dusk among the Pelungas, an' then he effected a landin' on the water.'

[1] Never mind.

'A nasty wet business—landin' that way, Dinah. *We* know,' said Jerry into the keen little cocked ear in his lap.

'Then he taxied about in the dark till he taxied on to a coral-reef and couldn't get the machine off. Coral ain't like mud, is it?' The question was to Jerry, but the insult was addressed to The Damper, who had lately spent eighteen hours on a soft and tenacious shoal off the East Coast. The Damper launched a kick at his host from where he lay along the settee.

'Then,' Duckett went on, 'this Baxter man got busy with his wireless and S O S'ed like winkie till the tide came and floated the old bus off the reef, and they taxied over to another island in the dark.'

'Thousands of islands in All the Pelungas,' Jerry murmured. 'Likewise reefs—hairy ones. What about the reefs?'

'Oh, they kept on hittin' reefs in the dark, till it occurred to them to fire their signal lights to see 'em by. So they went blazin' an' stinkin' and taxyin' up and down the reefs till they found a gap in one of 'em and they taxied bung on to an uninhabited island.'

'That must have been good for the machine,' was Jerry's comment.

'I don't deny it. I'm only tellin' you what my Sub told me. Baxter wrote it all home to his people, and the letters have been passed round the family. Well, then, o' course, it rained. It rained all the rest of the night, up to the afternoon of the next day. (It always does when you're in a hole.) They tried to start their engine in the intervals of climbin' palm-trees for coconuts. They'd only a few biscuits and some water with 'em.'

'Don't like climbin' palm-trees. It scrapes you raw,' The Damper moaned.

A FLIGHT OF FACT

'An' when they weren't climbin' or crankin' their engine, they tried to get into touch with the natives on the next nearest island. But the natives weren't havin' any. They took to the bush.'

'Ah!' said Jerry sympathetically. 'That aeroplane was too much for 'em. Otherwise, they're the most cosy, confidential lot *I* ever met. Well, what happened?'

'Baxter sweated away at his engine till she started up again. Then he flew round lookin' for his ship some more till his petrol ran out. Then he landed close to *another* uninhabited island and tried to taxi up to it.'

'Why was he so keen on *un*inhabited islands? I wish I'd been there. *I'd* ha' shown him round the town,' said Jerry.

'I don't know his reasons, but that was what he wrote home to his people,' Duckett went on. 'Not havin' any power by that time, his machine blew on to another reef and there they were! No grub, no petrol, and plenty of sharks! So they snugged her down. I don't know how one snugs down an aeroplane,' Duckett admitted, 'but Baxter took the necessary steps to reduce the sail-area, and cut the spanker-boom out of the tail-tassels or whatever it is they do on an aeroplane when they want her to be quiet. Anyhow, they more or less secured the bus to that reef so they thought she wouldn't fetch adrift; and they tried to coax a canoe over that happened to be passing. Nothin' doin' *there*! Canoe made one bunk of it.'

'He tickled 'em the wrong way,' Jerry sighed. 'There's a song they sing when they're fishing.' He began to hum dolefully.

'I expect Baxter didn't know that tune,' Duckett interrupted. 'He an' his observer cursed the canoe a good deal, an' then they went in for swimmin' stunts all among the sharks, until they fetched up on the *next* island when they came to it—it took 'em an hour to swim there—but the minute they landed the natives all left. Seems to me,' said Duckett thoughtfully, 'Baxter and his observer must have spread a pretty healthy panic scullin' about All the Pelungas in their shirts.'

'But why shirts?' said Jerry. 'Those waters are perfectly warm.'

'If you come to that, why *not* shirts?' Duckett retorted. 'A shirt's a badge of civilisation——'

'*Maskee* your shirts. What happened after that?' said The Damper.

'They went to sleep. They were tired by that time—oddly enough. The natives on *that* island had left everything standin' when they bunked—fires lighted, chickens runnin' about, and so forth. Baxter slept in one of the huts. About midnight some of the bold boys stole back again. Baxter heard 'em talkin' just outside, and as he didn't want his face trod on, he said "Salaam." That cleared the island for the second time. The natives jumped three foot into the air and shoved off.'

'Good Lord!' said Jerry impatiently. '*I'*d have had 'em eatin' out of my hand in ten seconds. "Salaam" isn't the word to use at all. What he ought to have said——'

'Well, anyhow, he didn't,' Duckett replied. 'He and his observer had their sleep out an' they woke in the mornin' with ragin' appetites and a strong sense of decency. The first thing they annexed was some native loin-cloths off a bush. Baxter wrote all this home to his people, you know. I expect he was well brought up.'

'If he was "Beloo" Baxter no one would notice——' The Damper began.

'He wasn't. He was just a simple, virtuous Naval Officer—

like me. Him an' his observer navigated the island in full dress in search of the natives, but they'd gone and taken the canoe with 'em. Baxter was so depressed at their lack of confidence that he killed a chicken an' plucked it an' drew it (I bet neither of you know how to draw fowls) an' boiled it and ate it all at once.'

'Didn't he feed his observer?' The Damper asked. 'I've a little brother what's an observer up in the air. I'd hate to think he——'

'The observer was kept busy wavin' his shirt on the beach in order to attract the attention of local fishin' craft. That was what *he* was for. After breakfast Baxter joined him an' the two of 'em waved shirts for two hours on the beach. An' that's the sort of thing my Sub prefers to servin' with me!— *Me!* After a bit, the Pelungaloos decided that they must be harmless lunatics, and one canoe stood pretty close in, an' they swam out to her. But here's a curious thing! Baxter wrote his people that, when the canoe came, his observer hadn't any shirt at all. Expect he's expended it wavin' for succour. But Baxter's shirt was all right. He went out of his way to tell his people so. An' my Sub couldn't see the humour of it one little bit. How does it strike you?'

'Perfectly simple,' said Jerry. 'Lootenant Baxter as executive officer in charge took his subordinate's shirt owin' to the exigencies of the Service. I'd ha' done the same. Pro-ceed.'

'There's worse to follow. As soon as they got aboard the canoe and the natives found they didn't bite, they cottoned to 'em no end. Gave 'em grub and dry loin-cloths and betel-nut to chew. What's betel-nut like, Jerry?'

'Grateful an' comfortin'. Warms you all through and makes you spit pink. It's non-intoxicatin'.'

'Oh! I've never tried it. Well, then, there was Baxter

spittin' pink in a loin-cloth an' a canoeful of Pelungaloo
fishermen, with his shirt dryin' in the breeze. Got that? Well,
then his aeroplane, which he thought he had secured to the
reef of the next island, began to drift out to sea. That boy
had to keep his eyes open, I tell you. He wanted the natives
to go in and makee-catchee the machine, and there was a big
palaver about it. They naturally didn't care to compromise
themselves with strange idols, but after a bit they lined up a
dozen canoes—no, eleven, to be precise—Baxter was awfully
precise in his letters to his people—an' tailed on to the aeroplane an' towed it to an island.'

'Excellent,' said Jerry Marlett, the complete Lieutenant-
Commander. 'I was gettin' worried about His Majesty's property. Baxter must have had a way with him. A loin-cloth ain't
uniform, but it's dashed comfortable. An' how did All my
Pelungaloos treat 'em?'

'We-ell!' said Duckett, 'Baxter was writin' home to his people, so I expect he toned things down a bit, but, readin'
between the lines, it looks as if—an' *that*'s why my Sub wants
to take up flyin', of course!—it looks as if, from then on, they
had what you might call Garden-of-Eden picnics for weeks an'
weeks. The natives put 'em under a guard o' sorts just for the
look of the thing, while the news was sent to the Headman,
but as far as I can make out from my Sub's reminiscences of
Baxter's letters, their guard consisted of the entire male and
female population goin' in swimmin' with 'em twice a day.
At night they had concerts—native songs *versus* music-hall—
in alternate what d'you call 'em? Anti-somethings. 'Phone,
ain't it?'

'They *are* a musical race! I'm glad he struck that side of
their nature,' Jerry murmured.

'I'm envious,' Duckett protested. 'Why should the Flyin''

Corps get all the plums? But Baxter didn't forget his Majesty's aeroplane. He got 'em to tow it to his island o' delights, and in the evenings he an' his observer, between the musical turns, used to give the women electric shocks off the wireless. And, one time, he told his observer to show 'em his false teeth, and when he took 'em out the people all bolted.'

'But that's in Rider Haggard. It's in *King Solomon's Mines,*' The Damper remarked.

'P'raps that's what put it into Baxter's head then,' said Duckett. 'Or else,' he suggested warily, 'Baxter wanted to crab his observer's chances with some lady.'

'Then he was a fool,' The Damper snarled. 'It might have worked the other way. It generally does.'

'Well, one can't foresee everything,' said Duckett. 'Anyhow, Baxter didn't complain. They lived there for weeks and weeks, singin' songs together and bathin' an'—oh, yes!—gamblin'. Baxter made a set of dice too. He doesn't seem to have neglected much. He said it was just to pass the time away, but I wonder what he threw for. I wish I knew him. His letters to his people are too colourless. What a life he must have led! Women, dice, and song, an' your pay rollin' up behind you in perfect safety with no exertion on your part.'

'There's a dance they dance on moonlight nights,' said Jerry, 'with just a few banana leaves—— Never mind. Go ahead!'

'All things bright and beautiful—fineesh,' Duckett mourned. 'Presently the Headman of All the Pelungas came along——'

' 'My friend? I hope it was. A first-class sportsman,' said Jerry.

'Baxter didn't say. Anyhow, he turned up and they were taken over to the capital island till they could be sent back to their own ship. The Headman did 'em up to the nines in every respect while they were with him (Baxter's quite enthusiastic over it, even in writin' to his own people), but, o' course, there's nothing like first love, is there? They must have felt partin' with their first loves. *I* always do. And then they were put into the full uniform of All the Pelungaloo Army. What's that like, Jerry? You've seen it.'

'It's a cross between a macaw an' a rainbow-ended mandrill. Very tasty.'

'Just as they were gettin' used to that, and they'd taught the Headman and his Court to sing: "Hello! Hello! Who's your lady friend?" they were embarked on a dirty common sailin' craft an' taken over the ocean and returned to the *Cormorang*, which, o' course, had reported 'em missing an' dead months before. They had one final kick-up before returnin' to duty. You see, they'd both grown torpedo-beards in the Pelungas, and they were both in Pelungaloo uniform. Consequently, when they went aboard the *Cormorang* they weren't recognised till they were half-way down to their cabins.'

'And then?' both Captains asked at once.

'That's where Baxter breaks off—even though he's writin' to his own people. He's so apologetic to 'em for havin' gone missin' and worried 'em, an' he's so sinful proud of havin' taught the Headman music-hall songs, that he only said that they had "some reception aboard the *Cormorang*." It lasted till midnight.'

'It is possible. What about their machine?' said Jerry.

'The *Cormorang* ran down to the Pelungas and retrieved it all right. But *I* should have liked to have seen that reception. There is nothing I'd ha' liked better than to have seen that reception. And it isn't as if I hadn't seen a reception or two either.'

A FLIGHT OF FACT

'The leaf-signal is made, sir,' said the Quartermaster at the door.

'Twelve-twenty-four train,' Duckett muttered. 'Can do.' He rose, adding, 'I'm going to scratch the backs of swine for the next three days. G'wout!'

The well-trained servant was already fleeting along the edge of the basin with his valise. *Stephanotis* and *Phlox* returned to their own ships, loudly expressing envy and hatred. Duckett paused for a moment at his gangway rail to beckon to his torpedo-coxswain, a Mr. Wilkins, a peace-time sailor of mild and mildewed aspect who had followed Duckett's shady fortunes for some years.

'Wilkins,' he whispered, 'where *did* we get that new starboard fender of ours from?'

'Orf the dredger, sir. She was asleep when we came in,' said Wilkins through lips that scarcely seemed to move. 'But our port one come orf the water-boat. We 'ad to over'aul our moorin's in the skiff last night, sir, and we—er—found it on 'er.'

'Well, well, Wilkins. Keep the home fires burning,' and Lieutenant-in-Command H. R. Duckett sped after his servant in the direction of the railway-station. But not so fast that he could outrun a melody played aboard the *Phlox* on a concertina to which manly voices bore the burden:

'When the enterprisin' burglar's not a-burglin'—not a-burglin',
   When the cut-throat isn't occupied with crime—'pied with
      crime.
He loves to hear the little brook a-gurglin'——'

Moved, Heaven knows whether by conscience or kindliness, Lieutenant Duckett smiled at the Policeman on the Dockyard gates.

THE BURNING OF THE *SARAH SANDS*

1898

THE BURNING OF THE *SARAH SANDS*

Men have sailed the seas for so many years, and have there done such amazing things in the face of danger, difficulty, and death, that no one tale of heroism exists which cannot be equalled by at least scores of others. But since the behaviour of bodies of untried men under trying circumstances is always interesting, and since I have been put in possession of some facts not very generally known, I am trying to tell again the old story of the Sarah Sands, *as an example of long-drawn-out and undefeatable courage and cool-headedness.*

SHE WAS A SMALL FOUR-MASTED, iron-built screw-steamer of eleven hundred tons, chartered to take out troops to India. That was in 1857, the year of the Indian Mutiny, when anything that could sail or steer was in great demand; for troops were being thrown into the country as fast as circumstances allowed—which was not very fast.

Among the regiments sent out was the 54th of the Line, now the Second Battalion of the Dorset Regiment—a good corps, then about a hundred years old, with a very fair record of service, but in no special way differing, so far as one could see, from many other regiments. It was despatched in three ships. The Headquarters—that is to say, the Lieutenant-Colonel, the Regimental books, pay-chest, Band, and Colours, which last represent the very soul of a Battalion—and some fourteen officers, three hundred and fifty-four rank and file, and perhaps a dozen women, left Portsmouth on the 15th of August all packed tight in the *Sarah Sands*.

Her crew, with the exception of the engineers and firemen, seem to have been foreigners or pier-head jumpers picked up at the last minute. They turned out bad, lazy, and insubordinate.

The accommodation for the troops was generously described as 'inferior,' and what men called 'inferior' in 1857 would now be called unspeakable. Nor, in spite of the urgent need, was there any great hurry about the *Sarah Sands*. She took two long months to reach Cape Town, and she stayed there five days to coal, leaving on the 20th of October. By this time, the crew were all but openly mutinous, and the troops, who must have picked up a little seamanship, had to work the ship out of harbour.

On the 7th of November, nearly three weeks later, a squall struck her and carried away her foremast; and it is to be presumed that the troops turned to and cleared away the wreckage. On the 11th of November the real trouble began, for, in the afternoon of that day, ninety days out from Portsmouth, a party of soldiers working in the hold saw smoke coming up from the after-hatch. They were then, maybe, within a thousand miles of the island of Mauritius, in half a gale and a sea full of sharks.

Captain Castles, the master, promptly lowered and provisioned the boats; got them over-side with some difficulty and put the women into them. Some of the sailors—the engineers, the firemen, and a few others behaved well—jumped into the long-boat, lowered it and kept well away from the ship. They knew she carried two magazines full of cartridges, and were taking no chances.

The troops, on the other hand, did not make any fuss, but

under their officers' orders cleared out the starboard or right-hand magazine, while volunteers tried to save the Regimental Colours. These stood at the end of the saloon, probably clamped against the partition behind the Captain's chair, and the saloon was full of smoke. Two Lieutenants made a dash thither but were nearly suffocated. A ship's quartermaster—Richard Richmond was his name—put a wet cloth over his face, managed to tear down the Colours, and then fainted. A private—and his name was W. Wiles—dragged out both Richmond and the Colours, and the two men dropped senseless on the deck while the troops cheered. That, at least, was a good beginning; for, as I have said, the Colours are the soul of every body of men who fight or work under them.

The saloon must have been one of the narrow, cabin-lined, old-fashioned 'cuddies,' placed above the screw, and all the fire was in the stern of the ship, behind the engine-room. It was blazing very close to the port or left-hand magazine, and, as an explosion there would have blown the *Sarah Sands* out like a squib, they called for more volunteers, and one of the Lieutenants who had been choked in the saloon recovered, went down first and passed up a barrel of ammunition, which was at once hove overboard. After this example, work went on with regularity.

When the men taking out the ammunition fainted, as they did fairly often, they pulled them up with ropes. Those who did not faint, grabbed what explosives they could feel or handle in the smother, and brought them up, and an official and serene quartermaster-sergeant stood on the hatch and jotted down the number of barrels so retrieved in his notebook, as they were thrown into the sea. They pulled out all except two barrels which slid from the arms of a fainting man—there was a fair amount of fainting that evening—and rolled out of reach. Besides these, there were another couple of barrels of signalling powder for the ship's use; but this the troops did not know, and were the more comfortable for their ignorance.

Then the flames broke through the after-deck, the light attracting shoals of sharks, and the mizzen-mast—the farthest aft of all the masts—flared up and went over-side with a crash. This would have veered the stern of the ship to the wind, in which case the flames must have swept forward; but a man with a hatchet—his name is lost—ran along the bulwarks and cut the wreck clear, while the boat full of women surged and rocked at a safe distance, and the sharks tried to upset it with their tails.

A Captain of the 54th—he was a jovial soul, and made jokes throughout the struggle—headed a party of men to cut away the bridge, the deck-cabins, and everything else that was inflammable—this in case of the flames sweeping forward again —while a provident Lieutenant, with some more troops, lashed spars and things together for a raft, and other gangs pumped water desperately on to what was left of the saloon and the magazines.

One record says quaintly: 'It was necessary to make some deviation from the usual military evolutions while the flames were in progress. The men formed in sections, countermarched round the forward part of the ship, which may perhaps be better understood when it is stated that those with their faces to the after part where the fire raged were on their way to relieve their comrades who had been working below. Those proceeding "forward" were going to recruit their exhausted strength and prepare for another attack when it came to their turn.'

No one seemed to have much hopes of saving the ship so long as the last of the powder was unaccounted for. Indeed,

Captain Castles told an officer of the 54th that the game was up, and the officer replied, 'We'll fight till we're driven overboard.' It seemed he would be taken at his word, for just then the signalling powder and the ammunition-casks went up, and the ship seen from midships aft looked like one floating volcano.

The cartridges spluttered like crackers, and cabin doors and timbers were shot up all over the deck, and two or three men were hurt. But—this is not in any official record—just after the roar of it, when her stern was dipping deadlily, and all believed the *Sarah Sands* was settling for her last lurch, some merry jester of the 54th cried, 'Lights out,' and the jovial Captain shouted back, 'All right! We'll keep the old woman afloat yet.' Not one man of the troops made any attempt to get on to the rafts; and when they found the ship was still floating they all went back to work double tides.

At this point in the story we come across Mr. Frazer, the Scotch engineer, who, like most of his countrymen, had been holding his trump-card in reserve. He knew the *Sarah Sands* was built with a water-tight bulkhead behind the engine-room and the coal-bunkers; and he proposed to cut through the bulkhead and pump on the fire. Also, he pointed out that it would be well to remove the coal in the bunkers, as the bulkhead behind was almost red-hot, and the coal was catching light.

So volunteers dropped into the bunkers, each man for the minute or two he could endure it, and shovelled away the singeing, fuming fuel, and other volunteers were lowered into the bonfire aft, and when they could throw no more water on it they were pulled up half roasted.

Mr. Frazer's plan saved the ship, though every particle of wood in the after part of her was destroyed, and a bluish vapour hung over the red-hot iron beams and ties, and the sea for miles about looked like blood under the glare, as they pumped and passed water in buckets, flooding the stern, sluicing the engine-room bulkhead and damping the coal beyond it all through the long night. The very sides of the ship were red-hot, so that they wondered when her plates would buckle and wrench out the rivets and let the whole misery down to the sharks.

The foremast had carried away on the squall of the 7th of November; the mizzen-mast, as you know, had gone in the fire; the mainmast, though wrapped round with wet blankets, was alight, and everything abaft the mainmast was one red furnace. There was the constant danger of the ship, now broadside on to the heavy seas, falling off before the high wind, and leading the flames forward again. So they hailed the boats to tow and hold her head to wind; but only the gig obeyed the order. The others had all they could do to keep afloat; one of them had been swamped, though all her people were saved; and as for the long-boat full of mutinous seamen, she behaved infamously. One record says that 'She not only held aloof, but consigned the ship and all she carried to perdition.' So the *Sarah Sands* fought for her own life alone, with the sharks in attendance.

About three on the morning of the 12th of November, pumping, bucketing, sluicing, and damping, they began to hope that they had bested the fire. By nine o'clock they saw steam coming up from her insides instead of smoke, and at mid-day they called in the boats and took stock of the damage. From the mizzen-mast aft there was nothing that you could call ship except just the mere shell of her. It was all one steaming heap of scrap-iron with twenty feet of black, greasy water flooding across the bent and twisted rods, and in the middle of it all four huge water-tanks rolled to and fro, thundering against the naked sides.

Moreover,—this they could not see till things had cooled down—the powder explosions had blown a hole right through her port quarter, and every time she rolled the sea came in there green. Of the four masts only one was left; and the rudder-head stuck up all bald, black, and horrible among the jam of collapsed deck-beams. A photograph of the wreck looks exactly like that of a gutted theatre after the flames and the firemen had done their worst.

They spent the whole of the 12th of November pumping water out as zealously as they had pumped it in. They lashed up the loose, charging tanks as soon as they were cool enough to touch. They plugged the hole at the stern with hammocks, sails, and planks, and a sail over all. Then they rigged up a horizontal bar gripping the rudder-head. Six men sat on planks on one side and six at the other over the empty pit beneath, hauling on to the bar with ropes and letting go as they were told. That made the best steering-gear that they could devise.

On the 13th of November, still pumping, they spread one sail on their solitary mast—it was lucky that the *Sarah Sands* had started with four of them—and took advantage of the trade winds to make for Mauritius. Captain Castles, with one chart and one compass, lived in a tent where some cabins had once been; and at the end of twelve more days he sighted land. Their average run was about four knots an hour; and it is no wonder that as soon as they were off Port Louis, Mauritius, Mr. Frazer, the Scotch engineer, wished to start his engines and enter port professionally. The troops looked down into the black hollow of the ship when the shaft made its first revolution, shaking the hull horribly; and if you can realise what it means to be able to see a naked screw-shaft at work from the upper deck of a liner, you can realise what had happened to the *Sarah Sands*. They waited outside Port Louis for the daylight, and were nearly dashed to pieces on a coral reef. Then the gutted, empty steamer came in—very dirty, the men's clothes so charred that they hardly dared to take them off, and very hungry; but without having lost one single life. Port Louis gave them all a public banquet in the market-place, and the French inhabitants were fascinatingly polite as only the French can be.

But the records say nothing of what befell the sailors who 'consigned the ship to perdition.' One account merely hints that 'this was no time for retribution'; but the troops probably administered their own justice during the twelve days' limp to port. The men who were berthed aft, the officers and the women, lost everything they had; and the companies berthed forward lent them clothes and canvas to make some sort of raiment.

On the 20th of December they were all re-embarked on the *Clarendon*. It was poor accommodation for heroes. She had been condemned as a coolie-ship, was full of centipedes and other animals picked up in the Brazil trade; her engines broke down frequently; and her captain died of exposure and anxiety during a hurricane. So it was the 25th of January before she reached the mouth of the Hugli.

By this time—many of the men probably considered this quite as serious as the fire—the troops were out of tobacco, and when they came across the American ship *Hamlet*, Captain Lecran, lying at Kedgeree on the way up the river to Calcutta, the officers rowed over to ask if there was any tobacco for sale. They told the skipper the history of their adventures, and he said: 'Well, I'm glad you've come to me, because I have some tobacco. How many are you?' 'Three hundred men,' said the officers. Thereupon Captain Lecran got out four hundred pounds of best Cavendish as well as one thousand Manila cigars for the officers, and refused to take payment on the grounds that Americans did not accept anything from shipwrecked people. They were not shipwrecked at the time, but evidently they had been shipwrecked quite enough for Captain Lecran, because when they rowed back a second time and insisted on paying, he only gave them grog, 'which,' says the record, 'caused it to be dark when we returned to our ship.' After this 'our band played "Yankee-Doodle," blue lights were burned, the signal-gun fired'—that must have been a lively evening at Kedgeree—'and everything in our power was had recourse to so as to convey to our American cousins our appreciation of their kindness.'

Last of all, the Commander-in-Chief issued a general order to be read at the head of every regiment in the Army. He was pleased to observe that 'the behaviour of the 54th Regiment was most praiseworthy, and by its result must render manifest to all the advantage of subordination and strict obedience to orders under the most alarming and dangerous circumstances in which soldiers can be placed.'

This seems to be the moral of the tale.

THE LAST LAP

How do we know, by the bank-high river,
  Where the mired and sulky oxen wait,
And it looks as though we might wait for ever,
  How do we know that the floods abate?
There is no change in the current's brawling—
  Louder and harsher the freshet scolds;
Yet we can feel she is falling, falling,
  And the more she threatens the less she holds.
Down to the drift, with no word spoken,
  The wheel-chained wagons slither and slue. . . .
Achtung! The back of the worst is broken!
  And—lash your leaders!—we're through—we're through!

How do we know, when the port-fog holds us
  Moored and helpless, a mile from the pier,
And the week-long summer smother enfolds us—
  How do we know it is going to clear?
There is no break in the blindfold weather,
  But, one and another, around the bay,
The unseen capstans clink together,
  Getting ready to up and away.
A pennon whimpers—the breeze has found us—
  A headsail jumps through the thinning haze.
The whole hull follows, till—broad around us—
  The clean-swept ocean says: 'Go your ways!'

How do we know, when the long fight rages,
  On the old, stale front that we cannot shake,

And it looks as though we were locked for ages,
  How do we know they are going to break?
There is no lull in the level firing,
  Nothing has shifted except the sun.
Yet we can feel they are tiring, tiring—
  Yet we can tell they are ripe to run.
Something wavers, and, while we wonder,
  Their centre-trenches are emptying out,
And, before their useless flanks go under,
  Our guns have pounded retreat to rout!

THE PARABLE OF BOY JONES

1910

THE PARABLE OF BOY JONES

This tale was written several years before the War, as
you can see for yourselves. It is founded on fact, and it is
meant to show that one ought to try to recognise facts,
even when they are unpleasant and inconvenient.

THE LONG SHED of the Village Rifle Club reeked with the
oniony smell of smokeless powder, machine-oil, and creosote
from the stop-butt, as man after man laid himself down and
fired at the miniature target sixty feet away. The Instructor's
voice echoed under the corrugated iron roof.

'Squeeze, Matthews, squeeze! Jerking your shoulder won't
help the bullet. . . . Gordon, you're canting your gun to the
left. . . . Hold your breath when the sights come on. . . .
Fenwick, was that a bull? Then it's only a fluke, for your last
at two o'clock was an outer. You don't know where you're
shooting.'

'I call this monotonous,' said Boy Jones, who had been
brought by a friend to look at the show. 'Where does the fun
come in?'

'Would you like to try a shot?' the Instructor asked.

'Oh—er—thanks,' said Jones. 'I've shot with a shot-gun, of
course, but this'—he looked at the miniature rifle—'this isn't
like a shot-gun, is it?'

'Not in the least,' said the Friend. The Instructor passed Boy
Jones a cartridge. The squad ceased firing and stared. Boy
Jones reddened and fumbled.

'Hi! The beastly thing has slipped somehow!' he cried. The

tiny twenty-two cartridge had dropped into the magazine-slot and stuck there, caught by the rim. The muzzle travelled vaguely round the horizon. The squad with one accord sat down on the dusty cement floor.

'Lend him a hair-pin,' whispered the jobbing gardener.

'Muzzle *up*, please,' said the Instructor (it was drooping towards the men on the floor). 'I'll load for you. Now—keep her pointed towards the target—you're supposed to be firing at two hundred yards. Have you set your sights? Never mind, I'll set 'em. *Please* don't touch the trigger till you shoot.'

Boy Jones was glistening at the edges as the Instructor swung him in the direction of the little targets sixty feet away. 'Take a fine sight! The bull's-eye should be just sitting on the top of the fore-sight,' the Instructor cautioned. 'Ah!'

Boy Jones, with a grunt and a jerk of the shoulder, pulled the trigger. The right-hand window of the shed, six feet above the target, starred and cracked.

The boy who cleans the knives at the Vicarage buried his face in his hands; Jevons, the bricklayer's assistant, tied up his bootlace; the Fellow of the Royal Geographical Society looked at the roof; the village barber whistled softly. When one is twenty-two years old, and weighs twelve-stone-eight in hard condition, one does not approve of any game that one cannot play very well.

'I call this silly piffle,' said Boy Jones, wiping his face.

'Oh, not so bad as that,' said the Instructor. 'We've all got to begin somehow. Try another?' But Boy Jones was not practising any more that afternoon. He seemed to need soothing.

'Come over to the big range,' said the Friend. 'You'll see the finished article at work down there. This is only for boys and beginners.'

A knot of village lads from twelve to sixteen were scuffling for places on the shooting-mat as Boy Jones left the shed. On his way to the range, across the windy Downs, he preserved a silence foreign to his sunny nature. Jevons, the bricklayer's assistant, and the F.R.G.S. trotted past him—rifles at the carry.

'Awkward wind,' said Jevons. 'Fish-tail!'

'What's a fish-tail?' said Boy Jones.

'Oh! It means a fishy, tricky sort of a wind,' said the Friend. A shift in the uneasy north-east breeze brought them the far-away sob of a Service rifle.

'For once in your young life,' the Friend went on, 'you're going to attend a game you do not understand.'

'If you mean I'm expected to make an ass of myself again——' Boy Jones paused.

'Don't worry! By this time I fancy Jevons will have told the Sergeant all about your performance in the shed just now. *You* won't be pressed to shoot.'

A long sweep of bare land opened before them. The thump of occasional shots grew clearer, and Boy Jones pricked his ears.

'What's that unholy whine and *wop*?' he asked in a lull of the wind.

'The whine is the bullet going across the valley. The *wop* is when it hits the target—that white shutter thing sliding up and down against the hillside. Those men lying down yonder are shooting at five hundred yards. We'll look at 'em,' said the Friend.

'This would make a thundering good golf-links,' said Boy Jones, striding over the short, clean turf. 'Not a bad lie in miles of it.'

'Yes, wouldn't it?' the Friend replied. 'It would be even prettier as a croquet-lawn or a basket-ball pitch. Just the place for a picnic too. Unluckily, it's a rifle-range.'

Boy Jones looked doubtful, but said nothing till they reached the five-hundred-yard butt. The Sergeant, on his stomach, binoculars to his eyes, nodded, but not at the visitors. 'Where did you sight, Walters?' he said.

'Nine o'clock—edge of the target,' was the reply from a fat, blue man in a bowler hat, his trousers rucked half-way to his knees. 'The wind's rotten bad down there!' He pointed towards the stiff-tailed wind-flags that stuck out at all sorts of angles as the eddy round the shoulder of the Down caught them.

'Let me try one,' the Sergeant said, and reached behind him for a rifle.

'Hold on!' said the F.R.G.S. 'That's Number Six. She throws high.'

'She's *my* pet,' said Jevons, holding out his hand for it. 'Take Number Nine, Sergeant.'

'Rifles are like bats, you know,' the Friend explained. 'They differ a lot.'

The Sergeant sighted.

'He holds it steady enough,' said Boy Jones.

'He mostly does,' said the Friend. 'If you watch that white disc come up you'll know it's a bull.'

'Not much of one,' said the Sergeant. 'Too low—too far right. I gave her all the allowance I dared, too. That wind's funnelling badly in the valley. Give your wind-sight another three degrees, Walters.'

The fat man's big fingers delicately adjusted the lateral sight. He had been firing till then by the light of his trained judgment, but some of the rifles were fitted with wind-gauges, and he wished to test one.

'What's he doing that for?' said Boy Jones.

'You wouldn't understand,' said the Friend. 'But take a

squint along this rifle, and see what a bull looks like at five hundred yards. It isn't loaded, but don't point it at the pit of my stomach.'

'Dash it all! I didn't *mean* to!' said Boy Jones.

'None of 'em mean it,' the Friend replied. 'That's how all the murders are done. Don't play with the bolt. Merely look along the sights. It isn't much of a mark, is it?'

'No, by Jove!' said Jones, and gazed with reverence at Walters, who announced before the marker had signalled his last shot that it was a likely heifer. (Walters was a butcher by profession.) A well-centred bull it proved to be.

'Now how the deuce did he do it?' said Boy Jones.

'By practice—first in the shed at two hundred yards. We've five or six as good as him,' said the Friend. 'But he's not much of a snap-shooter when it comes to potting at dummy heads and shoulders exposed for five seconds. Jevons is our man then.'

'Ah! talking of snap-shooting!' said the Sergeant, and—while Jevons fired his seven shots—delivered Boy Jones a curious little lecture on the advantages of the foggy English climate, the value of enclosed land for warfare, and the possibilities of well-directed small-arm fire wiping up—'spraying down' was his word—artillery, even in position.

'Well, I've got to go on and build houses,' said Jevons. 'Twenty-six is my score-card—sign, please, Sergeant.' He rose, dusted his knees, and moved off. His place was taken by a dark, cat-footed Coastguard, firing for the love of the game. He only ran to three cartridges, which he placed—magpie, five o'clock; inner, three o'clock; and bull. 'Cordery don't take anything on trust,' said the Sergeant. 'He feels his way in to the bull every time. I like it. It's more rational.'

While the F.R.G.S. was explaining to Boy Jones that the

rotation of the earth on her axis affected a bullet to the extent of one yard in a thousand, a batch of six lads cantered over the hill.

'We're the new two-hundred-ers,' they shouted.

'I know it,' said the Sergeant. 'Pick up the cartridge-cases; take my mackintosh and bag, and come on down to the two-hundred range, quietly.'

There was no need for the last caution. The boys picked up the things and swung off in couples—scout-fashion.

'They are the survivors,' the Friend explained, 'of the boys you saw just now. They've passed their miniature rifle tests, and are supposed to be fit to fire in the open.'

'And are they?' said Boy Jones, edging away from the F.R.G.S., who was talking about 'jump' and 'flip' in rifle-shooting.

'We'll see,' said the Sergeant. 'This wind ought to test 'em!'

Down in the hollow it rushed like a boulder-choked river, driving quick clouds across the sun: so that one minute the eight-inch Bisley bull leaped forth like a headlight, and the next shrunk back into the grey-green grass of the butt like an engine backing up the line.

'Look here!' said the Sergeant, as the boys dropped into their places at the firing-point. 'I warn you it's a three-foot wind on the target, *and* freshening. You'll get no two shots alike. Any boy that thinks he won't do himself justice can wait for a better day.'

Nothing moved except one grin from face to face.

'No,' said the Sergeant, after a pause. 'I don't suppose a thunderstorm would shift you young birds. Remember what I've been telling you all this spring. Sighting shots, from the right!'

They went on one by one, carefully imitating the well-observed actions of their elders, even to the tapping of the cartridge on the rifle-butt. They scowled and grunted and compared notes as they set and reset their sights. They brought up their rifles just as shadow gave place to sun, and, holding too long, fired when the cheating cloud returned. It was unhappy, cold, nose-running, eye-straining work, but they enjoyed it passionately. At the end they showed up their scorecards; one twenty-seven, two twenty-fives, a twenty-four, and two twenty-twos. Boy Jones, his hands on his knees, had made no remark from first to last.

'Could I have a shot?' he began in a strangely meek voice.

But the chilled Sergeant had already whistled the marker out of the butt. The wind-flags were being collected by the youngsters, and, with a tinkle of spent cartridge-cases returned to the Sergeant's bag, shooting ended.

'Not so bad,' said the Sergeant.

'One of those boys was hump-backed,' said Boy Jones, with the healthy animal's horror of deformity.

'But his shots aren't,' said the Sergeant. 'He was the twenty-seven card. Milligan's his name.'

'I should like to have had a shot,' Boy Jones repeated. 'Just for the fun of the thing.'

'Well, just for the fun of the thing,' the Friend suggested, 'suppose you fill and empty a magazine. Have you got any dummies, Sergeant?'

The Sergeant produced a handful of dummy cartridges from his inexhaustible bag.

'How d'you put 'em in?' said Boy Jones, picking up a cartridge by the bullet end with his left hand, and holding the rifle with his right.

'Here, Milligan,' the Friend called. 'Fill and empty this magazine, will you, please?'

The cripple's fingers flickered for an instant round the

rifle-breech. The dummies vanished clicking. He turned towards the butt, pausing perhaps a second on each aimed shot, ripped them all out again over his shoulder. Mechanically Boy Jones caught them as they spun in the air; for he was a good fielder.

'Time, fifteen seconds,' said the Friend. 'You try now.' Boy Jones shook his head. 'No, thanks,' he said. 'This isn't my day out. That's called magazine-fire, I suppose.'

'Yes,' said the Sergeant, 'but it's more difficult to load in the dark or in a cramped position.'

The boys drew off, larking among themselves. The others strolled homewards as the wind freshened. Only the Sergeant, after a word or two with the marker, struck off up the line of firing-butts.

'There seems to be a lot in it,' said Boy Jones, after a while, to his friend. 'But you needn't tell me,' he went on in the tone of one ill at ease with himself, 'don't tell *me* that when the hour strikes every man in England wouldn't—er—rally to the defence of his country like one man.'

'And he'd be *so* useful while he was rallying, wouldn't he?' said the Friend shortly. 'Imagine one hundred thousand chaps of your kidney introduced to the rifle for the first time, all loading and firing in your fashion! The hospitals wouldn't hold 'em!'

'Oh, there'd be time to get the general hang of the thing,' said Boy Jones cheerily.

'When that hour strikes,' the Friend replied, 'it will already have struck, if you understand. There may be a few hours—perhaps ten or twelve—there will certainly not be more than a day and a night allowed us to get ready in.'

'There will be six months at least,' said Boy Jones confidently.

'Ah, you probably read that in a paper. I shouldn't rely on it, if I were you. It won't be like a county cricket match, date settled months in advance. By the way, are you playing for your county this season?'

Boy Jones seemed not to hear the last question. He had taken the Friend's rifle, and was idly clicking the bolt.

'Beg y' pardon, sir,' said the Marker to the Friend in an undertone, 'but the Sergeant's tryin' a gentleman's new rifle at nine hundred, and I'm waiting on for him. If you'd like to come into the trench'—a discreet wink closed the sentence.

'Thanks awfully. That 'ud be quite interesting,' said Boy Jones. The wind had dulled a little; the sun was still strong on the golden gorse; the Sergeant's straight back grew smaller and smaller as it moved away.

'You go down this ladder,' said the Marker. They reached the raw line of the trench beneath the targets, the foot deep in the flinty chalk.

'Yes, sir,' he went on, 'here's where all the bullets ought to come. There's fourteen thousand of 'em this year, somewhere on the premises, but it don't hinder the rabbits from burrowing, just the same. *They* know shooting's over as well as we do.' You come here with a shot-gun, and you won't see a single tail; but they don't put 'emselves out for a rifle. Look, there's the Parson!' He pointed at a bold black rabbit sitting half-way up the butt, who loped easily away as the Marker ran up the large nine-hundred-yard bull. Boy Jones stared at the bullet-splintered framework of the targets, the chewed edges of the woodwork, and the significantly loosened earth behind them. At last he came down, slowly it seemed, out of the sunshine, into the chill of the trench. The Marker opened an old cocoa-box, where he kept his paste and paper patches.

'Things get mildewy down here,' he explained. 'Mr. Warren,

our sexton, says it's too like a grave to suit *him*. But as I say, it's twice as deep and thrice as wide as what *he* makes.'

'I think it's rather jolly,' said Boy Jones, and looked up at the narrow strip of sky. The Marker had quietly lowered the danger flag. Something yowled like a cat with her tail trod on, and a few fragments of pure white chalk crumbled softly into the trench. Boy Jones jumped, and flattened himself against the inner wall of the trench. 'The Sergeant is taking a sighting-shot,' said the Marker. 'He must have hit a flint in the grass somewhere. We can't comb 'em all out. The noise you noticed was the nickel envelope stripping, sir.'

'But I didn't hear his gun go off,' said Boy Jones.

'Not at nine hundred, with this wind, you wouldn't,' said the Marker. 'Stand on one side, please, sir. He's begun.'

There was a rap overhead—a pause—down came the creaking target, up went the marking disc at the end of a long bamboo; a paper patch was slapped over the bullet-hole, and the target slid up again, to be greeted with another rap, another, and another. The fifth differed in tone. 'Here's a curiosity,' said the Marker, pulling down the target. 'The bullet must have ricochetted short of the butt, and it has keyholed, as we say. See!' He pointed to an ugly triangular rip and flap on the canvas target face. 'If that had been flesh and blood, now,' he went on genially, 'it would have been just the same as running a plough up you. . . . Now he's on again!' The sixth rap was as thrillingly emphatic as one at a spiritualistic séance, but the seventh was followed by another yaa-ow of a bullet hitting a stone, and a tiny twisted sliver of metal fell at Boy Jones's rigid feet. He touched and dropped it. 'Why, it's quite hot,' he said.

'That's due to arrested motion,' said the F.R.G.S. 'Isn't it a funking noise, though?

THE PARABLE OF BOY JONES

A pause of several minutes followed, during which they could hear the wind and the sea and the creaking of the Marker's braces.

'He said he'd finish off with a magazine-ful,' the Marker volunteered. 'I expect he's waiting for a lull in the wind. Ah! here it comes!'

It came—eleven shots slammed in at three-second intervals; a ricochet or two; one on the right-hand of the target's framework, which rang like a bell; a couple that hammered the old railway ties just behind the bull; and another that kicked a clod into the trench, and key-holed up the target. The others were various and scattering, but all on the butt.

'Sergeant can do better than that,' said the Marker critically, overhauling the target. 'It was the wind put him off, or' (he winked once again) 'or . . . else he wished to show somebody something.'

'I heard 'em all hit,' said Boy Jones. 'But I never heard the gun go off. Awful, I call it!'

'Well,' said his friend, 'it's the kind of bowling you'll have to face at forty-eight hours' notice—*if* you're lucky.'

'It's the key-holing that I bar,' said Boy Jones, following his own line of thought. The Marker put up his flag and ladder, and they climbed out of the trench into the sunshine.

'For pity's sake, look!' said the Marker, and stopped. 'Well, well! If I 'adn't seen it, I wouldn't have credited it. You poor little impident fool! The Sergeant *will* be vexed.'

'What has happened?' said Boy Jones, rather shrilly.

'He's killed the Parson, sir!' The Marker held up the still kicking body of a glossy black rabbit. One side of its head was not there.

'Talk of coincidence!' the Marker went on. 'I know Sergeant 'll pretend he aimed for it. The poor little fool! Jumpin' about after his own businesses and thinking he was safe; and then to have his head fair mashed off him like this. Just look at him! Well! Well!'

It was anything but well with Boy Jones. He seemed sick.

A week later the Friend nearly stepped on him in the miniature-rifle shed. He was lying at length on the dusty coir matting, his trousers rucked half-way to his knees, his sights set as for two hundred, deferentially asking Milligan the cripple to stand behind him and tell him whether he was canting.

'No, you aren't now,' said Milligan patronisingly, 'but you were.'

A DEPARTURE

Since first the White Horse Banner blew free,
  By Hengist's horde unfurled,
Nothing has changed on land or sea
  Of the things that steer the world.
(As it was when the long-ships scudded through the gale,
  So it is where the Liners go.)
Time and Tide, they are both in a tale:—
  'Woe to the weaker—woe!'

No charm can bridle the hard-mouthed wind
  Or smooth the fretting swell.
No gift can alter the grey Sea's mind,
  But she serves the strong man well.
(As it is when her uttermost deeps are stirred,
  So it is where the quicksands show,)
All the waters have but one word:—
  'Woe to the weaker—woe!'

The feast is ended, the tales are told,
  The dawn is overdue,
And we meet on the quay in the whistling cold
  Where the galley waits her crew.
Out with the torches, they have flared too long,
  And bid the harpers go.
Wind and warfare have but one song:—
  'Woe to the weaker—woe!'

Hail to the great oars gathering way,
  As the beach begins to slide!

LAND AND SEA TALES

Hail to the war-shields' click and play
As they lift along our side!
Hail to the first green over the bow—
Slow for the sea-stroke! Slow!—
All the benches are grunting now:—
'Woe to the weaker—woe!'

THE BOLD 'PRENTICE

1895

THE BOLD 'PRENTICE

*This story is very much of the same sort as 'An Un-
qualified Pilot,' and shows that, when any one is really
keen on his job, he will often find some older man who is
even keener than he, who will give him help and instruction that could not be found in a whole library of books.
Olaf Swanson's book of 'Road-Locos Repair or The
Young Driver's Vademecome,' was well known in the
Railway sheds in its day, and was written in the queerest
English ever printed. But it told useful facts and, as you
will see, saved a train at a pinch. It may be worth notic-
ing that young Ottley's chance did not come to him till
he had worked on and among engine-repairs for some
five or six years and was well grounded in practical
knowledge of his subject.*

YOUNG OTTLEY'S FATHER came to Calcutta in 1857 as fireman
on the first locomotive ever run by the D.I.R., which was then
the largest Indian railway. All his life he spoke broad Yorkshire, but young Ottley, being born in India, naturally talked
the clipped sing-song that is used by the half-castes and Eng-
lish-speaking natives. When he was fifteen years old the D.I.R.
took him into their service as an apprentice in the Locomotive Repair Department of the Ajaibpore workshops, and
he became one of a gang of three or four white men and
nine or ten natives.

There were scores of such gangs, each with its hoisting and

515

overhead cranes, jack-screws, vices, and lathes, as separate as separate shops, and their work was to mend locomotives and make the apprentices behave. But the apprentices threw nuts at one another, chalked caricatures of unpopular foremen on buffer-bars and discarded boilers, and did as little work as they possibly could.

They were nearly all sons of old employees, living with their parents in the white bungalows of Steam Road or Church Road or Albert Road—on the broad avenues of pounded brick bordered by palms and crotons and bougain-villeas and bamboos which made up the railway town of Ajaibpore. They had never seen the sea or a steamer; half their speech was helped out with native slang; they were all volunteers in the D.I.R. Corps—grey with red facings—and their talk was exclusively about the Company and its affairs.

They all hoped to become engine-drivers earning six or eight hundred a year, and therefore they despised all mere sit-down clerks in the Store, Audit, and Traffic departments, and ducked them when they met at the Company's swimming-baths.

There were no strikes or tie-ups on the D.I.R. in those days, for the reason that the ten or twelve thousand natives and two or three thousand whites were doing their best to turn the Company's employment into a caste in which their sons and relatives would be sure of positions and pensions. Everything in India crystallises into a caste sooner or later—the big jute and cotton mills, the leather, harness, and opium factories, the coal-mines and the dockyards, and, in years to come, when India begins to be heard from as one of the manu-facturing countries of the world, the labour Unions of other lands will learn something about the beauty of caste which will greatly interest them.

THE BOLD 'PRENTICE

Those were the days when the D.I.R. decided that it would be cheaper to employ native drivers as much as possible, and the 'Sheds,' as they called the Repair Department, felt the change acutely; for a native driver could misuse his engine, they said, more curiously than any six monkeys. The Company had not then standardised its rolling-stock, and this was very good for apprentices anxious to learn about machines, because there were, perhaps, twenty types of locomotives in use on the road. They were Hawthornes; E types; O types; outside cylinders; Spaulding and Cushman double-enders and short-run Continental-built tank engines, and many others. But the native drivers burned them all out impartially, and the apprentices took to writing remarks in Bengali on the cabs of the repaired ones where the next driver would be sure to see them.

Young Ottley worked at first as little as the other apprentices, but his father, who was then a pensioned driver, taught him a great deal about the insides of locomotives; and Olaf Swanson, the red-headed Swede who ran the Government Mail, the big Thursday express, from Serai Rajgara to Guldee Haut, was a great friend of the Ottley family, and dined with them every Friday night.

Olaf was an important person, for besides being the best of the mail-drivers, he was Past Master of the big railway Masonic Lodge, 'St. Duncan's in the East,' Secretary of the Drivers' Provident Association, a Captain in the D.I.R. Volunteer Corps, and, which he thought much more of, an Author; for he had written a book in a language of his own which he insisted upon calling English, and had printed it at his own expense at the ticket-printing works.

Some of the copies were buff and green, and some were pinkish and blue, and some were yellow and brown; for Olaf did not believe in wasting money on high-class white paper. Wrapping-paper was good enough for him, and besides, he said the colours rested the eyes of the reader. It was called 'The Art of Road-Locos Repair or The Young Driver's Vademecome,' and was dedicated in verse to a man of the name of Swedenborg.

It covered every conceivable accident that could happen to an engine on the road; and gave a rough-and-ready remedy for each; but you had to understand Olaf's written English, as well as all the technical talk about engines, to make head or tail of it, and you had also to know personally every engine on the D.I.R., for the 'Vademecome' was full of what might be called 'locomotive allusions,' which concerned the D.I.R. only. Otherwise, it would, as some great locomotive designer once said, have been a classic and a text-book.

Olaf was immensely proud of it, and would pin young Ottley in a corner and make him learn whole pages—it was written all in questions and answers—by heart.

'Never mind what she *means*,' Olaf would shout. 'You learn her word-perfect, and she will help you in the Sheds. I drive the Mail,—*the* mail of all India,—and what I write and say is true.'

'But I do *not* wish to learn the book,' said young Ottley, who thought he saw quite enough of locomotives in business hours.

'You *shall* learn! I haf great friendship for your father, and so I shall teach you whether you like it or not.'

Young Ottley submitted, for he was really fond of old Olaf, and at the end of six months' teaching in Olaf's peculiar way began to see that the 'Vademecome' was a very valuable help in the repair sheds, when broken-down engines of a new type came in. Olaf gave him a copy bound in cartridge-paper

and hedged round the margins with square-headed manu-
script notes, each line the result of years of experience of
accidents.

'There is nothing in this book,' said Olaf, 'that I have not
tried in my time, and I say that the engine is like the body of
a man. So long as there is steam—the life, you see,—so long,
if you know how, you can make her move a little,—so!' He
waggled his hand slowly. 'Till a man is dead or the engine she
is at the bottom of a river, you can do something with her.
Remember that! *I* say it and I know.'

He repaid young Ottley's time and attention by using his
influence to get him made a Sergeant in his Company, and
young Ottley, being a keen Volunteer and a good shot, stood
well with the D.I.R. in the matter of casual leave. When
repairs were light in the Sheds and the honour of the D.I.R.
was to be upheld at some far-away station against the men of
Agra or Bandikui, the narrow-gauge railway-towns of the west,
young Ottley would contrive to get away, and help to uphold
it on the glaring dusty rifle-ranges of those parts.

A 'prentice never dreamed of paying for his ticket on any
line in India, least of all when he was in uniform, and young
Ottley was practically as free of the Indian railway system
as any member of the Supreme Legislative Council who wears
a golden General Pass on his watch-chain and can ride where
he chooses.

Late in September of his nineteenth year he went north
on one of his cup-hunting excursions, elegantly and accurately
dressed, with one-eighth of one inch of white collar showing
above his grey uniform stock, and his Martini-Henry rifle
polished to match his sergeant's sword in the rack above him.

The Rains were out, and in Bengal that means a good deal
to the railways; for the rain falls for three months lavishly,

till the whole country is one sea, and the snakes take refuge on the embankment, and the racing floods puff out the brick ballast from under the iron ties, and leave the rails hanging in graceful loops. Then the trains run as they can, and the permanent-way inspectors spend their nights flourishing about in hand-carts pushed by coolies over the dislocated metals, and everybody is covered with the fire-red rash of prickly heat, and loses his temper.

Young Ottley was used to these things from birth. All he regretted was that his friends along the line were so draggled and dripping and sulky that they could not appreciate his gorgeousness; for he considered himself very consoling to behold when he cocked his helmet over one eye and puffed the rank smoke of native-made cigars through his nostrils. Until night fell he lay out on his bunk, in his shirt-sleeves, reading the works of G. W. M. Reynolds, which were sold on all the railway bookstalls, and dozing at intervals.

Then he found they were changing engines at Guldee Haut, and old Rustomjee, a Parsee, was the new driver, with Number Forty in hand. Young Ottley took this opportunity to go forward and tell Rustomjee exactly what they thought of him in the Sheds, where the 'prentices had been repairing some of his carelessness in the way of a dropped crown-sheet, the result of inattention and bad stoking.

Rustomjee said he had bad luck with engines, and young Ottley went back to his carriage and slept. He was waked by a bang, a bump, and a jar, and saw on the opposite bunk a subaltern who was travelling north with a detachment of some twenty English soldiers.

'What's that?' said the subaltern.

'Rustomjee has blown her up, perhaps,' said young Ottley, and dropped out into the wet, the subaltern at his heels. They found Rustomjee sitting by the side of the line, nursing a scalded foot and crying aloud that he was a dead man, while the gunner-guard—who is a kind of extra-hand—looked respectfully at the roaring, hissing machine.

'What has happened?' said young Ottley, by the light of the gunner-guard's lantern.

'*Phut gya* [She has gone smash],' said Rustomjee, still hopping.

'Without doubt; but where?'

'*Khuda janta!* [God knows]. I am a poor man. Number Forty is broke.'

Young Ottley jumped into the cab and turned off all the steam he could find, for there was a good deal escaping. Then he took the lantern and dived under the drive-wheels, where he lay face up, investigating among spurts of hot water.

'Doocid plucky,' said the subaltern. '*I* shouldn't like to do that myself. What's gone wrong?'

'Cylinder-head blown off, coupler-rod twisted, and several more things. She is very badly wrecked. Oah, yes, she is a tottal wreck,' said young Ottley between the spokes of the right-hand driver.

'Awkward,' said the subaltern, turning up his coat-collar in the wet. 'What's to be done, then?'

Young Ottley came out, a rich black all over his grey uniform with the red facings, and drummed on his teeth with his finger-nails, while the rain fell and the native passengers shouted questions and old Rustomjee told the gunner-guard to walk back six or seven miles and wire to some one for help.

'I cannot swim,' said the gunner-guard. 'Go and lie down.' And that, as you might say, settled that. Besides, as far as one could see by the light of the gunner-guard's lantern, all Bengal was flooded.

'Olaf Swanson will be at Serai Rajgara with the Mail. He will be particularly angry,' said young Ottley. Then he ducked under the engine again with a flare-lamp and sat cross-legged, considering things and wishing he had brought his 'Vademe-come' in his valise.

Number Forty was an old reconstructed Mutiny engine, with Frenchified cock-nosed cylinders and a profligate allow-ance of underpinning. She had been through the Sheds sev-eral times, and young Ottley, though he had never worked on her, had heard much about her, but nothing to her credit.

'You can lend me some men?' he said at last to the sub-altern. 'Then I think we shall disconnect her this side, and perhaps, notwithstanding, she will move. We will try—eh?'

'Of course we will. Hi! Sergeant!' said the subaltern. 'Turn out the men here and do what this—this officer tells you.'

'Officer!' said one of the privates, under his breath. 'Didn't think I'd enlisted to serve under a Sergeant o' Volunteers. 'Ere's a 'orrible street accident. Looks like mother's tea-kettle broke. What d'yer expect us to do, Mister Civilian Sergeant?'

Young Ottley explained his plan of campaign while he was ravaging Rustomjee's tool-chest, and then the men crawled and knelt and levered and pushed and hauled and turned spanners under the engine, as young Ottley told them. What he wanted was to disconnect the right cylinder altogether, and get off a badly twisted coupler-rod. Practically Number Forty's right side was paralysed, and they pulled away enough iron-mongery there to build a culvert with.

Young Ottley remembered that the instructions for a case like this were all in the 'Vademecome,' but even he began to feel a little alarmed as he saw what came away from the engine and was stacked by the side of the line. After forty minutes of the hardest kind of work it seemed to him that everything movable was cleared out, and that he might venture to give her steam. She leaked and sweated and shook, but she moved —in a grinding sort of way—and the soldiers cheered.

Rustomjee flatly refused to help in anything so revolutionary as driving an engine on one cylinder, because, he said, Heaven had decreed that he should always be unlucky, even with sound machines. Moreover, as he pointed out, the pressure-gauge was jumping up and down like a bottle-imp. The stoker had long since gone away into the night; for he was a prudent man.

'Doocid queer thing altogether,' said the subaltern, 'but look here, if you like, I'll chuck on the coals and you can drive the old jigamaroo, if she'll go.'

'Perhaps she will blow up,' said the gunner-guard.

'Shouldn't at all wonder by the sound of her. Where's the shovel?' said the subaltern.

'Oah no. She's all raight according to my book, I think,' said young Ottley. 'Now we will go to Serai Rajgara—if she moves.'

She moved with long *ssghee! ssghee's!* of exhaustion and lamentation. She moved quite seven miles an hour, and—for the floods were all over the line—the staggering voyage began.

The subaltern stoked four shovels to the minute, spreading them thin, and Number Forty made noises like a dying cow, and young Ottley discovered that it was one thing to run a healthy switching-locomotive up and down the yards for fun when the head of the yard wasn't looking, and quite another to drive a very sick one over an unknown road in absolute darkness and tropic rain. But they felt their way along with their hearts in their mouths till they came to a distant signal, and whistled frugally, having no steam to spare.

'This *might* be Serai Rajgara,' said young Ottley, hopefully.

'Looks more like the Suez Canal,' said the subaltern. 'I say, when an engine kicks up that sort of a noise she's a little impatient, isn't she?'

'That sort of a noise' was a full-powered, furious yelling whistle half a mile up the line.

'That is the Down Mail,' said young Ottley. 'We have delayed Olaf two hours and forty-five minutes. She must surely be in Serai Rajgara.'

'Don't wonder she wants to get out of it,' said the subaltern. 'Golly, what a country!'

The line here dipped bodily under water, and young Ottley sent the gunner-guard on to find the switch to let Number Forty into the siding. Then he followed and drew up with a doleful *wop! wop! wop!* by the side of the great forty-five-ton, six-wheel, coupled, eighteen-inch inside-cylinder Number Twenty-five, all paint and lacquer, standing roaring at the head of the Down Mail. The rest was all water—flat, level, and solid from one point of the horizon to the other.

Olaf's red beard flared like a danger-signal, and as soon as they were in range some knobby pieces of Giridih coal whizzed past young Ottley's head.

'Your friend very mad?' said the subaltern, ducking.

'Aah!' roared Olaf. 'This is the fifth time you make delay. Three hours' delay you make *me*—Swanson—the Mail! Now I will lose more time to break your head.' He swung on to the foot-board of Number Forty, with a shovel in one hand.

'Olaf!' cried young Ottley, and Olaf nearly tumbled backward. 'Rustomjee is behind.'

'Of course. He always is. But you? How you come here?'

'Oah, we smashed up. I have disconnected her and arrived here on one cylinder, by your book. We are only a—a diagram of an engine, I think.'

'My book! My very good book! My "Vademecome"! Ottley, you are a fine driver. I forgive my delays. It was worth. Oh, my book, my book!' and Olaf leapt back to Number Twenty-five, shouting things about Swedenborg and steam.

'Thatt is all right,' said young Ottley, 'but where is Serai Rajgara? We want assistance.'

'There is no Serai Rajgara. The water is two feet on the embankment, and the telegraph office is fell in. I will report at Purnool Road. Good-night, good boy!'

The Mail train splashed out into the dark, and Ottley made great haste to let off his steam and draw his fire. Number Forty had done enough for that night.

'Odd chap, that friend of yours,' said the subaltern, when Number Forty stood empty and disarmed in the gathering waters. 'What do we do now? Swim?'

'Oah no! At ten-forty-five thiss morning that is coming, an engine will, perhaps, arrive from Purnool Road and take us north. Now we will lie down and go to sleep. You see, there *is* no Serai Rajgara. You could get a cup of tea here once on a time.'

'Oh, my Aunt, what a country!' said the subaltern, as he followed Ottley to the carriage and lay down on the leather bunk.

For the next three weeks Olaf Swanson talked to everybody of nothing but his 'Vademecome' and young Ottley. What he said about his book does not matter, but the compliments of a mail-driver are things to be repeated, as they were, to people in high authority, the masters of many engines. So young Ottley was sent for, and he came from the Sheds buttoning his jacket and wondering which of his sins had been found out this time.

It was a loop line near Ajaibpore, where he could by no

possibility come to harm. It was light but steady traffic, and a first-class superintendent was in charge; but it was a driver's billet, and permanent after six months. As a new engine was on order for the loop, the foreman of the Sheds told young Ottley he might look through the stalls and suit himself.

He waited, boiling with impatience, till Olaf came in, and the two went off together, old Olaf clucking, 'Look! Look! Look!' like a hen, all down the Sheds, and they chose a nearly new Hawthorne, No. 239, which Olaf highly recommended. Then Olaf went away, to give young Ottley his chance to order her to the cleaning-pit, and jerk his thumb at the cleaner and say, as he turned magnificently on his heel, 'Thursday, eight o'clock. *Mallum?* Understand?'

That was almost the proudest moment of his life. The very proudest was when he pulled out of Atami Junction through the brick-field on the way to his loop, and passed the Down Mail, with Olaf in the cab.

They say in the Sheds that you could have heard Number Two hundred and Thirty-nine's whistle from Ranigunge clear to Calcutta.

THE NURSES

When, with a pain he desires to explain to his servitors, Baby
Howls himself black in the face, toothlessly striving to curse;
And the six-months-old Mother begins to inquire of the Gods
    if it may be
Tummy, or Temper, or Pins—what does the adequate Nurse?

See! At a glance and a touch his trouble is guessed; and,
    thereafter,
She juggles (unscared by his throes) with drops of hot water
    and spoons,
Till the hiccoughs are broken by smiles, and the smiles pucker
    up into laughter,
And he lies o'er her shoulder and crows, and she, as she nurses
    him, croons!

When, at the head of the grade, tumultuous out of the cutting
Pours the belated Express, roars at the night, and draws clear,
Redly obscured or displayed by her fire-door's opening and
    shutting—
Symbol of strength under stress—what does her small engi-
    neer?

Clamour and darkness encircle his way. Do they deafen or
    blind him?
No!—nor the pace he must keep. He, being used to these
    things,
Placidly follows his work, which is laying his mileage behind
    him,

While his passengers trustfully sleep, and he, as he nurses her,
sings!

When, with the gale at her heel, the ship lies down and
recovers—
Rolling through forty degrees, combing the stars with her tops,
What says the man at the wheel, holding her straight as she
hovers
On the summits of wind-screening seas; steadying her as she
drops?

Behind him the blasts without check from the Pole to the
Tropic, pursue him,
Heaving up, heaping high, slamming home, the surges he
must not regard:
Beneath him the crazy wet deck, and all Ocean on end to undo
him;
Above him one desperate sail, thrice-reefed but still buckling
the yard!

Under his hand fleet the spokes and return, to be held or set
free again;
And she bows and makes shift to obey their behest, till the
master-wave comes
And her gunnel goes under in thunder and smokes, and she
chokes in the trough of the sea again—
Ere she can lift and make way to its crest; and he, as he nurses
her, hums!

These have so utterly mastered their work that they work
without thinking;

THE NURSES

Holding three-fifths of their brain in reserve for whatever
    betide.
So, when catastrophe threatens, of colic, collision, or sinking,
They shunt the full gear into train, and take that small thing
    in their stride.

THE SON OF HIS FATHER

1894

THE SON OF HIS FATHER

'It is a queer name,' Mrs. Strickland admitted, 'and none of our family have ever borne it; but, you see, he *is* the first man to us.'

So he was called Adam, and to that world about him he was the first of men—a man-child alone. Heaven sent him no Eve for a companion, but all earth, horse and foot, was at his feet. As soon as he was old enough to appear in public he held a levee, and Strickland's sixty policemen, with their sixty clanking sabres, bowed to the dust before him. When his fingers closed a little on Imam Din's sword-hilt they rose and roared till Adam roared too, and was withdrawn.

'Now that was no cry of fear,' said Imam Din afterwards, speaking to his companions in the Police lines. 'He was angry —and so young! Brothers, he will make a very strong Police officer.'

'Does the Memsahib nurse him?' said a new recruit, the dye-smell not yet out of his yellow cotton uniform.

'Ho!' said an up-country Naik scornfully; 'it has not been known for *more* than ten days that my woman nurses him.' He curled his moustaches as lordlily as ever an Inspector could afford to do, for he knew that the husband of the foster-mother of the son of the District Superintendent of Police was a man of consideration.

'I am glad,' said Imam Din, loosening his belt. 'Those who drink our milk become of our own blood, and I have seen, in those thirty years, that the sons of Sahibs once being born here return when they are men. Yes, they return after they have been to Belait [Europe].'

'And what do they in Belait?' asked the recruit respectfully.

'Get instruction—which thou hast not,' returned the Naik. 'Also they drink of *belaitee-panee* [soda-water] enough to give them that devil's restlessness which endures for all their lives. Whence we of Hind have trouble.'

'My father's uncle,' said Imam Din slowly, with importance, 'was Ressaldar of the Long Coat Horse; and the Empress called him to Europe in the year that she had accomplished fifty years of rule. *He* said (and there were also other witnesses) that the Sahibs there drink only common water even as do we; and that the *belaitee-panee* does *not* run in all their rivers.'

'He said that there was a Shish Mahal—a glass palace—half a mile in length, and that the rail-trains ran under roads; and that there are boats bigger than a village. He is a great talker.' The Naik spoke scornfully. He had no well-born uncles.

'*He* is at least a man of good birth,' said Imam Din, and the Naik was silent.

'Ho! Ho!' Imam Din reached out to his pipe, chuckling till his fat sides shook again. 'Strickland Sahib's foster-mother was the wife of a gardener in the Ferozepur district. I was a young man then. This child also will be suckled here and he will have double wisdom, and when he is a Police officer it will be very bad for the thieves in this part of the world. Ho! Ho!'

'Strickland Sahib's butler has said,' the Naik went on, 'that they will call him Adam—and no jaw-splitting English name. Udaam. The *padre* will name him at their church in due time.'

'Who can tell the ways of Sahibs? Now Strickland Sahib knows more of the Faith than ever I had time to learn— prayers, charms, names and stories of the Blessed Ones. Yet he is not a Mussulman,' said Imam Din thoughtfully.

'For the reason that he knows as much of the Gods of Hindustan, and so he rides with a rein in each hand. Remember that he sat under the Baba Atal, a fakir among fakirs, for ten days; whereby a man came to be hanged for the murder of a dancing-girl on the night of the great earthquake,' the Naik replied.

'True—it is true. And yet—the Sahibs are one day so wise— and another so foolish. But he has named the child well; Adam. Huzrut Adam. Ho! Ho! Father Adam we must call him.'

'And all who minister to the child,' said the Naik quietly, but with meaning, 'will come to great honour.'

Adam throve, being prayed over before the Gods of at least three creeds, in a garden almost as fair as Eden. There were gigantic clumps of bamboos that talked continually, and enormous plantains, trees on whose soft, paper skin he could scratch with his nails; green domes of mango-trees as huge as the dome of St. Paul's, full of parrots as big as cassowaries and grey squirrels the size of foxes. At the end of the garden stood a hedge of flaming poinsettias higher than anything in the world, because, child-like, Adam's eye could not carry to the tops of the mango-trees. Their green went out against the blue sky, but the red poinsettias he could just see. A nurse who talked continually about snakes and pulled him back from the mouth of a fascinating dry well, and a mother who believed that the sun hurt little heads, were the only drawbacks to this loveliness. But, as his legs grew under him, he found that by scaling an enormous rampart—three feet of broken-down mud wall at the end of the garden—he could come into a ready-made kingdom, where every one was his slave. Imam Din showed him the way one evening, and the Police troopers, cooking their supper, received him with rapture, and gave him pieces of very indigestible, but altogether delightful, spiced bread.

Here he sat or sprawled in the horse-feed where the Police

were picketed in a double line, and he named them, men and
beasts together, according to his ideas and experiences, as his
First Father had done before him. In those days everything
had a name, from the mud mangers to the heel-ropes, for things
were people to Adam exactly as people are things to folk in
their second childhood. Through all the conferences—one
hand twisted into Imam Din's beard, and the other on his
polished belt-buckle—there were two other people who came
and went across the talk—Death and Sickness—persons greater
than Imam Din, and stronger than the heel-roped horses.
There was Mata, the smallpox, a woman in some way connected with pigs; and Heza, the cholera, a black man, according to Adam; and Booka, starvation; and Kismet, who settled
all questions, from the untimely choking of a pet mongoose in
the kitchen-drain to the absence of a young Policeman who
once missed a parade and never came back. It was all very
wonderful to Adam, but not worth much thinking over; for
a child's mind is bounded by his eyes exactly as a horse's view
of the road is limited by his blinkers. Between these objectionable shadowy vagrants stood a ring of kind faces and strong
arms, and Mata and Heza would never touch Adam, the First
of Men. Kismet might do so, because—and this was a mystery
no staring into his looking-glass would solve—Kismet was
written, like Police orders for the day, in or on Adam's head.
Imam Din could not explain how this might be, and it was
from that grey, fat Mohammedan that Adam learned through
every inflection that *Khuda janta* [God knows!] that settles
everything in the mind of Asia.

Beyond the fact that 'Khuda' [God] was 'a very good man
and kept lions', Adam's theology did not run far. Mrs. Strickland tried to teach him a few facts, but he revolted at the story
of Genesis as untrue. A turtle, he said, upheld the world, and

one-half the adventures of Huzrut Nu [Father Noah] had never been told. If Mamma wanted to hear them she must ask Imam Din.

'It's awful,' said Mrs. Strickland, half crying, 'to think of his growing up like a little heathen.' Mrs. Strickland had been born and brought up in England, and did not quite understand Eastern things.

'Let him alone,' said Strickland. 'He'll grow out of it all, or it will only come back to him in dreams.'

'Are you sure?' said his wife.

'Quite. I was sent home when I was seven, and they flicked it out of me with a wet towel at Harrow. Public schools don't encourage anything that isn't quite English.'

Mrs. Strickland shuddered, for she had been trying not to think of the separation that follows motherhood in India, and makes life there, for all that is written to the contrary, not quite the most desirable thing in the world. Adam trotted out to hear about more miracles, and his nurse must have worried him beyond bounds, for she came back weeping, saying that Adam-*baba* was in danger of being eaten alive by wild horses.

As a matter of fact he had shaken off Juma by bolting between a couple of picketed horses, and lying down under their bellies. That they were old personal friends of his, Juma did not understand, nor Strickland either. Adam was settled at ease when his father arrived, breathless and white, and the stallions put back their ears and squealed.

'If you come here,' said Adam, 'they will hit you kicks. Tell Juma I have eaten my rice, and I wish to be alone.'

'Come out at once,' said Strickland, for the horses were beginning to paw.

'Why should I obey Juma's order? She is afraid of horses.'

'It is not Juma's order. It is mine. Obey!'

'Ho!' said Adam. 'Juma did not tell me that'; and he crawled out on all-fours among the shod feet. Mrs. Strickland was crying bitterly with fear and excitement, and as a sacrifice to the home gods Adam had to be whipped. He said with perfect justice:

'There was no order that I should *not* sit with the horses, and they are *my* horses. Why is there this *tamasha* [fuss]?'

Strickland's face showed him that the whipping was coming, and the child turned white. Mother-like, Mrs. Strickland left the room, but Juma, the foster-mother, stayed to see.

'Am I to be whipped here?' he gasped.

'Of course.'

'Before that woman? Father, I am a man—I am not afraid. It is my *izzat*—my honour.'

Strickland only laughed—(to this day I cannot imagine what possessed him), and gave Adam the little tap-tap with a riding-cane that was whipping sufficient for his years.

When it was all over, Adam said quietly, 'I am little and you are big. If I had stayed among my horse-folk I should not have been whipped. *You* are afraid to go there.'

The merest chance led me to Strickland's house that afternoon. When I was half-way down the drive Adam passed me without recognition, at a fast run. I caught one glimpse of his face under his big hat, and it was the face of his father as I had once seen it in the grey of the morning when it bent over a leper. I caught the child by the shoulder.

'Let me go!' he screamed; though he and I were the best of friends, as a rule. 'Let me go!'

'Where to, Father Adam?' He was quivering like a haltered colt.

'To the well. I have been beaten. I have been beaten before a woman! Let me go!' He tried to bite my hand.

'That is a small matter,' I said. 'Men are born to beatings.'

'*Thou* hast never been beaten,' he said savagely (we were talking in the native tongue).

'Indeed I have; times past counting.'

'Before women?'

'My mother and my *ayah* saw. *By* women, too, for that matter. What of it?'

'What didst thou do?' He stared beyond my shoulder up the long drive.

'It is long ago, and I have forgotten. I was older than thou art; but even then I forgot, and now the thing is only a jest to be talked of.'

Adam drew one big breath and broke down utterly in my arms. Then he raised his head, and his eyes were Strickland's eyes when Strickland gave orders.

'Ho! Imam Din!'

The fat orderly seemed to spring out of the earth at our feet, crashing through the bushes, and standing at attention.

'Hast *thou* ever been beaten?' said Adam.

'Assuredly. By my father when I was thirty years old. He beat me with a plough-beam before all the women of the village.'

'Wherefore?'

'Because I had returned to the village on leave from the Government service, and said of the village elders that they had not seen the world. Therefore he beat me to show that no seeing of the world changes father and son.'

'And thou?'

'I stood up to the beating. He was my father.'

'Good,' said Adam, and turned on his heel without another word.

Imam Din looked after him. 'An elephant breeds but once

in a lifetime, but he breeds elephants. Yet I am glad I am no father of tuskers,' said he.

'What is it all?' I asked.

'His father beat him with a whip no bigger than a reed. But the child could not have done what he desired to do without leaping through me. And I am of some few pounds weight. Look!'

Imam Din stepped back through the bushes, and the pressed grass showed that he had been lying curled round the mouth of the dry well.

'When there was talk of beating, I knew that one who sat among horses such as ours was not like to kiss his father's hand. He might have done away with himself. So I lay down in this place.' We stood still looking at the well-curb.

Adam came along the garden path to us. 'I have spoken to my father,' he said simply. 'Imam Din, tell thy Naik that his woman is dismissed my service.'

'*Huzoor!* [Your Highness!]' said Imam Din, stooping low.

'For no fault of hers.'

'Protector of the Poor!'

'And to-day.'

'*Khodawund!* [Heaven-born!]'

'It is an order. Go!'

Again the salute, and Imam Din departed, with that same set of the back which he wore when he had taken an order from Strickland. I thought that it would be well to go too, but Strickland beckoned me from the veranda. When I came up he was perfectly white, rocking to and fro in his chair.

'Do you know he was going to chuck himself down the well—because I tapped him just now?' he said helplessly.

'I ought to,' I replied. 'He has just dismissed his nurse—on his own authority, I suppose?'

'He told me just now that he wouldn't have her for a nurse

any more. I never supposed he meant it for an instant. I suppose she'll have to go.'

Now Strickland, the Police officer, was feared through the length and breadth of the Punjab by murderers, horse-thieves, and cattle-lifters.

Adam returned, halting outside the veranda.

'I have sent Juma away because she saw that—that which happened. Until she is gone I do not come into the house,' he said.

'But to send away thy foster-mother!' said Strickland with reproach.

'*I* do not send her away. It is *thy* blame,' and the small forefinger was pointed at Strickland. 'I will not obey her. I will not eat from her hand. I will not sleep with her. Send her away!'

Strickland stepped out and lifted the child into the veranda.

'This folly has lasted long enough,' he said. 'Come now and be wise.'

'I am little and you are big,' said Adam between set teeth. 'You can beat me before this man or cut me to pieces. But I will *not* have Juma for my *ayah* any more. She saw me beaten. I will not eat till she goes. I swear it by—my father's head.'

Strickland sent him indoors to his mother, and we could hear sounds of weeping and Adam's voice saying nothing more than 'Send Juma away!' Presently Juma came in and wept too, and Adam repeated, 'It is no fault of thine, but go!'

And the end of it was that Juma went with all her belongings, and Adam fought his own way into his little clothes until the new *ayah* came. His address of welcome to her was rather amazing. In a few words it ran: 'If I do wrong, send me to my father. If you strike me, I will try to kill you. I do not wish my *ayah* to play with me. Go and eat rice!'

From that Adam forswore the society of *ayahs* and small na-

tive boys as much as a small boy can, confining himself to
Imam Din and his friends of the Police. The Naik, Juma's
husband, had been presuming not a little on his position,
and when Adam's favour was withdrawn from his wife he
thought it best to apply for a transfer to another post. There
were too many companions anxious to report his shortcomings
to Strickland.

Towards his father Adam kept a guarded neutrality. There
was not a touch of sulkiness in it, for the child's temper was as
clear as a bell. But the difference and the politeness worried
Strickland.

If the Policemen had loved Adam before the affair of the
well, they worshipped him now.

'He knows what honour means,' said Imam Din. 'He has
justified himself upon a point thereof. He has carried an order
through his father's household as a child of the Blood might
do. Therefore he is not altogether a child any longer. Wah!
He is a tiger's cub.' The next time that Adam made his little
unofficial inspection of the lines, Imam Din, and, by consequence, all the others, stood upon their feet with their hands
to their sides, instead of calling out from where they lay,
'Salaam, Babajee,' and other disrespectful things.

But Strickland took counsel with his wife, and she with the
cheque-book and their lean bank account, and they decided
that Adam must go 'home' to his aunts. But England is not
home to a child who has been born in India, and it never
becomes home-like unless he spends all his youth there. Their
bank-book showed that if they economised through the summer by going to a cheap hill-station instead of to Simla (where
Mrs. Strickland's parents lived, and where Strickland might be
noticed by the Government) they could send Adam home in
the next spring. It would be hard pinching, but it could be
done.

Dalhousie was chosen as being the cheapest of the hill-stations;—Dalhousie and a little five-roomed cottage full of mildew, tucked away among the rhododendrons.

Adam had been to Simla three or four times, and knew by name most of the drivers on the road there, but this new place disquieted him. He came to me for information, his hands deep in his knickerbocker pockets, walking step for step as his father walked.

'There will be none of my *bhai-bund* [brotherhood] up there,' he said disconsolately, 'and they say that I must lie still in a *dooli* [palanquin] for a day and a night, being carried like a sheep. I wish to take some of my mounted men to Dalhousie.'

I told him that there was a small boy, called Victor, at Dalhousie, who had a calf for a pet, and was allowed to play with it on the public roads. After that Adam could not sufficiently hurry the packing.

'First,' said he, 'I shall ask that man Victor to let me play with the cow's child. If he is *muggra* [ill-conditioned], I shall tell my Policemen to take it away.'

'But that is unjust,' said Strickland, 'and there is no order that the Police should do injustice.'

'When the Government pay is not sufficient, and low-caste men are promoted, what *can* an honest man do?' Adam replied, in the very touch and accent of Imam Din; and Strickland's eyebrows went up.

'You talk too much to the Police, my son,' he said.

'Always. About everything,' said Adam promptly. 'They say that when I am an officer I shall know as much as my father.'

'God forbid, little one!'

'They say, too, that you are as clever as Shaitan [the Evil One] to know things.'

'They say that, do they?' and Strickland looked pleased. His pay was small, but he had his reputation, and it was dear to him.

'They say also—not to me, but to one another when they eat rice behind the wall—that in your own heart you esteem yourself as wise as Suleiman [Solomon], who was cheated by Shaitan.'

This time Strickland did not look so pleased. Adam, in all innocence, launched into a long story about Suleiman-bin-Daoud, who once, out of vanity, pitted his wits against Shaitan, and because God was not on his side Shaitan sent 'a little devil of low caste,' as Adam put it, who cheated him utterly and put him to shame before 'all the other Kings.'

'By Gum!' said Strickland, when the tale was done, and went away, while Adam took me to task for laughing at Imam Din's stories. I did not wonder that he was called Huzrut Adam, for he looked old as all time in his grave childhood, sitting cross-legged, his battered little helmet far at the back of his head, his forefinger wagging up and down, native-fashion, and the wisdom of serpents on his unconscious lips.

That May he went up to Dalhousie with his mother, and in those days the journey ended in fifty or sixty miles of uphill travel in a palanquin along a road winding through the Himalayas. Adam sat in the *dooli* with his mother, and Strickland rode and tied with me, a spare *dooli* following. The march began after we got out of the train at Pathankot, one wet hot night among the rice and poppy fields.

II

It was all new to Adam, and he had opinions to advance—notably about a fish that jumped in a wayside pond. '*Now* I know,' he shouted, 'how God puts them there! First He makes them up above and then He drops them down. That was a new one.' Then, lifting his head to the stars, he cried: 'Oh, God, do it again, but slowly, so that I, Adam, may see.'

But nothing happened, and the *dooli*-bearers lit the noisome, dripping rag-torches, and Adam's eyes shone big in the dancing light, and we smelt the dry dust of the Plains that we were leaving after eleven months' hard work.

At stated times the men ceased their drowsy, grunting tune, and sat down for a smoke. Between the guttering of their water-pipes we could hear the cries of the beasts of the night, and the wind stirring in the folds of the mountain ahead. At the changing-stations the voice of Adam, the First of Men, would be lifted to rouse the sleepers in the huts till the fresh relay of bearers shambled from their cots and the relief pony with them.

Then we would re-form and go on, and by the time the moon rose Adam was asleep, and there was no sound in the night except the grunting of the men, the husky murmur of some river a thousand feet down in the valley, and the squeaking of Strickland's saddle. So we went up from date-palm to deodar, till the dawn wind came round a corner all fresh from the snows, and we snuffed it. I heard Strickland say, 'Wife, my overcoat, please,' and Adam, fretfully, 'Where is Dalhousie and the cow's child?' Then I slept till Strickland turned me out of the warm *dooli* at seven o'clock, and I stepped into all the splendour of a cool Hill day, the Plains sweltering twenty miles back and four thousand feet below. Adam waked too, and needs must ride in front of me to ask a million questions, and shout at the monkeys and clap his hands when the painted pheasants bolted across our road, and hail every wood-cutter and drover and pilgrim within sight, till we halted for breakfast at a resthouse. After that, being a child, he went out to play with a train of bullock-drivers halted by the roadside, and we had to chase him out of a native liquor-shop, where he was bargaining with a native seven-year-old for a parrot in a bamboo cage.

Said he, wriggling on my pommel as we went on again, 'There were four men *behosh* [insensible] at the back of that house. Wherefore do men grow *behosh* from drinking?'

'It is the nature of the waters,' I said, and, calling back, 'Strick, what's that grog-shop doing so close to the road? It's a temptation to any one's servants.'

'Dunno,' said a sleepy voice in the *dooli*. 'This is Kennedy's District. 'Twasn't here in *my* time.'

'Truly the waters smell bad,' Adam went on. 'I smelt them, but I did not get the parrot even for six annas. The woman of the house gave me a love-gift that I found playing near the veranda.'

'And what was the gift, Father Adam?'

'A nose-ring for my *ayah*. Ohé! Ohé! Look at that camel with the muzzle on his nose!'

A string of loaded camels came cruising round the corner as a fleet rounds a cape.

'Ho, Malik! Why does not a camel salaam like an elephant? His neck is long enough,' Adam cried.

'The Angel Jibrail made him a fool at the beginning,' said the driver, as he swayed on the top of the leading beast, and laughter ran all along the line of red-bearded men.

'That is true,' said Adam solemnly, and they laughed again.

At last, in the late afternoon, we came to Dalhousie, the loveliest of the hill-stations, and separated, Adam hardly able to be restrained from setting out at once to find Victor and the 'cow's child.' I found them both, something to my trouble, next morning. The two young sinners had a calf on a tight rope just at a sharp turn in the Mall, and were pretending that he was a Rajah's elephant who had gone mad; and they shouted with delight. Then we began to talk, and Adam, by way of crushing Victor's repeated reminders to me that he and not 'that other' was the owner of the calf, said, 'It is true I have no cow's child; but a great *dacoity* [robbery] has been done on my father.'

'We came up together yesterday. There could have been nothing,' I said.

'It was my mother's horse. She has been *dacoited* with beating and blows, and now is *so* thin,' He held his hands an inch apart. 'My father is at the telegraph-house sending telegrams. Imam Din will cut off *all* their heads. I desire your saddle-cloth for a howdah for my elephant. Give it me!'

This was exciting, but not lucid. I went to the telegraph office and found Strickland in a black temper among many telegraph forms. A dishevelled, one-eyed groom stood in a corner whimpering at intervals. He was a man whom Adam invariably addressed as *'Be-shakl, be-ukl, be-ank'* [ugly, stupid, eyeless]. It seemed that Strickland had sent his wife's horse up to Dalhousie by road, a fortnight's march, in the groom's charge. This is the custom in Upper India. Among the foot-hills, near Dhunnera or Dhar, horse and man had been violently set upon in the night by four men, who had beaten the groom (his leg was bandaged from knee to ankle in proof), had incidentally beaten the horse, and had robbed the groom of the bucket and blanket, and all his money—eleven rupees, nine annas. Last, they had left him for dead by the wayside, where some woodcutters had found and nursed him. Then the one-eyed man howled with anguish, thinking over his bruises. 'They asked me if I was Strickland Sahib's servant, and I, thinking the Protection of the Name would be sufficient, spoke the truth. Then they beat me grievously.'

'H'm!' said Strickland. 'I thought they wouldn't dacoit as a business on the Dalhousie road. This is meant for me person-ally—sheer *badmashi* [impudence]. All right!'

In justice to a very hard-working class it must be said that the thieves of Upper India have the keenest sense of humour. The last compliment that they can pay a Police officer is to rob him, and if, as once they did, they can loot a Deputy Inspector-General of Police, on the eve of his retirement, of everything except the clothes on his back, their joy is complete. They cause letters of derision and telegrams of condolence to be sent to the victim; for of all men thieves are most compelled to keep abreast of progress.

Strickland was a man of few words where his business was concerned. I had never seen a Police officer robbed before, and I expected some excitement, but Strickland held his tongue. He took the groom's deposition, and then retired into himself for a time. Then he sent Kennedy, of the Pathankot District, an official letter and an unofficial note. Kennedy's reply was purely unofficial, and it ran thus: 'This seems a compliment solely intended for you. My wonder is you didn't get it before. The men are probably back in your District by now. My Dhunnera and foot-hill people are highly respectable culti-vators, and, seeing my Assistant is an unlicked pup, and I can't trust my Inspector out of my sight, I'm not going to turn their harvest upside down with Police investigations. I'm run off my feet with vaccination Police work. You'd better look at home. The Shubkudder Gang were through here a fortnight back. They laid up at the Amritzar Serai, and then worked down. No cases against them in my charge; but, remember, you imprisoned their head-man for receiving stolen goods in the Prub Dyal burglary. They owe you one.'

'Exactly what I thought,' said Strickland. 'I had a notion

it *was* the Shubkudder Gang from the first. We must make it pleasant for them at Peshawur, and in my District, too. They're just the kind that would lie up under Imam Din's shadow.'

From this point onward the wires began to be worked heavily. Strickland had a very fair knowledge of the Shubkudder Gang, gathered at first hand.

They were the same syndicate that had once stolen a Deputy-Commissioner's cow, put horse-shoes on her, and taken her forty miles into the jungle before they lost interest in the joke. They added insult to insult by writing that the Deputy-Commissioner's cows and horses were so much alike that it took them two days to find out the difference and they would not lift the like of such cattle any more.

The District Superintendent at Peshawur replied to Strickland that he was expecting the Gang, and Strickland's Assistant, in his own District, being young and full of zeal, sent up the most amazing clues.

'Now that's just what I want that young fool not to do,' said Strickland. 'He's an English boy, born and bred, and his father before him. He has about as much tact as a bull, and he won't work quietly under my Inspector. I wish the Government would keep our service for country-born men. Those first five or six years in India give a man a pull that lasts him all his life. Adam, if only you were old enough to be my Assistant!' He looked down at the little fellow in the veranda. Adam was deeply interested in the dacoity, and, unlike a child, did not lose interest after the first week. On the contrary, he would ask his father every evening what had been done, and Strickland had drawn him a map on the white wall of the veranda, showing the different towns in which Policemen were on the look-out for thieves. They were Amritzar, Jullunder, Phillour,

Gurgaon, Rawal Pindi, Peshawur, and Multan. Adam looked
up at it as he answered:

'There has been great *dikh* [trouble] in this case?'

'Very great trouble. I wish that thou wert a young man and
my Assistant to help me.'

'Dost thou need help, my father?' Adam asked curiously,
with his head on one side.

'Very much.'

'Leave it all alone. It is bad. Let loose everything.'

'That must not be. Those beginning a business continue to
the end.'

'Thou wilt continue to the end? Dost thou not *know* who
did the dacoity?'

Strickland shook his head. Adam turned to me with the
same question, and I answered it in the same way.

'What foolish people!' he said, and turned his back on us.

He showed plainly in all our dealings afterwards how we
had fallen in his opinion. Strickland told me that he would
sit at the door of his father's workroom and stare at him for
half an hour at a time as he went through his papers. Strickland seemed to work harder over the case than if he had been
in office in the Plains.

'And sometimes I look up and I fancy the little chap's
laughing at me. It's an awful thing to have a son. You see, he's
your own and *his* own, and between the two you don't quite
know how to handle him,' said Strickland. 'I wonder what in
the world he thinks about.'

I asked Adam this later on, quietly. He put his head on one
side for a moment and replied: 'In these days I think about
great things. I do not play with Victor and the cow's child any
more. Victor is only a *baba*.'

At the end of the third week of Strickland's leave, the result of Strickland's labours—labours that had made Mrs. Strickland more indignant against the dacoits than any one else—came to hand. The Police at Peshawur reported that half of the Shub-kudder Gang were held at Peshawur to account for the possession of some blankets and a horse-bucket. Strickland's Assistant had also four men under suspicion in his charge; and Imam Din must have stirred up Strickland's Inspector to investigations on his own account, for a string of incoherent telegrams came in from the Club Secretary in which he entreated, exhorted and commanded Strickland to take his 'mangy Policemen' off the Club premises. 'Your men, in servants' quarters here, examining cook. Billiard-marker indignant. Steward threatens resignation. Members furious. Grooms stopped on roads. Shut up, or my resignation goes to Committee.'

'Now I shouldn't in the least wonder,' said Strickland thoughtfully to his wife, 'if the Club was not just *the* place where the men would lie up. Billy Watson isn't at all pleased, though. I think I shall have to cut my leave by a week and go down to take charge. If there's anything to be told, the men will tell me.'

Mrs. Strickland's eyes filled with tears. 'I shall try to steal ten days if I can in the autumn,' he said soothingly, 'but I must go now. It will never do for the gang to think that they can burgle *my* belongings.'

That was in the forenoon, and Strickland asked me to lunch to leave me some instructions about his big dog, with authority to rebuke those who did not attend to her. Tietjens was growing too old and too fat to live in the Plains in the summer. When I came, Adam had climbed into his high chair at table, and Mrs. Strickland seemed ready to weep at any moment over the general misery of things.

'I go down to the Plains to-morrow, my son,' said Strickland.

'Wherefore?' said Adam, reaching out for a ripe mango and burying his head in it.

'Imam Din has caught the men who did the dacoity, and there are also others at Peshawur under suspicion. I must go to see.'

'*Bus!* [Enough],' said Adam, between sucks at his mango, as Mrs. Strickland tucked the napkin round his neck. 'Imam Din speaks lies. Do not go.'

'It is necessary. There has been great *dikh-dari* [trouble-giving].'

Adam came out of the fruit for a minute and laughed. Then, returning, he spoke between slow and deliberate mouthfuls.

'The dacoits live in Beshakl's head. They will never be caught. All people know that. The cook knows, and the scullion, and Rahim Baksh here.'

'Nay,' said the butler behind his chair hastily. 'What should *I* know? Nothing at all does the Servant of the Presence know.'

'*Achcha!* [Good],' said Adam, and sucked on. 'Only it *is* known.'

'Speak, then, son,' said Strickland to him. 'What dost thou know? Remember my groom was beaten insensible.'

'That was in the bad-water shop where I played when we came up here. The boy who would not sell me the parrot for six annas told me that a one-eyed man had come there and drunk the bad waters and gone mad. He broke bedsteads. They hit him with a bamboo till he was senseless, and fearing he was dead, they nursed him on milk—like a little *baba*. When I was playing first with the cow's child, I asked Beshakl if he were that man, and he said no. But *I* knew, because many woodcutters in Dalhousie asked him whether his head were whole now.'

'But why,' I interrupted, 'did Beshakl tell lies?'

'Oh! He is a low-caste man, and desired to get consideration. Now he is a witness in a great law-case, and men will go to the jail on his account. It was to give trouble and obtain notice that he did it.'

'Was it all lies?' said Strickland.

'Ask him,' said Adam, through the mango-pulp.

Strickland passed through the door. There was a howl of despair in the servants' quarters up the hill, and he returned with the one-eyed groom.

'Now,' said Strickland, 'it is known. Declare!'

'Beshakl,' said Adam, while the man gasped. 'Imam Din has caught four men, and there are some more at Peshawur. *Bus! Bus! Bus!* [Enough].'

'Thou didst get drunk by the wayside, and didst make a false case to cover it. Speak!'

Like a good many other men, Strickland, in possession of a few facts, was irresistible. The groom groaned.

'I—I did not get drunk till—till—Protector of the Poor, the mare rolled.'

'*All* horses roll at Dhunnera. The road is too narrow before that, and they smell where the other horses have rolled. This the bullock-drivers told me when we came up here,' said Adam.

'She rolled. So her saddle was cut and the curb-chain lost.'

'See!' said Adam, tugging a curb-chain from his pocket. 'That woman in the shop gave it to me for a love-gift. Beshakl said it was not his when I showed it. But *I* knew.'

'Then they at the grog-shop, knowing that I was the Servant of the Presence, said that unless I drank and spent money they would tell.'

'A lie! A lie!' said Strickland. 'Son of an owl, speak the truth now at least.'

'Then I was afraid because I had lost the curb-chain, so I cut the saddle across and about.'

'She did *not* roll, then?' said Strickland, bewildered and angry.

'It was only the curb-chain that was lost. Then I cut the saddle and went to drink in the shop. I drank and there was a fray. The rest I have forgotten till I recovered.'

'And the mare the while? What of the mare?'

The man looked at Strickland and collapsed.

'She bore faggots for a week,' he said.

'Oh, poor Diamond!' said Mrs. Strickland.

'And Beshakl was paid four annas for her hire three days ago by the woodcutter's brother, who is the left-hand man of our rickshaw-men here,' said Adam, in a loud and joyful voice. 'We *all* knew. We all knew. I and the servants.'

Strickland was silent. His wife stared helplessly at the child; the soul out of Nowhere that went its own way alone.

'Did no man help thee with the lies?' I asked of the groom.

'None, Protector of the Poor—not one.'

'They grew, then?'

'As a tale grows in telling. Alas! I am a very bad man!' and he blinked his one eye dolefully.

'Now four men are held at my Police-station on thy account, and God knows how many more at Peshawur, besides the questions at Multan, and my honour is lost, and my mare has been pack-pony to a wood-cutter. Son of Devils, what canst thou do to make amends?'

There was just a little break in Strickland's voice, and the man caught it. Bending low, he answered, in the abject fawning whine that confounds right and wrong more surely than most modern creeds, 'Protector of the Poor, is the Police Service shut to—an honest man?'

'Out!' cried Strickland, and swiftly as the groom departed he must have heard our shouts of laughter behind him.

'If you dismiss that man, Strick, I shall engage him. He's a genius,' said I. 'It will take you months to put this mess right, and Billy Watson won't give you a minute's peace.'

'You aren't going to tell him?' said Strickland appealingly.

'I couldn't keep this to myself if you were my own brother. Four men arrested with you—four or forty at Peshawur—and what was that you said about Multan?'

'Oh, nothing. Only some camel-men there have been——'

'And a tribe of camel-men at Multan! All on account of a lost curb-chain. Oh, my Aunt!'

'And whose Memsahib [lady] was thy aunt?' said Adam, with the mango-stone in his fist. We began to laugh again.

'But here,' said Strickland, pulling his face together, 'is a very bad child who has caused his father to lose his honour before all the Policemen of the Punjab.'

'Oh, *they* know,' said Adam. 'It was only for the sake of show that they caught people. Assuredly they all knew it was *benowti* [make-up].'

'And since when hast thou known?' said the first Policeman in India to his son.

'Four days after we came here, after the woodcutter had asked Beshakl after the health of his head. Beshakl all but slew one of them at the bad-water place.'

'If thou hadst spoken then, time and money and trouble to me and to others had all been spared. *Baba,* thou hast done a wrong greater than thy knowledge, and thou hast put me to shame, and set me out upon false words, and broken my honour. Thou hast done *very* wrong. But perhaps thou didst not think?'

'Nay, but I *did* think. My father, *my* honour was lost when that beating of me happened in Juma's presence. Now it is made whole again.'

And with the most enchanting smile in the world Adam climbed up on to his father's lap.

AN ENGLISH SCHOOL

1893

AN ENGLISH SCHOOL

OF ALL THINGS in the world there is nothing, always excepting a good mother, so worthy of honour as a good school.
Our School was created for the sons of officers in the Army
and Navy, and filled with boys who meant to follow their
fathers' calling.

It stood within two miles of Amyas Leigh's house at
Northam, overlooking the Burrows and the Pebble Ridge, and
the mouth of the Torridge whence the *Rose* sailed in search of
Don Guzman. From the front dormitory windows, across the
long rollers of the Atlantic, you could see Lundy Island and
the Shutter Rock, where the *Santa Catharina* galleon cheated
Amyas out of his vengeance by going ashore. If you have ever
read Kingsley's *Westward Ho!* you will remember how all
these things happened.

Inland lay the rich Devonshire lanes and the fat orchards,
and to the west the gorse and the turf ran along the tops of
the cliffs in combe after combe till you come to Clovelly and
The Hobby and Gallantry Bower, and the homes of the
Devonshire people that were old when the Armada was new.

The Burrows, lying between the School and the sea, was a
waste of bent rush and grass running out into hundreds of
acres of fascinating sandhills called the Bunkers, where a few
old people played golf. In the early days of the School there
was a small Club-house for golfers close to the Pebble Ridge,
but, one wild winter night, the sea got up and drove the
Pebble Ridge clean through the Club basement, and the walls

fell out, and we rejoiced, for in those days golfers wore red coats and did not like us to use the links. We played golf as a matter of course and thought nothing of it.

Now there is a new Club-house, and cars take the old, red, excited men to and from their game, and all the great bunkers are known and written about; but we were there first, long before golf became a fashion or a disease, and we turned out one of the earliest champion amateur golfers of all England.

It was a good place for a school, and that School considered itself the finest in the world, excepting perhaps Haileybury, because it was modelled on Haileybury lines and our caps were Haileybury colours; and there was a legend that, in the old days when the School was new, half the boys had been Haileyburians.

Our Head-master had been Head of the Modern Side at Haileybury, and, talking it over with boys from other public schools afterwards, I think that one secret of his great hold over us was that he was not a clergyman, as so many Head-masters are. As soon as a boy begins to think in the misty way that boys do, he is suspicious of a man who punishes him one day and preaches at him the next. But the Head was different, and in our different ways we loved him.

Through all of five years I never saw him lose his temper, nor among two hundred odd boys did any one at any time say or hint that he had his favourites. If you went to him with any trouble you were heard out to the end, and answered without being talked at or about or around, but always *to*. So we trusted him absolutely, and when it came to the choice of the various ways of entering the Army, what he said was so.

He naturally knew boys better than their fathers knew them, and considerably better than they knew themselves. When the time came to read for the Final Army Examinations, he knew the temper and powers of each boy, the amount of training each would stand and the stimulus or restraint that each needed, and handled them accordingly till they had come through the big race that led into the English Army. Looking back on it all, one can see the perfect judgment, knowledge of boys, patience, and, above all, strength, that the Head must have had.

Some of the masters, particularly on the Classical side, vowed that Army examinations were making education no more than mark-hunting; but there are a great many kinds of education, and I think the Head knew it, for he taught us hosts of things that we never found out we knew till afterwards. And surely it must be better to turn out men who do real work than men who write about what they think about what other people have done or ought to do.

A scholar may, as the Latin masters said, get more pleasure out of his life than an Army officer, but only little children believe that a man's life is given him to decorate with pretty little things, as though it were a girl's room or a picture-screen. Besides, scholars are apt, all their lives, to judge from one point of view only, and by the time that an Army officer has knocked about the world for a few years he comes to look at men and things 'by and large,' as the sailors say. No books in the world will teach that knack.

So we trusted the Head at school, and afterwards trusted him more.

There was a boy in the Canadian Mounted Police, I think, who stumbled into a fortune—he was the only one of us who ever did—and as he had never drawn more than seven shillings a day, he very properly wrote to the Head from out of his North-Western wilds and explained his situation, proposing that the Head should take charge of and look after all his wealth till he could attend to it. He was a little impatient when the Head pointed out that executors and trustees and that sort of bird wouldn't hand over cash in that casual way. The Head was worth trusting—he saved a boy's life from diphtheria once at much greater risk than being shot at, and nobody knew anything about it till years afterwards.

But I come back to the School that he made and put his mark upon. The boys said that those with whom Cheltenham could do nothing, whom Sherborne found too tough, and whom even Marlborough had politely asked to leave, had been sent to the School at the beginning of things and turned into men. They were, perhaps, a shade rough sometimes. One very curious detail, which I have never seen or heard of in any school before or since, was that the Army Class, which meant the Prefects, and was generally made up of boys from seventeen and a half to nineteen or thereabouts, was allowed to smoke pipes (cigarettes were then reckoned the direct invention of the Evil One) in the country outside the School. One result of this was that, though these great men talked a good deal about the grain of their pipes, the beauty of their pouches, and the flavour of their tobacco, they did not smoke to any ferocious extent. The other, which concerned me more directly, was that it went much harder with a junior whom they caught smoking than if he had been caught by a master, because the action was flagrant invasion of their privilege, and, therefore, rank insolence—to be punished as such. Years later, the Head admitted that he thought something of this kind would happen when he gave the permission. If any Head-master is anxious to put down smoking nowadays, he might do worse than give this scheme a trial.

The School motto was, 'Fear God, Honour the King'; and so the men she made went out to Boerland and Zululand and

India and Burma and Cyprus and Hongkong, and lived or died as gentlemen and officers.

Even the most notorious bully, for whom an awful ending was prophesied, went to Canada and was mixed up in Riel's rebellion, and came out of it with a fascinating reputation of having led a forlorn hope and behaved like a hero.

All these matters were noted by the older boys, and when their fathers, the grey-whiskered Colonels and Generals, came down to see them, or the Directors, who were K.C.B.'s and had been officers in their time, made a tour of inspection, it was reported that the School tone was 'healthy.'

Sometimes an old boy who had blossomed into a subaltern of the Queen would come down for a last few words with the Head-master, before sailing with the regiment for foreign parts; and the Lower School boys were distracted with envy, and the Prefects of the Sixth Form pretended not to be proud when he walked with one of their number and talked about 'my men, you know,' till life became unendurable.

There was an unwritten law by which an old boy, when he came back to pay his respects to the School, was entitled to a night in his old dormitory. The boys expected it and sat up half the night listening to the tales of a subaltern that the boy brought with him—stories about riots in Ireland and camps at Aldershot, and all his first steps in the wonderful world.

Sometimes news came in that an old boy had died with his men fighting, and the School said, 'Killed in action, of course,' as though that were an honour reserved for it alone, and wondered when its own chance would come.

It was a curiously quiet School in many ways. When a boy was fourteen or fifteen he was generally taken in hand for the Army Preliminary Examination, and when that was past he was put down to 'grind' for the entrance into Sandhurst or

Woolwich; for it was our pride that we passed direct from the School to the Army, without troubling the 'crammers.' We spoke of 'The Shop,' which means Woolwich, as though we owned it. Sandhurst was our private reserve; and the old boys came back from foreign parts and told us that India was only Westward Ho! spread thin.

On account of this incessant getting ready for examinations there was hardly time for us (but we made it) to gather the beautiful Devonshire apples, or to ferret rabbits in the sand-hills by the golf-links, and saloon-pistols were forbidden because boys got to duelling-parties with dust-shot, and were careless about guarding their eyes.

Nor were we encouraged to lower each other over the cliffs with a box-rope and take the young hawks and jackdaws from their nests above the sea. Once a rope broke, or else the boys above grew tired of holding it, and a boy dropped thirty feet on to the boulders below. But as he fell on his head nothing happened, except punishment at the other ends for all concerned.

In summer there was almost unlimited bathing from the Pebble Ridge, a whale-backed bank four miles long of rounded grey boulders, where you were taught to ride on the rollers as they came in, to avoid the undertow, and to watch your time for getting back to the beach.

There was a big sea-bath, too, in which all boys had to qualify for open bathing by swimming a quarter of a mile, at least; and it was a matter of honour among the School Houses not to let the summer end with a single boy who could not 'do his quarter,' at any rate.

Boating was impossible off that coast, but sometimes a fishing-boat would be wrecked on Braunton Bar, and we could see the lifeboat and the rocket at work; and once just after chapel there was a cry that the herring were in. The School ran down to the beach in their Sunday clothes and fished them out with umbrellas. They were cooked by hand afterwards in all the studies and form-rooms till you could have smelt us as far off as Exeter.

But the game of the School, setting aside golf, which every one could play if he had patience, was football. Both cricket and football were compulsory. That is to say, unless a boy could show a doctor's certificate that he was physically unfit to stand up to the wicket or go into the scrimmage, he had to play a certain number of afternoons at the game of the season. If he had engagements elsewhere—we called it 'shirking'—he was reasonably sure of three cuts with a ground-ash, from the Captain of the Games, delivered cold in the evening. A good player, of course, could get leave off on any fair excuse, but it was a beautiful rule for fat boys and loafers. The only unfairness was that a master could load you with an imposition to be shown up at a certain hour, which, of course, prevented you from playing and so secured you a licking in addition to the imposition. But the Head always told us that there was not much justice in the world, and that we had better accustom ourselves to the lack of it early.

Curiously enough, the one thing that the School did not understand was an attempt to drill it in companies with rifles, by way of making a volunteer cadet corps. We took our lickings for not attending *that* cheerfully, because we considered it 'playing at soldiers,' and boys reading for the Army are apt to be very particular on these points.

We were weak at cricket, but our football team (Rugby Union) at its best devastated the country from Blundell's—we always respected Blundell's because 'Great John Ridd' had been educated there—to Exeter, whose team were grown men.

Yet we, who had been taught to play together, once drove them back over the November mud, back to their own goal-posts, till the ball was hacked through and touched down, and you could hear the long-drawn yell of 'Schoo-*ool*! Schoo-*ool*!' as far as Appledore.

When the enemy would not come to us our team went to the enemy, and if victorious, would return late at night in a three-horse brake, chanting:

> *It's a way we have in the Army,*
> *It's a way we have in the Navy,*
> *It's a way we have in the Public Schools,*
> *Which nobody can deny!*

Then the boys would flock to the dormitory windows, and wave towels and join in the 'Hip-hip-hip-hurrah!' of the chorus, and the winning team would swagger through the dormitories and show the beautiful blue marks on their shins, and the little boys would be allowed to get the sponges and hot water.

Very few things that the world can offer make up for having missed a place in the First Fifteen, with its black jersey and white—snow-white—knickerbockers, and the velvet skull-cap with the gold tassel—the cap that you leave out in the rain and accidentally step upon to make it look as old as if you had been in the First Fifteen for years.

The other outward sign of the First Fifteen that the happy boy generally wore through a hard season was the 'jersey-mark'—a raw, red scrape on ear and jawbone where the skin had been fretted by the rough jerseys in either side in the steady drive of many scrimmages. We were trained to put our heads down, pack in the shape of a wedge and shove, and it was in that shape that the First Fifteen stood up to a team of trained men for two-and-twenty counted minutes. We got the ball through in the end.

At the close of the winter term, when there were no more football teams to squander and the Christmas holidays were coming, the School set itself to the regular yearly theatricals—a farce and a three-act play all complete. Sometimes it was *The Rivals,* or sometimes an attempt at a Shakespearean play; but the farces were the most popular.

All ended with the School Saga, the *'Vive la Compagnie!'* in which the Senior boy of the School chanted the story of the School for the past twelve months. It was very long and very difficult to make up, though all the poets of all the forms had been at work on it for weeks; and the School gave the chorus at the top of its voice.

On the last Sunday of the term the last hymn in chapel was 'Onward, Christian Soldiers.' We did not know what it meant then, and we did not care, but we stood up and sang it till the music was swamped in the rush. The big verse, like the 'tug-of-war' verse in Mrs. Ewing's *Story of a Short Life,* was:

> *We are not divided,*
> *All one body we,*
> *One in hope and doctrine,*
> *One in charity.*

Then the organ would give a hurricane of joyful roars, and try to get us in hand before the refrain. Later on, meeting our men all the world over, the meaning of that hymn became much too plain.

Except for this outbreak we were not very pious. There was

a boy who had to tell stories night after night in the dormitory, and when his stock ran out he fell back on a book called *Eric, or Little by Little,* as comic literature, and read it till the gas was turned off. The boys laughed abominably, and there was some attempt to give selections from it at the meeting of the Reading Society. That was quashed by authority because it was against discipline.

There were no public-houses near us except tap-rooms that sold cider; and raw Devonshire cider can only be drunk after a long and very hot paper-chase. We hardly ever saw, and certainly never spoke to, anything in the nature of a woman from one year's end to the other; for our masters were all unmarried. Later on, a little colony of mothers came down to live near the School, but their sons were day-boys who couldn't do this and mustn't do that, and there was a great deal too much dressing-up on week-days and going out to tea, and things of that kind, which, whatever people say nowadays, are not helpful for boys at work.

Our masters, luckily, were never gushing. They did not call us Dickie or Johnnie or Tommy, but Smith or Thompson; and when we were undoubtedly bad we were actually and painfully beaten with an indubitable cane on a veritable back till we wept unfeigned tears. Nobody seemed to think that it brutalised our finer feelings, but everybody was relieved when the trouble was over.

Canes, especially when they are brought down with a drawing stroke, sting like hornets; but they are a sound cure for certain offences; and a cut or two, given with no malice, but as a reminder, can correct and keep corrected a false quantity or a wandering mind more completely than any amount of explanations.

There was one boy, however, to whom every Latin quantity was an arbitrary mystery, and he wound up his crimes by suggesting that he could do better if Latin verse rhymed as decent verse should. He was given an afternoon's reflection to purge himself of his contempt; and feeling certain that he was in for something rather warm, he turned *'Donec gratus eram'* into pure Devonshire dialect, rhymed, and showed it up as his contribution to the study of Horace.

He was let off, and his master gave him the run of a big library, where he found as much verse and prose as he wanted; but that ruined his Latin verses and made him write verses of his own. There he found all the English poets from Chaucer to Matthew Arnold, and a book called *Imaginary Conversations* which he did not understand, but it seemed to be a good thing to imitate. So he imitated and was handed up to the Head, who said that he had better learn Russian under his own eye, so that if ever he were sent to Siberia for lampooning the authorities he might be able to ask for things.

That meant the run of another library—English Dramatists this time; hundreds of old plays; as well as thick brown books of voyages told in language like the ringing of bells. And the Head would sometimes tell him about the manners and customs of the Russians, and sometimes about his own early days at college, when several people who afterwards became great were all young, and the Head was young with them, and they wrote wonderful things in college magazines.

It was beautiful and cheap—dirt-cheap, at the price of a permanent load of impositions, for neglecting mathematics and algebra.

The School started a Natural History Society, which took the birds and plants of North Devon under its charge, reporting first flowerings and first arrivals and new discoveries to learned societies in London, and naturally attracting to itself every boy in the School who had the poaching instinct.

Some of us made membership an excuse for stealing apples

and pheasants' eggs and geese from farmers' orchards and gentlemen's estates, and we were turned out with disgrace. So we spoke scornfully of the Society ever afterwards. None the less, some of us had our first introduction to gunpowder in the shape of a charge of salt which stings like bees, fired at our legs by angry game-keepers.

The institution that caused some more excitement was the School paper. Three of the boys, who had moved up the School side by side for four years and were allies in all things, started the notion as soon as they came to the dignity of a study of their own with a door that would lock. The other two told the third boy what to write, and held the staircase against invaders.

It was a real printed paper of eight pages, and at first the printer was more thoroughly ignorant of type-setting, and the Editor was more completely ignorant of proof-reading, than any printer and any Editor that ever was. It was printed off by a gas-engine; and even the engine despised its work, for one day it fell through the floor of the shop, and crashed—still working furiously—into the cellar.

The paper came out at odd times and seasons, but every time it came out there was sure to be trouble, because the Editor was learning for the first time how sweet and good and profitable it is—and how nice it looks on the page—to make fun of people in actual print.

For instance, there was friction among the study-fags once, and the Editor wrote a descriptive account of the Lower School, —the classes whence the fags were drawn,—their manners and customs, their ways of cooking half-plucked sparrows and imperfectly cleaned blackbirds at the gas-jets on a rusty nib, and their fights over sloe-jam made in a gallipot. It was an absolutely truthful article, but the Lower School knew nothing about truth, and would not even consider it as literature.

It is less safe to write a study of an entire class than to discuss individuals one by one; but apart from the fact that boys throw books and inkpots with a straighter eye, there is very little difference between the behaviour of grown-up people and that of children.

In those days the Editor had not learned this; so when the study below the Editorial study threw coal at the Editorial legs and kicked in the panels of the door, because of personal paragraphs in the last number, the Editorial Staff—and there never was so loyal and hard-fighting a staff—fried fat bacon till there was half an inch of grease in the pan, and let the greasy chunks down at the end of a string to bob against and defile the lower study windows.

When that lower study—and there never was a public so low and unsympathetic as that lower study—looked out to see what was frosting their windowpanes, the Editorial Staff emptied the hot fat on their heads, and it stayed in their hair for days and days, wearing shiny to the very last.

The boy who suggested this sort of warfare was then reading a sort of magazine, called *Fors Clavigera*, which he did not in the least understand,—it was not exactly a boys' paper,—and when the lower study had scraped some of the fat off their heads and were thundering with knobby pokers on the door-lock, this boy began to chant pieces of the *Fors* as a war-song, and to show that his mind was free from low distractions. He was an extraordinary person, and the only boy in the School who had a genuine contempt for his masters. There was no affectation in his quiet insolence. He honestly *did* despise them; and threats that made us all wince only caused him to put his head a little on one side and watch the master as a sort of natural curiosity.

The worst of this was that his allies had to take their share of his punishments, for they lived as Communists and Socialists hope to live one day, when everybody is good. They were bad, as bad as they dared to be, but their possessions were in common, absolutely. And when 'the Study' was out of funds they took the most respectable clothes in possession of the Syndicate, and leaving the owner one Sunday and one week-day suit, sold the rest in Bideford town. Later, when there was another crisis, it was *not* the respectable one's watch that was taken by force for the good of the Study and pawned, and never redeemed.

Later still, money came into the Syndicate honestly, for a London paper that did not know with whom it was dealing, published and paid a whole guinea for some verses that one of the boys had written and sent up under a *nom de plume*, and the Study caroused on chocolate and condensed milk and pilchards and Devonshire cream, and voted poetry a much sounder business than it looks.

So things went on very happily till the three were seriously warned that they must work in earnest, and stop giving amateur performances of *Aladdin* and writing librettos of comic operas which never came off, and worrying their House-masters into grey hairs.

Then they all grew very good, and one of them got into the Army; and another—the Irish one—became an engineer; and the third one found himself on a daily paper half a world away from the Pebble Ridge and the sea-beach. The three swore eternal friendship before they parted, and from time to time they met boys of their year in India, and magnified the honour of the old School.

The boys are scattered all over the world, one to each degree of land east and west, as their fathers were before them, doing much the same kind of work; and it is curious to notice how little the character of the man differs from that of the boy of sixteen or seventeen.

The general and commander-in-chief of the Study, he who suggested selling the clothes, never lost his head even when he and his friends were hemmed round by the enemy—the Drill-Sergeant—far out of bounds and learning to smoke under a hedge. He was sick and dizzy, but he rose to the occasion, took command of his forces, and, by strategic manœuvres along dry ditches and crawlings through tall grass, out-flanked the enemy and got into safe ground without losing one man of the three.

A little later, when he was a subaltern in India, he was bitten by a mad dog, went to France to be treated by Pasteur, and came out again in the heat of the hot weather to find himself almost alone in charge of six hundred soldiers, and his Drill-Sergeant dead and his office clerk run away, leaving the Regimental books in the most ghastly confusion. Then we happened to meet; and as he was telling his story there was just the same happy look on his face as when he steered us down the lanes with the certainty of a superior thrashing if we were caught.

And there were others who went abroad with their men, and when they got into tight places behaved very much as they had behaved at football.

The boy who used to take flying jumps on to the ball and roll over and over with it, because he was big and fat and could not run, took a flying jump on to a Burmese dacoit whom he had surprised by night in a stockade; but he forgot that he was much heavier than he had been at school, and by the time he rolled off his victim the little dacoit was stone dead.

And there was a boy who was always being led astray by bad advice, and begging off punishment on that account. He got into some little scrape when he grew up, and we who knew him knew, before he was reprimanded by his commanding officer, exactly what his excuse would be. It came out almost word for word as he was used to whimper it at school. He was cured, though, by being sent off on a small expedition where he alone would be responsible for any advice that was going, as well as for fifty soldiers.

And the best boy of them all—who could have become anything—was wounded in the thigh as he was leading his men up the ramp of a fortress. All he said was, 'Put me up against that tree and take my men on'; and when his men came back he was dead.

Ages and ages ago, when Queen Victoria was shot at by a man in the street, the School paper made some verses about it that ended like this:

> *One school of many, made to make*
> *Men who shall hold it dearest right*
> *To battle for their ruler's sake,*
> *And stake their being in the fight,*
>
> *Sends greeting, humble and sincere,*
> *Though verse be rude and poor and mean,*
> *To you, the greatest as most dear,*
> *Victoria, by God's Grace, our Queen!*
>
> *Such greetings as should come from those*
> *Whose fathers faced the Sepoy hordes,*
> *Or served you in the Russian snows*
> *And, dying, left their sons their swords.*

AN ENGLISH SCHOOL

For we are bred to do your will
By land and sea, wherever flies
The Flag, to fight and follow still,
And work your Empire's destinies.

Once more we greet you, though unseen
Our greetings be, and coming slow.
Trust us, if need arise, O Queen!
We shall not tarry with the blow.

And there are one or two places in the world that can bear witness how the School kept its word.

A COUNTING-OUT SONG

A COUNTING-OUT SONG

WHAT IS THE SONG the children sing
When dooryard lilacs bloom in Spring,
And the Schools are loosed, and the games are played
That were deadly earnest when Earth was made?
Hear them chattering, shrill and hard,
After dinner-time, out in the yard,
As the sides are chosen and all submit
To the chance of the lot that shall make them 'It.'
  (Singing) *'Eenee, Meenee, Mainee, Mo!*
        Catch a nigger by the toe!
        If he hollers let him go!
        Eenee, Meenee, Mainee, Mo!
         You—are—It!'

Eenee, Meenee, Mainee, and Mo
Were the First Big Four of the Long Ago,
When the Pole of the Earth sloped thirty degrees,
And Central Europe began to freeze,
And they needed Ambassadors staunch and stark
To steady the Tribes in the gathering dark:
But the frost was fierce and flesh was frail,
So they launched a Magic that could not fail.
  (Singing) *'Eenee, Meenee, Mainee, Mo!*
        Hear the wolves across the snow!
        Some one has to kill 'em—so
        Eenee, Meenee, Mainee, Mo
         Make—you—It!'

Slowly the Glacial Epoch passed,
Central Europe thawed out at last;
And, under the slush of the melting snows,
The first dim shapes of the Nations rose.
Rome, Britannia, Belgium, Gaul—
Flood and avalanche fathered them all;
And the First Big Four, as they watched the mess,
Pitied Man in his helplessness.
    (Singing) *'Eenee, Meenee, Mainee, Mo!*
                Trouble starts when Nations grow.
                Some one has to stop it—so
                Eenee, Meenee, Mainee, Mo
                Make—you—It!'

Thus it happened, but none can tell
What was the Power behind the spell—
Fear, or Duty, or Pride, or Faith—
That sent men shuddering out to death—
To cold and watching, and, worse than these,
Work, more work, when they looked for ease—
To the day's discomfort, the night's despair,
In the hope of a prize that they never would share.
    (Singing) *'Eenee, Meenee, Mainee, Mo!*
                Man is born to toil and woe.
                One will cure the other—so
                Eenee, Meenee, Mainee, Mo
                Make—you—It.'

Once and again, as the Ice went North,
The grass crept up to the Firth of Forth.
Once and again, as the Ice came South,
The glaciers ground over Lossiemouth.

A COUNTING-OUT SONG

But, grass or glacier, cold or hot,
The men went out who would rather not,
And fought with the Tiger, the Pig, and the Ape,
To hammer the world into decent shape.
  (Singing) *'Eenee, Meenee, Mainee, Mo!*
        What's the use of doing so?
        Ask the Gods, for we don't know;
        But Eenee, Meenee, Mainee, Mo
        Make—us—It!'

Nothing is left of that terrible rune
But a tag of gibberish tacked to a tune
That ends the waiting and settles the claims
Of children arguing over their games;
For never yet has a boy been found
To shirk his turn when the turn came round;
Nor even a girl has been known to say
'If you laugh at me I shan't play.'
  For—   *'Eenee, Meenee, Mainee, Mo,*
        (Don't you let the grown-ups know!)
        You may hate it ever so,
        But if you're chose you're bound to go,
        When Eenee, Meenee, Mainee, Mo
        Make—you—It!'

THE TABU TALE

1903

THE TABU TALE

THE MOST IMPORTANT THING about Tegumai Bopsulai and his dear daughter, Taffimai Metallumai, were the Tabus of Tegumai, which were all Bopsulai.

Listen and attend, and remember, O Best Beloved; because *we* know about Tabus, you and I.

When Taffimai Metallumai (but you can still call her Taffy) went out into the woods hunting with Tegumai, she never kept still. She kept very unstill. She danced among dead leaves, she did. She snapped dry branches off, she did. She slid down banks and pits, she did—quarries and pits of sand, she did. She splashed through swamps and bogs, she did; and she made a horrible noise!

So all the animals that they hunted—squirrels, beavers, otters, badgers, and deer, and the rabbits—knew when Taffy and her Daddy were coming, and ran away.

Then Taffy said, 'I'm awfully sorry, Daddy, dear.'

Then Tegumai said: 'What's the use of being sorry? The squirrels have gone, and the beavers have dived, the deer have jumped, and the rabbits are deep in their buries. You ought to be beaten, O Daughter of Tegumai, and I would, too, if I didn't happen to love you.' Just then he saw a squirrel kinking and prinking round the trunk of an ash-tree, and he said, 'H'sh! There's our lunch, Taffy, if you'll only keep quiet.'

Taffy said, 'Where? Where? Show me! Show!' She said it in a raspy-gaspy whisper that would have frightened a steam-cow, and she skittered about in the bracken, being a 'citable child; and the squirrel flicked his tail and went off in large, free, loopy-legs to about the middle of Sussex before he ever stopped.

Tegumai was severely angry. He stood quite still, making up his mind whether it would be better to boil Taffy, or skin Taffy, or tattoo Taffy, or cut her hair, or send her to bed for one night without being kissed; and while he was thinking, the Head Chief of the Tribe of Tegumai came through the woods all in his eagle-feathers.

He was the Head Chief of the High and the Low and the Middle Medicine for the whole Tribe of Tegumai, and he and Taffy were rather friends.

He said to Tegumai, 'What is the matter, O Chiefest of Bopsulai? You look angry.'

'I *am* angry,' said Tegumai, and he told the Head Chief all about Taffy's very unstillness in the woods; and about the way she frightened the game; and about her falling into swamps because she *would* look behind her when she ran; and about her falling out of trees because she wouldn't take good hold on both sides of her; and about her getting her legs all greeny with duckweed from ponds and places, and bringing it sploshing into the Cave.

The Head Chief shook his head till the eagle-feathers and the little shells on his forehead rattled, and then he said, 'Well, well! I'll see about it later. I wanted to talk to you, O Tegumai, on serious business.'

'Talk away, O Head Chief,' said Tegumai, and they both sat down politely.

'Observe and take notice, O Tegumai,' said the Head Chief. 'The Tribe of Tegumai have been fishing the Wagai river ever so long and ever so much too much. Consequence is, there's hardly any carp of any size left in it, and even the little carps are going away. What do you think of putting the big Tribal Tabu on it, so as to stop every one fishing there for six months?'

'That's a good plan, O Head Chief,' said Tegumai. 'But what will the consequence be if any of our people break tabu?'

'Consequence will be, O Tegumai,' said the Head Chief, 'that we will make them understand it with sticks and stinging-nettles and dobs of mud; and if *that* doesn't teach them, we'll draw fine, freehand Tribal patterns on their backs with the cutty edges of mussel-shells. Come along with me, O Tegumai, and we will proclaim the Tribal Tabu on the Wagai river.'

Then they went up to the Head Chief's head house, where all the Tribal Magic of Tegumai belonged; and they brought out the Big Tribal Tabu-pole, made of wood, with the image of the Tribal Beaver of Tegumai and the other animals carved on top, and all the Tribal Tabu-marks carved underneath.

Then they called up the Tribe of Tegumai with the Big Tribal Horn that roars and blores, and the Middle Tribal Conch that squeaks and squawks, and the Little Tribal Drum that taps and raps.

They made a lovely noise, and Taffy was allowed to beat the Little Tribal Drum, because she was rather friends with the Head Chief.

When all the Tribe had come together in front of the Head Chief's house, the Head Chief stood up and said and sang: 'O Tribe of Tegumai! The Wagai river has been fished too much, and the carp-fish are getting frightened. Nobody must fish in the Wagai river for six months. It is tabu both sides and the middle; on all islands and mud-banks. It is tabu to bring a fishing-spear nearer than ten man-strides to the bank of the river. It is tabu, it is tabu, it is most specially tabu, O Tribe of Tegumai! It is tabu for this month and next month and next month and next month and next month and next month. Now go and put up the Tabu-pole by the river, and don't let anybody pretend that they haven't understood!'

Then the Tribe of Tegumai shouted, and put up the Tabu-pole by the banks of the Wagai river, and swiftly they ran down both banks (half the Tribe on one side and half on the other), and chased away all the small boys who hadn't attended the meeting because they were looking for crayfish in the river; and then they all praised the Head Chief and Tegumai Bopsulai.

Tegumai went home after this, but Taffy stayed with the Head Chief, because they were rather friends. She was very much surprised. She had never seen a tabu put on anything before, and she said to the Head Chief, 'What does Tabu mean azactly?'

The Head Chief said, 'Tabu doesn't mean anything till you break it, O Only Daughter of Tegumai; but when you break it, it means sticks and stinging-nettles and fine, freehand Tribal patterns drawn on your back with the cutty edges of mussel-shells.'

Then Taffy said, 'Could I have a tabu of my own—a little small tabu to play with?'

Then the Head Chief said, 'I'll give you a little tabu of your own, just because you made up that picture-writing, which will one day grow into the ABC.' (You remember how Taffy and Tegumai made up the Alphabet?[1] That was why she and the Head Chief were rather friends.)

He took off one of his magic necklaces—he had twenty-two of them—and it was made of bits of pink coral, and he said: 'If you put this necklace on anything that belongs to you your own self, no one can touch that thing until you take the neck-

[1] See 'How the Alphabet was Made' in *Just So Stories*.

lace off. It will only work inside your own Cave; and if you have left anything of yours lying about where you shouldn't, the tabu won't work till you have put that thing back in its proper place.'

'Thank you very much indeed,' said Taffy. 'Now, what d'you truly s'pose it will do to my Daddy?'

'I'm not quite sure,' said the Head Chief. 'He may throw himself down on the floor and shout, or he may have cramps, or he may just flop, or he may take Three Sorrowful Steps and say sorrowful words, and then you can pull his hair three times if you like.'

'And what will it do to my Mummy?' said Taffy.

'There aren't any tabus on people's Mummies,' said the Head Chief.

'Why not?' said Taffy.

'Because if there were tabus on people's Mummies, people's Mummies could put tabus on breakfasts, and dinners, and teas, and that would be very bad for the Tribe. Long and long ago the Tribe decided not to have tabus on people's Mummies anywhere—for anything.'

'Well,' said Taffy, 'do you know if my Daddy has any tabus of his own that will work on me—s'posin' I broke a tabu by accident?'

'You *don't* mean to say,' said the Head Chief, 'that your Daddy has never put any tabus on you yet?'

'No,' said Taffy; 'he only says "Don't!" and gets angry.'

'Ah! I suppose he thought you were a kiddy,' said the Head Chief. 'Now, if you show him that you've a real tabu of your own, I shouldn't be surprised if he put several real tabus on *you*.'

'Thank you,' said Taffy; 'but I have a little garden of my own outside the Cave, and if you don't mind I should like you to make this tabu-necklace work so that if I hang it up on the wild roses in front of the garden, and people go inside, they won't be able to come out until they have said they are sorry.'

'Oh, certainly, certainly,' said the Head Chief. 'Of course you can tabu your very own garden.'

'Thank you,' said Taffy; 'and now I will go home and see if this tabu truly works.'

When she got back to the Cave, it was nearly time for dinner; and when she came to the door, Teshumai Tewindrow, her dear Mummy, instead of saying, 'Where have you been, Taffy?' said, 'O Daughter of Tegumai, come in and eat,' same as if she had been a grown-up person. That was because she saw a tabu-necklace on Taffy's neck.

Her Daddy was sitting in front of the fire waiting for dinner, and he said the very same thing, and Taffy felt *most* important.

She looked all round the Cave, to see that her own things (her private mendy-bag of otter-skin, with the shark's teeth and the bone needles and the deer-sinew thread; her mud-shoes of birch-bark; her spear and her throwing-stick and her lunch-basket) were all in their proper places, and then she slipped off her tabu-necklace quite quickly and hung it over the handle of the little wooden water-bucket that she used to draw water with.

Then her Mummy said to Tegumai, her Daddy, quite accidental, 'O Tegumai! Won't you get us some fresh drinking-water for dinner?'

'Certainly,' said Tegumai, and he jumped up and lifted Taffy's bucket with the tabu-necklace on it. Next minute he fell down flat on the floor and shouted; then he curled himself up and rolled round the cave; then he stood up and flopped several times.

'My dear,' said Teshumai Tewindrow, 'it looks to me as if you had rather broken somebody's tabu somehow. Does it hurt?'

'Horribly,' said Tegumai. He took Three Sorrowful Steps and put his head on one side, and shouted, 'I broke tabu! I broke tabu! I broke tabu!'

'Taffy, dear, that must be *your* tabu,' said Teshumai Tewindrow. 'You'd better pull his hair three times, or he will have to go on shouting till evening; and you know what Daddy is like when he once begins.'

Tegumai stooped down, and Taffy pulled his hair three times; and he wiped his face, and said, 'My Tribal Word! That's a dreadful strong tabu of yours, Taffy. Where did you get it from?'

'The Head Chief gave it me. He told me you'd have cramps and flops if you broke it,' said Taffy.

'He was quite right. But he didn't tell you anything about Sign Tabus, did he?'

'No,' said Taffy. 'He said that if I showed you I had a real tabu of my own, you'd most likely put some real tabus on me.'

'Quite right, my only daughter dear,' said Tegumai. 'I'll give you some tabus that will simply amaze you—Stinging-Nettle Tabus, Sign Tabus, black and white tabus—dozens of tabus. Now attend to me. Do you know what this means?'

Tegumai skiffled his forefinger in the air snaky-fashion. 'That's tabu on wriggling when you're eating your dinner. It is an important tabu, and if you break it, you'll have cramps—same as I did—or else I'll have to tattoo you all over.'

Taffy sat quite still through dinner, and then Tegumai held up his right hand in front of him, the fingers close together. 'That's the Still Tabu, Taffy. Whenever I do that, you must stop *as* you are, whatever you are doing. If you are sewing, you must stop with the needle halfway through the deerskin. If you're walking, you stop on one foot. If you're climbing, you stop on one branch. You don't move until you see me go like this.'

Tegumai put up his right hand, and waved it in front of his face two or three times. 'That's the sign for Carry On. You can go on with whatever you are doing when you see me make *that*.'

'Aren't there any necklaces for that tabu?' said Taffy.

'Yes. There is a red-and-black necklace, of course, but how can I come tramping through the fern to give you a Still Tabu necklace every time I see a deer or a rabbit, and want you to be quiet?' said Tegumai. 'I thought you were a better hunter than that. Why, I might have to shoot an arrow over your head the minute after I had put Still Tabu on you.'

'But how would I know what you were shooting at?' said Taffy.

'Watch my hand,' said Tegumai. 'You know the three little jumps a deer gives before he starts to run off—like this?' He looped his finger three times in the air, and Taffy nodded. 'When you see me do that, you'll know we've found a deer. A little jiggle of the forefinger means a rabbit.'

'Yes. Rabbits run like that,' said Taffy, and jiggled her forefinger the same way.

'Squirrel's a long, climby-up twist in the air. Like this!'

'Same as squirrels kinking round trees. *I* see,' said Taffy.

'Otter's a long, smooth, straight wave in the air—like this.'

'Same as otters swimming in a pool. *I* see,' said Taffy.

'And beaver's just as if I was smacking somebody with my open hand.'

'Same as beavers' tails smacking on the water when they are frightened. *I* see.'

'Those aren't tabus. Those are just signs to show you what

I am hunting. The Still Tabu is *the* thing you must watch, because it's a big tabu.'

'I can put the Still Tabu on, too,' said Teshumai Tewindrow, who was sewing deerskins together. 'I can put it on you, Taffy, when you get too rowdy going to bed.'

'What happens if I break it?' said Taffy.

'You can't break a tabu except by accident.'

'But s'pose I *did*,' said Taffy.

'You'd lose your own tabu-necklace. You'd have to take it back to the Head Chief, and you'd just be called Taffy again, not Daughter of Tegumai. Or perhaps we'd change your name to Tabumai Skellumzulai—the Bad Thing who can't keep a Tabu—and very likely you wouldn't be kissed for a day and a night.'

'Umm!' said Taffy. 'I don't think tabus are fun at all.'

'Well, take your tabu-necklace back to the Head Chief, and say you want to be a kiddy again, O Only Daughter of Tegumai!' said her Daddy.

'No,' said Taffy. 'Tell me more about tabus. Can't I have some more of my very own—my very own—strong tabus that give people Tribal Fits?'

'No,' said her Daddy. 'You aren't old enough to be allowed to give people Tribal Fits. That pink necklace will do quite well for you.'

'Then tell me more about tabus,' said Taffy.

'But I am sleepy, daughter dear. I'll just put tabu on any one talking to me till the sun gets behind that hill, and we'll go out in the evening and see if we can catch rabbits. Ask Mummy about the other tabus. It's a great comfort that you are a tabu-girl, because now I shan't have to tell you anything more than once.'

Taffy talked quietly to her Mummy till the sun was in the

right place. Then she waked Tegumai, and they both got their hunting things ready and went out into the woods. But just as she passed her little garden outside the Cave, Taffy took off her tabu-necklace and hung it on a rose-bush. Her garden-border was only marked with white stones, but she called the Rose the real gate into it, and all the Tribe knew it.

'Who do you s'pose you'll catch?' said Tegumai.

'Wait and see till we come back,' said Taffy. 'The Head Chief said that any one who breaks that tabu will have to stay in my garden till I let him out.'

They went along through the woods and crossed the Wagai river on a fallen tree, and they climbed up to the top of a big bare hill where there were plenty of rabbits in the fern.

'Remember you're a tabu-girl now,' said Tegumai, when Taffy began to skitter about and ask questions instead of hunting for rabbits; and he made the Still Tabu sign, and Taffy stopped as if she had been all turned into one solid stone. She was stooping to tie up a shoestring, and she stayed still with her hand on the string (*We* know that kind of tabu, don't we, Best Beloved?) only she looked hard at her Daddy, which you always must do when the Still Tabu is on. Presently, when he had walked a long way off, he turned round and made the Carry On sign. So she walked forward quietly through the bracken, always looking at her Daddy, and a rabbit jumped up in front of her. She was just going to throw her stick, when she saw Tegumai make the Still Tabu sign, and she stopped with her mouth half open and her throwing-stick in her hand. The rabbit ran towards Tegumai, and Tegumai caught it. Then he came across the fern and kissed his daughter and said, 'That is what I call a superior girl-daughter. It's some pleasure to hunt with you now, Taffy.'

A little while afterwards, a rabbit jumped up where Tegumai couldn't see it, but Taffy could, and she knew it was coming towards her if Tegumai did not frighten it; so she held up her hand, made the Rabbit Sign (so as he should know she wasn't in fun), and she put the Still Tabu on her own Daddy! She did—indeed she did, Best Beloved!

Tegumai stopped with one foot half lifted to climb over an old tree-trunk. The rabbit ran past Taffy, and Taffy killed it with her throwing-stick; but she was so excited that she forgot to take off the Still Tabu for quite two minutes, and all that time Tegumai stood on one leg, not daring to put his other foot down. Then he came and kissed her and threw her up in the air, and put her on his shoulder and danced and said, 'My Tribal Word and Testimony! This is what I call having a daughter that *is* a daughter, O Only Daughter of Tegumai!' And Taffy was most tremenenssly and wonderhugely pleased.

It was almost dark when they went home. They had five rabbits and two squirrels, as well as a water-rat. Taffy wanted the water-rat's skin for a purse. (People *had* to kill water-rats in those days because they couldn't buy purses, but *we* know that water-rats are just as much tabu, these particular days, for you and me as anything else that is alive.)

'I think I've kept you out a little too late,' said Tegumai, when they were near home, 'and Mummy won't be pleased with us. Run home, Taffy! You can see the Cave-fire from here.'

Taffy ran along, and that very minute Tegumai heard something crackle in the bushes, and a big, lean, grey wolf jumped out and began to trot quietly after Taffy.

Now, all the Tegumai people hated wolves and killed them whenever they could, and Tegumai had never seen one so close to his Cave before.

He hurried after Taffy, but the wolf heard him, and jumped

back into the bushes. Those wolves were afraid of grown-ups, but they used to try and catch the children of the Tribe. Taffy was swinging the water-rat and singing to herself—her Daddy had taken off all tabus—so she didn't notice anything.

There was a little meadow close to the Cave, and by the mouth of the Cave Taffy saw a tall man standing in her rose-garden, but it was too dark to make out properly.

'I do believe my tabu-necklace has truly caught somebody,' she said, and she was just running up to look when she heard her Daddy say, 'Still, Taffy! Still Tabu till I take it off!'

She stopped where she was—the water-rat in one hand and the throwing-stick in the other—only turning her head towards her Daddy to be ready for the Carry On sign.

It was the longest Still Tabu she had had put upon her all that day. Tegumai had stepped back close to the wood and was holding his stone throwing-hatchet in one hand, and with the other he was making the Still Tabu sign.

Then she thought she saw something black creeping side-ways at her across the grass. It came nearer and nearer, then it moved back a little and then it crawled closer.

Then she heard her Daddy's stone throwing-hatchet whirr past her shoulder just like a partridge, and at the same time another hatchet whirred out from her rose-garden; and there was a howl, and a big grey wolf lay kicking on the grass, quite dead.

Then Tegumai picked her up and kissed her seven times and said, 'My Tribal Word and Tegumai Testimony, Taffy, but you *are* a daughter to be proud of. Did you know what it was?'

'I'm not sure,' said Taffy. 'But I think I guessed it was a wolf. I knew you wouldn't let it hurt me.'

'Good girl,' said Tegumai, and he stooped over the wolf and picked up both hatchets. 'Why, here's the Head Chief's hatchet!' he said, and he held up the Head Chief's magic throwing-hatchet, with the big greenstone head.

'Yes,' said the Head Chief from inside Taffy's rose-garden, 'and I'd be very much obliged if you would bring it back to me. I came to call on you this afternoon, and accidentally I stepped into Taffy's garden before I saw her tabu-necklace on the rose-tree. So, of course, I had to wait till Taffy came back to let me out.'

Then the Head Chief all in his feathers and shells took the Three Sorrowful Steps with his head on one side, and said, 'I broke tabu! I broke tabu! I broke tabu!' and bowed solemnly and statelily before Taffy, till his tall eagle-feathers nearly touched the ground, and he said and he sang: 'O Daughter of Tegumai, I saw everything that happened. You are a true tabu-girl. I am very pleased at you. At first I wasn't pleased, because I had to wait in your garden since six o'clock, and I know you only put tabu on your garden for fun.'

'No, not fun,' said Taffy. 'I truly wanted to see if my tabu would catch anybody; but I didn't know that a little tabu like mine would work on a big Head Chief like you, O Head Chief.'

'I told you it worked. I gave it to you myself,' said the Head Chief. 'Of course it would work. But I don't mind. I want to tell you, Taffy, my dear, that I wouldn't have minded staying in your garden from twelve o'clock instead of only six o'clock to see how beautifully you kept that last Still Tabu that your Daddy put on you. I give you my Chiefly Word, Taffy, that a great many men in the Tribe wouldn't have kept that tabu as you kept it, with that wolf crawling up to you across the grass.'

'What are you going to do with the wolfskin, O Head Chief?' said Tegumai, because any animal that the Head Chief threw his hatchet at belonged to the Head Chief by the Tribal Custom of Tegumai.

'I am going to give it to Taffy, of course, for a winter cloak, and I'll make her a magic necklace of her very own out of the teeth and claws,' said the Head Chief; 'and I am going to have the story of Taffy and the Still Tabu painted on wood on the Tribal Tabu-Count, so that all the girl-daughters of the Tribe can see and know and remember and understand.'

Then they all three went into the Cave, and Teshumai Tewindrow gave them a most beautiful supper, and the Head Chief took off his eagle-feathers and all his necklaces; and when it was time for Taffy to go to bed in her own little cave, Tegumai and the Head Chief came in to say good-night, and they romped all round the cave, and dragged Taffy over the floor on a deerskin (same as some people are dragged about on a hearth-rug), and they finished by throwing the otter-skin cushions about and knocking down a lot of old spears and fishing-rods that were hung on the walls. At last things grew so rowdy that Teshumai Tewindrow came in, and said, 'Still! Still Tabu on every one of you! How do you ever expect that child to go to sleep?' And they said the really good-night, and Taffy went to sleep.

After that, what happened? Oh, Taffy learned all the tabus just like some people we know. She learned the White Shark Tabu, which made her eat up her dinner instead of playing with it (and that goes with a green-and-white necklace, you know); she learned the Grown-Up Tabu, which prevented her from talking when Neolithic ladies came to call (and, you know, a blue-and-white necklace goes with that); she learned the Owl Tabu, which prevented her staring at strangers (and a black-and-blue necklace goes with that); she learned the Open Hand Tabu (and we know a pure white necklace goes with that), which prevented her snapping and snarling when people borrowed things that belonged to her; and she learned five other tabus.

THE TABU TALE

But the chief thing she learned, and the one that she never broke, not even by accident, was the Still Tabu.

That was why she was taken *everywhere* that her Daddy went.

THE END